THE TURNING SWORD

The TURNING SWORD

A Van Kill Novel of Detection by
SPENCER BAYNE

WILDSIDE PRESS

THE TURNING SWORD

〜〜

"WHICH proves again," Mr. Frederick Pough was saying, "that you never need execute an important job in person." He paused. "So long as you can trust it to Betty."

"Or an office boy," said Miss Elizabeth Hargrave, respectfully bitter. She pushed a Descat roller hat further back upon her light amber curls.

A smile ran easily over the Miami-browned face of the president and editorial director of Po Publications, Inc. He made a deprecatory gesture.

"All right," his editorial assistant said. "Tell me I'm unreasonable. Tell me it isn't like me to get bored on the job." Her blue eyes were almost sulky.

Pough asked, "Why, for instance?"

"Well, for instance, everything," the girl burst out impatiently. "For the steenth time in five months, nothing new to report."

Betty Hargrave shifted position in the big chair and put down a small brightly-manicured hand to adjust her rice-grained tweed skirt. She was the sort of young business woman who puts a month's salary into a *tailleur* and gets her evening dresses in Union Square.

"Same old door-to-door diddling of housewives and storekeepers," she went on, "with the same old anti-Semitic boycott and promises. Same kind of contributions from soap manufacturers' widows and safety vault lice. Same letters of appreciation for me to type. Same old Burke and Lee. They just keep rolling along, damn 'em."

"That's what interests us," Pough said quietly. "The steady roll. I gave the Christian Cavaliers six months for a test run, when you started investigating them in July, remember. It may take longer than that. It isn't our policy to shoot half-primed."

"I know." The girl nodded more brightly than she felt. "Even at skunks."

As editorial assistant in this chain magazine firm, it was Betty

Hargrave's business to know. She liked to call herself an investigator rather than a writer. Dispatching questionnaire cards, "setting up telephone polls," as she liked to say, taking field trips to sound out public sentiment, she helped create the trend-aware policy of Po Publications, Inc. If *he* was going to diagram it now . . . Betty Hargrave settled back in the deep green chair across from Frederick Pough and heaved a voiceless sigh . . .

Pough put a pair of yachtsman's calloused palms on the uncluttered surface of his teakwood desk. He leaned toward the girl who sat on the other side of it, facing the broad window behind him.

Betty Hargrave nodded in all the right spots . . . What the public is thinking before they know it themselves . . . but wait until they *want* to know . . . Sampling . . .

"Particularly at skunks," Pough got around to the girl's wisecrack. "From what you've uncovered in the past five months it's plain the Christian Cavaliers are organized to advance cautiously." He shifted metaphors with editorial ease. "They know the value of having a variety of roots against any kind of gale."

Betty looked at Pough with the childlike gaze of admiring attention which was part of her professional self and often enough sincere. It was a good boss, an amiable creature, could be humored, although on the ultimate decisions, it listened only to itself . . .

There was an intimate but strictly office kind of understanding between Frederick Pough and his chain magazine gang. His business and private lives were so definitely defined that his wife could take a holiday trip to Miami without raising the least speculation. Betty found herself thinking, irrelevantly, about that now as Pough continued to hold forth upon the vagaries of the public mind.

As an intelligent executive Pough never meddled in his employees' private lives, the girl knew. As a self-made man he held no person's background against him unless it rose up to interfere with the business at hand.

Similarly the many publications housed on the various floors of the Popub Building near Radio City functioned with a minimum of interplay. Before Christmas annually a banquet presided over by the woman's magazine *Hearth* was given in honor of the publication making the largest rise in circulation. Otherwise the links in Pough's chain were like members of an aviary carrying on the processes of reproduction within arbitrarily marked boundaries . . .

This year the circulation race had gone neck and neck between *Lo!* the world's greatest pictorial news weekly and *Carnage* the world's greatest "fact" detective magazine. But at the stretch *Carnage* had nosed *Lo!* out and won the banquet, and Betty had rashly offered to manage it . . . The small blonde girl gave a moment's thought to this circumstance, which she found unreasonably depressing. She let her mind rove on among a variety of subjects irrelevant to Popub, Inc. This hour's out-of-the-world mood was unaccountable and made her annoyed . . .

Pough, discoursing upon a favorite, perhaps because debatable, theme of publishing as a profession, had no idea that Betty Hargrave was only half listening to him. Yet he knew better than most the serpent wisdom behind her dove-blue eyes. He knew she had too candid a nature to take full advantage of the discrepancy between her appearance and her brains, yet it frequently happened that people gave themselves away to Betty by taking her too lightly. She was useful therefore to Frederick Pough in the office of the Christian Cavaliers, the "business promotion agency" which she had been quietly investigating for nearly six months in the guise of part-time secretary to its manager, Thomas Carroll Burke.

Pough was telling her once more why Burke and the Cavaliers were dangerous. Not like the *Bund*. "Americans," he said. "They know American attitudes. Americans like to think they think for themselves, believe they're capable as experts at it. But we're lazy-minded and we'll swallow propaganda that's properly packaged. Not as Truth or Facts, but Inside Stuff, the Lowdown."

Betty Hargrave's eyes wandered left around the boss's smoothly working jaw to the respectable bulk of the Times Building. At its bottom the electric band would run bright that evening with destruction and death. Bombers shot down. Irreplaceable treasures, ordinary people and ordinary decencies wiped out . . . And she was supposed to go leisurely on the Cavaliers assignment, occupy her mind with the *Carnage* banquet, for instance . . .

Pough wasn't even thinking about her any longer, the girl decided, watching him stroke the fingers of his left hand from square chin to iron-gray temple along a lineless cheek. His light brown, she called them golden oak eyes when she felt rebellious, had an inward look. A perfect picture of fifty justifying itself for not taking a chance, she thought, and immediately asked herself if she wasn't falling a victim of war nerves. Did it matter anyway . . .

Betty shook herself loose to hear herself being talked to, not apprised any more for her own good. There was a quirk of personal amusement in Pough's well-schooled voice.

"You're under thirty, Betty," he said, "that's your trouble."

"An incurable romantic." The girl smiled. "Usually out of hours though."

He did not let it drop at that. "Enamored," he said, "of bright-faced danger in swinging cloak and Sandeman port sombrero."

"True, melud, this once," Betty answered, looking at him with more attention and wondering if Pough appreciated how completely her phony allegiance to the Christian Cavaliers as their part-time secretary had altered her private life and soured her attitude toward humanity. "But just for once I wish they'd do something rash. Their slow, tame, despicable efficiency gets me. Do I spy, or don't I?"

Pough offered her a cigarette, lit one himself, and inhaled deliberately. "They won't," he said. "And you do. And most of them who're worth their secret ink," he smiled, "have spells."

"Like mine?"

"Like yours. Most espionage work *is* prosaic as selling pork and beans." Smoke wavered about Pough's pleasant executive face. "This thing is bigger than you realize. More dangerous, perhaps. As you've discovered, it has ramifications beyond anti-Semitism. We need a little more on it before we go to town, but there's no hurry."

"I hope we can break it soon," Betty said doubtfully. "What I've given you already shows how they cover the ground." She nodded toward the safe which bulked against the wall. Here had been deposited a list of the Cavaliers' small contributors and sympathizers as the names had come under Betty's hands.

"Promise me you'll be careful," Pough interrupted, "as George was. I think you underestimate Stock," he said, referring to the art editor of *Carnage* magazine. "For all he's so quiet that lad's got brains to spare."

George Stock, Pough went on to point out, had been a member of the *Bund* for a year while investigating it for *Lo!* He never got into any trouble because he kept his emotions, his unquestionable loyalty, and his motor impulses separate.

"It's a matter of divorcing the cerebrum from the cerebellum and the viscera, Betty," Pough said with a smile.

"Stock, yes." Betty went on as if she hadn't heard. "I haven't gotten into the Cavaliers' confidential files, you see. That's where I'll get the dope on their big angels like 'True American.' Trouble is—" She bit her lower lip with reflective irritation and looked deceptively like a pouting child. "Burke isn't careless with his keys. Always one of that gaggle of spinsters hanging around." And she herself couldn't hang around the office of the Christian Cavaliers too much and maintain her pose of a young lady looking for something better than a part-time job with a downtown business firm, Miss Hargrave indicated. "But I'll get into those files. See if I don't."

Pough laughed, but he cautioned her again to be careful. "Because you might be disappointed," he said. "I've told you about Burke, his labor activities on the coast. A man with his background keeps his secrets in his hat. Your guess that the person who writes the True American editorials in the Cavaliers' *Lance* could be their big supporter is only a guess, Betty."

"But I'm good at guessing," the girl exclaimed. "It's my job, here at Popub, I mean, and ——"

She stopped. Pough had raised a hand and was looking beyond her. The office door was opening. Echo Newman, creamily brunette in slim secretarial blue, was raising a hand to knock again when Pough spoke.

"Yes, Jael." Miss Newman's employer was one of the few who called her by that triumphant Hebraic name. Firmly self-effacing, Echo never used a word of her own when someone else would supply it. Betty Hargrave rose and walked to the window with the suspicion of a flounce.

"I'm sorry." Miss Newman advanced over the green rug, a cameo figure in the huge office, but carrying efficiency like an almost visible nimbus on her dark head. "Mr. Snell is on the phone. He said he'd missed you at lunch and wanted to ask ——"

Pough's casual glance had traveled from the girl at the window to the one before him. It was curious, Pough thought, that his editorial assistant, who's been brought up expecting to support herself, should regard business as a kind of game, while his secretary, who hadn't, was so earnest about every office affair.

"Is it the usual?" Pough asked.

"Yes, Mr. Pough. About this lot of ——"

"War babies?" Echo nodded. "Tell him to let them go. One point is always enough."

Outside the window where Betty stood the mild December day hung dim and bodiless over the familiar streets toward Times Square. Four more shopping days till Christmas, she thought, trying to put down her vexation at Mr. Pough's male obtuseness . . . A newsboy's bark came up clear, but somehow ghostly, from the Radio City corner on the east. . . .

Betty Hargrave had overheard Richard Lee, assistant manager of the Cavaliers, saying, "They stink under refrigeration, all of 'em," and Burke, "I'd print the *Shema Isroel* on the front page every issue if it had the same result." . . . Well, the article signed "True American" was the only thing that appeared regularly on the front page of *The Lance*.

Mr. Pough was just a victim of holiday vegetation, the girl reflected charitably. He had nothing on his mind except the dummy for the March *Carnage*, which was late as usual, and the *Carnage* banquet. No wonder he wasn't putting two and two together. . . .

Five days until Christmas . . . By the time she got into it Betty Hargrave was too deeply concerned to remember the sense of questing unease which possessed her now. Even so she would probably not have labeled it a premonition of the whirlpool of events into which she was about to step. She was not, as she had told Pough, an incurable romantic.

Five days before Christmas and five days after loomed as an uneventful stretch to Betty Hargrave. Before that time had passed the shape of many things as she knew them now would be changed. The newsboy barking on the corner would, along with holocausts and devastation, incidentally bark about her. An incurable romantic frequently gets into trouble, but by virtue of this faculty he sometimes manages to avoid it too. Betty Hargrave was a wide-eyed blond with frivolous fingernails and if she was more romantic than an adding machine, she was also as little inclined to take advice. . . .

"I thought I told him that before so it stuck." Pough's irritation at the insistent Mr. Snell flowed over onto his secretary. "Tell him *one* point is enough."

Echo, following the custom of office hierarchies, shed the injustice by sending a look that was strictly a misdemeanor at the back of the girl in brown tweed. "Yes, Mr. Pough," she said, turned on her heel and was gone as noiselessly as she had come.

"These reckless brokers," Pough remarked as Betty sat down again, jerking a curl into line at the nape of her neck. Seeing Echo Newman always made her wonder if her stocking seams were straight.

"I'll admit you'd never think the Cavaliers were getting any money from the looks of their lair." Betty took up the discussion where it had left off.

"I've driven by there," Pough admitted. "Not a slum, one of those quietly depressed areas. Ideal for their purpose. Has the landlady loosened up on the heat?"

Betty said no, but she was sure now that the woman drank. "Don't get the idea that I'm fleshpotting." She smiled, indicating Pough's spacious office with a charming two-handed gesture. "But Burke's economies with typewriter ribbons alone would make your personal jewel hang up her harp—Bible," she added saucily when her boss did not respond. "I was brought up properly by a maiden aunt."

"You told me you had an old threshing machine to type on." Pough laughed tardily. "And a dictaphone Burke bought from a bankrupt school for the blind. Have you got so expert with that equipment you're angling for Jael's job?"

"Not blind. Deaf," Betty said. "You have to be careful of the volume control. Does she—" Pough's personal spy stabbed a red-tipped index finger toward his reception room. "Does Echo——"

"Yes, of course," Pough told her. "Purely as a routine precaution. Nobody else knows what you're up to with the Cavaliers. But if I should die——"

"God fabbid!" Betty Hargrave interjected piously. She was beginning to feel a little better.

"—— Jael would have to protect you and all of Popub from Montefiore."

For an instant Betty and her boss wore identical expressions of amused exasperation at Mr. David Montefiore, who was Popub's minority stockholder.

"None of my business, I suppose," the girl went on, "but I heard something when I was down talking about the *Carnage* banquet to Miss Treach. She said the blond menace had fallen for Echo. Cane over spats. Aren't you afraid——"

"My word, I'm counting on her to be a good influence," Pough said with feeling. He asked, "What about the banquet?"

"Going to be lovely," Betty declared. "Roast beef rare, naturally, for *Carnage*. No stuffed tomatoes, nor anything creamed in timbales. Treach is planning an article for *Hearth* on it. Telling the housewife what men really like to eat. Sensational idea, I told her. She won't mention my cake though. It's designed to put rough boys on their good behavior."

Pough flashed one of those looks that people frequently sent Betty when she walked right over a private misgiving, but she was prattling along. "Reason I asked if anybody else was onto my Cavaliers job was Mr. Harris has noticed the irregularity of my comings and goings here. I told him I had a drag."

"*Lo!* will handle the Cavaliers' story when we break it," the president of Popub stated. "Mr. Harris has sprouted ambition since his baby won the banquet, but the Cavaliers wouldn't interest him. There's no police angle."

"Maybe Harris can make one," Betty suggested, grinning inwardly at Pough's reference to *Carnage's* usual subject matter. *Police angle* was one way of describing the magazine's concentration on sex, murder, dope, prostitution, and all the least savory problems of law enforcement. She shrugged a neat shoulder, dismissing the ambitious Paul Harris, editor of *Carnage* magazine, and asked about Pough's out-of-town reports on organizations similar to the Cavaliers.

"Still about the same as yours," he said. "The regulation pre-lobby setup apparently. All sorts of small business coming in with them. Not much trace of higher connections, not *any* trace of a conspiratorial connection between these scurvy little boycott outfits and printing firms over the country where they get their material. That's where they play safe. They all operate under different names."

Pough leaned back in his chair and went on thoughtfully. "If some operative connection could be proved between them," he said, "they might be brought up for a boycott conspiracy to obstruct or interfere with interstate commerce. Unfortunately the Federal anti-trust statutes are limited to the protection of interstate commerce and we haven't any really enforceable local laws against the incitement of that kind of racial intolerance."

"I know it," Betty said. "The fact the Christian Frontiers were practically patted on the back last year. The Cavaliers know it too. That's what makes me burn. I *do* hope we break it soon."

"We'll coordinate all of our local and out-of-town stuff before we give it to *Lo!*" Frederick Pough's voice was noncommittal. "In a month, say."

"Okay," Betty said more cheerfully, picking up her gloves. "I'll get into their files by then." She went on in a breath because Pough looked as if he meant to interrupt. "I think you exaggerate the danger." He frowned a mild dissent. "If Burke or Lee caught me snooping, they'd simply heave me out and call the cops. Sure they would. With them it's business as usual. They're not fanatics. It would be embarrassing to get caught, and I don't intend to, but I don't think there's the least danger." She wound up a trifle breathless and added, "I hope."

"From them," Pough said. "But we must keep all the possibilities in mind. It's the zealots I'm afraid of for you. The underpaid, the unemployed and the incompetent who look for salvation in every bright-colored garbage can. There's martyr stuff in that lot, and you can never trust a martyr."

"Burke, for instance?" Betty's face was scornful. "That Hibernian perisher. He won't even smile for fear somebody'll steal his teeth."

"Even Burke," Pough replied. "You need more than economic theory to get up horsepower. You need slogans, gas for the honor machine. You need, well, religion." He rose as Betty got to her feet.

"You need the wacky types that come prowling around the Cavaliers' office," Betty countered. "Down-and-out clerks. Disgruntled DAR's. They wouldn't admit Chaym Solomon staked their little revolution if they read it in *The Lance*. But," she added as Pough took the topcoat that matched her suit and helped her into it, "they're not running the machine."

"We think not," her employer cautioned. "But remember what I said—yes, Jael?"

"Sorry to interrupt you again," Miss Newman said. "Mr. Montefiore's down the hall, waiting for Mr. Harris. Miss O'Bryan phoned. You said you'd like to know when he ——"

"I would." Pough chuckled. "If he catches me, he'll have to talk a lot less than he usually does."

~~~~~~

THE editor of *Carnage* swiveled away from his visitor across the desk and hoisted his feet onto a table piled thick with magazines. He tilted his head, which was noticeably too large for his slim body, to one side and cocked back a light-brown hat with a green feather as if to equalize the weight of the whole. Paul Harris possessed a news ghoul's facility for fitting people into journalistic pigeonholes and David Montefiore irritated him. Montefiore had irritated other rats.

The visitor whom the editor of *Carnage* was studying through eyes the color of slate-streaked coal might have modeled for a German health poster. Not only did he talk too much, but his appearance, Mr. Montefiore had been told when asked to terminate his tour of the Reich a few months before the war, was almost as unfortunate as his blood. His hyacinthine gold head was misleading, his Danube eyes and the proud flare of his coin portrait nose were a mockery.

For his part Paul Harris would have been only too glad to call David Montefiore a handsome screwball and dismiss him from his mind . . . Mr. Montefiore had just compared Mr. Harris to a witch's bantling newly ridden back from a technically successful sabbat . . . And the editor of *Carnage* had exactly that aspect of unsatisfied malevolence in his narrow face, the unscrupulous hungry curiosity of a carrion bird as he took his feet down suddenly and spoke.

"Will you for the last time get the hell out of here and let me work? You may not be busy. I am." Paul Harris put his feet up again.

"*J'y suis*," said Montefiore. He leaned forward and lifted his hat from the copy of *Carnage* it had been lying on as if the juxtaposition of the magazine with his admirable Homburg had suddenly become too repulsive to bear. The shiny cover showed a screaming girl in a badly torn dress against a red background. "And since you ask me, *J'y reste.*"

Harris reached for his telephone. "Don't put any calls through in the next ten minutes," he said. An affectionate cackle answered him from the receptionist's room next north by the elevator bank. Mr. Harris smiled superciliously, said, "Okay, Baby," and snapped the receiver into its cradle.

"Now then," he drawled in his nose, "Mister MontyfeeOHree. First you drift in here where you've no damn business. Right? You tell me I'm a rotten editor. Right?"

"Oh, very," said David inattentively. He seemed to be listening to the tinny gabble of a typewriter in an office at his left.

"Who asked *you*?" demanded the editor. "You offer me money to quit the job." Harris consulted his hatbrim about the enormity of this and shifted his feet. "You make childish threats."

"Moral," said Montefiore, who sat very straight. "Moral only. Anyway you ought to be fair." He waved a graceful but competent-looking hand. "I'm making the effort myself. I even told you I'd see you stayed on here if you put out the kind of magazine I want."

"Stayed on!" Harris mewed. "What the hell have you got to do with hiring and firing around here? The kind of magazine he wants, he says. What for God's sake do you know about putting out my kind of book?"

"Magazine, please," David murmured. "For your kind a committee of well-disposed madams ——"

The typewriter next door had ceased firing with a final spurt and slam of its bell. A door opened. Special Investigator and Crime-scribe Poynton Darcy's mournful horse face loomed in the entrance of the consultation room which Harris shared with *Carnage's* art editor. The mat of hair which fell nearly to Darcy's horn-rimmed spectacles in an unkempt bang was totally white. But he was no older than the thirty to forty-five years which Editor Harris owned according to his mood and his vis-à-vis' vital information.

Darcy's big loose frame shambled toward the editorial desk. Something hangdog, ignorantly knowing, in Darcy's manner proclaimed ex-newspaper hack. His clothes had never been hung up properly since they were new and his shoes looked as if he habitually wore them out to the barnyard to slop the hogs. As a matter of fact, David Montefiore reflected, that was what Poynton Darcy had been doing. Poynton Darcy's title of Special Investigator was hung onto a variety of noms de plume by a variety of True Crime Magazines like *Carnage*, as a tribute to his facility at reproducing his own and his fellow crimescribes' literary output.

Harris snatched the manuscript which Darcy held out. "Well, Poynton," he said waspishly, rattling the yellow paper, "I didn't think when I asked you to hop over here and fix up this piece of crap you'd take all day to it. You must be slipping. How much have you got?"

"A thousand. What you asked for," Darcy said. His articulation was slack-lipped and matched his grooming. "Didn't take me an hour."

"You must be slipping," Harris repeated, taking a look that was more like a cautious sniff at the manuscript.

"Read it," said Darcy without conviction.

"Don't need to." The editor took another cautious sniff in another place. "Swell," he said brusquely. "Swell. And don't go getting the idea you're writing for *Harpers* again. Want to cheat the readers? That stuff you had in the middle there would put 'em to sleep."

Neither man was paying him the least attention, but Montefiore got the definite sense that he was being treated to a staged episode.

"Maybe I didn't dress it up enough," Poynton was saying, "but after you cut out half of my flagellation piece ——"

"Not on moral grounds, my boy," Harris barked. "Gotta think of my budget. You've got three in this number. Whatinell are you kicking about?"

"Well," Darcy said doubtfully. He turned his mournful backside full on Montefiore and spoke into Harris's ear. It was not an act, David saw now, but a scene which had fallen into grooves through repetition. Apart from his horrendous virtuosity at the typewriter Poynton probably didn't think fast. Montefiore heard the editor

mumble something about putting the check through right away as
he got up and guided Darcy toward the hall door. . . .

David promptly reached over and plucked Darcy's manuscript
from the welter of papers on Harris's cigarette-scarred desk . . .
Saintly Siren, the little gem which Darcy had been engaged in
rubbing up, was evidently the memoirs of a repentant madam . . .

Sixteen and I had already held a rendezvous with life . . . Had
a baby, interpreted the reader, who had lately done some research
groping in the field . . . Husband got in jail. Demanded his young
wife, the memoirist, do anything to get him out. Blindly she yielded
to others those charms she had vowed to keep as love's pledge for
husband alone, and sent him the money. . . .

"Gee, Paul," Montefiore heard the earnest salivary voice of Poynton Darcy. "Do you know you're into me for a century already?"

David went back to his platter of cold cuts . . . She trod the
garden of disillusionment then, ah, then, walked valley of betrayal,
knowing now that girl who pawns pearl of greatest price for pelf
is doomed . . .

Darcy's muffled whine struck in, "You put me in a hell of a position, Paul. You've been ——"

Harris (Montefiore could tell from fragments of the talk which
he was obviously not meant to hear) had interrupted to tell Darcy
that he had been the most generous of editors. Hadn't he brought
Poynton up from a pup? Bought his tripe when nobody else
would? . . .

David grimaced and dove in again . . . Now though she longed
for humble but spotless cabin of her innocent childhood, her feet
were set on way that has no turning. Return she dared not. Her
mother's wise old eyes would tear tinsel from gaudy lie that was
in her heart . . . Slumped and sobbing beside the beast, she begged
him to let her go. But he would not. Like some beast of the jungle,
licking his dry lips with hot tongue, sordid lecherous sneer twist-
ing cruel corners of his heavy cruel mouth, his eyes were agleam
with savage urge of physical desire. He struck her twice across ripe
curving body upon her white flesh. Her senses reeled . . .

She got over it all right, Mr. Montefiore observed. He waved the manuscript back and forth and noticed that from where he sat it looked as if the greatest crimescribe was giving in . . .

Her eyes became tombstones of soul as she allowed playboys to paw her remorselessly. Modesty forbade her even to recall weird sex rites she had indulged with some of them. But, oh, the burning memories of that night . . . Mr. Darcy here recalled some of them and burned for a number of lines. . . .

The night when he clasped her nude in his nude arms before loud mad throng of revelers whose greedy grasp for pleasure left even hardened bartenders staring dumbly. When he ran upstairs with her, threw her on bed among silken cushions . . . Montefiore skipped the rest of what Mr. Darcy had just now gone all out to substitute for the half-baked sociological musings to which Mr. Harris had objected.

"Long shot in the third," Mr. Harris was saying to his creature . . .

Montefiore skimmed over the inevitable close . . . Now, old in body, though still young in years, she stumbled through littered alleys fawning on rabble for kind word, chance favor. Shivering, she stared into cold future and saw no hope there. Be warned, girls, she declared, CRIME CANNOT PAY. . . .

David sighed, threw the manuscript back on the desk and glanced up to see Darcy fumbling in his coat.

"You *will* put the check through right away, won't you, Paul?" the special investigator said as Harris's hand came more than half-way and extracted the bill from his fingers. . . .

www

"AUTHORS!" Mr. Harris crossed the room and sank down as if exhausted at his desk. Privately he was making a vigorous note to write Darcy's yarn up himself before Darcy got around to it. *Dependable Detective* would take it and maybe *Elementary Detective* as well. *Ghastly Detective* and *Privy Detective* had accepted his paraphrasing of Poynton's last. . . .

"Writing!" he snarled to Montefiore. "God, what a phony racket!"

"About madams." David crossed an elegant knee. "As I was saying. A well-organized committee of them could do your kind of thing with less overhead. Distribute through their syndicates. They wouldn't act in restraint of trade either by describing unsuccessful colleagues. Were you planning to publish that recrement of Darcy's?"

"March issue of *Carnage*, front position," Paul answered with a kind of relishing insolence. "Cover line and picture. If it suits Mr. Pough, what can *you* do about it?"

"I could line up every pest I can locate out of your past," David's eyes showed a flash of blue contempt, "to camp on you. There must be plenty. That wouldn't suit Mr. Pough."

"Oh, yeah?" Harris's sneer was a trifle inept.

"I'll needle every vice society in the country to descend on you." David's anger was either quite evanescent or superbly covered. This quality in it bothered Harris more than Montefiore's ability to exchange insults.

"I've got a bishop warning youth about big city vice, editorial page. Why, you forty-nine per cent short-ender—" Harris's indignation was sincerely righteous. "Think of the investment. Over ten million ——"

"Yes, yes, I know. Ten million morons read the crime books every month," David replied. "But," he got to his feet and stood over Harris, "they go to the better movies and listen to decent radio programs too. Maybe they buy your stuff in spite of the fact that it stinks."

"So what?" Harris kicked his feet off the table and shouted. "So you're an aesthetic saperino who thinks another *Journal of Criminology* is what the public wants? Mr. Pough," he continued with satisfied security, "likes the idea of having a horse of every color in his stable. I wish you'd remember, Mr. Monteefeeohree, that Mr. Pough is satisfied with *Carnage* and Mr. Pough owns fifty-one per cent of the Popub stock."

"He'll own a hundred per cent if I die." David laughed with a characteristic turn of mood. "If *he* goes first, *I* will. A mutual arrangement before I was interested, Harris. Pough is perfectly healthy of course, but so am I and he's much older."

David swayed on his toes and chuckled good-naturedly at Harris's startled face. "Since your loyalty is motivated by those two per cent, you really ought to have that information to wallow around with, my dear fellow. Because if I got it all, it would be pop goes the weasel, you know."

A door slammed. George Stock, *Carnage's* art editor, a short wiry bustling man in his early thirties, shouldered his way between David and the desk. His sandy complexion was darkroom-bleached, his conscious efficiency combined with the manners of a post-office clerk. He tossed a bunch of photographs into Harris's lap.

"Pop goes *you*, too," said David cheerfully to George Stock.

"Here, Paul." The art editor's voice had a quick harsh quality. "Here's what Tiptop and Superba sent around." Harris riffled the photographs with some interest. "Don't like any of them myself," Stock went on. "But here's my angle. Run the torso, legs, head together, see? Anatomical composograph, just as they're found. Spread cops digging in between. All up against some big pix of the Pennsylvania Peach——"

"—— as she was before Fate drove her into a ghastly web of circumstance," David interrupted. He had come around to stand behind Harris's padded swivel chair and was looking over the editor's shoulder. "That soon bore sinister fruit in one of the most bizarre and fantastic catastrophes that ever rocked the nation," he finished smoothly.

Mr. Stock's invisible eyebrows twitched and he spoke before he thought. "That's right," he said. He bent over Harris with a hostile glance at Montefiore, who had circled the magazine table and paused at a cupboard with glass-paneled doors which stood between two windows on the Sixth Avenue side.

This cabinet contained a hugger mugger of torn lingerie, sharp and blunt instruments, strangling devices, buttons found on scenes, and a number of guns. His Black Chamber of Crime, Mr. Harris had called it with the magniloquence of a schoolboy. A reform schoolboy, David amended to himself, turning to encounter the gaze of Stock.

The art editor had halted in the doorway to scan David target-wise. David returned the stare casually and Stock's eyes fell. He slammed the door after him. . . .

"So," David said, "bishop one, madam two, torso disappearance fortified with heavy sex three, for March."

"A clairvoyant," Harris said. "Sure. The bishop makes it moral."

"Your competitor, *Authentic Detective,* has an educator this month," David said, moving over to the table and stirring about in the pile of magazines there. "A dean of men who says one can find considerable sin in coeducational colleges after dark. There was a trunk murder on the other side of his picture with a photographic layout remarkably like the one Mr. Stock just invented. When you held the page up to the light," Montefiore illustrated with the copy of *Carnage* which he had recently disassociated from his hat, "the dean seemed an integral, I might say intimate part of the trunk arrangement. I've wondered why you and your brethren don't really go in for transparencies, Harris."

"Those special processes cost money," the editor answered, caught himself, and barked, "I should walk right in your parlor, huh? Listen, dope, the farmers love the two bits' worth I give 'em. Did you know most crime mag subscriptions are RFD's? Our advertisers offer novelty art studies," Harris added in a lower tone and repeated, "the bishop makes it moral."

"It's a pity the bishop can't exorcise your grammar," David answered. "Truth, you say on your editorial page, is often stranger than fiction, but, 'An author has to show me his story fits the facts I can accept it.' Your very words, sir. What pidgin!"

"Sure." Harris set his hat over his eyes. "I could have written it. I write, dictate that is, such a lot. It's the only efficient way. I'm not a stenographer." He adjusted his feet and wondered if Montefiore knew that the position was beginning to be irksome. "Pardon me while I nap for two minutes. If you don't haul your freight by then, I'll call the guard."

"Oh, no," David answered pleasantly, "I like it here. I like looking at you sitting in front of your homicidal collection revolving your criminous preoccupations in your criminal mind." Harris's foot twitched involuntarily. "It reminds me, with the gray winter sky behind you, of a tableau at Madame Tussaud's." Harris peered up like a suspicious crow while Montefiore drew a breath. "And all the while I was waiting for you to come in from your noon expedition taking candy away from babies, I was wondering if you realized that, in addition to contributing to the delinquency of delinquents and the perversion of perverts, you had helped develop a new contribution to English literature."

There was a pushbutton in the base of his telephone which would have summoned the guard, but Harris sat quiet under his hat. He knew that letting Montefiore engage in a rumpus would result in newspaper publicity.

"Take," David said, "your number four ruby, entitled, WHO SLAYED THE RED-HEADED JULIET? PASSION IN THE PAWNEE RANGE OR THE MYSTERIOUS RIDDLE OF THE CHEATING ROMEO AND THE BATTERED BRIDE. THE BIZARRE HORROR OF A CRIMSON FLASK LEADS POLICE ON THE TRAIL OF A COLD-HEARTED KILLER. BY SHERIFF ELMER PIGG AS TOLD TO PEVERILL PEAKE, SPECIAL INVESTIGATOR FOR *Carnage* MAGAZINE.

"That title," Montefiore declared enthusiastically, "has its roots firmly in the Newgate Calendar for all it's as modern as air sickness."

Harris raised his head at David's recitation of the title, but he said nothing. Mr. Harris had a rather remarkable memory for extraneous detail, although he was quite without originality or critical sense. He habitually kept quiet when confronted by circumstances or people he did not understand. After he figured them out, he acted according to his own peculiar lights.

The editor of *Carnage* magazine was to be confronted by a number of circumstances in the next few days, most of which he misunderstood completely. At present he had no more suspicion than Betty Hargrave that the sort of thing he dressed for market might come to life in his hands . . . Montefiore was still speaking. . . .

"The epic opens quietly in the Smoggs family mansion outside the peaceful little town of Quagmire. Present at the time are Grandma Smoggs, a negro maid who is of course humming *Swing Low*, and little Orville Quander who has come with his dog Spot to dig potatoes. Some sinister portent of grim doom hits all four at the same time, it seems. They all make for the parlor. Let me read it to you, Mr. Harris:

"On the threshold a grim sight met their eyes. Upon the rug which was akimbo lay the battered body of Madeleine Smoggs, whose slim figure revealed the outlines of ripening womanhood through the damp dress clinging weirdly to her form. It was an appalling discovery. A pattern of red writhing horror etched itself on the rug, fed by five sinister rivulets from five black holes in the young girl's breast. Some fiend had hacked her with an ax until her face bore no slightest semblance of humanity and thrown water upon her helpless form. Her unclosed eyes were foggy gray blurs. The blood had jellied on her marred face among black and blue clotted spots. . . . The trio shrank back in stark stunned powerless amazement. Something, they thought, must be strangely amiss. . . ."

"You got a nice refined voice," Harris spoke cautiously.

"What a service to humanity!" David cried. "Think of the poor souls who spring from warm beds to run out to traffic accidents, and how frequent their disappointment! Here is exactly what they are looking for and how elegantly expressed!"

Harris eased his right foot to the floor. "You could talk on the *Carnage* Radio Hour, if we get it," he said. "You're really inter-

ested in true crime. If you'd get rid of your asinine prejudice against
the glamour we have to give the trade ——"

"Faced by these suspicious circumstances," David interrupted
conversationally, "grandma instantly summons police. As always in
your art form, these arrive instantly. They are commanded, Adonai
be my witness, by none other than those vigilant investigators
Sheriff Elmer Pigg and Trooper Taswell Trice, who viewing the
scene also feel that there must be a dark background of ominous
tragedy lurking pantherwise behind this gruesome discovery.

"There follows," David sitting on the desk spoke directly down
at Harris's hat, "a fruity recapitulation of the grim macabre spec-
tacle for the benefit of those who came in late . . . The sight makes
Pigg thrust out his jaw stubbornly, a gesture which has rendered
him feared by malefactors far and wide . . . Consider," David
flipped a page, "the machine-like coolness of Sheriff Pigg's mind.
'In the event that the culprit emerges shooting, men,' he says, 'do
not hesitate to reach for your guns.' "

David dropped his voice. "I am enthralled by Sheriff Pigg."

Harris had both feet on the floor now. He sat with his chin up
and listened to Popub's minority stockholder.

"Pigg disarms the culprit by a lucky shot through the door which,
when broken down, reveals none other than Madeleine's friend, the
manicurist, Doll Beaver. Now, all along we have posited a lust-
driven bestial he-slayer behind this baffling inscrutable enigma, but
Pigg knows at once that Doll is the killer. Why? She is smoking a
cigar and besides she has shifty blue eyes. All murderers have shifty
blue eyes, Harris. Why is that?"

Harris jerked his elbow and his chair squeaked.

David went on, reading and glossing, but with an experimental
note in his voice and more frequent glances at the editor's face.

"Defiant, Doll was garbed in a smartly tailored suit and sport oxfords,
sneering sullenly at her captors. 'I'm Sheriff Pigg,' Pigg said icily to the
haughty beauty. 'We're tired of being made monkeys of.' . . . 'So what?'
Doll Beaver sneered. 'So this,' Sheriff Pigg volleyed. Unbeknown to her,
Pigg had been *appraised* by the microscope . . ."

David's delivery, which has become increasingly declamatory, wavered on a note of pleased surprise.

". . . *appraised* that the crimson fragments of glass were the ominous relicts of the manicurist's nail polish . . ."

"To relieve the suspense," David said, forgetting himself, "as the dawn broke, Doll did too."

" 'I know,' Doll told Pigg, her gaze falling to the floor with a sob, 'I know that the taking of a human life is bound to stigmatize any girl in the eyes of her fellow man, but I resolved that if I could not, Madeleine Smoggs should never have Malachi Snodgrass for her own. Now I only want to lift this hideous weight from my soul in the thought that some other girl, tempted to stray from the narrow path, may reflect that CRIME DOES NOT CANNOT PAY.' Sobbing wildly, her jailers led her away, A Crushed And Broken Butterfly."

The young aesthete spoke the last words with a sob in his own voice and looked at Harris. He went on watching the man almost continuously and with no more than a random glance at his script.

"Now she stands, now, staring at iron bars behind grim prison walls, a living corpse, a passion-betrayed butterfly. Beyond is life, she thinks. Life, life. Autumn leaves turning crimson as her crime, hearth fires gleaming, a child calling for its mother. Mother, mother . . . But for her white body, to which sex and its weird rites beckoned overpoweringly, there awaits only the current that will slam her taut against the cruel straps, redden and blister her flesh, searing it beyond the clasp of the strongest man's arm. Does she, the beautiful and the damned, on loveless nights that she spends in her murder-haunted cell, hear the choked screams of her rival, feel the dead girl's flesh once again hacking away under her hands?"

Montefiore ended on a high note and dusted his fingers. He looked closely at Harris now. What he saw enraged him. The more because those lines which had clinched the effect had been largely

Montefiore. Harris, hat far back, eyes wide, sat rapt. Like a gull his mind soared, a gull hard after a flushing vent.

"You liked it," Montefiore asserted with rising fury. "You really liked that—*you*. It isn't the bloody public, it's you! You rotten root, you abominable branch. Yoy! You apocatharsis, you, you dump!"

David tore his copy of *Carnage* to shreds. Pieces hit the table, fluttered in the air.

"Hey!" mewed Harris, flapping down out of it.

Purposefully Montefiore scooped up a handful of true crime publications and rounded the table toward Harris's desk.

"Go away," said the editor of *Carnage* as his hat was jerked down over his eyes.

"Siddown," growled the young aesthete. David's free hand shoved hard at Harris's shoulder so that he and his chair were set too well against the desk.

The editor of *Carnage* was pinned thus, with streamers of *Elementary*, *Ghastly*, and *Privy Detective* still descending upon his head, when the eagle nose of Mr. George Stock came slowly through a crack in the consultation room door. The art editor himself came no further.

Montefiore adjusted his own hat and marched with dignified exhilaration toward the hall exit. Here an object, hanging on a costumer, commanded his eye, Harris's topcoat, huge shepherd's plaid wedges of maroon and white.

Harris, clawing blindly, caught between chair and rim of desk, was beginning to curse a little. A smile crossed Montefiore's fine mouth. He snatched down the overcoat, swung it matadorwise with the happy inspiration of a sentiment which rose to his lips.

"You," said Montefiore, sailing the coat through the air. It settled over Harris like a canvas top. *"You should live so."*

David Montefiore left then, whistling quietly, and sauntered toward the far end of the hall.

The part owner of *Carnage* had only an antiquarian interest in Tin Pan Alley, and Echo Newman had not lived long when the tune in question was composed. But out of that fund of surplus knowledge which made her so good an office wife she recognized it. She took off a dictaphone headpiece when David appeared in Pough's outer office and regarded him solicitously.

"Have you been—in with—Mr. Harris all this time?"

Montefiore stopped whistling, removed his hat, and bowed European fashion.

"Have I been annoying Mr. Harris, you mean?" He smiled. "Past all recounting I have been annoying Mr. Harris, my Shulamite, you dern betcha."

Mr. Pough was out, Echo said. David's overcoat which he had left with her, professing a fear of thieves in Harris's domain, was there. She pointed.

"Are you angry with me, acushla?"

"No, but I will be if you don't go," she answered with the worried half-maternal expression which David's vagarious manner always brought out. "I'll see you tonight. I have a job to do here. You go."

"I have a job to do here too," David assured her and commenced his almost soundless whistle again. But he did go.

A job, the minority stockholder was thinking, on which he would, he was bound he would enlist the help of a certain stubborn long-legged friend of his . . . *Dead girl's flesh hacking away under her hands,* David reflected as he passed the offices of *Lo!* . . . A one- or two-horse hack? . . . Peculiar, how reading Harris's product aloud made you realize its eminent loathsomeness. The ear absorbed what the eye flinched away from. *That,* David remembered with the self-approbation which he always accorded himself for dredging up a scrap of technical knowledge, was what Hal had told him one did to test the style of a disputed document.

Well, David asked his absent opposition, the Poynton Darcy *opera* were documents, weren't they? And would Hal Van Kill deny that he, David, was disputing them? . . . *Hacking away under her hands* . . .

Poor Butterfly the tune was in the office, *Poor Butterfly* it still was and louder as Montefiore ambled thoughtfully toward the elevator rank . . . Echo turned back to dictaphone and typewriter with a sigh. . . .

IV

〜〜〜

THE region around Random Street is close enough to the Battery to remind those who loiter there in cold weather that New York City is near the ocean front. Random Street is close enough to Wall to give a kind of deliberation to its shabbiness. But part of the suggestion of imminent fog that hangs over the eateries, independent brokerage establishments, small dress shops and secondhand office equipment stores following Random Street's unorthodox curve around Random Place comes from the ancient basements beneath them, which tend to collect water.

No appreciable warmth came on this particular afternoon from the winter-thinned sun. The tall young man, who blocked what lingering beams would have fallen on the stall of throwaways in front of Benjamin De Porta's Random Place bookstore, had an aspect of alert content which irritated the elderly female watching him from the window. His cheerful silhouette Miss Daisy Goff identified with the animal tranquillity of the affluent even before she noticed the unassuming perfection of his Chesterfield overcoat.

Hendrik Van Kill, examiner of questioned documents and licensed investigator, continued to examine a furry specimen from the seventeen-cent rack as if he hadn't caught the running glitter of her pince-nez chain. There was a wink of light as his ungloved hand turned a page. The thin wattles on the lady clerk's chin jerked once. Many gentlemen affected big rings nowadays. But the ring plus the fluid awareness of the hand that wore this one made Miss Goff think of her boss. Musicians and artists were supposed to have fingers like that, one saw them in family portraits, and most annoyingly among the tribe of Ben De Porta. The bookseller's nephew, David Montefiore, for instance.

The bookseller's lady clerk snapped her eyeglasses back onto her bosom, turned away from the window, and so missed the reactions of two young ladies in skating costumes who circled the boundary of the furthest projecting stall, fell out of step for an instant, and passed behind the young man in the Chesterfield with a more definitely marked swing.

The young man did not raise his head. In recognition of this indifference a darling little mitten with a red heart on the palm had come up to pat the back of its matching Sonja bonnet when there fell on the ears of the wearers of both little bonnets a sound like that of a cow removing its hoof from deep mud.

The black velveteen skirt switched its red facing in rhythm with the blue velveteen skirt's flash of yellow and the shoulders of the little quilted jackets came around in unison. The horrid sound had not been one of derision and two pairs of patent eyelashes narrowed at the appearance of an improper gambit. For the young man had not moved. He stood there with his generous aura of knowing all the answers and not caring, but he was not looking at them.

His companion was, however. The skating costumes teetered on thin heels, the faces under the bonnets assumed personality when they finally noticed the boy.

Close to the young man, leaning back in the angle of a table so as to be hidden on their approach was a small figure, compact in riding clothes and vital curiosity. He seemed pleased. The dark eyes which dominated the essentially childish contours of the boy's face looked at the girls with an intent yet impersonal interest which followed their accelerated progress around the curve of Random Street where it leads into Barclay.

"'Oh what a lovely baby,'" Master Cameron quoted reflectively. "'How nice it would go with gravy.'" He shifted his elbows on the guard rail of the table, crossed one shiny boot over the other and twisted his neck to study his guardian's noncommittal features. "Do you think they thought I was a midget?"

"Not awfully." Hendrik Van Kill answered comment and question economically without raising his eyes from his book. "You'll come to recognize, quite common phenomena. How tall do you think?" he asked with the tone of disinterested challenge which always made his charge rise like a trout.

"Height five feet two and three without heels," Edward recited promptly. "Weight, average 110 pounds, dolichocephalic types, prominent noses, brown eyes and marked pituitarism. Hair naturally straight and dark, permanently curled in both cases, and the black and red outfit bleached."

The young man's wide rather thin mouth lengthened a bit as he considered the face of Edward. Edward with lowered lids and chin tilted toward the grimy heavens was summoning the inward eye. Van Kill would never have considered himself, an individual of unconventional opinions and no settled habits, as a suitable mentor for a lad of nine years. But this particular specimen was a particularly special kettle of I.Q. Van Kill was conscious of a perfectly human satisfaction in beholding a development which must be the result of his own influence.

"Age?" he asked, telling himself not to be fatuous.

"You know I can never tell age. There are girls in the ninth grade at Webster look to me like women of thirty-five with three children. They squat when they walk. *I* think it's mostly a matter of height and bearing——"

The boy halted as if minded to expound this further, but went on. "I guess those two, who are *not* going skating, are about nineteen. The whites of their eyes were clear. The bleached one had rickets in infancy which probably accounts for the malocclusion——"

"Do they work together?" Van Kill had stepped back from the table and was looking down the street.

"I think they work in the same place and probably live together. They wore stockings of the same shade, which would be economical." Edward took the weight off his shoulders and stood up. "I don't care to think about those girls any more. Is that man who looks like Monty Woolley, Mr. De Porta? I believe those girls are waitresses. That would account for their dresses being fresh and their stockings having been worn all day."

The boy and the young man waited there, a disparate couple tranquilly en rapport, watching the plump gentleman with the white imperial who was approaching them. Small fawn-spatted feet carried him along with an abstracted yet purposeful meander in front of, more than in, a fur-lined overcoat of Droshka proportions. Above the little beard was a Buddha face enlivened by pleasant malice. He did not see them until Van Kill spoke.

"Why don't you take it off, Ben, if it's too hot for you?"

"Hendrik, my boy!" The overcoat billowed around the three of them while De Porta shook hands with Van Kill. "It is so long since I have seen you."

These were black eyes of the sharpest, the child observed, as Benjamin De Porta looked Van Kill up and down with frank approval. Merchant's eyes that probed and snapped admirably unvarnished facts to the brain behind them. But they were surrounded by laugh wrinkles which pointed to eyebrows suddenly tipped up at the ends so that Edward felt the plump gentleman's nicely balanced conclusions were irresponsibly catalogued by a light and mischievous heart. Even without seeing his guardian's long countenance drop the amenable shell which it turned to the outside world, Edward thought he would have known much of this.

"Not since you returned from the corn belt in such happily altered circumstances," De Porta was saying. "Circumstances almost —of a family man." The intimate note dropped from his slightly accented voice as Van Kill introduced the boy.

"I think we have met after a fashion? Over the telephone," the bookseller said, releasing the child's hard paw. Being assured now that De Porta did not consider friendship with Van Kill as license to pat Edward Lindsay Cameron on the head, Edward relaxed.

"I remember of course," he replied. "Hal was upstate."

"Ah, yes, a disputed document case, was it, Hendrik? David told me something about it. It is so right, I think, that you are interesting yourself in that sort of scholarship. It would have pleased your father. But—" De Porta shrugged his overcoat onto his shoulders "—you must be cold. I am beginning to be grateful for this rug."

Van Kill's long hand tweaked the lapel of De Porta's coat. "I saw it," he said in the tone of one speaking of a family pet. "Clinging to the wall when we came by Moskowitz's. I knew you'd be along directly, so we didn't go in and disturb the post-prandial chess."

"I have known a time," the bookseller smiled at the boy, "when in a guise of scholarly abstraction your guardian would have pretended our meeting was accidental. Is this change because he now admits to being a professional investigator?"

"He is the same sort of detective that he is a scholar," Edward answered thoughtfully. "It's Yanni, Mr. Mavromicháli, who is practical. Hal says scholarship is static, while a detective must weigh the abilities and limitations of other human elements than himself, but—" Edward's eyes rolled at Van Kill and his cheeks rounded with disapproval "—he takes the *same selective attitude*."

De Porta had heard rumors of the Cameron heir's views on practical economics. He was commendably grave. "Just so," he said, turning toward the shop door. "And without any claim to intuitive deduction, Hendrik, I wonder if you did not stay outside to wait for me because you saw my poor Miss Goff. She lies in wait for good-looking *Goyim* to take their money for dressed calf with lots of gilding."

"My interest in robbery is usually well-controlled as my interest in reform," Van Kill parried.

De Porta slid out of his coat with a sigh. He had a horror of cold and was almost always too warm. "By which you mean you consider my nephew David's project to improve the reading habits of the general public as hopeless?" The bookseller shook his thatch of hair, black and white like watered silk, and retrieved his hat from a display of Christmas cards where he had tossed it. "Have you time to come upstairs and klatsch about the last of the Montefiores?"

"Quite hopeless by the methods dear Dizzy has proposed," the document examiner agreed, moving after his friend. De Porta had begun to drift toward the semi-enclosed staircase at the rear. This structure clambered over a private office past a low balcony and deviously through a fire door to the rear of Ben's own living quarters. A telephone was ringing in the office.

De Porta never hurried. He could pad through his shop after a three-hour absence, nod to his clerks and know how events moved.

No man in the book trade had a better set of antennae, Van Kill reflected. Which made it difficult to account for the lady who had just come out of the office.

She said, "Telephone, Mr. De Porta," in a female seminary voice and with the air of one granting a concession.

De Porta turned back. "Thank you, Miss Goff. I'll take it down here." He shifted his greatcoat and wagged a free hand toward the stairs. "You and the boy go along up, Hendrik. You know the—" He felt in a pocket and tossed a key.

The young man caught it, stepped aside for an outgoing customer with a war map, and stood with his face bent over the bright metal. Its edges were still sharp from the cutting. He hoped the woman would go away.

"Why, it's Dr. Van Kill," she said, coming over to him. "Imagine seeing you here!" Here in this *stew*, her tone implied. Compared with her manner toward De Porta her urgent friendliness now was like a suddenly wrenched faucet.

It involved no effort for Van Kill to reassure her protestations that he wouldn't remember *her* from the class in Late Latin Poets which he had taken over at International University when Professor Devries had influenza. Van Kill did as a matter of fact recall Miss Goff as a type which should never attempt to look ingratiating.

"You really made them *live*!" Miss Goff cried. "Though I knew it wasn't your *field*. I used to see you coming down from the Papyrus Gallery in the Old Library."

"Various scholars have agreed that I have a lamentable tendency to skip around," the document examiner acknowledged. From the office he could hear De Porta, whose telephone voice was more Viennese than usual. . . . He was wondering where Edward had taken himself and was absently observing how without any real peculiarity of dress the woman seemed to be wearing a boned net collar from 1910.

"I've heard how you skipped around." Daisy Goff startled Van Kill's full attention with a burst of ghastly archness. "I am not *completely* cut off from Olympus, you know! You skipped all over

Europe with a perfectly marvelous child prodigy and got back with the greatest *difficulty*, Professor Devries said."

Van Kill looked away from the painful creases of the lady clerk's smile. "Not quite all over. Devries makes it sound very irresponsible," he complained, twitching the triangle of handkerchief in his breast pocket as if it were the Latin professor's loose tongue. From the corner of his eye he could see the gleam of Edward's approaching boots.

"Oh, dear no, Dr. Van Kill!" The spinster's hand made a nervous apologetic movement and her thumb caught in her glasses' chain. "Don't misunderstand me. The responsibility of guiding the education of the sort of child Dr. Devries was telling about would be a *full-time* occupation for the *average* person!" Miss Goff's voice soared to a veritable trill on the last words.

So that was it. Repressing a desire to hoot, Van Kill looked at her closely. Here, he saw, was indeed another female who had got the idea that the Cameron heir must need a woman's influence in his young life.

"Tell me," Miss Goff went on hurriedly. The soft-spoken young man's blank gray regard had unshuttered a glint of steel and she was uncomfortable. "Is it true that you speak nothing but Latin together?" She rounded her colorless lips reverently. Behind Van Kill the voice he had been anticipating spoke with an intonation which matched Miss Goff's for clipped precision:

"We commonly speak Latin from nine to eleven every day."

Daisy Goff's eyes fled from Van Kill's uncommunicative face to a spot behind and to the right of his elbow. "Why here he is now."

Variation 3-B, the document examiner ticketed the major rearrangement of her features, Pleasure at Meeting Juveniles. But no surprise.

This, he discovered when he turned to introduce the boy, was because of Edward's nice judgment of what Miss Goff would expect to see. The most tangible changes were the neatly slicked hair and the huge black-rimmed spectacles. Under them the child's face had dwindled to a pinched wedge which was nearly all eyes and much too small for his head.

Van Kill knew that Edward could pull the tip of his retroussé nose into a straight line. His upper lip then acquired an adenoidal length which contributed much to this admirably loathsome impression of a standard infant prodigy. It was the hollow cheeks, sustained in conjunction with the contemptuous enunciation of a BBC broadcaster that excited his guardian's admiration.

" 'The ancient languages are the scabbard which holds the mind's sword,' " Edward quoted hollowly. Little Rollo was even managing to stand as if he had a weak chest, Van Kill observed.

"Well, isn't that lovely!" Miss Goff was all beginning-of-term pedagogue. "I've never had a chance to *talk* Latin much, but I'm awfully good on forms. Probably I could help *you* there."

"I know all my forms," said the little monster flatly.

He very nearly did too, Van Kill reflected during the ensuing pause. "We are beginning our Greek," he volunteered out of a kind of revolted pity.

"Greek!" She snatched at the remark as if it had been a lamppost in a blackout. "There's nothing like Greek. *You* know, Dr. Van Kill, how it is. I'm devoted to Latin, but I know how you feel too. There's nothing like Greek."

Van Kill agreed that there was nothing like Greek.

"Latin's my first love, but I used *regularly* to put myself to *sleep* with the *mee* verbs," Miss Goff bleated rustily. "*Tithaymee, tithays, tithaysee.*" She bounced on the accents like an aging parrot looking for a billet, was Van Kill's uncomfortable thought. "*Tithemen, tithete, tithéasee.* See?" she demanded, creasing her cheeks in triumph. "The future begins, *tháyso, tháysayss,*" she resumed, just as he had feared. "And it's the imperfect that has the catch in the first person singular active—eta *not* epsilon iota ——"

"Give the second-person-singular-second-aorist-middle-imperative of *tithaymee,*" said the child prodigy.

"Second aorist middle—" Daisy Goff struggled with her memory and her expression. She looked from the boy to the young man, an ugly blue flush creeping around her ears. Van Kill made an involuntary movement to put himself between Edward and the woman, covered it with a casual wave at De Porta, emerging from the office.

"Happily Miss Goff is' never troubled by insomnia." Van Kill dropped the words neatly into the spreading pool of silence. And such was the nature of the woman that their meretriciously face-saving quality was acceptable to her. The basilisk smile was adjusted at its unlovely best as Edward and his guardian took leave of her, but she realized that her ambitions toward their domestic life had died aborning.

V

〰〰

"THAT was David on the phone," De Porta told Van Kill. "He wants us to meet him for dinner at your Greek protégé's place in Pye Street."

"I have already had an argument with Dizzy today," the young man replied, following De Porta up the stairs.

"He says he has something new to tell you."

Van Kill made a skeptical noise in his throat. "Something he's found out, or something new he's thought of?"

"It doesn't really matter if the food is good." De Porta stopped on the landing which was also the roof of his office. "Besides I want to meet your Greek partner in crime. David said he knew you'd want to dine late on account of the boy."

"Edward's private life and mine do not overlap," Van Kill said, looking down at his ward. "We have our arrangements."

"These spectacles," Edward took them off and said a shade defensively when they emerged on the balcony, "are plain optical glass." Ahead of them De Porta quite obviously hesitated to listen before he opened the heavy door that led through a party wall into his apartment. "I got them from a man on Fourteenth Street for thirty-nine cents including tax and had the earpiece fixed for a quarter."

"Oh," said Van Kill.

"It's the anonymity of the big city," Van Kill explained, tossing a match into De Porta's open fire. "Edward's been spared the usual prodigy publicity. One must hand it to the late professor for that." Van Kill's upper lip tightened against his teeth as he referred to Edward's father. "Still, around Brampton and in Cameron County the boy couldn't go far without being recognized."

De Porta's arrangements for living were, Van Kill had often said, as elaborate and as practical as his mind. The bookseller had a finicking taste in porcelains, but they were set out of the way

34

of people reaching for ash trays. Van Kill had spent many contented hours in this apartment.

There were bagel, two kinds of cheese and several varieties of Jewish pastry on the end of a long Biedermeier table near De Porta's silk-jacketed shoulder. The two men were sitting in the dining room, mostly on account of an unbeautiful cohesion of silversmith's and plumber's art which created matchless coffee. De Porta had acquired the copper and silver marvel by means which were always a trifle obscure in the telling, from an Argentinian collector of incunabula. Van Kill had always claimed that the Argentine was buried in the cellar under the bookstore.

"You will have your coffee now, Hendrik, even if a fuse blows." The bookseller nodded at a feather of vapor which was edging from a spout at the top of the contraption.

"I can see," he went on speaking of the boy, "how such forays *au Raschid*, accompanied by this Greek who is you say almost superstitiously devoted to the boy, must be safe enough. Having the seclusive Lady Diana Brown on the same terrace is adventurous too of course. Her latest thriller isn't moving so fast. Possibly Edward will be a leavening influence. His play acting is a childlike manifestation."

De Porta put a certain emphasis on the last words and inclined his black and white crest toward the living room. There behind closed French doors Edward, fortified by a plate of food and a brandy sniffer full of milk, was improving the shining hour with Ben's collection of Arabian phonograph records. Every now and then a vocal passage would be interrupted and the boy's voice heard conscientiously echoing a quarter-tone sequence. "It *surprises* me," he had explained his self-appointed task. "It doesn't surprise Arabs."

"Eminently safe," De Porta repeated. "And practical. How much undisturbed browsing would the Cameron prodigy do in my shop if my poor Miss Goff identified him? Where an urchin who wanders in from the public school around the corner——"

Edward Lindsay Cameron was nine years old and large for his age. His adjustment to the imbalance between his understanding and his experience was excellent. When his face was in repose or when, as now, he was eating, he looked as vague as the bland-eyed child in the Renoir over his head.

Lately he had proved to himself that he could beat people who had their growth at their own games. He was even fairly confident of his ability to anticipate such difficulties as they might create . . .

The voice on the record he was playing turned on itself suddenly and the boy winced as the tone line shattered against his ears. As if the singer's sweetheart had stepped on her cat. Edward acknowledged to himself that he was surprised. It was probably, he reflected, because he had stopped listening with part of his mind and begun to wonder about something else . . .

In general, Master Cameron admitted he had been wondering for a long time if Van Kill really approved, as he knew Yanni disapproved, of his scraping an acquaintance with Rudi Smart at the World's Fair this fall? Did Van Kill really approve of him and Yanni riding with Rudi in Central Park? People had noticed that he looked like Rudi superficially, which had pleased Master Cameron in some obscure way which he could not yet understand.

The fact that he could not annoyed Edward now. The fact that he had shown it a few minutes ago by asking Van Kill if he thought the girls in the skating costumes thought he looked like a midget provoked him too. But more specifically, Van Kill's ward admitted, he was beginning to wonder whether the truant officer had called at the Matapan that afternoon.

Edward Cameron selected a variety of blintz that was foreign to him and prepared to concentrate on the music. He would not have admitted that he was worried at all . . .

Three men, Yanni Mavromicháli privately reckoned two and a half men, sat in a corner of the Matapan Restaurant's gleaming pantry and drank his whisky. Yanni had proposed a toast to their improved understanding and having done so, was fairly certain this was the sort of thing Van Kill meant when he said that a Greek's coals of fire might be classed with his gifts.

"It is as you say, tsust big misonderstanding," Mavromicháli

repeated and poured the agent from the Society another drink.
Reaching across the table, he gave the little figure on the step stool
another drink too. "Big misonderstanding."

Black-browed Yanni, devious and proud as Lucifer, was enjoying the teeter-totter of apology. The agent, whose work in the
defense of underprivileged children had given him an excusable
arrogance, was not so good at it. He had the manner and appearance of an old-time plain-clothes man and he was aggrieved.

"My informant," he said, and it was obvious where his grievance
lay, "gave me to understand that Article 44 of Section 486 would
apply to one of your busboys."

"An habitual truant," Rudi said in his most cultivated bass voice.
"Not to mention Section 490 which would make Mr. Mavromicháli,"
his small hand described a histrionic arc toward Yanni, "responsible
for my delinquency and guilty of a misdemeanor! It is to laugh,
is it not, officer?"

"I only mentioned them article and section numbers from the
Penal Law once," the man from the Society said with admiration.

"It's my business to live up to my name," the midget replied
glibly. "I do a mind-reading act. It all depends on memory really."
Rudi Smart cinched up the corners of his mouth and closed his
eyes.

As if this action had rendered the manikin deaf, the agent
whispered, "Very sensitive, these Little People. I'm glad this business didn't hurt his feelings."

Yanni, who had promised Rudi ten dollars for this business,
did not think his feelings were hurt. The Greek had constantly
to remind himself that little burros were just as self-centered and
lecherous as full-sized asses in order to tolerate Rudi at all.

However, the little fellow had put on what Yanni conceded was
a very nice act of outraged professional pride. He had torn open
his shirt to show the agent the indubitable hair on his diminutive
chest, he had used words that Yanni would never have countenanced from a genuine employee, he had flung his professional
card at the Society's agent and flourished a scrapbook of press-
clippings for the past ten years to prove that he was a man.

The representative of the Society dedicated to the defense of children had had many sharp contacts with theatrical people. The card which he accepted read: COUNT RUDI SMART—MINUTE MAN, MIGHTY MIND. The agent knew better than to get involved with the press clippings.

"I'll see that you're not bothered again," he told Yanni Mavromicháli now . . .

De Porta stretched in his big chair and crossed his slippered feet. "As a matter of fact," he was saying, "I dare say the outfit which your ward wears on the afternoons he chooses to spend among his chronological contemporaries at Webster would put him on the free soup list at a public school ——"

Van Kill, who was examining the inlay on the coffee machine's reservoir with the lens attached to his ring, acknowledged that the gilded scions who attended Webster dressed as if momentarily expecting a relief investigator. "Republican swank," he elaborated, uncurling his long frame and moving over to lean against the mantelpiece. His attitude was casual, but the bookseller moved uneasily under his gaze.

"It is a good thing to harmonize with one's background," De Porta said as the fingers of one hand started brushing up and down at his beard. "For instance, that mirror behind you gives back a Rembrandt light from the fire, Hendrik. You have the neutral greeny brown hair too. All you need is a ruff. What assertive fluid Dutch blood must be."

"The British Museum had a Thirteenth Dynasty statuette of *you* wearing the double crowns of the—" Van Kill broke off with a laugh. "You *are* a wily Jew, Ben. I came to tell *you* why I can't help Dizzy in his plot against an editor named Harris because your beamish nephew can't seem to focus on its impracticality."

"I know that David's plans are frequently visionary and impractical." De Porta spoke with feeling.

"I have been trying to tell him they were also dangerous," Van Kill said crisply. He moved across the hearth and dropped onto a footstool beside his friend. De Porta was wearing an uncle-intoils-of-persistent-child look. "Since when have you been locking your back door?"

"Since October." The bookseller sounded as if he had expected a different question. "It occurred to me that keeping the Evelyn Letters up here, anyone could come up through the shop and——"

"You have always had the Evelyn Letters," the young man cut in.

"I didn't miss anything," De Porta said rather apologetically. "But the excellent Mrs. Horowitz wouldn't disturb my papers. She puts my shirts away according to a system of her own of course——"

"But the system is part of the harmonic background you were recommending," Van Kill interrupted. "It is the disharmony of Dizzy's interference with Popub which really disturbs me." Van Kill swung around on the footstool and stretched his long legs.

De Porta glanced at the coffee machine, decided he had time for a cigar. He chuckled gently while he lit it. "But for, shall we say family pull, that nickname might have been yours, Hendrik, at the time David acquired it. You have changed a great deal since your undergraduate days, but there is something about David of the young Disraeli still."

"I have never," Van Kill declared, "owned an opera cape."

"It is in my mind, Hendrik," De Porta pursued his main theme placidly, "that you should understand this *Carnage* vagary of David's better than anyone. Part of his attitude, I fear, springs from sheer prejudice against Frederick Pough. Most of his reasons do not interest me as a businessman. But I had thought they might interest you with your, I had almost said deplorable, fondness for psychology." The bookseller smiled.

"What David says amounts to this. Catering to every form of public taste, Pough has lost every ideal he might ever have possessed. He no longer knows what he likes, except that he likes what brings in the cash. Only an excuse for David's hostility to *Carnage*, in my opinion," said De Porta on a meditative puff of smoke. "He has no real objection to Pough's other magazines. I myself sell books which nothing could induce me to read."

"The same might be said of many businessmen," observed Van

Kill. "I gather the real trouble is Pough doesn't take our Dizzy seriously."

"Oh, he listens to David seriously enough, but he never *does* anything. And there is David with ideas which would make both of them a mint of money," De Porta said, his eyes twinkling.

"I can *quite* understand," said Hendrik Van Kill.

On the masculine side at least David Montefiore had no better friends than these two who proceeded so genially to take him apart now . . . Little Theaters, Little Forums, Little Movements from Left to Right were well in character, they agreed, for a dilettante patron of the arts. The fact that David had always given money to refugee organizations and refrained from embarrassing them with offers of personal assistance seemed to show he knew his limitations. . . .

Yet now he was inspired to scuttle a profitable publication because he could not control its policy. Disassociating himself from his forty-nine per cent holding in Po Publications, Inc., was not enough. *Carnage,* he said, must be destroyed.

"Galling to an artistic soul," Van Kill remarked, "but many artists are practical."

Montefiore's uncle took his cigar out of his mouth to tug at his beard. He reminded Van Kill that David was no artist. "He is only a rich young aesthete and his attitude reflects on me."

"You mean you managed his affairs when he lived abroad," Van Kill asserted. "David told me he was at Oxford when he inherited the stock."

"I suppose *I* reflected that the vicarious thrill slayers, harlots and bank robbers who liked the *Carnage* type of ordure were always assured that inevitably cops and wormwood grew at the end of the road. It was a matter of business and I am a businessman." De Porta drew his heavy black brows together at Van Kill.

"Of course, Ben," the document examiner said soothingly. "I have noticed that where matters of business are concerned you are always a businessman."

De Porta continued to frown at Van Kill, who had only tightened his mouth. "So tell me, Hendrik, does a Catholic businessman pull out of a rubber company because it manufactures sanitary items?"

"Granted he does," Van Kill mused. "Granted that the Prevention-of-Disease-Only stamp butters no more parsnips for him than the Crime-Does-Not-Pay tag on every *Carnage* article does for Dizzy. Must he still sabotage the rubber goods factory? Why should Dizzy, who is essentially a believer in every man's right to kiss the cow of his choice, be so hot to strafe *Carnage* that he offers me twenty-five thousand dollars to get something that will stick on the chief engineer?"

The chief engineer, De Porta corrected his young friend, was Frederick Pough. An astute businessman, Pough, a gentleman of many interests.

"He has recently acquired, through very reliable channels, I understand, a letter from Ludwig Geyer to Richard Wagner's mother," De Porta remarked and added dryly, "It is supposed to establish the secret of Wagner's pedigree . . . The point about Popub, my dear Hendrik," the bookseller went on, "is that the big boss has a general library rather than a set of bound volumes on his shelf. The magazines are not interdependent. They stand—or fall alone."

David's assumption that Harris and *Carnage* were synonymous was essentially sound, De Porta thought. "Undoubtedly this Harris is remarkably proficient in his own questionable field." Without him the circulation of Popub's *Carnage* would probably trickle back to its seventeen-odd competitors. Frederick Pough could be depended upon to eliminate a failing *Carnage* before David Montefiore had time to exercise his rights as a minority stockholder in the firm.

Van Kill got up and rather crossly poked at Ben's fire. "All very true," he said. "Dizzy will not see that Harris's refusal to be bought shows that *Carnage* is a slimier pond than the surface scum would indicate. Dizzy points to Frederick Pough on his mountaintop, bulwarked by *Lo!* and *Brief* and *Here* and *Hearth* and *You Yourself*, all respectable adjuncts of American life. A stink from *Carnage* could hurt them," he went on. "Pough *is* a businessman. Dizzy claims it all operates in favor of my getting something on Paul Harris over the week end that will make Frederick Pough cut *Carnage's* throat on Monday."

"So far I see nothing that could not with a little care be made perfectly legal," De Porta said easily. "I suppose David made other suggestions which you have not bothered to tell me."

"I explained that to your nephew too," Van Kill said in an impatient tone. "Harris is always within the law. He has extra-mural contacts—oh, nothing tangible," the document examiner added as De Porta made a sudden movement. "Buying their confessions and the reminiscences of their molls, how can he help knowing a rat here, an ex-con there? I do myself. But whereas I might commission one to swipe me a piece of necessary evidence, Harris wouldn't baulk at hiring one to put a knife in David's back."

"Hendrik!" The bookseller waved the mouthpiece of his cigar holder at Van Kill. "I find all this talk about throat cutting and back stabbing very distasteful. A corrupt and generally untrustworthy individual was all the impression David gave me of Harris and I intended to urge you to help him with his crusade . . . Because," Ben answered Hal's raised eyebrows, "as David said when he complained to me about your unco-operative spirit, twenty-five thousand dollars is not hay. Now *I* will pay you twenty-five thousand dollars if you will keep David out of it."

Van Kill hung the poker where it belonged without clatter and remarked that David and his uncle were fine ones to talk about people who could not distinguish between twenty-five thousand dollars and hay.

"I thought the blond ape understood that it was not because the project is visionary or dangerous that I turned him down. It's because," the young man's voice rose, "it's so damn footling! I have not given up trying to argue him out of it, Ben. I am doing well enough so that I can help a friend turn a private furrow."

"You must never give a professional service to a friend who can pay you, Hendrik. If you fail, he can always say it was because you were doing it for nothing."

Van Kill wandered across the room and listened to the coffee machine, which was beginning to provide a not inappropriate accompaniment to the thread of Arabian music from the next room. The contraption's modest eructations told him that the green coffee beans and water, which had been introduced at one end, had severally roasted and ground, boiled and filtered, and come together at the other. His nostrils sought the faint aroma that had begun to rise and flickered thoughtfully.

"Ben," he said, "do you suppose there could be a woman mixed up anywhere in this business?"

A woman in the case was devoutly to be hoped for, David's uncle said after he had poured the coffee. "Waning and waxing love affairs have distracted his attention from numerous enterprises. If there is one here, David will soon forget about Mr. Harris and his dirty little publication."

"Book," Van Kill murmured over his cup. "The people who nurture *Carnage* and its fictional and confessional cousins call them books. There must be a deep, bitter and ominous significance for you in that, Ben, if you could find it . . . No brandy, thanks . . . David ought to get married."

"Have your responsibilities *in loco parentis* of this *Wunderkind* made a demi-benedict out of you, Hendrik?" De Porta measured a careful drop of the liqueur into his coffee and sat holding the crystal stopper. "David says he will never marry. But I feel that the right female, combined with a milieu which would appeal to David's anachronistically romantic fancy, would do the trick . . ."

"The literature of chivalry describes two kinds of knightly behavior," Van Kill remarked. "Knight number one rescues lady from ogre and beats it with her. Knight number two, a social-minded critter, had to demolish the ogre and clean out the castle first. I believe he seldom lived to be anyone's ancestor."

De Porta rose to his feet. "More coffee, Hendrik? It's been long since you tasted this brew of mine. Has it magicked your brain? Ordinarily you are not so devious but that I can follow you."

"More coffee, Ben. *My* wits are not bewitched," the young man said lazily. And then, "What about this incubus *you* have assumed, this Goff?"

Ben De Porta, an elegant, plump, suddenly unhappy little man, stood moodily over the coffee cups. "I had hoped you wouldn't insist on asking about my poor Miss Goff, Hendrik."

"She'd scratch your face, probably, if she heard you call her your poor Miss Goff. I don't have to ask about her, I'll tell you. Divorced from her job because the suburban high school where she's taught Caesar, Cicero and Virgil for twenty years asked her to double in Spanish, English, bookkeeping or maybe all three."

"Just English," De Porta admitted unwillingly.

"She wouldn't even try, no?" Van Kill snorted. "Oh, I'll concede you, it's tragic. But you have no idea what Brahmins these types are. And the sympathy of Latin fanciers like you, Ben—" Van Kill pointed a finger "—Chris Morleyish dilettantes who prattle of esoterica like Ovid and read Latin for fun is hardest of all to bear. Why, you don't know all your forms!"

"Is that it really, Hendrik?" De Porta asked. "I discovered Miss Goff couldn't make head or tail of Juvenal, but she was happy enough here for a few days. Then apparently she discovers I am Jewish." De Porta's brocade housecoat rustled as he shrugged deliberately. "Shouldn't she know?"

"For your sake I wish she had," Van Kill said wryly. "Be warned, Ben. There is no good will in her. It is what Yanni would call a blasted soul."

VI

〰〰

AT FIVE o'clock on this winter Wednesday, an hour before Van
Kill and De Porta sat down to their *apéritif* in the Matapan Restaurant, Miss Daisy Goff sat down to her real day's work in the
office of the Christian Cavaliers. Between Monday and Friday,
thanks to De Porta's easygoing ways, she was able to reach her post,
a front basement apartment in the West Nineties, that early each
afternoon. Saturday she had entirely free, thanks to her employer's
superstition, she was happy to say. . . .

By seven o'clock, when David Montefiore and Echo Newman
were entering the Matapan, Miss Goff had finished running the
addressograph and shoved it to one side on the dilapidated light-
oak table in the Cavaliers' mailing room where she habitually
worked. Neatly she had put the addressograph's little lead name
plates back in their proper compartments in the long table drawer.
. . . By seven o'clock she was ready to stuff and seal the last in
a week's batch of several hundred large plain envelopes. . . .

Miss Goff patted the neatly wrapped pile of stationery boxes on
the table in front of her neatly into line. Stretching her long stiff-
knuckled fingers for the last envelope, she gave a little half-frozen
suspiration of relief. It was not colder than usual in the room where
Miss Goff sat near a draughty vestibule giving on an alley, but her
absorption in the job often left her nearly paralyzed.

Reverently she took up fillers from what had been six high stacks
at her right hand. She believed what they said. The mind of Miss
Goff was virgin of politics, of economics, and logic, though she had
always taught authors bearing on these lines.

With a tiny rattle two pamphlets, THUS SPEAKS THE TALMUD, and
WHY ARE THE JEWS PERSECUTED FOR THEIR RELIGION? went into the
envelope. . . . A saving remnant, that's what we are, Miss Goff
reflected—like those who held the Republic together before Augus-
tus, she thought, easily disremembering the special privileges ac-

corded The People by Great Julius and by the first Roman emperor. . . .

Miss Goff's fingers relaxed with her mood and a square sticker fluttered to the floor. It looked up at her, a bilious yellow and black. . . .

Jesus Christ, it shouted, *Martin Luther, Mohammed, Pope Clement VIII, Benjamin Franklin, Ulysses Grant, James A. Garfield, and Henry Ford, unite with 50 other famous personages in saying:* JEWS *are* TRAITORS *to America and should not be trusted.* BUY GENTILE, it said. . . .

This was the *main* gospel, Miss Goff knew. She stooped down and retrieved the sticker tenderly. Its recipient could put it to good use on a shop door or windshield or in a public toilet. . . .

Three badly printed pamphlets followed the sticker into the last envelope. Badly written, too. Their rambling incoherence baffled Van Kill when he came to grips with it. The pamphlets were aimed several cultural levels below Van Kill, but essentially they preached what the Christian Cavaliers uttered for the higher brackets in *The Lance.* . . .

Night, day, through the alleys and in the high places of America and the world, a gang of international cutthroats slink, stalk brazenly, subsidized by the Big International Jewish Bankers of the Universe. Mostly these thugs commit the huge international crimes: depression, war, famine, and plague. But they also dispatch purely domestic jobs, most of the robbery, rape, and murder, most of the kidnaping in America. The police, all venal, make no effort to seize the real criminals, but arrest harmless bums. . . .

Wake up, America, the pamphlets cried at their close. *Blot out the real criminals. Rub out the Jewish Reds. Don't let warmongering Jew capitalists drain your boy's blood. Stay out of European politics and European wars,* they ordered. BUY GENTILE, HIRE GENTILE, they shouted. BRING BACK THE GOOD OLD DAYS. . . .

Miss Goff shook her streamlined Protocols of Zion into place, wet the flap of the envelope, and smoothed it down. She let her narrow shoulders droop and rubbed her hands. The bone at the top of her spine burned like acid, but she straightened up. In the blind alley which parted this brownstone walk-up from the next one east she heard the scuffling of shoes. Across the barred window which gave upon the alley passed the shadows of several boys. A single tread sounded through the alley, then, and advanced through the vestibule where stairs angled up to the first floor. The footsteps did not ascend the stairs, but turned near their base through the vestibule and toward the room where Daisy Goff sat. . . .

"All ready, Miss Goff?" said a heavy male voice and Thomas Burke's face appeared in the door at Daisy's right.

Miss Goff pointed to the pile on the table top. "All ready, Mr. Burke," she said with what she intended for bright and energetic tones.

"Okay, boys," he said, "stop shoving now," and pushed back a too-eager rabbit-faced lad. "Pass 'em back along the line, same as usual," Burke ordered, and started handing boxes through the door.

Meanwhile a questing tomcat wailed in the maze of back yards behind the offices of the Christian Cavaliers. "Immoral animal," mumbled Daisy Goff directly at the bullet-scarred cheek of Mr. Thomas Burke, who was clearing off the last of the pile.

Miss Goff's epithet, meant entirely for the cat, would have been more apt for Richard Lee, assistant manager of the Christian Cavaliers, whose office, shared with Manager Burke, was reached directly by a door in the mailing room behind the table at which De Porta's lady clerk was still seated. But Mr. Lee and Mr. Burke had both been *wonderful* to her. Mr. Burke had showed her, yes, deference. The manager of the Christian Cavaliers might be a graduate of a goon squad, but having worked up to bigger and better things, Thomas Burke kept his manners like his teeth firmly in place all the time. And fine ingratiating manners they were, even when hinting to shopkeepers who wouldn't sign the pledge that co-operation was a pretty elastic term.

Mr. Burke stayed well within the law now, and a willing sucker if I ever saw one, that old dame, he was thinking as he shooed the rear guard of his delivery boys down the alley. No brains either, thought Mr. Burke, not like that Hargrave girl who might have too much for her own good. . . .

Burke managed delivery for the Christian Cavaliers and did it well. The retired or working newsboys whom he employed could talk their way around anything this side murder. They made their deliveries honestly and within the hour. They had better, they knew. Mr. Burke was partial to his notion that dinner left this night's readers and tomorrow's shoppers in a receptive mood. . . .

The sound of the last footstep had died away. Miss Goff was alone. Something Burke had said recently started a tired wave of half thought flowing. The glaring overhead light hurt her eyes. She reached for the card and clicked it off. . . . There's going to be a lot of changes made. The Classics, sure the Classics are coming back, all the good old things, the old-time religion and respect, he had said. *You* know who's responsible for everything that's wrong, don't you? he had asked. And Miss Goff, bearing in mind that Language supervisor who favored English had answered, yes. . . .

Respect—Miss Goff felt herself at her desk once more, receiving it, dealing out culture with an impartial hand. Whether those big boys, she'd sometimes had nightmares about them, were thankful didn't matter. They needed it, said the conventional busts of Caesar, Cicero, Virgil, no pagans but respectable Christians all, who saluted her from the illustrated pages of the well-thumbed texts she saw herself using once more. . . .

Again came the call of the cat, summoning Miss Goff back to the present with a shock. *Horrid things,* she told herself in the darkness and shivered at the sound of her voice. What a lot of them there were around here, and that one was a he cat all right, which made it worse. People left money to animals like that when women like herself, not so good but like, might be starving.

The cry of the cat sounded again, or rather there were two, the second, Miss Goff thought, disagreeably human, inviting the first and the first accepting the call. . . .

Miss Goff sat up rigidly and forced herself to recite. But she could not go much beyond the division of Gaul, Catiline's abuse of Cicero's patience, or Virgil's arms. The very forms, the sacred forms rolled sluggishly.

In the darkness she could feel a mist on the lenses of her spectacles. She took them off, polished them, and hooked them to her bosom. No, she was not, she told herself, grasping for control that eluded her, *not* at her own familiar desk. Where had it gone and where were they, the high school principals of her spring, respectable, quiet men who revered the Classics and respected her?

Gone, and she was here, not even in the inner office. Not as important as that taffy-headed made-up chit who flirted with Mr. Lee. She was here, here at this old scarred table in the dark, she a priestess whose altar had been overturned by a bearded Baal. . . .

A lot of changes, Mr. Burke had said. The phrase rose to Daisy Goff's lips and caught in a jarring sob. She wanted to believe it. There's going to be a lot, she said it again, a *lot* of changes made. In the darkness Daisy Goff laid her head on the table and wept.

VII

"Oristikós . . . Decidedly." Standing under the sign of the Cerberus which decorated the entrance to his restaurant, Yanni Mavromicháli fortified his resolution to use English even while thinking. The young kyrios, Yanni made an automatic gesture warding off evil influences, had so advised. The little kyrios, Yanni breathed a prayer for the boy's welfare now. It was true, as Van Kill had said—and the Greek saw nothing odd in it, that when Yanni referred to the document examiner or any other gentleman as *kyrios* it meant little more than *mister*. But when he spoke of Edward Cameron, the word took on its ancient shading and become *Lord*.

In any language this was, Yanni calculated, one of the few good alleys in New York. For Pye Street, originating in that knot of byroads which wander south of Wall and one way and another get into Hanover Square and the locale of Captain Kidd's season of respectability, is itself only a very clean blind passageway which gets nowhere. It had been a good place for his Matapan Restaurant, Yanni thought.

The Greek ran an appreciative hand along the lapel of his blameless dinner coat (a garment so well contrived by the Kyrios Van Kill's pet tailor that it nearly molded without revealing too much of Yanni's considerable muscle and disclosed no sign of the quite considerable weapon under his arm). Yanni was looking ahead to the summer. Then some latticework, a few potted trees, and some whitewash would make an outdoor dining room. The Greek's dark face showed a smile. His teeth gleamed under the street lamp near the door.

Yes, Yanni reflected, it had been a good place and healthy for the new-old roots that every Greek must put down. Here, Van Kill had told him, had been an *agora*, a public common, three hundred years ago. Here, a long length of ticker tape west, white men had made their first huts on the island; within cheering distance George Washington had assumed the presidency; and, more significant to Yanni, a businessman-patriot named Revere had operated . . .

Oristikós, decidedly Yanni was thankful to his Uncle Yoryos for buying the site and, Yanni wrinkled his classic nose, for managing it so calamitously. Yoryos was a good whittler, but he was not the type of Greek who becomes an American businessman by spelling his name George. Yanni, reverencing every furrow in his uncle's guileless brow, had bought him out at a loss.

At the alley's mouth now only an occasional car rolled by. The Greek noted how, as the December chill deepened, noisier echoes grew out of the silence. Kyrios Van Kill liked to bring friends down the dusky alley at this hour and into the Matapan's leisurely warmth. He would be along any moment now with his learned and rich friend the bookdealer. . . .

Yanni turned under the wooden Cerberus and went inside.

He walked down four polished steps of dark wood and stood scanning the quiet interior. The center tables were empty, perhaps half a dozen of the booths at the side walls had occupants. (Yanni was cultivating the post-theater crowd.) His gaze roved back to the kitchen embrasure where Antoine in a tall cap moved against a comely array of gleaming copper pans past Phil Dukas. His headwaiter and his best waiter, Yanni was wont to say, a mere Spartan, he could show the others who were Maniotes a thing or two.

He could indeed. Yanni lifted his chin. By a tall booth of grained black walnut, one of a row on the far side and out of the headwaiter's line of vision, a wretched thing was going on. Teekee, the redheaded busboy who wore the Greek fustanella, bent over like a crane, his ballet skirt swung high . . . Yanni picked his path around the tiled fishpool and across the burgundy carpet.

Young Panayoteekee, under the Madonna's care by his name, snapped the garter on his high blue hose and saw a hand hovering behind him. Through Teekee's legs Yanni glimpsed the face of a sixteen-year-old imp caught out. The blue eyes closed. With a resounding smack Yanni's hand came down on the thin rump.

"Stockings you do in the kitsen," Yanni hissed. Dexterously he snatched the boy erect, pulled down the wings of the gay needle-work jacket, slapped the blue cap and tassel to a rakish set, and glared with spurious fury at the immaculate blue pompoms on Teekee's shoes.

The diminutive redhead started to speak. Yanni waved him silent and turned to the booth. His fury became real.

"So, Teekee. Is it thus the men of Mani make? The evzones, the well-girdled ones, freeze and fight in the mountains and you play games."

The service of glazed white on black, a vase pattern of Yanni's own, had been left on the table as brought. Likewise the woeful lad had dumped the silver all in a heap while he ministered to his dress.

"No explains," Yanni cut in as Teekee opened his mouth, "for your sinful pride. To the kitsen, you, and there you remain this evening the rest, unless comes someone without reservation."

The boy's lips quivered, the red head drooped.

"*Grégora. Káme grégora,*" Yanni said. "Make quickly."

Young Teekee took a sad step toward the kitchen and Yanni relented. "Thankful you sood be I let you serve the kyrios later. Now go."

He pointed his words with a second reminder in the rear, but Teekee's stride never broke. Like a swan the white ballet skirt swam off sedately. The way of the aspiring waiter is hard and Teekee was proud to be the focal point of the Matapan's foreign atmosphere with a difference.

Yanni rinsed his hands in the bowl that Phil Dukas had silently brought up, dried them on the proffered napkin, set the table to rights with a few flips of his wrist, and again made for the outer door.

He opened it to see Van Kill pointing with his stick at the sign. "Port ho, Ben. The Matapan at the Sign of the Cerberus."

De Porta looked up at the well-nourished monster who gazed down benevolently through his snaky mane. "Only two heads, Hendrik."

"He's continued within," Van Kill said, pulling De Porta

through the door and introducing him to Yanni. For an instant of frank silence they weighed each other, the man of food and the man of books who both admitted being in business. The verdict, Van Kill noted without surprise, was on both sides favorable.

"It is ancient design," Yanni explained as De Porta surveyed Cerberus's backward-looking third head and spiky rear elevation over the inner door. "But newly from the knife of my mother's brother."

Possibly because he had grubbed them out of the ground in his early youth and supervised their excavation as foreman of an archaeological dig when he was older, Yanni Mavromicháli had a sixth sense about classical antiquities which his art-fancying Wall Street customers found commercially valuable. But he had no stiff-necked prejudice against modern adaptations.

The bookseller remarked that the interior doghead was a sterner specimen than the two under the street lamp.

"The entire work is an impressionistic image of Yanni himself," Van Kill replied unfeelingly. "The big smile for the client, the teeth for the help."

"Herakles himself, kyrie." Leading the two men to their booth Yanni replied good-humoredly over his shoulder. "Not alone his dog to manage the help here. True Greeks they are almost all."

"In the opinion of Maniotes like Yanni the only true Greek is one from Mani," Van Kill commented with cheerful rudeness. "And Greeks from other sections habitually refer to such a one as *Maniátes maniakós*, a Maniote maniac. They agree that it takes a Maniote to handle a bunch of them."

Yanni lifted an eyebrow to summon Phil Dukas and went away wearing an expression of inscrutable good cheer.

"How you do needle him," De Porta remarked after they had ordered an *apéritif* against David's arrival.

"Yanni?" Van Kill grinned. "I can't help trying when he gets that archaic smirk on his handsome pan. It's the smile he turns upon the bright face of cash. That's why he wouldn't sit down with us. He knows you've been talking about money."

"He appears to have virtues you might emulate, Hendrik," De

Porta replied and asked, "Is the exception to his Maniote monopoly that redheaded Irish boy?"

Van Kill adjusted his long legs under the table and took a meditative sip of his Dubonnet. Ben had presented him with an opening for a delicate point.

"The non-Greeks by Maniote standards are Antoine in the kitchen, whose mother was an Athenian, and our gloomy Dukas here who comes from Sparta. Teekee—" Van Kill balanced a spoon on his forefinger and let it fall onto the carpet.

Panayoteekee's red head bobbed into view at once. De Porta watched the youngster change the spoon and pour water between glances of intense blue worship at Van Kill.

"Not Irish," De Porta said when the boy withdrew.

"Teekee," Van Kill went on, "was about a year old when Yanni's uncle found him crawling along in a pine forest, but he's undoubtedly a Maniote. Only a Maniote would lose a redheaded baby boy."

"You mean—" De Porta's placid countenance took on shock and incredulity. "You mean these people in the south of Greece are so backward and cruel they still practice infant exposure?"

"Not backward and cruel. Tradition-ridden and cautious. The people around Cape Matapan claim descent from the aboriginal stock. The blue-eyed invader from the north was repulsed. I myself have had horns made at me in Mani for want of a little pigment," Van Kill added, raising his gray eyes to De Porta. "An infant who retains Teekee's ill-omened coloring is almost surely a witch's changeling, a *vrykólakas*. Rear such a one and some midnight or high noon he may summon his own kind. They will come out of the secret places and help him eat you, your family, and goats."

"So," De Porta said after a moment. "Would he also undermine the national morale by subversive political activity?"

"Only by eating people," Van Kill said. "Tell me, Ben," he went on with a spurt of pace, "do you know any Big International Jewish Bankers?"

De Porta took a startled look at Van Kill's face and chuckled. "What insane tangent? Have you been reading the Protocols of the Elders of Zion? Or that energetic product of my own Vienna, Herr Rohling, perhaps?"

"The adjective is your own, Ben." Van Kill curled his lip. "I'm on no tangent. I'm thinking of David, who is incidentally late as usual. If he is carried over this *Carnage* crusade, what guarantee is there that he won't begin to generate heat against the international Semitic windmill? And David waves a wild lance."

De Porta moved his shoulders slightly as if to indicate that there was no guarantee. "I suppose you have gotten hold of some pamphlets, Hendrik," he said. "Bankers, then. You know we don't control Kuhn, Loeb any more. Seligman either exclusively. There's even Virginia Tidewater mixed up there. Counting them all—" The bookseller spoke with a kind of disinterested authority much as Van Kill would have outlined an historical period with which he wasn't particularly engaged. "—domestic and foreign, Landenburg, Lehman, and the rest, I would say that *we* have of the total perhaps ten per cent. Internationally we stand at the very bottom of the pile. We never did run to banking until the Middle Ages forced us to. Before that we were likely to be farmers as not, as you perfectly well know, Hendrik."

De Porta lit another of his small cigars and twinkled at the young man, who seemed to be leaning on his friend's words as if they formed a support for him to think against.

"We've always been buyers and sellers, though, if only of Canaanitish grapes. Why don't you ask about clothing and furs? About the buying of junk and tobacco? We stand on the top of those piles, though I *doubt* whether the less than five per cent of Jewish souls in this country control more than five per cent of its total business. You are inconsistent, Hendrik," David's uncle went on in the same reflective tone. "You do not care to look at the face of finance out of hours."

"It's for my own information, as Edward says. In other words, the Chosen People are worse short-enders generally than Dizzy is in Popub. Interesting," Van Kill observed, "and probably significant. That five per cent probably seems a handleable segment to the covetous. It also accounts for their reliance upon obscure and antique sources for their arguments . . . I have, as you suggested, got hold of some pamphlets, Ben. Not that I think percentages would bring Dizzy to a boil."

"I suppose you mean *The Talmud Jew*," De Porta said placidly.

"You're wonderful, Ben, aren't you? Yes, he was included in a batch of linotype lues I found shoved under the door of our private stair this evening. Whether they were intended for me or for Diana I don't know. Yanni burned them in the fireplace. With contrapuntal profanity . . . It was the usual sort of thing, I suppose."

Van Kill began drumming on the table with his fingers. He spoke angrily while the smoke from De Porta's cigar ascended in unhurried puffs.

"The Talmud is the Jew's secret cult, and by distorted and forged quotations from this 'secret lore' the anonymous compilers show how the sons of Israel are urged to break their promises to Gentiles in business and their oaths as citizens and public officials . . . Which accounts for American crime—and the New Deal . . . What I want to know—who takes the trouble to dump these galley droppings at my door?"

"That kind of thing has been distributed by the bale in America before," De Porta said smoothly.

"That kind of thing, more than their arms, has swept a certain sentimental gang of sado-masochists in triumph from the Channel to the Black Sea."

"Are you concerned about David? It is you who boil, Hendrik. At an ancient fire."

"Yes, yes," the young man agreed impatiently. "But I tell you—" He broke off and shook his head ruefully at the other's massive calm. "It's the Van Kill automatic blood boiler and gorge raiser, Ben. A handy little attachment guaranteed to counteract Dutch phlegm. For a small down payment you too may possess this——"

"We were talking about my nephew, David," De Porta remarked, caressing his beard with two fingers. "He is generally conceded to be a hotheaded and inconsequential young man."

"So why," Van Kill put down his empty glass, "mightn't he bare a fang at the anti-Semite? And can you stand any more of this red tonic we've been drinking?"

De Porta indicated that he was virtually awash with Dubonnet. "Thanks to David's lateness . . . It occurs to me that the answer to David as an anti-anti-Semite lies with Popub," he continued. And when Van Kill frowned a question, "Frederick Pough's picture magazine *Lo!* has done good work against Nazi organizations throughout the country. There is also his newly acquired Geyer letter. If, when Pough publishes this, it *does* establish Wagner as his stepfather's son and hence part Jew, it will be a very nasty pill for the Siegfrieds."

"You mean you'd expect Dizzy to refrain from biting the hand because of such general and putative nourishment?" Van Kill shook his head.

"Ah, well, Hendrik," De Porta sighed. "I am an old man and anti-Semitism is no new evil. But I have a very definite feeling that this *Carnage* affair is dangerous for David. My only nephew is worth more than an initial investment of $250,000. The $25,000 I offer you to protect it is less than ten per cent now. Why can't you look at it that way?"

"Precisely because I couldn't guarantee anything." Van Kill sighed in turn. "Not without interfering with David's personal freedom. I shall try to root up something equally colorful to divert his crusade at *Carnage*, but it won't be worth $25,000 if I succeed."

"When I sell a fifteenth-century block book, an *Apocalypse*, for more than that . . ."

"Did you?" the young man inquired with more animation than he had shown before. "The one with the Dutch cuts?"

"Six months," De Porta urged. "Ride herd on David until spring and he will have a love affair to distract him." De Porta went on speaking, although Van Kill's attention had been caught by Yanni making for the front of the restaurant. "Some woman will come into his life then and our troubles will be over."

"It looks to me as if you were less than half right, Ben." Leaning out of the booth now, Van Kill was following a moving object with pleased curiosity. "It's not just some woman. One look at your young relative will tell you that . . . And I've a feeling our troubles have only begun."

VIII

It was Yanni of course who saw them first, Yanni who observed
and later told Van Kill how they stood there at his entrance in Pye
Street, not far apart like midnight and dawn, the blond and the
brunette. To Yanni, relieving them of their outer garments and
disposing with particular reverence of David's top hat, it was clear
that they had quarreled on the way. He shepherded the pair to
their place in his most soothing manner. An incorrigible *promnéstria*
Van Kill called him. Yanni didn't mind being called a matchmaker.
Now he managed to bring Echo Newman and David Montefiore
close together, they were not too reluctant, while they walked. . . .

"A modern Judith, I might tell you, sultry in silver," Van Kill
was reporting to David's uncle, "though you, with your more sub-
stantial tastes, would say she lacks the necessary heft. It is an antique
head, however," he went on, watching Echo Newman's profile as
Yanni led the pair around the fishpool and across the room. He
noted the long well-turned neck, the fine ears, and the single clean
line of forehead and nose. "Nefertiti," he said. "Like you she has
an Egyptian face, Ben. How gratifying to see a woman with sense
enough to dress to type. You'll approve of this girl."

"Nefertiti was married to a reformer," De Porta commented as
they got up to receive the two.

Echo, seeming to be but escaping tall, armed with the shining
upswept burgonet of her thick black hair and tailored silver lamé
from throat to toe was, as David presented her, nearly as exotic
as Van Kill's long-range description. But her hand was warm and
firm, the slightly tilted eyes had a clear direct gaze, and De Porta
did approve of the girl. Echo after the fashion of women knew this
at once, recognized a friend in David's uncle, as she recognized
the impersonal connoisseur's appreciation in Van Kill's reflective
stare. Awareness gave her that indefinable mixture of tone and

58

relaxation which always bring beauty alive when there is any under it.

David looked away from the girl with somber pride and said he hoped Van Kill and his uncle had not interfered with his arrangements for dinner. "She had to dress. That's why we're a trifle late."

"That's more than I can bear," Echo appealed to De Porta. "If he hadn't made a scene——"

She was waiting for David when he and the delivery man with the silver gown had arrived at the desk of the business women's hotel where Echo lived. The London was one of those conservative institutions by Echo's account. Van Kill could imagine the powerful minority of decayed gentlewomen who inhabited the lounge with their knitting. And David had insisted on opening the box, examining the dress, and arguing about it there.

"Silly business, buying a new outfit for the lugs who'll be at the *Carnage* dinner," David said as Dukas turned a cupful of soup onto the plate in front of him.

"Your nephew," Echo remarked to De Porta, "knows a great deal about women's clothes."

The heartless laughter of his uncle and his friend might have ruffled David's mannered calm if Dukas had not intervened with two ducks. The presentation of the raw bird to patrons ordering pressed duck was a custom on which Antoine had sold Yanni. Van Kill called it unutterable swank. His instant co-operation with the mummery which David then inaugurated gave point to De Porta's belief that Van Kill ought to be able to anticipate his nephew.

Van Kill held the plump white carcass which David passed across the table to his ear and thumped it solemnly.

"The good die young," David said of his own bird.

"A wicked and adulterous generation," Van Kill countered, applying a lighted match to an obvious excrescence.

"The dook is not good, sor?" Dukas inquired. It was his presence which kept Teekee standing glassy-eyed at attention one pace behind.

"Only by inclination," Van Kill replied. "Not a tough duckling, no. Tender, yielding even. Saved by death from a fate worse than."

Dukas bowed and handed the platter with the ducks to Teekee, who skimmed away like a small boat yawing.

Echo took a drink of water and looked hard at De Porta, who had been steadily eating soup.

"No," the bookseller answered her unspoken question. "In the long run Hendrik has a sobering effect on David. One can, for instance, carry on quite a rational conversation with Hendrik for hours."

"About what?" Montefiore demanded. His performance with the ducks had raised his spirits.

"We discussed intolerance in general, international bankers, and we argued about the causes of anti-Semitism. But—" Van Kill turned the latter half of his reply accusingly at David "—we did not quarrel."

"Oh, Echo and I don't quarrel," David said cheerfully. "She's just so bighearted she thinks murdering thieves like Paul Harris ought to be let live."

"Next to blackmail there's nothing I like better than murder," Van Kill grinned. "This is nothing you can prove, I suppose."

"No," David answered as though proof were of negligible importance. "I don't suppose so. But it's a good idea."

"What he means," De Porta spoke to Echo, who was vainly trying to catch David's eye, "what Hendrik means is that there is never any excuse for blackmail."

This, David said, was the new approach to Harris that he had for Van Kill. "About Harris's stable of refugee artists."

David could have learned about Harris's stable of refugee artists from her, Echo put in. "Mr. Harris makes no secret of it."

"Sure," David replied in the tone of one going over an old argument. "I wouldn't have thought of Rabbi Fox in connection with Harris if our Paul hadn't told me Fox was an old guy didn't know what side his matzoths was buttered." Apparently the editor of *Carnage* had wanted to use the rabbi's name to legitimize a super-exposé of Nazi harems, he added.

"I just hunched that I might find out something that wasn't kosher, so I went to see Fox. He's a *shadchan*, you know," David interpolated with a certain emphasis. "A marriage broker. And after I convinced him I wasn't immediately interested in marrying a Polish countess, Fox told me this Lithuanian soprano who suicided in the Ladies Room at the Continental last week was a protégée of Harris. It was suicide all right, but I say Harris was responsible. The rabbi thought so too."

Echo asked Van Kill to remember that the rabbi was interested in refugees too. "And it's much easier to marry them off when they have a little money."

De Porta made no comments on his nephew's story, but it may have started him on a certain line of thought. He noticed that Van Kill looked as if he had stopped listening.

Yet, Echo's protestations and his own tangential characterizations of Harris aside, David Montefiore gave a succinct account of his suspicions as the meal progressed. Paul Harris had been handling public relations for newly landed foreign artists since before the war. David had known this from the time he had first got his knife out for Harris.

"There didn't seem to be anything to take hold of," he admitted. It was to be expected that Harris would bilk his clients as long as they remained ignorant of the language and currency. Huge fees for Sunday magazine spreads that didn't cost Harris a cent, kickbacks on photographs and professional coaching, cartage for pianos, claque money, "bribes" for critics and columnists, fees for free radio auditions, most of Harris's artists broke away from him soon enough.

"Tell about those who didn't break away," Van Kill suggested suddenly. "What have they in common with the Lithuanian soprano? That was a strychnine case incidentally, David. She told them at Bellevue it was Hitler's fault. I beg your pardon, Miss Newman?"

"One long howl," Echo said flatly. "That's what they have in common. I've heard some of them. If Harris can overcharge them for his services, it's because no other impresario will have them."

With an attitude of endless patience David said it was quite true they weren't first-rate artists. "It was the fact that they all had money that interested me, because it's obviously what interested Harris." The majority were women, the rabbi had said, and none of them seemed to have any relatives in this country. "Which was why they, the Jewish ones anyway, complained to Fox."

"And he," Echo commented dryly, "told David."

De Porta, who had been giving most of his attention to the duck, its first slices, what Dukas called break pieces, and the blazing black juice from the press, regarded the girl thoughtfully. He had no liking for women who were credited with that dubious quality, a masculine mind.

The burden of Echo's appeal to Van Kill was specifically personal. Frederick Pough, she said with a meaningful glance at David, was a competent humanitarian. If there was anything in David's notion that Harris's greed was driving his refugees to suicide, Pough would put a stop to it.

"Mr. Pough knows what's going on in his organization," Echo said. "There isn't any phase of it he couldn't handle himself if he wanted to."

De Porta had an instant's glimpse of the efficient private secretary behind David's silver lady, saw too a vein of crystal practicality that would need more than his nephew's antic charm to dent. The bookseller took a slow draught of his *Nuits Saint George* and began wondering about the clasp on his dead wife's pearls. Fania De Porta had been a sapphire blond. David would perhaps want to put emeralds on this girl. Though the three others who dined with him that night at the Matapan were to know fear and doubt about the shape of their lives in the next few days, Benjamin De Porta never lost the vision which came to him then of David standing beside Echo and Fania's pearls around Echo's neck.

"It's tiresome of you, Dizzy, not to know whether these female refugees are married or not."

"Well, you can ask Harris," David sent a glance that was at once triumphant and pleading at Echo. He could tell as well as De

Porta that Van Kill was interested. The document examiner's face had a shuttered look, doubtful, rather bored, and very Dutch.

Van Kill's brisk, "I shall, tomorrow," startled the girl.

"I thought surely you'd discourage David," she exclaimed. She sat back and lowered her lids. "I was certain."

"Don't worry," Van Kill told her. "I mean I shall find out. I shan't inject a bass note into Popub's even tenor. Now if I sent my partner—Yanni's method is to go and ask. Me, I lack the scopolamine eye and Ben will tell you I am naturally devious. I'll ask Mr. Pough to let me see his Geyer letter, but I shan't do anything to disturb him."

Something in Van Kill's tone disturbed De Porta's reflection that in times like these one should adhere to orthodox forms. Was Hendrik implying that Echo had more than a faithful employee's interest in her boss? Studying the girl's cool chiseled features, De Porta refused to believe stupidity of that sort threatened. He went back to his decision that if he lived, Echo and David would stand under a canopy on the occasion that Echo first wore those pearls.

The young people fell silent while Dukas, competently tense, made *pêches flambées* at the open end of the table. The blue flames of the burning spirit cast alabaster highlights on Echo's cheekbones and colored the peak of hair on David's forehead so that he looked like a sulky faun. Van Kill's self-absorbed silence might have meant anything or nothing.

De Porta was to remember this dinner as a small promontory of content. Over the coffee and Cointreau he remembered thinking that he was old enough to find exhilaration in the subdued irritation of a pair of lovers. Van Kill was not, and it was Van Kill who dragged him away at the end of the meal.

"We're going to pubcrawl. Even if you won't come along, we've all the time in the world to kill," David protested and his tone said plainly that he would rather they killed it alone.

De Porta and Van Kill went back to the kitchen to pay their compliments to Antoine and returned with Yanni, making a small parade of their progress through the tables.

"My book on Julian, Ben?" Echo and David saw Van Kill halt opposite their booth and heard him laugh. "I'll certainly have it done before the Julianic bimillennium."

"Twenty-three hundred A.D., Hendrik?" De Porta asked as they moved out of sight.

They were evidently, Montefiore told the girl, embarking on one of their arguments about Neoplatonism and Christianity in the fourth century A.D. This could go on all night, he said, with Van Kill supporting Iamblichus and the Apostate Julian and De Porta backing the Church.

"Twenty-three hundred A.D., Echo," David added bitterly. "Our greatest great-grandchildren will all be killed off by then——"

"A bit previous, aren't you, David?" Echo answered lightly. David's moods of despair about marriage for any of their kind were largely affectation, she believed. In any case better not discussed, that or anything connected with it. "I'm sure you'd make as creditable an attempt at fatherhood as Dr. Van Kill." Echo had reserved judgment on the document examiner.

"I hope you wouldn't expect to produce the kind of problem *he* has," David exclaimed. Edward Cameron rather frightened him. "Hal can cope of course, but ordinary people like you and me— let's talk about us."

And so they did for a time. They talked and the talk dwindled. Dark head and the light came close together then and passing the booth on cat feet, Yanni Mavromicháli also was glad. . . .

〰〰

IX

By noon the next day Hendrik Van Kill, examiner of questioned documents, had left Rabbi Lionel Fox and was waiting in the lobby of the Popub Building for an up car. It came, saluted as arriving elevators frequently are by the sound of tapping heels. This was Van Kill's presage of the woman, the sound he was afterward to associate with Morna Maye.

Not an employee, Van Kill decided as he stepped back to let her enter the car. Desirable San Quentin Quail at one time, Broadway bargain basement now and plump. He could not help notice her noticing him. A blonde who had not laundered well, he thought indifferently, but Morna Maye, before the affair of *Carnage* had run its course, would throw Hendrik Van Kill into the most unreasoning panic of his life. He faced front and put his mind onto his immediate purpose. . . .

Rabbi Lionel Fox after some coaxing had made bold to state that most of the refugee artists in question had been married shortly before they reached America, and that some of the marriages "had not turned out so well." Marriages made for the sole purpose of getting them into the country, Van Kill could clearly see. . . .

On the twentieth floor he discovered that callers at *Carnage* could take immediate cover in its reception room directly across from the elevator. By following the main corridor and turning right beyond a sign which read arrestingly *Lo!* one came to the presidential suite. Far enough away, as Montefiore expressed it, so that Pough was not disturbed by sounds of strife from *Carnage*, but close enough to make Harris careful about throwing bodies into the hall.

"Mr. Harris is in conference," said the telephone girl. "With Sheriff Orin Hitchcock of Nebraska," she revealed after she had looked the document examiner over and giggled experimentally. Her name was O'Bryan, but male persons of more than thirty minutes acquaintance were at liberty to call her Baby. She was a slimmer simulacrum, Van Kill noticed, of the plump blonde who had tapped in behind him. The blonde perched in a chair facing a door with a long panel of ground glass which led into Harris's office. Baby returned Morna Maye's unmistakable glare with a look of tolerant indifference. She evidently thought the older blonde was with Van Kill and he let the inference stand.

He took a copy of *Carnage* for January from a smoking stand, sat down beside it in a chair next to Harris's door, lit a cigarette, and began leafing the magazine. The strange blonde had not said a word. It was hard to believe that a woman so obviously sitting could be half rising as well. Like a well-nourished partridge with something on its mind.

Van Kill glanced back at the caption under his finger tip on page thirteen: THE WEIRD RIDDLE OF THE BORDEAUX WINE. One of Mr. Harris's desperate midden-sweepers had plucked Commissaire Gustave Macé's most famous investigation, the Voirbo homicide, out of the year 1869 and dumped it into modern times, equipped with cops in prowl cars and murderer Voirbo trying to flit on the *Ile de France*.

Carnage's fictioneer had changed murderer Voirbo's name and made him jump off a beetling cliff instead of slitting his weasand. But he had carelessly let Macé's own name stand. Puzzling to a scholar, the document examiner thought. He glanced up to see a brazen, yet oddly furtive little man strut over to Baby at the telephone desk and greet her effusively. Baby gave out as befitting Mr. Stock's photographer of torsos and legs whose bills Mr. Harris sometimes paid. She told him to step right in.

"Mr. Harris wants that matter straightened out now," Baby said.

Van Kill tried to ticket this creature, who was not a pimp, yet possessed all of the characteristics. He put the train of thought on a siding for future reference and listened.

"Everything's gunna be copaseetic, Baby," Louie Lenz spoke over his shoulder as he shoved open the door beside Van Kill. He closed it after him and Van Kill could hear nothing at first.

Shortly, however, Mr. Lenz's jaunty *derrière* could be seen pressed against the glass panel.

"Those flagellation pix'll all be copaseetic, Paul," the document examiner heard Lenz say with husky insinuation. "Just wait'll you see 'em. *Boy!*"

Harris was not visible, but his unenthusiastic reply was distinct. "I want 'em now, Louie, right now, not New Year's. Think you're working for *National Geographic?*"

"Tomorrow afternoon," Louie said in an arrogant wheedling tone. "I'll get Darcy over for the retakes. Before five, positive."

The rest was a mumble. David would have recognized its relation to a scene he had witnessed between Harris and Darcy the day before. It ended with Louie Lenz edging hastily but stubbornly out of the door. Harris's voice came after him.

"You're not the only fotog in town, you tight-orificed little tramp."

Voice and words were harsh, but Morna Maye, Van Kill observed brightened toward them like a woman who has heard an angel speak.

Behind the door the voice could still be heard. Van Kill pushed the door open an inch with his copy of *Carnage.*

"I always co-operate with officers of the law, Sheriff Hitchcock. But I don't pay a cent for by-lines, see?"

Morna Maye put a hand on the arm of her chair. The gentleman whose voice she recognized never paid for anything if he could help it, she knew.

"I could get J. Edgar Hoover's for half a yard a month," Harris declared. "It isn't worth that to me. It means nothing to our readers if you did come East to crash a quiz hour and win a case of irradiated dog food. Girls who die for unwise love are a dime a dozen and yours has no color, see?"

Morna Maye rose. She fluttered past Baby's desk and into Harris's sanctum like a clock work hen, leaving the door wide ajar. Van Kill could see Harris now, standing over his sheriff, whom he had apparently harangued into a complete slump.

"My god," the editor of *Carnage* said to the cigarette which was half way to his mouth, "I thought I left that behind in Albany."

"Paulie," Morna Maye spoke at last. "Paulie *dar*ling, it's really you."

"Well, blow me down?" Baby inquired when the door closed. She looked over at Van Kill, but he was absorbed in *Carnage*.

The sheriff from Nebraska and the blonde from Albany were evidently dispatched through a door direct from Harris's sanctum into the corridor, though Van Kill had no sure knowledge of the order of their going. By one o'clock at any rate a tender kind of *status quo* had been established in Harris's spirit.

"You're the fellow they used to call the savant sleuth," he said accusingly when the document examiner sat down.

Van Kill didn't bother expressing his aversion to the title. He meant to get Harris's reaction to a single question and leave.

But Harris, whether for reasons of his own or nothing more than monkeylike curiosity about the reactions of his visitor had commenced talking. About authors and women chiefly. Van Kill did his best and his best was an excellent blank to exhibit no reactions whatever. There were times when the professorial manner was expected.

Listening, Van Kill concluded that Harris's low literary bent had deflected him from a completely criminal career and that the sublimation was unfortunate.

Authors, Harris deplored. "Why, I could write the great American novel myself," he declared, his restless little black eyes busy on Van Kill's face. "I've got a camera-plate brain of course, I notice everything, but I could do it without going further for my stuff than what I see here every day."

What he saw was girls mostly, girls who sold him photographs (stolen from newspaper morgues and consequently cut-rate, Van Kill knew), girls who wanted to sell him the story of their misspent lives. Harris knew them all, real characters. He learned a lot of languages, too, the savant sleuth could understand how *that* was—

Spanish from a Spaniard, Czech from a Czech, Polish, Austrian, and so on.

David Montefiore had not overestimated Harris's horrid charm, Van Kill reflected. He had an essential innocence, like a degenerate child. If Harris suspected the document examiner of sicking a blonde out of his past on him, there was no least hint of resentment in his manner.

"One Egyptian I had to put a screen up so I could stick to the language." Harris licked his lips. *"Leiltak s' aida.* May your night be happy. I learn too much on this job to wanta quit." He broke into an ugly cackle.

"Resourceful of you." The document examiner ignored Harris's last remark. It was the nearest he came to mentioning Montefiore or any suspicion he may have had that Montefiore had sent Van Kill to him.

"Speaking of foreign women," Van Kill went on easily, "I've run onto a story you could use if you cared to. With a national defense angle, maybe."

"Yeah?" Harris sounded interested. "An individual like you, doc, has a certain follow-up value, even if the story's lousy. Do you still wear a ring with a lens? Hinged over a carved—wait a minute— a goat's head crest, that's it. I remember reading it belonged to your old man. Well, that kind of crap is what you call glamour."

Harris's offensiveness was not entirely deliberate, Van Kill saw with a twinge of amusement. It was largely this interesting rascal's peculiar naïveté. The man was studying him with the expression of a poolroom track expert looking at his first horse.

"That's what that hick sheriff I had in here couldn't understand." The editor of *Carnage* tilted his big head confidentially. "I might have used his by-line on the piece I'm going to write if anything like it had happened to him before. Matter of fact the story has, in another state."

He'd used it in *Carnage* right after he took over, Harris said. A nice little tie-up could be effected again, using the sheriff's story (but not the sheriff) and some historical stuff for the Scientific Detection Department. . . .

"I even got the weapons from that first case." Harris leaned back to jerk open the door of his Black Chamber and indicated a Colt Frontier Model revolver hanging on a hook over a ragged silk stocking.

"Ah, yes." Van Kill exhibited polite enthusiasm. "The old Peacemaker. The little .44 Frankie had under her kimona. Takes the same cartridge as your Winchester 1873 there. Is that connected with the story?"

Harris looked at the rifle on the bottom shelf of his unhealthy little museum. Looking like a frustrated curator, he closed the door.

"That *is* the story," he admitted. "You find those rifles still in use out West, and if some broad out pottin' rabbits with a 44.40 gets shot with an old Winchester 1873, the defense can always claim reasonable doubt of suicide."

"There's no doubt that this case I have in mind was suicide, I'm afraid," Van Kill bored into his story again.

Harris's face assumed an editorial expression so immediately that Van Kill gave him credit for knowing what was up all along. "Never use 'em unless they try a window and show a lot of leg," he sniffed.

"This girl," the document examiner pursed his lips as if trying to be professorially honest, "took a fairly good picture." He sketched the history of the Lithuanian singer whose marriage to an American had facilitated her entry into this country and who had paid such exorbitant fees to her agent (unnamed) that she was almost completely beggared when she killed herself.

"Suicide." Harris smirked. "Suicide used to be a felony if you weren't successful. We use 'em in the Cavalcade of Crime Department if they've got glamour. But suicide's no crime."

Neither, in practice, was driving a person to it. (Van Kill had recently discussed the matter with Detective Swann of the Manhattan Homicide Squad. Swann, who had digested a number of arguable theories out of Menninger for use during dull periods in the squad room, maintained that all suicides were caused by other people ultimately, and what could you do about it?)

"Are you building up to another refugee horror yarn, doctor?" Harris asked in a professional tone. "There's a million kicking around every crime book office from here to K.C. And what I get of yours, doctor, I'm sorry to say, stinks."

"I'm glad you notice it." Van Kill was sure that it was unnatural for Harris to talk so much without being nastier. "Most people have a distaste for blackmail. A respectable, not-too-bright young emigree whose American wedding ring has a fishy gleam is an ideal subject. Our trouble here has been a notion that all our latter-day immigrants are smart. Government and private agencies are tightening up now. That kind of moral sabotage will be too dangerous for a man with a permanent business address."

Van Kill finished his speech with a professorial flourish, but he had not succeeded in catching Harris's roving eyes. Harris closed them now and moved his head slowly from side to side. "I'm afraid you haven't studied our publication to get our slant," he said regretfully.

"I'm giving you the slant," Van Kill said in a quiet voice. "A historical now-it-can-be-told vein, warning your readers that the white slave racket out of Lisbon is the only safe refugee racket left. That of course has never been the sort of thing a man with a permanent business address could engage in."

Harris's eyes opened and for the first time met the other man's cool stare. There was a dark back alley look in them, but all he said was:

"Try us with something else, doctor, if you want to crash *Carnage* first time off." He continued with a provocative overtone. "Like the grim saga of how you tracked down the fiendish duo of Danforth kidnapers who crushed out of Sing Sing and brought your savant father to an untimely end."

"That's a matter of common knowledge," Van Kill said carelessly.

"Not the inside story of the mug who didn't live to stand trial," Harris said suavely. "If you want to write that, I'll pay you top rate, extra for by-line and pictures, cash *in* advance."

Van Kill laughed. He had displayed no emotion to Harris beyond

a vague scholarly smile and his mirthless bark as he stood up to
go was out of character.

"I'm a man with a permanent business address now, too, but I
leave no loose ends." He dropped lightly into his former manner.
"That's for my memoirs, Harris. It wouldn't do for you, Harris.
No woman interest."

Behind his own hooded gaze Van Kill was thinking that he had
got more than he had hoped to out of this visit. The strange (but
not to Harris) blonde, a still-to-be-thought-out notion from looking
at Louie Lenz, Harris's unguarded reference to Kansas City, and
several glimmers from Harris's many-faceted character were all, in
Van Kill's phrase, interesting and possibly significant.

Van Kill knew that the Lithuanian's suicide had made it too late
to trip Harris on the phony marriage brand of extortion. The time
to catch a blackmailer is when none of his victims has rebelled.

Very politely Harris accompanied Van Kill as far as the corridor
door. Looking straight up at the document examiner there, he said
and his words were arsenic sweet, "I'm sorry I didn't like your story,
doctor."

Van Kill could see that he didn't, but on none of the occasions
which followed was he really prepared for the steps Harris took to
satisfy his grudge. He did not, having seen the man, qualify any of
the statements he had made about Harris to De Porta. But the little
man with the big head and the gaudy clothes, being dark, ominous,
sinister and mysterious in a way no criminal in his right mind would
dare to, amused Hendrik Van Kill. And though he denied it, Hendrik Van Kill's sense of humor sometimes took his mind off his
work.

"A *lusus naturae* as conscientiously scrupleless as a Radcliffe vil-
lain," the document examiner told Benjamin De Porta from the
phone booth outside *Lol*'s office in the Popub corridor. "Surely I
can say he's funny without underestimating him," Van Kill protested. "A barrel of monkeys with hydrophobia . . ."

"*Aber ernsthaft,*" he dropped into German. "Seriously, though,
your nephew was right about the refugee racket. There has been

one. And blackmail. Called it protection, I dare say. *Aber der Selbstmord hat das alle geendet,*" he went on. "But the suicide has put a stop to all that. The fact that he has been a blackmailer shows us where he may strike next, though, indicates there is nothing to which he cannot easily stoop . . . *Natürlich interessier' ich mich.* Of course I'm interested. I want to know if this fellow has a hold on the big boss . . . My immediate need is for someone who knows more than your nephew about *all* the activities of this firm."

Van Kill found that someone more quickly than De Porta would have supposed possible. When he came out under the glass and metal marquee which ornamented the entrance to the Popub Building he had a blonde young woman with him.

X

〜〜

"Pye Street," Betty Hargrave said as Van Kill parked the Hermes coupé at the entrance to Yanni's alley. "Mr. Pough comes down to this neighborhood to lunch with his broker." She looked up at him consideringly from under the rim of a shredded ostrich bird bath. Morna Maye, Van Kill reflected, would have been taken up on suspicion for wearing such a hat. "I wouldn't have supposed you were a person with active financial interests."

"No," he said, "I leave them to my youngers and betters."

Hendrik Van Kill recognized that Betty Hargrave was additionally refreshing for having burst upon his sight not long after he left Paul Harris. He liked the knowledgeable Midwestern co-ed with a top dressing of metropolitan business woman. Van Kill had no objection to people who were wholesome if they didn't make a cult of it. And this little wench was attractive enough to make the occupant of a passing taxi look out behind.

On the sidewalk the two stood still for a moment, each looking at the other with the honest conceit of a person deciding that his companion's appearance is a worthy complement of his own. Amused gray eyes sought for a spark of self-knowledge in blue and they both laughed.

All the way downtown from the Popub offices Miss Hargrave had been absolving her conscience for spending her Christmas money on gauds. Get yourself something you need, her aunt had said . . . Walking along the alley now with Van Kill's fingers at her elbow, Betty told herself that the embroidered gilet was an essential link between her suit and the hat. And the hat was in memory of adolescent heartburning during the Eugénie period.

"You write the Letter to Aunt Louella in *Hearth*, do you?" Van Kill was saying as they halted under the Cerberus. "Big city pleasures and palaces glamooriously described with an undercurrent of nostalgia for Aunt Louella's pickles."

"Glamoorious," Betty agreed, "but proper. The *Hearth* letter is a drop in the bucket to wash out the big bad city legend."

"In other words," Van Kill pulled open the Matapan's front door, "you wouldn't tell your Aunt Louella you came here with a man you picked up in the hall outside your office."

"Dali ballet!" the girl exclaimed as she stepped onto the railed foyer. Her eyes had lit on the white-kilted Teekee running interference for a waiter with two flaming sword spits of *arnì soúvla*. "Never mind how the conscientious columnist got here."

Van Kill inspected the crowded room. The comfortable dusk of the Matapan's daytime character was giving off its usual smooth buzz of mostly male relaxation. The big spits at the kitchen end were turning brightly, the considered peace of the patrons intensified by the quiet activity of Yanni's staff. Van Kill wondered what had become of Yanni. He was sure he had caught sight of the Greek's smooth head through the door.

Dukas came up. "Mr. Mavromicháli's compliments, he was not expecting you," the poker-faced Spartan said and announced as if he were responsible for the timing, "I have a booth which is vacating for you, sor."

Van Kill noticed two men getting into their coats by a very acceptable location across the room. One of them put out a hand and stopped Yanni, who had just come out of the kitchen and headed toward Van Kill.

"It's Mr. Pough," Betty said as they reached the booth.

The man talking to Yanni turned. "Miss Hargrave," he said, distantly cordial. Pough's light-brown eyes passed casually over Van Kill and he went on speaking to Yanni.

The Greek hadn't looked so uncomfortable since the day when Van Kill had insisted on going to live in a house full of vampires. The great publisher seemed to be making a species of apology, Van Kill thought, as he settled Betty in the booth and told Dukas to bring them a Pernod to start.

"If you like it, you can go on with it," he told the girl.

Why should an apology from Pough make Yanni unhappy? The Maniote had no false humility. But the "big misonderstanding" which Van Kill heard him repeat at intervals held more than his usual quota of MPs and THs and was full of an urgent desire for Mr. Pough to be gone.

"It doesn't taste as nice as it looks," Betty qualified her decision to go on with the Pernod. "But then drinks don't."

Van Kill indicated the holiday aspect of the Pernod's clouded green and her amazing fingernails. He had allotted half an eye to her hands ever since she had stripped off her gloves. They were thin-boned, delicately sinewed, the hands of a woman executive. The collegiate length and redness of the nails were interesting anomalies, he thought.

She followed Van Kill's recommendation of *kottópoulo bámies* with a cryptic, "Just so it's not chicken and okra *southern* style."

"Your boss maintains a distant attitude toward his serfs in public," Van Kill commented. . . .

He heard Pough outside the booth saying, "The little man scarcely speaks a word when he's helping around the tables," and wondered what Teekee had been up to now. "As the officer said, midgets are very touchy about their size."

Hendrik Van Kill lifted his head like a dreamer awakened to day. His companion saw the pupils of his eyes contract.

"You haven't heard a word I said," Betty accused.

"You said," Van Kill replied promptly, "that if Mr. Pough had known I was a friend of Mr. Montefiore, he would have stopped to chat." His smile was companionable, but he was still looking through her.

"After telling you that it's my job to have a finger in every Popub pie," Betty grinned, "you thought I didn't know how Mr. Montefiore feels about *Carnage*." She leaned toward Van Kill. "Why, even Queen Echo disapproves. Though if you ask me, he wouldn't have had the idea if he hadn't fallen for her."

Yanni came up and asked if they liked the table and if they had thought of anything not on the menu. The Greek's black eyes glowed with an expression Van Kill recognized when Betty was established as *Miss* Hargrave, but they did not meet Van Kill's.

"I agree that David wouldn't have stayed with the idea except for Echo Newman," the document examiner said when Yanni was gone. Betty put her nose into her Pernod to hide her chagrin. Divided before, the man's thoughts were leaping along at least three tangents now. She raised her eyes to find Van Kill looking at her.

"Why don't you like Echo?" It was his faraway gaze, still impersonal, but concentrated on her now. She was sure she didn't like it.

"Because—because she's so sure of herself," Betty faltered. (She resents my job spying on the Cavaliers. She thinks I'm helping make more trouble. She's the kind believes you can stop pogroms by ignoring them.) "Echo—" Van Kill's suddenly withdrawn attention was like a lifted weight. "Echo thinks I'm light-minded," Betty finished easily. "She doesn't approve of *me*."

"A good female reason," the young man said mildly.

This sweet, not unintuitive child whom he had picked up on the spur of the desire for companionship knew something useful. Something dangerous? One hand executed an idle four-finger exercise on the table. Four little thuds on the bare wood like (Van Kill looked down at his hand, repeated the movement) like the ominous summoning notes of the opening of Beethoven's Fifth, he thought irritably.

But she didn't think it was dangerous. She had it in the front of her consciousness like a little girl with a Christmas secret. Twice as if by compulsion she had skirted a threshold which she didn't intend to cross.

Van Kill pivoted his arm and for an instant laid his hand lightly on hers. She was a darling and she was going to be difficult to pump. "If you'll excuse me," he said, rising. "Before our meal arrives there's somebody I want to see in the kitchen. Or in the potato bin maybe. Drink up your Pernod," he suggested. . . .

A little confused but, she assured herself, normal in all her reflexes, the young woman opened her purse and took out her mirror. She made sure there was no lipstick on her teeth and admired her hat. Something you need, her aunt had said. It occurred to Betty that she was what her aunt's generation called an old maid. This restlessness that even Mr. Pough had noticed . . . Miss Hargrave finished her Pernod. . . .

XI

EDWARD had had plenty of time to change his clothes after Yanni spotted Van Kill arriving, but he was still wearing his embroidered jacket and fustanella when his guardian found him in the pantry. The boy was perched out of the way on the step stool, Yanni standing beside him, when Van Kill slid his long body through the ordered frenzy of the Matapan behind scenes and bore down on them.

Having silently considered Edward from the tassel on his cap to the pompoms on his slippers, Van Kill said, "Your desire to learn the restaurant business from every angle is very praiseworthy, Edward. But surely you could have saved yourself this embarrassment by letting Yanni tell Mr. Pough who you were."

"It was Mr. Pough who was embarrassed," Edward replied with a more than childlike satisfaction. He rolled his dark eyes at Yanni. "I told you he'd know all about it if he saw you and Pough together."

"I can't help overhearing some of your joyless conversations over the financial page," Van Kill told the pair. "I thought Edward's grasp of stock-market esoterica had increased while I was away." Yanni considered the little boy's flair for speculation as nearly supernatural. Van Kill had seen no valid reason to interfere with the two. Both had what he regarded as an almost morbid caution where money was concerned. "It was running around with bread and water for customers' men that did it, I see."

"They think—" Edward began. "They *assumed* I was a little Greek boy who didn't understand English. They used to call me Papadopolus." He looked pained for an instant. "They like—that is, they liked to send me between tables with messages." The pained expression became that of a practical-minded mystic. "I couldn't *help* noticing when things they said reminded me of things I'd read in the papers, and I would tell Yanni."

"Stand up, Edward," Van Kill said. "Walk over to the silver polisher."

Edward got up and walked away from them with admirable aplomb. But whereas the legs of the native Teekee skimmed under the fustanella like doves, on the last of the Camerons it tilted and swayed with a sidewinding series of flips above his small rump.

"You can see, kyrie, how it takes mind off," Yanni remarked. Van Kill could see how it might engender such mirth as to distract any broker from ordinary caution.

"I am glad the kyrios is not annoyed," the Greek said unnecessarily.

Van Kill shrugged. Risking the loss of one of the Matapan's patrons was Yanni's worry, he said. "You palmed that little homunculus Rudi Smart off on Pough's investigator, I suppose."

"Calls himself a good American," Edward burst out suddenly. "A conscientious American citizen doing his duty," the boy chattered with cheeks that matched his jacket. Edward's squirrel rages were brief and almost always ended on a note of dramatic self-pity. "Doing his duty! Spoiling the innocent amusement of a poor little boy, doing his duty! . . . I *had* to let him see me today, but there wasn't any *fun* in it."

Van Kill sat down on the step stool. "Your decision to stop this masquerade now is only discreet," he said quietly. "But how about the midget? Even if he doesn't know whom he was fooling, a hint to any gossip writer——"

"He will not hint," Yanni interrupted with Doric calm. "The little Smart has job now with Uncle Yoryi's cousin Spiros who is owner three-four movie theaters with vaudeville in Yonkers"

"Yanni says Rudi will be grateful," the boy put in.

"He will be grateful," the Greek declared. He looked at Van Kill, ran his lower lip along the shining edge of his upper teeth in a way that was surprisingly threatening for so small a grimace, and added in the vernacular, "Because I promised otherwise to cut his miserable little throat."

"*Kalá.* Excellent, Yanni." Van Kill got up and walking around

Edward, availed himself of a privilege which more than one diner at the Matapan had assumed with less cause.

Edward rose on his toes when he was swatted and remarked, "That is the end of the busboy."

It was not until some days later that Van Kill remembered a note of reservation in his ward's voice which set him thinking that the career of Edward Lindsay Cameron, busboy, had had a more significant end than he or Yanni suspected.

They talked about Betty throughout the lunch proper, of her philosophy of life, and about her job. For city-minded country mice and the thousands of unassimilated small-towners in the city, too, she was, Betty informed Van Kill, Popub's emulsient elixir.

"*Hearth* was the first of the mother-wife-mistress magazines to have a heroine achieve happiness by divorcing her husband and marrying the other man," Miss Hargrave said. "I told them Peoria was ready for it. *I* am the Pulse of Peoria."

Betty's eyes had taken on a liquid sheen and a curl had come loose above her eyebrow when she took her hat off. As a prospective pumpee Betty Hargrave had been nursed along very carefully by Van Kill. Once this girl felt she was on the way to getting drunk, she would dry up.

"You have become a city-wise little piece though," he told her seriously. "I'm sure you can bore through a subway rush like a Bronx seamstress on her way to Thirty-fourth Street. Sooner or later your Letter to Aunt Louella will get a New Yorkerish taint and Mr. Pough is a businessman."

"You must realize that I really have an Aunt Louella," Betty replied. "When I said I lived my job, I fore God meant it. Why, I even live in a southern apartment house. You know." Miss Hargrave tucked in the corners of her red mouth and dropped her consonants. "One of those lil islands of Dixie culcha. They run in with presents of beaten biscuit and ask you what your mother's maiden name was."

"Horrible," said Van Kill.

"They think not knowing all about your neighbors is horrible. Why, they say, you might be living right next door to a murderer."

With a certain air of abstraction Van Kill agreed that this was possible, and asked what function her fine provincial hand had in the magazine *Carnage.*

"I tell 'em what they can't get by with," Betty chuckled. "They're pretty cocky over their circulation now. They got the Popub dinner this year for it," she explained parenthetically. "We figure the public for *Carnage* as a separate clientele. They may look at the pictures in *Lo!* But they never see *Brief* or *Chic* or *You Yourself.*"

"So." Van Kill laid down his fork and taunted lightly, "Like the apostle, Popub is all things to all men. A *Hearth* for mother and the girls, a *Carnage* for every sublimated rape killer."

Betty's corn-colored eyebrows were offended arcs above her third Pernod. "You said sublimated," she pointed out. "The people who read *Carnage* could be *doing* worse things."

"Not at the same time, my lamb." Van Kill grinned suddenly, baring his teeth at her. "Just offhand, mention something worse than a lurid description of murder by torture, though of course pulp fiction has it all over so-called true fact mags there. However," he went on, watching the tips of the girl's ears redden and her cheek line go square with anger, "take child murder, at which the worst fiction draws a line. Must Mr. Pough's readers also have *pictures* of the bloody body of a little girl?"

"It's to keep that sort of thing," Miss Hargrave's words spurted when they came as if they had been caught in her throat, "things that are only single instances from happening in numbers that Mr. Pough is spending most of his time and money right now." She flamed for an instant, her long lacquered nails digging into the table.

Van Kill leaned back and allowed his eyes to wander about the booth, on his face a glaze of courteous disbelief. Inwardly he felt a familiar upsurge of quickened interest which always came to him when reason emerged to justify instinct.

"Mr. Pough's an idealist," the girl burst out again. "But he knows in business it's just like politics, you have to support a lot of things you don't approve of to accomplish the big important things."

Van Kill contrived to add a shade of embarrassment to his impersonation of a young man being needlessly lied to.

"You ought to understand *that*." Betty was near tears. They had seemed to be understanding each other perfectly until now. "I—I admit everything you could say about *Carnage* is true, but I'm standing up for it. I was glad to take care of the cake for their old dinner for instance, because I know what good use Mr. Pough will make of the increased inc—increment."

Betty Hargrave, trying to cover the sob which rose up under increased increment was so charmingly pathetic that Van Kill almost forgot to curl his lip.

"You'll never have to go home to your Aunt Louella because you've become a weak and thready pulse," he said. "Milk funds and free clinics and scholarship foundations have always been worthy to salve big business conscience. Why, Al Capone had a soup kitchen."

"It isn't like that at all, damn you!"

Young Teekee, waiting outside the booth for a sign to clear away, heard the thump of a feminine fist on the table and turned his head in time to see Kyrios Van Kill sliding into the seat beside the young lady. Panayoteekee, under the care of the Madonna, again faced front, his hands at his sides, thumbs hidden in his fluted kilt and therefore wriggling slightly. He knew that for the present there was no table service wanted in the booth.

"Granted," said Van Kill as he stopped for the light at Fifty-ninth Street. Less than two hours had passed since he had badgered Betty Hargrave into telling him about the plot Frederick Pough of Popub had inaugurated against the Christian Cavaliers. Betty recognized the word as a patent notification that she was arguing off the point.

"Granted," Van Kill said, "that we Dutch and you Yankees were dampening sugar and watering milk, importing wooden nutmegs here and adding willow leaves to tea before the Chosen

People . . ." He released the brake and let the car filter across the circle toward the stream of traffic headed up Central Park West.

"Columbus," Betty interrupted. She pointed a brightly gloved hand over her left shoulder as they passed under the statue. "Columbus," she insisted, "Columbus was a Jew. I'm convinced of it."

"De Madariaga's theory?"

"It explains so many of those screwy and inconsistent things about his character," the girl said and twisted in her seat as they passed the IRT station to peer through the back window.

Van Kill, who was watching the rear vision mirror with particular attention, saw that she had been trying to look at Columbus on his pedestal. The gesture was appropriate to the Pulse of Peoria and, he thought, expressive of an integrated kind of patriotism. Pough, Kill reflected, had recognized Betty Hargrave's rock-ribbed Americanism before he put her on the Cavaliers job.

"Intellectual convictions aren't what you fight when you fight anti-Semitism," he said. "You fight underground sentiments."

"The underground sentiments have their authorities," Betty answered with an exasperated shake of her head. "The Cavaliers' anonymous contributor to *The Lance*, the 'True American' I was telling you about, quoted somebody named Ecker in his last."

"Jacob Ecker? Did he now!" Van Kill had abandoned his interest in the rear vision mirror and he seemed pleased. "Did you ever read any Ecker?"

"As if I'd touch the filthy stuff."

"That's my point exactly," Van Kill crowed. "Ecker was a nineteenth-century phony who stole a book by one Aaron Briman called *Mirror of the Jew* and published it as his own. Briman himself was a forger by trade of such meretricious technique that he was kicked out of Austria."

"Would you think better of him if ——"

"My dear, we have our standards. Briman, sometimes he called himself Dr. Justus, is almost a favorite in my collection of historical rogues."

Van Kill flashed a grin at Betty, who was giving him a long disapproving stare.

They rode by the Natural History Museum in silence. The building looked more like a slightly run-down school for backward children than usual, Van Kill thought, with a rheumy Salvation Army Santa huddled on the steps and covies of apathetic youngsters on pre-holiday field trips trailing past him.

"All right," Betty capitulated when the Santa's shivery little bell was left behind. "All right. What did Briman do?"

"Aaron Briman was a misdirected Vicar of Bray, who renounced Judaism to turn Catholic, left the Church to become a Protestant, and tried to complete the spiritual cycle by re-embracing Jerusalem. He published a denunciation of his *Mirror* under his own name as an instance of good faith, but the Jews wouldn't have him because he'd deserted his wife and children in the first place. So he went to Paris to study medicine."

"You mean," Betty Hargrave said after a moment, "how can we appeal to reason and justice when even stuff like Justus-Briman's can't be discredited? Don't you think Mr. Pough's right in saying we ought to have a line on people who go for it?"

Van Kill temporized. "And how would the line be played?"

They were approaching the yellow outcrop which Central Park's northwestern corner turns upon Porto Rican Harlem. Van Kill maneuvered left and gradually up into the crescent of Morningside Drive. "I mean this assumption of solidarity, in the face of so much ambivalence, is wrong," he said after a time. "Jews get on each other's nerves just as Christians do, and catty-cornered. But we persist in thinking in terms of groups. I wonder if Briman ever came to suspect that he just didn't like people."

"Probably that's what's really the matter with the Cavaliers," Miss Hargrave commented without enthusiasm. "You *are* the most peculiar driver. Now you're just crawling again."

"Would a tenth of your Cavaliers support an American Hitler without some reservations?" Van Kill demanded. "Even your Miss Goff possibly . . . I always go slowly here because of that green angel on Bishop Manning's back porch. It's bound to fall down some day and I'd hate to miss it by seconds."

"I told you," Betty insisted after she had sorted this out, "there's no promise of violence in the Cavaliers' activities. Mr. Pough says that's what makes their appeal so deadly. And," Betty's voice quavered in her throat, "you promised not to tell Mr. De Porta about Miss Goff, remember. I only hope I haven't—" She got her handkerchief out of her purse as they reached Amsterdam and stopped for the light.

"Darling, I am the grave." Van Kill gave her a cigarette. "I strongly suspect Ben De Porta knows the Goff is biting his hand," he added as they slid into 122nd Street. "That's neither here nor there. What's here," he said, turning left again into Broadway and casually pulling her over to him, "besides that fat-legged Barnard girl staring at your wanton hat, is the necessity for you to realize that your sudden doubts about me are a letdown from quite a lot of Pernod. You've a good head for a—" he glanced down at the head now resting against his shoulder "—so small a female."

Van Kill felt absurdly pleased at having poked through Miss Hargrave's mental baggage without rousing resentment. He could see the tips of her lashes through the smoke from her cigarette and the curve of her cheek, which reminded him of Edward's in dubious moments.

"Did you drive so far out of the way because you thought I might be taken drunk?" Betty asked without moving.

"And furthermore," Van Kill blew a strand of her ostrich feather away from his nose, "there is the necessity for you to realize that you are taking much too cavalier an attitude toward these American Nazis. Violence is implicit in their name. That's why your boss has told you to be careful in your snooping. For purely business reasons, while I——"

Betty slid away from him, threw her cigarette out of the window, and straightened her hat. "Telling me to be careful for *business* reasons makes me feel really secure," she said firmly. "It's the names of some of their big contributors, I've collected most of their little ones, that I expect to find in Burke's closet. Not machine-gun ammunition. Why should there be? The Cavaliers are fat rats right now. And too conceited by far to suspect me of being a cat in a mouse dress."

"Can you tell me then," Van Kill's voice was very casual, "if it's for business or for personal reasons that you've been followed since we left the Popub offices this noon?"

"Personal," Betty said just as casually. She turned to admire a small forest of Christmas trees outside a Reeves store and missed Van Kill's truly creditable suppression of surprise.

Betty explained about Dick Lee then. It must have been Dick Lee who looked out at them from the rear of a passing taxi as they entered Pye Street.

"A southern gentleman who can't believe a good girl would live alone in the big city. But harmless," she said with a quiver of remembered mischief around her mouth. She had taken him shopping that morning because she had had plans for keeping him on his feet during the afternoon too, and she had *let* him follow her to the Popub Building. "He thinks I do piece work somewhere around Fiftieth Street and Sixth Avenue. There's personal interest for you."

Van Kill pointed out that there was no place where Lee could have watched the Matapan and kept warm and cautioned her against regional intolerance. "Some of my best friends are Southerners," he declared smugly. But he was not altogether amused.

As they turned from Ninety-sixth Street into Amsterdam, Betty asked him to set her down a block away from the office of the Cavaliers. "So Mr. Lee will see how discreet I am."

Watching the small tawny blonde cross Amsterdam, Van Kill wondered at his own ferment of doubt and apprehension. The Cavaliers were, as she said, fat rats and she had promised to let him know before she attempted anything in the burgling line. . . .

She stopped and looked back after she had crossed the street, not at Van Kill apparently, but for Richard Lee in his taxicab. Van Kill knew that they had got rid of Lee at Columbus Circle. He started his car and went home to phone Paul Harris.

XII

"Oh, good Lord!" Betty spoke her disgust aloud and flipped the lever on the dictaphone. She looked around then to make sure she was still alone in the Burke-Lee office. The headquarters of the Christian Cavaliers had been deserted when she arrived, but she had been expecting Lee to tag her in before this.

Her disgust was for the letter Burke had composed thanking a lady on Riverside Drive for a contribution. Miss Hargrave, who had already taken the lady's name and address for Popub, wondered whether even a childless widowed DAR would fall for such guff. The treacly insinuations of personal regard looked much thicker on paper than they sounded in Burke's colorless tones on the dictaphone.

This was evidently one of Lee's personal clients. Burke, wire-jawed, cunning Burke had acquired many arts since his teeth had been shot out in a dock workers' strike. He had learned how to approximate the gallant Lee by letter . . . Betty drew one foot under her and took time out for a cigarette while she pondered Mr. Pough's warning against underestimating Burke.

"I don't," she told herself, "but he does me. He's never learned that a pretty girl can have brains. That type never does."

She got up then, remembering that she hadn't tried the door of Burke's closet. She crossed the room, tugged at the lock bolt, and petulantly, though with regard for her suede toes, kicked at the door. Van Kill had said he would help her get into that closet if she insisted, but . . .

Betty ground out her cigarette against the side of the wastebasket and admitted that Hendrik Van Kill was in the back of her mind. As she slipped on the dictaphone headpiece and went back to her typing, she wondered again what had become of Lee. She disliked the notion of his sliding into the room while her ears were full of Burke.

Mr. Lee came just as she was taking the letter out of the typewriter, bursting in through the alley door with a flurry of cold air and snow specks. "Well, well, Betty Lou," he sang out, coming through the mailing room from the alley vestibule and entering his office.

Richard Lee was a hearty young man with a curly crew haircut. He had a boyish smile incorporated with his personality for an effect many women found charming. He stamped his feet and rubbed his hands in a manner which Miss Hargrave recognized as a conversation starter designed to indicate that Mr. Lee, being from the South, felt the cold.

"Betty Lou workin' hard?" he inquired.

"I'm all through, Mr. Lee," Betty said, not smiling. "When Mr. Burke comes in, will you tell him the list of names ready for envelope three is in the mailing room on the addressograph, the list of number one's ready for envelope two is there in the basket underneath the letters?"

A typed copy and a carbon duplicate of the list of names was also in Betty's purse, from which it would be transferred to the safe in Mr. Pough's office, but she did not mention this.

Mr. Lee, taking off his overcoat, shook his head, and made a clicking noise with his tongue. "Sure is a shame pretty little ol' girl like you has to work so hard. Now if I'd my way—" Mr. Lee put one hand on Betty's desk and leaned forward confidentially "—pretty little girls wouldn't have to work."

"It isn't hard work." Betty, putting the typewriter away and covering the dictaphone, spoke lightly, but kept a weather eye out. Mr. Lee made passes by reflex action. "It isn't hard work," she repeated, putting her chair between herself and him. "I'm smart."

"Sure," Mr. Lee, left hovering intimately over the empty desk, agreed. "But you can't tell me that makes it right." He picked up the dictaphone cylinder that Betty had just taken out of the machine and waggled it at her. "Ol' Burke sittin' here talkin' onto that thing when you're not here to make work for you to do when you are." Lee tossed the cylinder in the air and caught it. "Pretty girl's got no business bein' so smart. And workin' so hard," he added with an extra layer of Old South vibrato.

Betty finished adjusting her hat. "It's experience," she said, and, "Don't break that," as Lee went on juggling the cylinder. "It's a discard, but sometimes Mr. Burke wants to check on the letters."

"Did you do the one in the drawer here?" Mr. Lee's time-killing movements were in direct contrast to Betty's purposeful tempo of imminent departure. He sat on the desk now in an atti-tude of boyish charm.

"Mr. Burke always leaves work on top of the desk," Betty said, snatching her coat from the costumer and getting into it quickly to frustrate any possible gallantry.

But Lee was reaching into the middle right-hand drawer of the desk. "Here's one Burke forgot, I reckon."

"No!" Betty's throat was tight with annoyance at herself. She was looking, not at the dictaphone cylinder Lee was taking from its box, but at the papers on which it had lain in the drawer. How many times she had investigated the desk drawers and found noth-ing of interest. Today she had forgotten.

Now three swift steps took her to the desk and she was ruffling through a pile of manuscript before Lee could have stopped her . . . WHAT MAKES DEPRESSION? . . . THE CRACKS IN OUR FOUNDATION . . . SEEDS OF DECAY . . . AMERICA FIRST . . . The headings flashed under her fingers. The papers were only a collection of essays by "True American" which had appeared in *The Lance*.

Disappointed the girl straightened up to see Lee bent over the dictaphone, its dust cover under his arm, trying to fit the cylinder from the drawer onto the spindle. "Just see whether this is a job for you too," he was saying.

Betty's ears pricked to a note of ill-concealed excitement. Her blue eyes narrowed speculatively on the eager hunch of Lee's shoulders. She saw more than ignorance of its ancient workings in his nervous fiddling with the machine which Burke had bought from a school for the deaf.

"Here," she said with what she hoped was a convincing tone of indifference. "You have to adjust this little dingus. Not the setscrew." She turned on the machine, pushed her hat back ruthlessly, and had the earpiece halfway to her head when Lee took hold of it.

"Let me," he said with false playfulness. "It was my idea. Lemme." His full mouth trembled, his enunciation was bayou thick as he tugged at the dictaphone headpiece.

The thing spoke: 'This is Burke, can you talk a little louder, sir?'

It *was* Burke's voice. Involuntarily Betty relaxed her grip.

"That's a girl." Lee wrested the receiver away. He clamped the attachment awkwardly on his head. "Telephone record, huh?" He stopped, eying Betty as if newly aware of her presence. "No, no," he murmured, catching her hand. His other arm went around her waist. "It's not for you, like you said, sugar, it's not for you. Be still now."

His lips automatically nuzzled toward her while his hands made play at her throat and breast. His attention was on the sounds which the dictaphone was giving to him exclusively.

Betty twisted in his arms. With her head pressed against Lee's she could hear a whisper of articulation, two voices it seemed, but not loud enough for her to catch anything. There were several things she could do, with teeth, elbows, and heels, to discommode Lee, and she *could* kick over the dictaphone. None of these would help her hear what Lee was listening to. Still, her right arm was free from the elbow and after she had reached the volume control on the machine, Betty heard very well.

'American business efficiency in control,' a strange tinny voice overflowed the headpiece.

Lee yelped, first with anguish, then with rage as he realized that the girl, who had been struggling to get away from him a moment before, was clinging to his wrist and keeping him from relieving his tortured ears.

"You—you bitch," he sobbed and tore away from her.

'The calm and unemotional guidance necessary to the conduct of your movement,' the metallic tones continued while Lee clawed at the headpiece. The voice lifted to a measured shout as he separated himself from it. 'Avoiding the extravagances which totalitarian governments have shown to be inefficient,' it boomed like radio thunder.

Lee held the instrument away from him and dashed the tears from his eyes. "You—you, shut it off," he said loudly.

Betty Hargrave backed away from him laughing and straightened her hat. "Not for me," she taunted.

'Private fortunes all over the country will rally to your support,' bugled the dictaphone voice. Lee smothered it under his arm.

"Betty," he begged, "you didn't ought to treat me like this."

'Yes, sir,' Burke's voice escaped from the receiver again, 'I think so, too.'

"Betty!" Lee made a spasmodic gesture toward the dictaphone and another toward the girl who was callously smoothing her gloves. "Betty, honey, *please* make it stop."

'But first get middle-class support,' Mr. Burke spoke from under Lee's arm.

"What goes on here?" Mr. Burke spoke from behind Betty.

She faced him, alert for what she hoped would prove an interesting exchange between the head Cavaliers, and gave him her best dumb-blonde smile. Burke's close-set eyes traveled from Lee's disheveled head back to the unruffled girl in the frivolous hat.

"It's just Mr. Lee playing with the dictaphone," she said sweetly.

"With the biscuit out of there?" Burke demanded, jerking his head toward the open drawer.

He was looking at Lee, Betty saw thankfully. She was exerting conscious effort to keep her hands clasped lightly on her purse and her stance casual while her pulse mounted in her throat.

"Just what, may I ask," Burke bit off his words deliberately, "just what inspired you to ransack that drawer the one time I go away and leave something in it?"

Betty knew excitement like a muscular ache in her chest. Burke's close-hauled fury was ample proof that the dictaphone record was important.

Lee shuffled his feet.

'Make haste slowly,' twanged the anonymous voice under his arm.

"Great day, Tom," Lee blotted it out again and spoke for the first time. "What the hell, ain't we partners?"

"Partners," Burke replied, setting his jaws on the word. "Partners in the fields in which you are useful. I thought you were calling on that prospect on Long Island today, for instance."

Lee did not want to say before Betty that the prospect's husband was at home with a cold. He stood still and said nothing. Like the Spartan boy hugging the dictaphone to his vitals, Betty observed with detachment.

"We are all partners," Burke went on, turning to the girl and stretching a smile beneath his angry eyes. "But I do not trouble people with matters which they cannot control or comprehend. *You* can understand that, can't you, Miss Hargrave?"

"Oh, yes," Betty heard herself say and from somewhere on top of her brain came applause for the dim-witted tone in which she was saying it. "I never could see any *sense* in political debates *myself*, but I know some folks just *dote* on them."

It seemed to Betty that the narrow speculative quality which she had sometimes imagined in his gaze faded completely then, as Burke looked at her. Certainly it was unfortunate that she was not close enough to the door to leave the instant Mr. Burke said, "I know I can rely on your discretion, Miss Hargrave."

For Dick Lee, easing his cramped elbow, released a final specimen of recorded Burke:

'You may, I assure you, rely upon my discretion,' it said earnestly.

And Betty, going out of the office via the mailing room, laughed. Not politely like a humorless steno reacting to a puzzling situation, not sympathetically as one making the best of an embarrassing accident, but wholeheartedly and with intelligent malice. Miss Hargrave laughed at the two Cavaliers so that all her teeth showed.

She had delivered the typewritten lists of Cavaliers contributors to Echo Newman and was nearly home before she remembered that during her display of mirth Thomas Burke's extension course smile had cracked, and that his effort was not at all enhanced by having his teeth in it. . . .

XIII

THE HONORABLE DIANA BROWN was a firm-bodied old lady who might have been more than handsome if she had taken some pains with herself. A kind of bare efficiency supplemented by plenty of money made her grooming unexceptionable. There was nothing about her superbly cut clothes that could get out of order and her white hair was cropped like a poodle's. She was a calm woman. The deceptively vague expression with which she regarded the world and the fact that she had all her own teeth probably accounted for her almost unlined face.

She wrote detective stories under the name of Lady Diana Brown and few people knew that birth and death and marriage had given her other titles and names sufficiently like the ones she used. The presumptuous who asked where she was listed in Debrett were apt to be told that she was in reality the Grand Duchess Anastasia still hiding from the Bolsheviks.

She sat now upon a divan near the east window of the Van Kill-Cameron-Mavromicháli living room in the Otranto Apartments with an animal which most people needed a second look at to identify as a cat. She was glancing at the boxed firs which adorned their common terrace and devoting a corner of her mind to speculation about Christmas lights for them . . . When Van Kill and Edward and Yanni had moved into this converted penthouse, Van Kill had discovered an old acquaintance in their next door neighbor. At her age, Lady Di said, she had met all kinds of people and in the time she had left preferred to create her own. As Ben De Porta had suggested, she was seclusive. However, she and Edward had begun spending a good deal of time together. Edward, who was something of a snob, liked to have her call for him at Webster and watch the genuflections of the headmaster who was a worse one. They went to concerts and prize fights together.

When cold weather came, Lady Di had remembered that in

pre-depression days the two apartments had been a single unit. The grande dame and the infant prodigy had bullied the management of the Otranto into unsealing a door behind the paneling between their two living rooms.

Because she was Lady Di this arrangement caused no invasion of privacy on either side and the fact that at any time after morning lessons were over Lady Di might tap on this door and come calling had a reconditely beneficial effect on the conduct of their bachelor hall. She saw to it that the Otranto maid service was adequate.

Yanni alone, perhaps because he had recently sustained a great disillusionment about old ladies, held off from Lady Di. Even Yanni admitted that, for notions like going around the house in nothing but a G string, Lady Di's influence with the young kyrios was excellent. And when Edward had to be left alone at night it was better to open the door between the apartments than to fee some unhappy hireling whose education the boy might get up out of bed to improve. . . .

Lady Di was thinking now about an isolation device for the thriller she was currently engaged on, and listening to Van Kill in his study talk over the telephone to the editor of *Carnage* magazine . . . She would, if asked, have said she was knitting. Actually her hands lay palm down and quiet on the olive wool in her lap. They were thin-knuckled hands, singularly young-looking.

Satisfied, Van Kill thought, as he stood in the doorway. It pleased him to reflect that the Honorable Diana's hands lay quietly on her life too, and neither clutched nor petitioned.

"About those mice," she said when he came into the room. Her accent was remotely English.

"I still think it's a very impractical way to get rid ot mice," the young man said. "Why not borrow Eo? And if you want to know what I was telephoning about, I'll tell you."

"So considerate of you, Hal, to save me the trouble of leading up to it. I came over with Eulalie to make sure she cleaned under the bed in Edward's room. He has a cow in there. Did you know? For his school play, I suppose."

The cat Eohippus, a Siamese-Persian with the tentative appearance of a horse, came forward to sniff polish on Van Kill's shoes and left the room.

"Eo's not interested in my mice," Diana continued. "I stayed after Eulalie left to keep him company. And you sailed in with that stirring in somebody else's soup expression and dove at the telephone without giving the poor beast so much as a word."

"Telling a man that his soup is being supplied with an inferior vegetable is merely an attention-diverger, Lady Di." Van Kill took his hat and overcoat to the closet in the foyer and went on talking. "The cook who believes I'm like to upset his soup should wonder why I take pains to tell him how to improve it."

He came back into the living room, smiled at Diana while he frisked himself for cigarettes, sat down beside her in the place the cat had vacated, and asked, "Has Edward made a good cow?"

Diana picked up the balaklava she was knitting. "Really, I think it's going to be very fierce for a cow, don't you? . . . Oh, you haven't seen it?"

"Since I helped him lug a secondhand bedspring and a sack of flour into his room, I haven't been consulted." Van Kill adopted the modern pedagogue's tone of self-abnegation.

"Did the owner of that soup you're dipping into consult you?" The Honorable Diana chuckled as her needles began to flash. "You weren't talking about soup on the phone anyway. I thought it was just as well Edward wasn't around. What did you mean by saying inattentive tail plus amateur talent wasn't equal to one efficient operation?"

"Operative," Van Kill coughed on an expiration of smoke. "The soup simile was yours. Before I gladly abandon it, consider that by throwing aspersions on the ingredients I hope to discover the size of the kettle."

"So that you can upset it," Diana agreed placidly. "But if you said *operative*, you were talking about detectives shadowing people." The knitting needles continued to rustle. "You're looking too erratic to be safe, Hal. I thought you were concentrating on indoor work."

"Lots of documents get out of doors. The signature on Uncle Jephtha's power of attorney most resembles that of the poweree because Uncle Jephtha was on horseback when he signed it."

The Honorable Diana's expression indicated her opinion of parables.

"Even a fuddy duddy of a document examiner who sees a nice girl like Betty Hargrave being *shadowed*, as your genteel readers would prefer, Diana, shadowed by, first an amateur who could double for King Wenceslaus's page, and second by a breakfast cereal sleuth who clings to the principle of following the follower so assiduously that he loses his quarry when his quarry shakes number one—even *he* might be curious." Van Kill took a breath.

"And in reply to the look on your face, I must add that anything touching David Montefiore's bête noir is my business now. Trouble is—" Van Kill hooked a finger into Diana's ball of wool and rolled it across the rug at Eo, who had come back from the kitchen. The cat ignored it. "Trouble is, there's so *much* touching him."

"Including Miss Hargrave?" the Honorable Diana asked. "Is this the Montefiore whose twenty-five thousand dollars Yanni was moaning at you about?"

"Betty has a special ten-foot pole to touch Paul Harris with," Van Kill answered. "It's a Montefiore relative, a related though still nebulous twenty-five thousand, and different reasons, but it's still the same Harris. Or are they different reasons?" Van Kill put his cigarette out and turned a quizzical eyebrow on the Honorable Diana. "Sorry, were you trying to edge in a word?"

Paul Harris had once done a rehash of a story quite personal to Lady Di, but he was not personally known to her, and she had not offered to speak. Counting stitches, her expression was even vaguer than usual.

"Only to say it seems complicated enough without *your* explaining anything."

Van Kill grinned. "What if I anticipate the development of that element whose lack you've always deplored in the stories I've brought you heretofore?"

"Really, my dear boy, I'm so glad. Is it the young lady whom this Mr. Harris is having followed?"

"You are quick, aren't you, Lady Di?" Van Kill put his feet on the floor and walked across the room to a cabinet which he opened. "Can I give you a drink or something?"

"Oh, a drink by all means." This was a ceremonial joke between them which never interrupted the pace of whatever talk was afoot. Van Kill put a decanter, glasses, and a bottle of seltzer on a tray and brought it to her.

The Honorable Diana worked at her knitting and drank whisky and soda while the young man talked. She was a good listener, like most old ladies with full lives behind them. Replenishing her glass from time to time and knitting steadily, she absorbed the story of Van Kill's refusal to go after the editor of *Carnage* merely *because* he edited *Carnage*, of Van Kill's dubious acceptance of De Porta's commission to protect David from his own zeal.

"The uncle's proposal is quite as impractical as the nephew's," Van Kill said. "That's why I regard this second twenty-five thousand dollars as a nebulous sum. To keep Dizzy out of trouble demands a change in world conditions. We can't send him on a world cruise. But when David told me Harris does so well as an impresario for refugee aritsts that one of them committed suicide recently, I agreed I'd anyway go look at the beast."

Harris *had* been indulging in a refugee racket until the suicide happened to put a stop to it, but probably one couldn't have proved anything even if the suicide hadn't happened, Van Kill added. "And that's that."

"But if you're investigating this Harris, you're doing what David wanted after all," Diana persisted. "You ought to collect twenty-five thousand from him too. Perhaps you can prove something else."

"You package things so neatly," Van Kill laughed. "Two jobs, you say. One, for the nephew, to catch the editor of *Carnage* with his hands so bloody that Frederick Pough will be forced to dispense with him and his magazine . . . Two, for the uncle, to keep nephew David out of trouble while I am engaged on job number one. Each job in its own little box as if the human elements weren't oozing back and forth like osmosis."

"For instance?" Diana Brown inquired serenely.

"For instance," Van Kill continued on a querulous note, "I discover Harris is apparently so interested in the confidential job Betty Hargrave is doing for their mutual boss on an anti-Semitic group in the West Nineties that he's put a second-rate tail on her. That annoys me. Betty deserves only the best. I called Harris up and told him so."

Diana suggested after a space of listening that Harris, who wouldn't admit it and did nothing but swear repetitively over the telephone at Van Kill, had the same reason for having Betty shadowed as Cavalier Lee, who probably would admit following her in person: an interest in Betty herself. . . .

The Honorable Diana Brown, replenishing her glass occasionally and knitting steadily, was a good listener and, as Van Kill had reason to know, she was discreet. The document examiner had many friends at whom he might have talked himself out, realists on the Manhattan Homicide Squad, theorists on the faculty at International University. But Lady Di was an idealist, Van Kill said, whose instinctive resistance to plot-thickeners sometimes proved illuminating. He was listening carefully when she made an alternative suggestion in which she showed no great interest.

"Your case may take a turn uptown," she said. "There may be some connection between *Carnage* and the Cavaliers which you don't know as yet."

Van Kill admitted this was a possibility. "Harris lives in the Cavaliers' neighborhood," he said. "Not significant of course, but I'd have put him in the Shady Seventies on a bet."

Diana's reactions were colored by the forthright emotions of her own characters. Like Betty Hargrave she thought David would surely want to avoid bothering Mr. Pough by harassing Harris when he discovered Mr. Pough was plotting the downfall of an anti-Semitic group.

"It's a question of ambivalence," Van Kill told Diana as he

had told Betty Hargrave a few hours before. "Pough, the defender of Judah, cannot whitewash Pough, publisher of *Carnage*, for David. Dizzy is in sympathy with every worker in the anti-anti-Semitic vineyard, we hope, but the red-chemised houris on the covers of *Carnage* are an active pain in his belly," Van Kill was saying as the outer door of the foyer clicked and Edward came in with Yanni.

There was an atmosphere of blatant secrecy about their entrance. Yanni was burdened with bundles, his forward progress hampered by Edward, who danced along beside him, holding up his coat as a screen while they steered past Van Kill and Diana on their way to Edward's room.

The boy came back at once to make his manners and Diana asked, "Do you still want to have a tree-trimming party Christmas Eve?"

"Oh, yes." Edward nodded vigorously. The spiritual depression under which he had labored at the Matapan was gone and he was cocky. There was a smudge of what looked like machine oil under his chin.

"Not a big party, you know." The boy winced and bent to disengage himself from the cat. Eo, his back bent like a bow was affectionately stretching his claws in the hem of Edward's short trousers. "Because of the war," Master Cameron continued. "And the price of champagne. Just a sort of family party."

"Champagne?" his guardian inquired.

"Edward believes it's a great mistake," Diana explained soberly, "for a boy to reach manhood with romantic notions about champagne."

"We can't have you having romantic notions," Van Kill said, leaning forward with a handkerchief to wipe Edward's chin.

The boy shied away, grinning. "Not at my age," he said, rubbing the grease off with the back of his hand. "But when people get to be your age, Hal—" He clucked to his cat and swaggered out toward the kitchen.

"Christmas." Yanni, holding a small jacket and a whiskbroom, appeared in the door of Edward's room. "The young kyrios is all excite' about Christmas."

"That's obvious," Diana chuckled. "Is this tree-trimming party an old Cameron County custom?"

"I think not," Van Kill said dryly. "Apparently he never looks back on life in Cameron County. Everything considered, it's probably a good thing," he added and began mixing himself another drink.

"Good thing for anyone," Diana held out her glass. "Take your experience with you, but don't look back where you got it."

"Yanni, Yannee!" Edward sang from the kitchen. "Bring me one of those newspapers from under my bed, will you? *Il faut changer le plat du chat!*"

XIV

THAT night about eight-thirty Van Kill went to call on Betty Hargrave at the Alabama Apartments. As he passed out of sight in the Alabama's lobby a wine-red sedan had parked across the street and well down the block . . . It was about midnight now and the car was still waiting there. . . .

From time to time the driver had glanced back casually with the merest roll of his eyes. His companion had sat silent except for a few muttered words. These, not in English, called a minor deity to witness how long a woman could keep a man and why.

The driver nodded slightly as Van Kill reappeared, brief case in hand, on the apartment house steps. Then for the first time the driver's companion looked around in a long stare which did not disturb the sharp angles of his brown face. He watched Van Kill start off toward Fifth Avenue, then pushing his gray hat down upon his left eyebrow, he got out of the sedan, which moved away toward Madison.

The man in the gray hat also made, but as if with no set purpose, for Fifth Avenue. He checked his step a moment when he saw another figure pass the Alabama entrance and overtake the man with the brief case across the street.

Van Kill turned at the light sound of footsteps behind him. "Yanni," he said as the Greek came alongside and fell into step. The pair moved on together at an easy gait. Yanni, just under six feet, was not appreciably shorter than his companion and was heavier in the torso. He smiled now, a somewhat embarrassed smile.

"Kyrie," he began.

Van Kill returned the smile with provoking deliberation. "Yes, I know," he said as they turned north on the Avenue. "You just happened along. You always do."

"I am taking walk," Yanni replied as if by rote. "Tsansing into this vicinity, I happen to remember, happening to be in this vicinity, I chance to remember you have engagement nearmpy and ——"

A muscle in Van Kill's cheek twitched. "Come off it, Yanni."

"When you go from home, I tell you," the Maniote continued in normal tones, "this golden *despoinís* will not like some dirty old books second hand. For her is flowers, candy, Schrafft's candy, and if books, poetry," Yanni specified. "And new. I see she have given them back." He indicated Van Kill's brief case with a mixture of self-justification and sorrow. "Her *kyría* mama says no too, I bet."

Van Kill was laughing openly now. "The *despoinís* received Eisenmenger's *Jewry Unmasked* with every indication of delight, though I told her it was not a good translation of *Entdecktes Judentum*. Likewise Dr. August Rohling's *Talmud Jew*. She put Briman on her bedside table . . . Miss Hargrave is an orphan, Yanni, like us. She lives alone. This—" Van Kill swung the brief case "—is full of trash of the sort you burned yesterday. For mutual aid, see?"

Yanni was struggling with thought. When he brought it to speech, it was hesitant but stubborn. "A man like you, kyrie," he said, "comes too easy to the hearts of women. Like me too," he acknowledged with a darkling glance, "and this is okay. But me, I know when time to marry how I should do. The good family, rich maybe, the daughter young, beautiful, with her I am not perhaps before acquaint', I am seek for wife. But you, kyrie, what a pity after it is—too late—you think to marry—" Yanni floundered delicately and fell into Greek. "For the wife," he said, adapting a famous line, *"henì zónan anerì lusaménan."*

For perhaps six long strides Van Kill was silent. Yanni watched him sidelong. "Have no fear," he said then with a sigh and the Greek let out a relieved breath. "Improving your vocabulary with *Hamlet* the other day, weren't you? Edward's doing, I suppose . . . 'Quoth she, before you tumbled me, You promised me to wed.'. . . Act Four, Scene Five . . . The bard was really more civilized than that, Yanni."

"Oímoi, civilization," Yanni replied in Greek. "What is it but a

thin skin, even on you, kyrie, and clothes—" He gestured. "So nearly the same this covering that how can a man tell an unfriend from his brother? Unless matters which concern brothers are afoot?"

"*Nai, nai,*" Van Kill said. " 'How should I your true love know, From another one?' " he reverted to English and quoted lightly.

He and Yanni had cicatrices on the inner surface of their left wrists. Mementos of a cold night in the Peloponnesus when they had crouched over a campfire, the wounds in their forearms unsanitarily tied together with a strip of Yanni's grandmother's petticoat while Yanni's Uncle Yoryos administered the blood oath. It was not the sort of thing one spoke of while walking on upper Fifth Avenue . . . They were approaching the Metropolitan Museum. . . .

"Civilization is nothing doing with love," Yanni declared. "You said Act Four, Scene Five, kyrie? Civilization is only money and law."

"Listen," Van Kill said. "Certainly it is the law."

The sound of a siren yelped nearer. A La Salle sedan flashed past them, checked its flight with an instant silent application of brakes, and backed up with a gentle growl at following traffic from its siren. Diagonally in front of the Metropolitan Museum loomed the Manhattan Homicide Squad's car. Its rear door opened.

"Sure it's the doc," a big voice said. A cigar, a derby, and then incongruously eyeglasses looked out. "Hi, doctor. Where in hell you been keeping yourself?"

"Sergeant Mars." Van Kill was delighted. "Captain McLone," he said, reaching into the car's shadowed interior to shake hands.

There were two other men in the back beside Sergeant Thomas Mars, Yanni observed, and considerable handshaking.

Not this kind of law, Yanni said to himself.

Van Kill said ambiguously that he had been around.

"Why in hell don't you come down to see us?" Mars boomed while the silhouette of McLone made hospitable gestures. "We got a good one tonight. Hop in. You and your friend."

"Dark?" Van Kill asked.

"We're headed for Harlem." Mars' cigar shifted in his face and pointed north. "Hop in, hop in. Maybe we'll find a piece of writing for you to look at."

Van Kill climbed over the equipment on the floor of the car, moved a couple of flood lights, and adjusted his long legs to the jack seat. His face, Yanni observed, had taken on something of the expectant noticing quality which all these men whose life-work was unnatural death, shared in common. "Come on, Yanni."

Yanni hung back. Unfortunately he had a great deal of work tomorrow and must get some sleep. He was too muts honored. . . .

Continuing briskly up Fifth Avenue carrying the brief case which Van Kill had handed him. Yanni thought it was all right for the kyrios to be friendly with *ee astynomía.* Through Van Kill, the police knew Yanni as an expert with a document camera, a man who could conjure a lump of charred paper into speech, but Yanni's attitude toward the police was retiring. He did not share Van Kill's regard for the work of their specialists in murder . . . In Yanni's opinion murder was often a private affair. There was no decency interfering unless there was something wrong about it.

He quickened his stride to reach a pseudo-medieval cathedral as the light went green. He crossed Fifth Avenue to the park side. Taking the left bank of the double staircase here, he struck across the bridle path onto the cinder track around the reservoir. Over the water he could see the four tower lights of the Otranto and home. Yanni had lived in pre-Mycenean palaces and in empty lofts. The penthouse in the Otranto was home to him now because the two *kýrioi* were there.

Head on as he walked Yanni saw and approved the bright panel which the Empire State laid against the sky. There was no wind and behind the high wire fence on his right the small, tame, black-watered lake was smooth as a good fifth-century glaze. The fine cinders were just moist enough to be silent and spring pleasantly under the feet, Yanni found as he hit the cement section in front of the water control house. He caught a flash of long levers through the open doorway at his right as he left it quickly behind.

His breath came freely, easily. He felt only the pleasure of blood moving through his legs and arms, the pleasure of half-mechanical thought and sight. Christmas was coming. It was a fact, as the little kyrios had said, that the gaudy pinnacles of the skyscrapers in the distance reminded you of the holiday at this season.

Still Yanni took no direct notice of these any more than he did of the familiar scroll of grass and trees on his left, contrastingly dark beyond the lights of the path, the rickety wooden bridge over the bridle path, and the police call box beside it.

The green lights of the Otranto's tower were straight ahead of him again. Yanni realized that his stride had crept up a notch toward the jog trot he used in his morning half-dozen around the reservoir track. The overcast night was brisk enough for one who took his time, but warm for an athlete in his stride.

Yanni slowed down to unbutton his overcoat, which was fortunate. It was lucky that he made the abrupt halt a split second before he sensed rather than saw the silent rush of a body behind him, of a forearm half raised. Yanni sprang for the cement coping at the base of the fence, a little eminence where, back against the wire, he had an instant's safety for the helpless moment when he shed his topcoat.

His attacker braked the overcharge and whirled back, a sharp-faced man with a drawn knife, but Yanni was ready for him. A little surprised the man was, though no more than a ripple of it showed in the impassive planes of his brown features. This would be more, it seemed to say, than the neat sticking he had been hired to do. Yanni had never laid eyes on the man in the gray hat before.

Yanni gave sharp-face no time for thought. Circling to test the ground, he sized his opponent up. A right-hander from the looks of things. Reach about three inches longer than his own, he judged. Too bad. But he himself had the same advantage in height . . . Moreover, long-arm was a little winded from stalking him along the bridle path and climbing the bank.

Circling wide to the left, Yanni shifted his own knife to his left hand, tried a practice lunge. No change. A left arm guard and a right arm attack. But the scoundrel had balance and a cool head. He had not been drawn off an inch. He was well-muscled on the breast, Yanni noted with the back of his mind. The heart was just at the top of a low fancy pocket under a blue handkerchief which deplorably matched tie, shirt and suit as well.

Suddenly long-arm feinted for the chest, right foot forward, lunged in hard, up and over for Yanni's face. His eyes did not telegraph the blow by a single flutter. Yanni caught the other's wrist on his left forearm, jumped backward a great leap at the counter rally which followed fast. With wary rage long-arm slashed in again, four furious thrusts that almost had Yanni off his feet. At the fourth, ducking under, he brought his knee up sharply into Yanni's groin.

"So," hissed the Greek, the only words spoken by either of them. "So, ntirty you fight."

Yanni, already aware that this mysterious attacker was set to cut rather than kill, now changed a decision he had made. Long-arm almost but not quite smiled.

Too soon, it appeared, for Yanni, circling left, was upon him left-handed in a flickering drive that left the other short of wind. Yanni was remembering thankfully that his technique was from the Cretan school of three knives, one in each hand and one in the teeth. He could make such flashing changes thus, boring in left after a right-hand rush.

Up, down, up. Three times the other cross-parried. Three times there was a ringing sound of knives whetted together in the air. Breathing lightly, the Greek jumped back, but long-arm caught his elbow in a powerful grasp, kicked viciously at his shin, shoved hard.

Yanni's knife flew wide as he fell, the assassin on top of him, thrusting with his right hand, which Yanni managed to grip, gouging with his left then for Yanni's eyes.

Twice over they coiled in a spray of fine cinders before the Greek landed a kick in the other's abdomen. He scrambled to his feet, recovered his knife, and waited disdainfully for long-arm to rise.

Yanni looked almost placid. Blood from a cinder scratch on his cheek ran down beside his mouth. His teeth gleamed as his tongue flicked out to touch it and his face was strangely calm. The other's as he rose was twisted with hurt and hate. Yanni could have ended it then with a couple of kicks and the long-armed one knew it. But the Greek, waiting contemptuously, had bethought him of a little exhibition trick, a wily Cretan trick, that might serve as a warning. . . .

So it was that in one breath Yanni stood relaxed like a pit-wise cock. In the next with the simultaneous co-ordination of a ballet figure he stepped forward, cracked down hard with his left forearm on the other's guarding left wrist, and was coolly describing an apprentice arc with his weapon. Almost thoughtfully, if the action of a flicker of lightning is thoughtful, the knife point flickered with a roughly triangular motion at the top of long-arm's breast pocket, carved the segment of cloth away so that the brown skin over his heart stood revealed. The blue silk handkerchief opened on the air and fell prettily. . . .

Too late Yanni whipped back his own left guard. Long-arm's lunge had slashed deep into his forearm. Blood poured out of Yanni's coat sleeve instantly.

Almost, again, long-arm smiled, but again too soon. Yanni, poised on the balls of his feet, feinted twice for his opponent's eyes. It felt as if hot milk were dribbling from the fingers of his left hand and Yanni knew he had no time to lose.

At his second try the other's guard came up just the necessary fraction of an inch. Veering, Yanni stamp-stepped hard, thrusting from close in. His blade went home with an audible small rip through the triangle of exposed flesh.

Yanni withdrew the knife. A little bubble of blood followed behind it. He stepped back, breathing, watching long-arm's face while he wiped the knife on his coat. He could hear the night murmur of traffic from Central Park West. Long-arm looked like a man swallowing a fruit pit. When he had swallowed it, he fell on his back with a choked invocation to a minor deity. The sudden muscular spasm clutched his fingers firmly onto the knife.

Yanni let his eyes dwell only an instant on the fall. He took a careful look along the cinder path both ways. Listened. Delicate moments like this too frequently produced last minute, incompetent witnesses . . . Not until he had reassured himself did Yanni care for his wound. From the pocket of his overcoat across the path he took his muffler, wiped his face on it, and with a mutter of annoyance at the necessity tore it lengthwise. Knotted and with the aid of his knife it made a rude tourniquet. Yanni put on his overcoat then and his gloves, which he had not been wearing when he was attacked. He was glad his hat hadn't fallen off during the fight. He noticed that long-arm's gray one had got all dirt when it rolled away from his head.

Viewing the terrain, Yanni saw that their scuffling had erased almost every sign of two separate pairs of feet. He attended to what was left. Gently, he wanted the knife to stay in the clenching hand, he rolled the body off onto the grass, knelt beside it. Swiftly he examined the clothing. Like the haberdashery it was new and bore no identifying tags. An overcoat, if there was one, abandoned among the trees, would probably be similarly anonymous, the Greek thought.

He replaced long-arm's hat, removed his own, and with a free mind crossed himself. Forehead, breast, right shoulder, left shoulder. Yanni prayed for the safety of those he loved and for the newly departed soul of one unknown. . . .

The body gave a convulsive twitch. Yanni shook his head disapprovingly at the interruption, took long-arm's clenching hand in his own fingers and gave him a *coup de grâce* . . . Yanni removed his hat again. . . .

"*Teèn eeméran dielthón, efcharistô* . . . Having come through the day, I thank thee, Lord. Grant that the night as the evening be without sin." Calmly Yanni finished his prayer. . . .

The Greek swayed a little when he got to his feet. Giddiness struck him again when he bent down for Van Kill's brief case and he hung on to the fence until the buildings reflected in the water looked like a runny but not a running color print.

He was all right after he started walking, but all he remembered afterward about getting out of the park was the policeman strolling away from him along the sidewalk which leads south from the Ninety-third Street exit. The same young cop probably who had once encountered Van Kill and the Greek walking on the reservoir after hours and expelled them from the park.

Yanni remembered smiling at this recollection and pulling himself together to meet the pre-Christmas pleasantries of Bertram the night elevator boy. The scarf around his arm had loosened and the inside of his coat pocket was getting sticky. He knew he was going to have to have help by the way his stomach behaved in the elevator. He told himself that the kyrios had always expressed great confidence in the Kyría, the Honorable Diana. . . .

"The matter is," he told her when she opened the door, "the matter is when I stop walking I cannot stand up."

"Keep walking then." She reached up out of her billowing flannel nightgown and grabbed him in time. "Ye puir callant, y're unco fashed," she said, steering him. "The trick with these things," she went on in comprehensible language after she had Yanni under the bright light in her bathroom, "is not to drip on the carpets."

She asked no question except, "Where's Hal?" She made no comment on the cause of Yanni's condition but, "So it's that way," when he muttered, "Cut sleeve, I mpurn all anyway."

At the time Yanni was too irritated at his own tendency to slide off the chair she had pushed under him to wonder at Lady Di's casual efficiency. She clucked at the wound when she uncovered it as if she were summoning the attention of a small animal, tightened Yanni's tourniquet again with the handle of her bath brush, and went away in the midst of her nightgown.

When he noticed her once more, she was putting a needle through the edges of his wound. A steaming enamel pan containing scissors, a pair of chop tongs, and a couple of extra needles threaded with white silk stood beside a pottery mug of soup on the floor. The

Honorable Diana's hands smelled of Clorox. He saw that she had fetched his dressing gown from his bedroom.

"One more," she said conversationally. "It's nerves, you know. Interests me to know you have some—quite a little bunch of them right around here that's making you so jangled. Not because you've lost a little blood."

Yanni stiffened his back. The witch woman must not think she had to talk at him because she was hurting him slightly. "It was my own fault," he told her. "For making show-off to a stranger."

XV

〰〰

A DIRECT consequence of Yanni's entering their apartment by way of Lady Di's was that Van Kill, on returning from his night out with the Homicide Squad, fell headlong over Edward's big construction job. The thing was resilient, but at the same time painfully knobby and it hummed when struck like the bedspring it was based on.

"Yanni!" shouted the examiner of questioned documents when he came to rest on his back. "Edward! What have I done to deserve this?" He opened his eyes when the light clicked on, took one look at the repellent muzzle of the beast his ward had fabricated and closed them again. "Holmes," Van Kill lamented, "a child has done this horrid thing."

"If you were hurt, you wouldn't moan so," Edward said from the living room door. "Yanni and I put it there for the shellac to dry after you went out. He said he'd move it back and cover it. I guess he forgot."

"Perhaps he was afraid to approach it alone," his guardian answered, sliding back on his elbows. "Lady Di said it was very fierce for a cow."

"It's a bull, a Mithra bull for the Webster Christmas program," Edward said. "You're just looking at one end." He stood on one foot to warm the other on his leg. His pajama trousers were rucked up to his knees and there was a pillow mark on one flushed cheek. "I didn't want you to see it until the performance," he added regretfully.

"I won't look at it any more," Van Kill promised, rolling over on his stomach and crawling away, "though I can't help feeling it."

Van Kill was, as Edward had said, not in the least hurt, but his insignificant contusions made him fail to notice that Yanni had slept through the ruckus. Yanni was up and away before the six o'clock snow covered the terrace, Edward announced while they were getting breakfast. This did not surprise Van Kill. Early rising was one of Yanni's few bad habits, and Van Kill had given Yanni a daily assignment at De Porta's apartment which, considering the human factor involved, had to be got at early.

"It looks so festive on the dark red bricks," Edward commented on the snow. "So proper for Christmas." He said this lying on the floor with the financial sheet of the *Times*. "A really heavy fall would be good for the wheat, but at the same time it would delay shipping. It's hard to decide, isn't it?"

The epidermis of Van Kill's mind was still bruised by his night out in Harlem. He grunted that he expected great things of Edward some day, but didn't anticipate his doing anything about the weather. He found his ward's jubilation over a "two to three cent advance in Chicago wheat yesterday" very trying. "It was the one bright spot in the most lethargic afternoon of trading for weeks," the Cameron heir quoted defensively.

It was nearly nine o'clock, Van Kill groaned. Would Edward trouble himself to give an eye to the Greek text of Aesop? . . .

The lesson period went off normally. Diana, when she came to take Edward to lunch, said nothing out of the way. Thus it happened that Van Kill kept his appointment with Frederick Pough in a preoccupied frame of mind. For he met Paul Harris on his way to the more remote and more respectable purlieus of Popub, Inc. The editor of *Carnage* bolted out of his reception room working hard to look like a hard-working man. In a hurry for a pre-lunch snifter, Van Kill reasoned. "Good morning," he said, sidestepping to avoid a collision.

After one glance of recognition Harris called, "Hold it, Sammie," to the boy on the elevator. He made a chin and shoulder gesture from Van Kill toward a window beyond the elevator rank, but he did not subsequently raise his eyes above the level of the other's collar.

He seemed such a comic menace, Van Kill thought, it was easy to understand how both writers and refugees fell into his clutches by underestimating him.

"I admire a white man," Harris scowled earnestly under his hat, "I admire a white man who's that handy with a knife . . . You won't have that kind of trouble again." He walked off abruptly as he had spoken.

Van Kill did not look after the man, but his steps as he retraced them down the corridor fell just a beat below their usual quick time. He was not weighing Harris at all beyond the first shock of useless alarm after the fact and the first rapid tip of decision. Something Edward had said not two hours ago was uppermost in his consciousness. . . .

They had been lining out Aesop's fable of the bird which is granted speech at the point of death from an arrow. *"Hetéra lúpe,"* Edward pronounced and rendered, "another trouble."

"Grief rather," Van Kill had amended. "The creature's dying, he's more than troubled. And it's a second grief, one of a pair, the first, that the eagle has to die in any way at all, understood," he had said and finished the line. "This is my *crowning* grief, to perish by my own feathers."

The verb from the noun stem signified to plume oneself in a flutter of boasting and excitement, a delicate connection hardly renderable here, he had pointed out . . . It all seemed pettily pedantic to Van Kill as he sat in Pough's office waiting for him to finish talking into a dictaphone. He also forced the Harris incident from his mind and gave his attention to Harris's boss.

"While appreciating the consideration which you urge," Van Kill caught the murmur, precise and well-routined, "I find by reference to your letter of November fifth that you voluntarily suggested this agreement. I deeply deplore any misunderstanding which may subsequently have arisen. . . ."

Van Kill reflected that Pough was probably everything that Echo and Betty claimed as an executive. He ignored the sense of Pough's words, while his own observation and thought wove against the background of their rhythms. The major stockholder of Popub had a strong humorous face, handsome in the American way that depends on health and regular exercise. Stubborn too, capable and well aware of it.

"But for any further discussion I must refer you to Mr. Harris," he was saying now.

Pough finished the letter in a strain which indicated a routine freeze to one of Harris's by-line victims, hung the dictaphone mouthpiece on its hook, and swiveled his chair around.

"Miss Newman tells me you're interested in my Geyer letter, Dr. Van Kill. I believe she said you collected Geyer items yourself."

"His handwriting, yes," Van Kill answered. It was the careful document examiner's habit, he said, to keep a representative collection of dated foreign and American scripts and photographs of scripts. "I am not interested in Richard Wagner's ancestry, however."

Pough smiled. "I see you've been listening to booksellers' gossip, which is only half correct."

Van Kill's perverse silence roused the collector's pride. "Don't you think we might more reasonably believe, Dr. Van Kill, just as a matter of hereditary probability that the real father of a genius like Richard Wagner was a, well a—" Pough halted measurably while his gaze went to the window "—a mercurial Jewish type such as Ludwig Heinrich Christian Geyer. Rather than an obscure police official like Karl Friedrich Wagner. It would help explain Richard's irresponsible conduct."

Betty Hargrave's argument for Columbus, Pough's for Wagner—and David Montefiore? Van Kill was amused. Pough knew that Van Kill was a friend of his irresponsible business associate.

"The Geyers," Van Kill spoke indifferently, "had only an infinitesimal drop of the blood by the time Ludwig was born. They'd been marrying into German Christian families for generations, exactly as Ludwig married Johanna Paetz, Richard's mother, soon after Karl Friedrich's death."

"Suspiciously soon," Pough retorted with the pleased annoyance of a man who has met some one capable of wrangling intelligently about his pet theory. He took a cigarette while he paused for a phrase, gave Van Kill one, and lit them both. "There is every kind of proof that that liaison which produced Geyer's first child Caecilie six months after his marriage to Johanna had been going on for a considerable time."

"The letters Geyer wrote Johanna between December, 1813 and February, 1814 don't establish that," Van Kill said. He regarded the tip of his cigarette. "I mean those we *know* to be genuine, Burrell's four and Bournot's one."

"*My* letter puts the Geyer paternity beyond a guess," said Frederick Pough. In the sort of man who obviously didn't admit to emotion during business hours this warmth was distinctly humanizing, Van Kill thought.

"It all depends," he said coolly, "upon whether Geyer was around Leipzig where the Wagners were living in the summer of 1812. He usually played there with the Franz Seconda troupe."

"My letter has to do with more than Geyer." In a gentlemanly fashion Pough was a little piqued. "It lays at rest a ludicrous Wagner family tradition."

"That Richard's mother Johanna was the natural daughter of Prince Friedrich Ferdinand Constantin of Weimar, the brother of Goethe's patron." Van Kill's smile was bland. "I realize that noblemen of the period bastardized the country pretty freely." Van Kill slid down in his chair a trifle and drew deeply on his cigarette. "Prince Friedrich would have been something like fifteen when he sired Johanna, if I remember my chronology, but that was *his* business, don't you think?"

"Yes," Pough said shortly. It was plain that Van Kill could discuss everything about the Wagner controversy except the contents of Pough's manuscript letter. And the mild-mannered young scholar had contrived to make the publisher feel that to say no more would be downright boorish.

"My letter offers proof that Johanna's father was neither baker nor nobleman," Pough said after a moment, "but a rich Jewish fancier of women and the arts. An eccentric and volatile individual by all accounts."

Once started Pough's reluctance left him. His voice rose a degree. "It fits everything we know of Richard Wagner's temperament. Our man corresponds entirely with Wagner's description of his mother's 'exalted paternal friend' who placed her in the select Leipzig school where she remained until 1793. The very year," Pough added triumphantly, "of her real father's death at the age of fifty-three."

"It's lovely." Van Kill wagged his head. "Some theories give Hitler a Jewish grandmother, don't they?"

Pough was not offended. "My document has an excellent pedigree." He smiled. "Nachmann of Lisbon bought it from a remote descendant of the Geyer clan in Prague before the war. It was submitted to Ernest Ainsworth the Wagner specialist in London. It has been in my office safe since I returned." Pough seemed to be watching Van Kill's face closely. "I have told no one but yourself about its exact contents."

Why? the document examiner asked himself. The specter of Montefiore rose again to answer. Van Kill's mind reverted to his original irritation, that everyone but himself should think it wrong of David to joggle the left hand of a man whose right was doing good. "You are very kind," Van Kill said. Now was the time. "I wonder if you would be additionally kind and allow my assistant to bring our document camera here. We could photograph the script without the letter going out of your sight."

Pough shook his head. "I'm sorry. If I granted one such request, I should in simple justice have to grant them all."

"Naturally," said Van Kill, telling himself not to jump to conclusions. "You aren't yet ready to face the inevitable publicity."

Pough seemed relieved that his caller had refrained from hinting at his inconsistency, but not too relieved.

"Have you shown the document to any of your staff?" Van Kill inquired. "Miss Newman or," the name dropped from his lips like an afterthought, "Mr. Harris?"

Pough laughed. "It's hardly up Mr. Harris's alley."

"Mr. Harris is a man of many interests," Van Kill answered and rose to leave. He was *certain* now that the editor of *Carnage* had no hold on the editor-in-chief of Popub.

"Harris," Pough said smiling, "keeps up my circulation." He got to his feet, held out his hand. "When the proper time comes for anyone to see the Geyer item, Dr. Van Kill," he promised, "I'll keep you in mind."

"Do that," the document examiner said.

"Obviously it was because Yanni took your brief case when you separated and the fellow thought he was still following you." The Honorable Diana glared at Van Kill over Yanni's head. "That's no reason why you should be so cross with him."

Yanni, who was reclining on the divan under compulsion, mumbled something around the thermometer the kyrios had thrust into his mouth.

"Quiet!" Van Kill commanded. "Perhaps I *have* got in the way of bouquets aimed at Yanni, but I didn't make a secretive martyr of myself. I'm not cross, I'm just terribly terribly hurt. Why should outsiders have to tell me these things?"

"Well, *he* isn't." Diana relieved Yanni of the thermometer and took it over to the window. "I knew he wouldn't be. That's why I promised not to say anything to you about it. A beautiful clean cut if ever I saw one."

Edward, who sat on the floor eating jelly beans, looked up from the atlas on his knees. Lady Di was great at describing Durbars and how to win the confidence of a kangaroo, but her stories always lacked details about herself. Edward was present at the conversation because no one ever suggested that he should absent himself from any conversation which occurred while he was awake. It was Van Kill's method of combatting Edward's tendency to eavesdrop.

"Going out in the cold this morning was taking a foolish chance," Van Kill said. Yanni sat up.

"This morning after I am asleep some, I am all right," he said impatiently. "And that old woman, that *grafa* who makes apartment clean for Kyrios De Porta is ready by seven o'clock with rag and furniture polish. If fingerprints Hitler himself is there, she clean them off before Kyrios De Porta eat breakfast."

"Hal, what is this?" Diana asked. "Why has Yanni been looking for fingerprints in Mr. De Porta's apartment? Has he been robbed?"

"Prowled," said Van Kill. "Instead of doing something positive about it Ben put a lock on the door that connects with his shop. I persuaded him to leave the key down in the office so that the prowling employee could get it conveniently. It's for the moral effect on Ben mostly," he added. "When Betty Hargrave told me Miss Goff was devoting her spare time to the Christian Cavaliers, I was sure she was the prowler."

Yanni made a disgusted noise at the Cavaliers.

"It isn't connected with De Porta's nephew and *Carnage* magazine then?" Diana said.

"Not yet." Van Kill took considerable time looking for his pipe and finding it on the music rack of the piano before he went on. "Miss Hargrave, who is Pough's official censor for *Carnage*, is connected with the Christian Cavaliers, as an assignment from Pough. Nobody else in Popub is supposed to know that except Pough's confidential secretary."

Lady Di let fall into Van Kill's half-troubled musing, "Do you know yet why Harris is having Miss Hargrave followed, Hal?"

"I wonder now if he isn't trying to get something on the big boss," said Van Kill. "That's the only thing I can think of that would justify his investment, trailing her, trying to scare me off."

"The girl may be in some danger herself," Diana Brown said reflectively.

"Not from Harris, I think, and not if she takes my advice," said Van Kill.

"This map," Edward remarked, pointing to an inside page of the *World-Telegram*, "puts the Galápagos as close to Panama as Jamaica is on the east." He selected three red jelly beans for himself after Van Kill said it was another New Deal plot and offered a yellow one to the cat, who batted it politely under the Honorable Diana's chair. Edward went back to his atlas.

Since they had stopped talking about Yanni, Edward had not bothered to listen. A man sent to cut up his guardian, if not to kill him, had mistakenly attacked Yanni. This man, a minor hoodlum with a record, had been found in the park by the police. The item in the paper on the other side of the inaccurate map of the Canal Zone said there were "circumstances indicating suicide."

Van Kill said this was probably because the police had taken Yanni's fancy knife work, cutting out a piece of the man's suit, as a sign of deliberation upon the part of the hoodlum. People committing suicide did such things.

Lady Di said she thought doctors could tell suicides by angles of direction and death.

Van Kill told her yes, sometimes. If they found a man with his throat cut, for instance, and one of the vertebrae was nicked, they knew it was murder. . . .

The interesting part of their conversation had automatically registered on Edward's mind. (Interesting things had been happening around the Cameron heir from the time when he first met Van Kill. Yanni's adventure was interesting, but Edward had not been along when it happened.) Yanni had apparently been fortunate in his angles of attack, so he could forget about the man in the park and save himself trouble. . . .

They were still talking about trouble, it seemed. "Ever since I discovered Goff was laboring on the anti-Semite front while taking De Porta's money," his guardian was saying, "I've had a feeling there ought to be a connection, aside from Betty I mean, between Popub and the Cavaliers. You suggested as much yesterday, Diana. Don't ask me how. It may be just that Harris's *Carnage* and the Cavaliers' *Lance* make such appropriate partners. Both on a level, spewing out muck."

Van Kill wandered over to the piano in a cloud of pipe smoke, put his left hand on the keys and fretfully played the first three measures of the Czerny exercise Edward was supposed to practice. He snorted. "Don't ask me how, it's just a feeling I've got."

"When the kyrios has feelings, it means trouble." Yanni adjusted the silk sling around his neck and grinned at Diana.

"We've already had some," Van Kill reminded him.

XVI

~~~~~~

ABOUT three o'clock that Friday afternoon George Stock sat down beside the magazine table in Harris's office and opened the dummy of *Carnage* for March which Harris had shoved at him.

"What's up?" he asked.

"Same old act." Harris tapped his own dummy with a nicotined nail. "Me and you with Pough and her Highness to see if our moron meat gets through the mail."

Stock did not resent the editor's tone, which was as nasty as if Stock had personally been responsible for this annoyance. Editors traditionally have gall bladders where their hearts ought to be and Mr. Stock was a great believer in tradition, though a stranger to the word.

"Arr," said Mr. Stock, meaning Betty Hargrave.

"Yes," Harris assented, propping his chair against his Black Chamber and gazing sidewise at the art editor. "And today we don't give an inch. Not a goddam inch. You know how our circulation stands."

"Right," said George Stock. In the perennial office arguments as to whether art or yarn made the book G. S. knew where *he* stood. "So we get to carry the banner at the Sunday-school picnic tonight," he added, referring to the Popub dinner. He fingered his dummy with worried pride.

"You'll see," Harris promised him. "You just keep your pants on, pal. I'll be a copper's by-line if we don't get a fiction book before the New Year's out."

Stock did not answer. The art editor of *Carnage* could never talk just to be talking. He saw with bitter clarity that all the staff of *Carnage* got for a phenomenal upping of their circulation was the chance to eat a fancy dinner with other members of Popub, most of whom held them cheap. They weren't even allowed to protect themselves against the minority stockholder's crazy pestering.

The mind of Editor Harris, by contrast, was so active he could scarcely keep up with it. When he was talking he truly believed he wanted Popub to let him manage a fiction book to complement *Carnage*. When he stopped talking his thoughts were of a nervous self-congratulatory nature. . . .

Boy, am I ever lucky. No connection. Nobody knows I knew that wop. Suit yourself, Angel, I tell him, all I want's the professor should keep his nose out of my business . . . Joke on Angel, all right . . . Shows what the bastard cops will do for a friend. Suicide. My money on him too. They'll use my money to bury Angel. No connection though. I'm shot with luck. . . .

Since Harris was thinking about the person Yanni Mavromicháli had killed, both men sitting with their backs to Harris's Black Chamber were silent when Frederick Pough entered. The editor of *Carnage* took off his hat and the president of Popub occupied a chair at the table's head.

Pough threw a few casual words into the silence and settled down doggedly with his dummy. So doggedly that even Stock noticed it and came to the eventual conclusion that the chief had something on his mind.

Paul Harris noticed too. Old iron puss was dreaming today, he thought, and imagined he knew what Pough was dreaming about. Harris's face wore something pretty close to a regulation *Carnage* leer when Betty Hargrave came in.

Light from the east window swam past the Crime Cabinet and closed up on a glint of red in the girl's hair. Betty palped the dummy's pages silently. When Frederick Pough was chairman, you waited before you spoke.

Pough meantime had been telling himself that the stuff under his eyes was not really worse than usual this time. It was only his bereft mood, a mood which Yanni Mavromicháli had noted that day when the president of Popub lunched at the Matapan. Twenty thousand, Pough tried to comfort himself, at an optimum four per cent, no better than a steady yield of eight hundred . . . But the trick, he knew it was a trick, still stung. . . .

And the familiar categories for the March number of *Carnage* were no help . . . Two exposés: the *Saintly Siren* and, after the hacksack disappearance case, a gentleman who styled himself "Warder of the Wacks" confessed everything about insane asylums. Mr. Stock and Louie Lenz had composed some elegant scenes from "nuthouse life": female lunatic (comely model) sticking knife in back of nurse (a model); doctor and attendant using clubs on another female (same comely model in different lingerie), who cowered at their feet . . . Pough went on to the *Parked Petter Assault Atrocity* and looked up impatiently.

"Harris," he said, "don't *men* ever get murdered?"

"Not for the March issue," Harris answered crisply. "*I* didn't have an after-Christmas slump last year. I don't mean to have one this."

Pough's nod was aloof. "Well, Miss Hargrave?" he asked for Betty's reactions and George Stock's face twitched with annoyance.

Betty flipped back to the front of the dummy and began to turn pages . . . The bishop and the madam got by her without comment. The hacksack murder of the Pennsylvania Peach was quite outside her provenance, but she gave a wicked little laugh when she came to the composograph of the Peach on which Mr. Stock had really extended himself.

The radio serial voice with which she read the caption brought a frowning chuckle from Pough: BIZARRE FATE DREW HER FROM RICHES AND LOVE TO A SORDID LITTLE FLOWER GARDEN IN A BACK YARD (BELOW) WHERE (SHOWN BY ARROW) OFFICERS MADE A SINISTER AND GRUESOME DISCOVERY.

Her work with the Cavaliers might be making her nervous, Pough thought worriedly. He cast a mollifying glance as his sour-faced *Carnage* minions just as she chose to say, "Harris, can't your backhouse art stand alone?" She smiled, unconsciously plagiarizing Van Kill's tone as well as his words. "Do you have to prop it up with that backhouse grand style of yours too?"

Pough laughed aloud then, the harsh hiccuping mirth of a man momentarily able to shake his gloom.

"What that dame needs," Stock grumbled at Harris out of the corner of his mouth, "is a damn good clip on the jaw."

Paul Harris shushed his subordinate with a shake of his head. Not that he wouldn't like to get the measure of the girl's neck. But he could wait. They would be certain to make some break before Mrs. Pough got back from Miami. The tail would get something definite and then the hell with this job. . . .

In her own mind Betty Hargrave was echoing Paul Harris's penultimate thought. What good had her outburst done? She remembered Van Kill, damn him, had said her boss was a good executive because he could pass such a slick buck to his ambassador without portfolio. Well——

"Did you see this, Mr. Pough?"

Frederick Pough looked. He saw the caption, NO EASTERN MORN FOR LITTLE JEAN, and the sentence immediately below the picture, "Slumped in a half-sitting position at the foot of the Easter-lily-adorned altar, lay a golden-haired girl of about twelve, her tender body betraying the first curving outlines of dawning womanhood."

Paul Harris looked. Granting his frequent assertion that he never read his stuff once he had dictated it, this was the first time he had ever seen:

"At her side, its china-blue eyes as stark and staring as those of the dead girl, lay a disheveled half-clad doll. The eyes of the doll and the eyes of the girl stared at a picture over the altar. It was a picture of Our Savior blessing a golden-haired, blue-eyed child."

George Stock looked. He had used a daring up-angle view of the body. With that montaged religious stuff he thought it had everything.

The author spoke first. "It's damn good writing and damn good art, if you ask me. Dramatic," Paul Harris said belligerently.

The tension of triple silence which followed was acute. Pough was pointedly waiting for Betty to say something.

"Religious," George Stock said suddenly. "Teaches a lesson."

Betty boiled over then. "It does, but not the kind *you* think."

So it was as always Pough who had the final word, cautious and soothing. Mr. Harris doubtless knew his market better than the rest of them. But in view also of recent policy complications (he did not mention David Montefiore by name) the story and picture might "as Miss Hargrave indicated, seem a trifle out of line."

Betty was trying to close her ears to the boss's words. Now (damn Van Kill) she could hear only too well that certain implication which Harris and Stock were supposed to catch. All these changes had to be made to satisfy a cross child from Peoria, who unfortunately represented the public view. The smile which regularly followed Pough's remarks was supposed to appease the cross child. Staring stonily out of the window beyond the Crime Cabinet, she ignored the smile this time.

Messrs. Stock and Harris, mindful of their agreement not to give an inch, had not been appeased either. The girl's flip remarks of a minute ago and the memory of every frustration she had given them in the past were all uncut venom in their eyes. Betty didn't notice.

"See here, Harris, is this in its final form?" Pough's glance went to the girl ignoring him. He added with a touch of displeasure, "Page forty, Miss Hargrave."

Drawing her gaze from the window, Betty saw the slightest of guilty colors in Harris's face. She heard the infinitesimal lacuna which goes before a lie as he answered:

"Yes."

Pough sat staring coolly at Harris and George Stock.

"You see," the art editor ventured.

"We thought," Paul Harris began and lapsed into a defensive sulk.

Pough's voice was quiet, but it seemed very loud in the room. "You know I will not allow any changes in the dummy as approved. Especially now." Harris said nothing.

Page forty. Betty got it in a flash when she really looked. She ought not, her old conscience returned despite her, to have slipped up on that. The picture spreads were definitely undercalid. Poynton's yarn fell into a recognized class: mad doctor revives ancient flagellation cult, high priestess tells all to Special Investigator.

In the foreground of the first spread the mad doctor sported a black-cowled robe with skull and crossbones motif and flourished a razor in his right hand. His left grasped the hair of a model in black lingerie, registering standard terror on Mr. Lenz's most sumptuous couch.

The picture's caption told the reader that the Mad Doctor with Machiavellian Fury (Poynton thought the adjective more dramatic than Devilish) had by means of a dagger with a weird oriental inscription dug into the white flesh of the sex rite priestess, above, until she was just a mass of bloody wounds. . . .

Ordinary Sunday Supplement stuff. So was the rest of the priestess and the story of her cult right back to the advertising for radio schools, virility tonics, and belts . . . Priestess decently clothed in white and rather adenoidal on an altar, shots that only hinted discreetly of a flagellation scene to come. . . .

Phooey, Betty thought. But just the proper kind of inserts in the story gaps that had been left for them, just the proper kind of pictures—and Pough took the words right out of her mouth.

"What kind of pictures did you intend to substitute, Harris?"

"Hotter," said the flustered editor of *Carnage*. "More dramatic," he corrected lamely.

"Call the fellow off," said Frederick Pough.

Harris scowled at Betty and reached for the telephone.

In the walk-up studio of Mr. Louie Lenz somewhere among the West Forties things were getting warmer right along.

"Mmyawff," Poynton Darcy groaned. He pushed back a lock of his white hair under the black cowl and dabbed at his moist panchromatic makeup. He got to his feet and rubbed his knees. "This," he said, "is a hell of a thing to ask a man to do at my age."

He was getting a big bang out of it all, the skull and crossbones gown, the pose with his whip before the altar of the high priestess, clad in nothing much but sheer devotion now. Poynton loved to identify himself with his art and Louie Lenz's cold little bird brain honored him for it.

"Positions, please," Louie commanded. "Take it again." He hopped over five bags of sand, used for seaside seductions, and scooted around on his little legs to the other side of the long room. He stood there, studying the scene.

Darcy's face had just the right shade of photogenic interest in his work as he raised his whip over the priestess, who recoiled, but not to suit Mr. Lenz. Nimbly dodging a chemically treated tree and a gate on which all rural true romances leaned for him, he scuttled to the center of the set.

"This is not a halitosis ad, see?" He adjusted the priestess's face. "You're gunna die maybe, but right now you don't care."

The priestess saw and Mr. Lenz was satisfied . . . I should be in Hollywood . . . The mad doc and the priestess are right in there, he thought . . . Behind them was a living frieze, six pairs of boys and girls in pseudo-classical draperies. Alternately, at miniature altars of their own, they mimicked Darcy and the priestess. Alternately, whips down, they fell into a swooning clinch.

Frowning, Lenz squinted at a slim brunette on the left end of the frieze. He stepped up to her. She was a recent high school graduate with a part-time job in a Fifth Avenue dress shop.

"No, darling," Lenz whispered patiently. The mascaraed lashes she batted at him were sticky wet under the hot floodlight. Her shining eyes were innocent. "You're not a Yosian takin' a gander at a boid." Lenz tilted her chin up and her head back in her slightly embarrassed young partner's arms. The girl stiffened and Lenz scowled. "Relax, sweetheart," he said. "This is passion. Don't you read no books? This is an org-ee, see?"

The rest were doing fine. "Too much," he said to an energetic blonde in the middle pair. "Tickle the customer. Don't hit him on the head."

Mr. Lenz adjusted a bit of drapery and an abdomen here, a bosom and a leg there. Clucking contentedly, he worked along the line to a bar by the south window used for all tavern trull yarns. He leaned against the bar.

"Swell," he said, moving toward the camera. "One hundred per cent copaseetic," he announced and was about to duck under the black cloth when the telephone rang. . . .

Lenz took it in the next room. "Speaking," he said and then, "What!"

"You heard me," Paul Harris's voice came scratching through. "Junk 'em."

"Who says?" said Louie Lenz.

"You ought to know," said Harris and hung up.

Lenz knew. "The Duchess," he said to Poynton Darcy, who had followed him out. "I could moiduh that broad."

The crimescribe had said this about Betty Hargrave so many times, it seemed superfluous now. The models would get their five smackers an hour anyway, Poynton's Percheron face contorted with the reflection while he watched the quickest of them trot out with her hat box. But *he* had lost four hours, maybe four thousand salable words. . . .

"Be seein' you, baby," he whickered gustily, though he never felt less like it in his life. They might decide to kill the whole damn flagellation yarn. . . .

This, finally, was what they did decide to do, though when it happened certain of those now consulting in the office of Mr. Paul Harris were no longer alive. To the last Harris insisted that people didn't pay two bits for pictures of church pageants any more than for tombstones and cops.

Frederick Pough had more important worries, his manner indicated as he left the room. Betty Hargrave followed him at a distance. She felt physically soiled and conscious of the futility of trying to clean around the edges of the *Carnage* machine. Futile, she told herself wryly, as taking a feather duster to the phone booth at Sixth Avenue and Fiftieth Street, where she went to phone Van Kill.

If this afternoon was any omen, the *Carnage* banquet would end in a brawl. Well, no, she told Van Kill, she didn't want it to. "I've gone to too much trouble with it now. But it seems to me you could give a girl a drink somewhere," she demanded.

"Come on up here," he suggested and gave her the address. "Come up and meet my ward. We're bringing our Eastern war map up to date and singing Christmas carols. You might as well know the worst."

XVII

POLITE, thought Van Kill, scowling into the eyepiece of his document microscope. Polite. That had been the word for it all through the cocktail hour. The Honorable Diana and Miss Elizabeth Hargrave had been killingly courteous to each other. Oh, his elderly neighbor had helped get Popub's distraught mechanic into a working frame of mind for the *Carnage* dinner. So much so that when he had put Betty into a taxi around five o'clock, she was intending to look in at the Cavaliers office before going home to dress.

But he did wish she and Diana could have been less edge of chair on their first meeting. Edward had been perhaps too British Public School on his best behavior, but the Honorable Diana had confined herself to one highball. Impossible to tell whether the two women liked each other or not, Van Kill concluded, and also that he himself had better get down to work.

He had been going after it more or less alone since dinner. Lady Di was in her own apartment up to her ears in galley proof, Yanni off to the Matapan, and Edward secluded in his bedroom, from which muffled whangings and thumps had emerged until Van Kill pounded on the door and ordered him to bed. He had a quiet apartment until the house telephone rang at eleven o'clock. He got up quickly to answer it and felt a wave of annoyance at his waiting mood.

"Montefiore?" He listened to the switchboard girl's ravished description and grunted, "Send him up."

"Come on in the office," Van Kill said when David, full of brittle exhilaration, stalked into the foyer. "While I work you can get off your mind whatever you fancy is on it now."

Montefiore pulled an easy chair near Van Kill's desk, flipped up his midnight blue coattails, sat down, and took a leisurely drink of the whisky-soda he had assembled on his way through the living room. "More enthusiasm, Hendrik," he demanded. "Can I help it if she didn't feel moved to come up here personally and tell you how my speech resurrected her dinner?"

Van Kill glanced at him. He moved the tuning-fork base of his microscope back a little, exposing another line of the document beneath. "It makes you short of breath to leap to conclusions."

"Had you there." David grinned. "I spotted the old Van Kill touch in the white poinsettia hair decor she was wearing. Oh, but instantly. However, I shall clam right up, as Harris and his pals would say, if you're going to be like this."

"I am," Van Kill said and gave the rack-and-pinion adjustment a breath of a turn. "I added the dwarf green orchids for background to convince the florist poinsettia didn't have to be sent in a pot."

"Not gaudy," David assured Van Kill, as if he had been asked. "Echo and Hargrave quite blotted that potential little piece Harris has in his reception room. You could see the *Carnage* cohorts licking their chops and wishing they were more reasonable."

"So, I take it, one *Carnage* non-supporter was wishing," Van Kill suggested.

David leaned toward the desk. "Disputed document?" he asked.

"Alliterative, but inaccurate," said Van Kill. "Most of my questioned documents never get disputed in court."

"Once a schoolmaster," David rejoined instantly. "Please, sir, I admire to see celebrated savant perform operations of miraculous skill and delicacy."

Van Kill laughed. "Mustn't touch though."

Montefiore pointed his fine nose at a fold of white letter paper with perhaps three lines of writing near its top.

"Fascinating," he said. "Last will and testament of L. O. Wheeler. Human document, yes."

"Rubbish," said Van Kill. "It's fascinating because it's a crossed-stroke problem. "Look." He showed Montefiore where the broad black stroke of the L in the signature seemed to ride over the lean Y in the last word *truly* of the text. "Which was made first?"

"I'd say, the text," David announced after the briefest consideration.

"So would any layman." Montefiore nodded meekly. "So do L. O. Wheeler's four weeping progeny by his first wife." Van Kill held the sheet out with a pair of rubber-lined tongs so that David could look at the strokes lengthwise. "Here's one thing that says they lied. Even with the naked eye you can see the nib marks of the Y stroke are continuous, not broken by the L."

"I can, actually," said Montefiore. His tone held the deference he usually managed to yield Van Kill, who was commanding him to mark the feathery fuzz spreading from the Y at the point where it crossed the L.

"That's where ink ran out of the Y stroke onto the L, although the signature was probably made some time before the text was jammed in above it."

"How long?" David asked as if he wanted to know.

"Dangerous to be dogmatic. Over two years probably. It takes at least that long for the temporary blue to get set in modern ink." Van Kill's voice had a kind of session-in-chambers authority. Useful, that quality of influence, David thought wistfully.

"The moral," Van Kill went on without urging, "is not to go around writing your name on blank sheets of paper. This job is easy because L. O. was an old vandal who bored in when he made his first. The nib marks of his L disturbed the fiber of the paper so that even after two years the Y stroke of the phony deathbed dictation flowed over into the nib tracks of his L where they crossed."

"Nib marks where they crossed, yes," David said.

Van Kill felt the switch of attention instantly. David was sitting well forward, blond as champagne in the strong light, bubbling with his own thoughts.

"Lecture's over," Van Kill said. "Course's open only by instructor's consent."

"I offered to pay the fee already, you know."

Van Kill ignored the overcasual lead. "All right," he said. "Go ahead and tell what you did at the dinner to bring me down in gray hairs."

"Thought I'd fetch you." David sat up even straighter and spoke over his glass, deliberately hurried, dramatizing himself. "The cake made it more appropriate."

"It?" Van Kill murmured. "I thought I had a lien on obscurity."

"My speech," David explained. "A regular monster of an ice cream cake. Miss Hargrave's idea. Marvelous, I told her. She had it put out to soften before we sat down. People circulated of course. A killing comment on Harris, Stock, and all their works. I told 'em so."

"Your infinite tact," said his friend.

"Not just the dolls," David continued rapidly. "The cake softened and—this is right in your line, Hal—before it was cut the F had run and the superscription turned out: CARNAGE—LET IT BE RIPE."

Van Kill raised his eyebrows, grinned.

"Hush," David went on at the same breathless rate. "I'll tell you about the dolls. Spun sugar like the wedding cake kind only more appropriate above the inscription. Gal on her back registering Standard Terror 69T menaced by brute registering Standard Brutality 69B—consult any cover of any crime mag. Harris didn't like it much, neither did Stock. But I detected a quiver on Pough's sour dial when they got caught in the mouse trap." David paused, savoring his recollection with a drink.

"Don't let me interrupt," Van Kill put in. "If you change the record while I'm gone, I shan't notice." He came back presently from the living room with a brandy for himself.

"I'm saying," David raised his voice at the door, "the wench on the cake had Spanish ruffles. Gesture toward Pan-American unity, I suppose."

"By which token the mouse trap under them represented the diplomatic snare?"

"Shut up," Montefiore said. "Even if you are ahead of me, this is *my* story. With your demoniacal insight you've realized that the doll-doxie was prostrate exposing quite a bit of limb. And unlike *Carnage* covers she was three-dimensional. What would a guy like Harris do in a case like that? And," David added, "what does a motherly old maid like Miss Harriet Treach do when somebody shows her a dressed doll? She looks to see if it has panties. It brought them all together, you know. Put the *Carnage* stamp on it and livened up their sordid little wake. Pough realized it too, I think."

"Wasn't Pough livened?"

"Pough crawled to his feet and let off the usual Rotarian drool. So veddy veddy nice for us all to be together and *Carnage* to take the cake. Incentive to other members of the Popub family, *you* know. I think he realized how sick-making it was, the one big family idea when he could see 'em all there together hating *Carnage*'s guts."

Van Kill inquired whether Mr. Pough looked sick before or after David's speech.

"Before." The blond young man was irritable. "Your Lady Di would say he felt the poisonous hatred which lay like a catafalque over their gayety. It was Harris' friend who really laid the old boy low. Harris wants to add a fiction book to their string, you see. So he rang in this mystery pulp writer to warm the boss up." Montefiore put a hand to his head. "And did he! La Hargrave herself said Pough was vaporing like the dry ice around the *Carnage* cake before Savage was through. And poor Miss Treach——"

"You understand—" David frowned and went on more slowly. Van Kill had moved out of the glare of light at the desk and was listening quietly. "I'm not trying to make this shindig sound funny. This pulpateer was a great hearty extrovert, serious as a self-help advertisement. Pough bore up noble as long as Savage descanted on how the bottom has dropped out of spontaneous combustion as a mystery-murder method and pooh-poohed tongues that balloon up with poison and choke the victim, ditto eyeballs that pop out and bones that crumble to a pulp. The public, Mr. Savage says, is more sophisticated, more interested in deep science now."

"Savage, you called him?" Van Kill asked. "Friend of Poynton Darcy's, isn't he?"

"Probably not his real name," David said. "He illustrated his point about the necrophilous public with a plug for a tale he has on the stands this month. Some new kind of drug makes the murderee disengage himself of his running gears. A nice fresh stomach is found alongside each successive victim. Treach went out on that one." David stuck out his lower lip like a ghoulish little boy. "Holding her face."

"I suppose that was where you came in," Van Kill said patiently, "to clear the air."

David caught the note of reproof. "I was tactful," he said defensively. "Not like you. I stole the show *and* settled their stomachs. What, I asked them, is contained in limestone, marble, and chalk, used by artists, teachers, and incidentally, dicks? Got 'em all guessing, see? What, I demanded, gathers in soda fountains, silos, disused closets, marshes, cellars, wells, beer vats, whisky vats, and geraniums?"

"To settle their stomachs?" Van Kill asked.

David was not in the least dashed. "Dithering, I said. They all guessed. CO_2, binary compound of oxygen and carbon, I said. Stock got it then. Quite pleased with himself. Popularly known when condensed and cooled as commercial dry ice."

Montefiore took another drink. His manner was complacent until Van Kill inquired, "And when they got it what did you tell them they could do with the stuff?"

"I said I could murder them with it and nobody would ever know," David blurted defiantly. "You can't trace it by any postmortem test. I said it would give me the greatest pleasure to shut certain people I could think of up in one of those little Popub offices with the dry ice that came with that cake."

"Dizzy, you didn't!" Van Kill's reaction was unguarded thinking aloud.

"Why not?" Montefiore snapped at him. "I meant to stir the animals up. Gave those specialists a brand-new murder method, painless and aesthetic. Just their dish with a sprinkle of reproof in it after Savage." David got up, put his glass on the desk, and began to pace the floor. "I gave the party tone. I ought to know, I was there."

"All of that, I dare say." Van Kill paused to sniff his brandy before he proceeded with musing disapproval. "You are prone, my

David, to enlarge upon Harris's lack of taste. I don't wonder Ben ——"

"Says I'm a damn idiot," Montefiore leaped at the goad. "Don't call me David and don't look at me like that when you do."

Van Kill had not glanced in Montefiore's direction for some time and remarked as much. "British detective authors began slaughtering folks with dry ice after the *First* German War. The Honorable Diana uses it to discourage mice. Eo who's a cupboard fancier won't set foot in her apartment. It's in the Household Hint class. Really, David, it's shocking to find a crime book publisher so far behind the times."

"God damn it!" Montefiore whirled from the window where he had been standing. "I come up here for consolation and you jump on me too."

One of Montefiore's most endearing qualities, Van Kill reflected. He never rationalized for long.

"Sorry," David said with a stiff sort of meekness and stopped where he was by Van Kill's chair. "Echo—" he began, "Echo was simply ——"

"David, look here." Montefiore met Van Kill's gray eyes sidewise like a restive golden colt. "David, did you ever see a person who'd been smothered?"

"No." The slightest of alarm tingled in the meekness of Montefiore's reply.

"When you find them," Van Kill spoke straight up at him in a deliberate cold voice, "their eyes are bloodshot and stick out. They've had convulsions, you see, spasms of the glottis. Painless, you said?" David did not answer. "The face and lips and fingernails are blue. Aesthetic . . ." The document examiner lowered his gaze from Montefiore's face and resumed a conversational tone. "A noble start for elevating *Carnage*," he said. Instantly Montefiore gave tongue.

"It isn't so!" he shouted at the top of his friend's head, stamped backward to get a line on Van Kill's face, and was disconcerted by a warning hiss from Eo, who had come to investigate the disturbance. "Sometimes they look pale," David insisted with a wary eye on the ruffled little beast. "The book *said*. It's just like going to sleep with dry ice."

Van Kill laughed. At the time he was merely delighted to see that Dizzy, poor harried and misunderstood Dizzy was plain colloquial mad. An honest sentiment, giving hope that Dizzy might become David in time. With Echo Newman's help of course. . . .

He stood for a long while at the French windows looking out on the terrace when Montefiore had gone. A light snow, he saw with pleasure, had begun to fall again, renewing itself. From here, inside, the parapet hid the city's brilliant spires. But as always nowadays a new emotion was engendered by the familiar red glow against the sky. A feeling of mingled pride and anxiety for the greatest and brightest city in the world, still arrogantly lighted at night.

A sudden vision of David escaping from his worries in an army truck shifted his mood for an instant. It was not impossible, Van Kill told himself, pushing the French window open and letting the wet wind dab at his face. Nothing was. He could hear the hum of traffic now and a clock striking midnight from somewhere near by. As the strokes died away, he became possessed with an odd desire, a desire connected with David, he thought. A crazy desire to rush down into the street and follow Montefiore wherever he might be bound. Or was it? Van Kill asked himself candidly. . . .

Was it Montefiore he was worrying about? He closed the window and decided he had better do his wondering over the microscope. When he finally came to answer the question he had posed, it was far too late . . . Yanni came in long after midnight and found Van Kill still working at his desk. . . .

XVIII

∿∿

IT LACKED twenty minutes of midnight and two men were following Betty Hargrave again. The man nearest her, the one in the dark overcoat, was about a block behind as she walked from Central Park West along a street in the Nineties. He was still a block behind when she disappeared under the L structure at Columbus and continued west.

He walked leisurely, but with absorbed assurance, unnoticing and unnoticed, this man of not much more than medium height who wore a dark overcoat. He passed a tavern at Columbus and looked around casually while he waited for the traffic light. He did not appear to observe the man following him then from a distance of perhaps half a block.

The second stalker, a man of about the same height as the first but considerably more noticeable in an overcoat of shepherd's plaid and a light hat took cover occasionally from one brownstone front to the next. He swore a little at the snow which was falling faster and shivered slightly when the wind veered down a service alley.

As he too passed the tavern his feet wavered toward it. The news butch across the street had his back turned now, dancing around in front of his stand to keep warm. But in the space of a quick one he might easily switch and be facing the tavern front. The second stalker decided against a drink and likewise crossed the Avenue. At this range the man ahead appeared to be carrying some sort of box or case. It blended most of the time with the color of his overcoat, which swirled out somewhat in the wind. Impossible safely to make sure. Man number two swore again and continued on. . . .

Betty Hargrave walked briskly, full of herself, exultantly aware of more than an immediate goal. The inspiration for what she was going to do now had held her above the gaps and tensions of the *Carnage* dinner and the memory of them was laid aside as definitely as she had shed her evening clothes for workaday tweed.

The flowers which remained in her hair lay against the back-turned brim of her hat and belonged to that remoter goal.

It was good to walk alone and independent in a New York street at night, she thought, liking the fall of snow on her face. She wrinkled her nose at a vagrant smell of baking which floated out from a neighborhood delicatessen near the avenue. She would stop and get a pastry to take home for breakfast after her work was done. She lifted her head to see the sky glow from the lofty apartments down by the Hudson as she approached the mouth of the narrow alley leading to the offices of the Christian Cavaliers. She entered it without looking back. . . .

The first stalker had closed up the distance between himself and the girl a trifle. Before she disappeared into the passage between the buildings, he glanced down the street. Nothing in sight but a solitary citizen on the opposite curb, holding the leash of a reluctant dog, his head bent against the snow. But the man in the dark overcoat took cover now for the first time in a tiny wooden entrance built out like a dovecot from a basement flat. He emerged only when he saw that the girl and the citizen too, evidently, were out of sight. Presently he himself reached the mouth of the alley, walked into it, and was blotted from sight as the second stalker came out from behind a bank of brownstone steps and went cautiously after the first. . . .

The shades were down and it was quite dark. With the contemptuous familiarity of long use Betty Hargrave did not turn on a light in the Cavaliers' mailing room, but she stopped once in her direct progress across the cold bare floor. A noise like the rustle of a dress in one corner. Then the yowl of a cat in the court, wailing, long drawn out. A familiar New York sound, particularly familiar in this neighborhood.

Accusing her nerves, the girl stepped into the inner office, switched on Lee's desk light, and by its mild illumination scanned the mailing room behind her. Piles of leaflets loomed palely where Miss Goff had stacked them that afternoon. A draft from the alley door would rustle the top ones. Betty Hargrave had a last look and closed the office door behind her.

The familiar room, where she had done so much routine work, vicious routine but tiresome, was reassuring, but the blond girl's mind was too narrowly focused to consider the need for reassurance. She laid her gloves and coat on Lee's desk, opened her purse and took a man's keyring out of a zipper compartment. The ring of keys dangled from a coral-enameled finger, clinked and flashed under the desk lamp for a moment. Moving then to the office door just behind her, she stood listening. All quiet in the outer room, but upon reflection she turned the knob, pulled it toward her, leaving the door open a crack.

The Yale lock responded smoothly to Burke's key. The closet door swung open with a breath of warm air. Betty Hargrave saw herself cleaning up her Cavaliers assignment on a pinnacle of business efficiency. A personal triumph. After that . . .

A luminescent dime-store button showed her the end of the light cord and the inside of the mysterious closet drew a little sigh of disappointment from the girl. She looked about twelve years old, standing there, sucking her lower lip, her hands in her jacket pockets, her wide hat well back on account of the white flowers on her forehead. A more commonplace-appearing layout could scarcely be conceived. A rank of four filing drawers with an unopened carton of dictaphone cylinders lying on top, an asbestos-wrapped steam pipe near the floor, that was all in perhaps a seven-foot square.

She stepped back and turned off the desk lamp. Solid darkness banked behind her now except where her shadow moved. A useful precaution, she told herself. If anyone came, as who should? Burke was set for the night, she was sure. Lee, she knew from experience, was gone for the week end. But if anyone did, she could flick off the light in a moment and be concealed. Her action was really just a fillip to enhance her ignoble snooping. Danger? Pough was a dear, but an idiot. Van Kill . . .

The bottom drawer was empty. Shutting it, she went to the one above, lifted out the first folder, and began to read. This was better than the small fry in the addressograph—packed to the gills with names listed against real contributions and dates. This was in fact much better. Mr. Pough would be delighted. Some of the names were News. Talk about biting off your own nose, Betty thought with amazement. She realized a new respect for Burke. Here was fruit for blackmail. . . .

She started suddenly, pulled the light cord, and stood listening. She leaned into the darkness, but the sound, whatever it was, had died down. Nerves, she told herself, lit the light, opened the folder again. But she had hardly got to the bottom of the second page when the rustling noise, unmistakably it was a rustling, sounded once more and to her tense ears it seemed to be coming from the outer room.

Betty stuck the folder back into the drawer with a little rap of annoyance and audibly damned her imagination. The whole place was drafty as a barn, she told herself. But better have a look around, make certainty sure so that she could come back and concentrate. Betty Hargrave hooked Burke's keys over her thumb, took her purse from the top of the filing cabinet where she had laid it beside the carton of dictaphone records, and a blow came from behind. A brief flash of pain stabbed inside above the blond girl's eyebrows, a *contre coup*. She fell forward instantly unconscious, slipped slowly down against the filing case then, and lay at last quietly upon the floor. . . .

Betty Hargrave awoke to darkness that buzzed and surged and seemed curiously to hold only a throbbing head. Faintly puzzled at her own indifference, she moved her head a little. Her movement increased the throbbing she could now plainly locate at her temples and the buzzing crackled like static in her ears. A twinge of nausea rose, subsided; it interested her only vaguely that there was room in this close darkness for her body as well as her head. Her pounding pulse quieted then. She even knew a brief pleasure, relapsing against whatever supported her.

Time passed, although she felt very remote from it. If she was very ill, if she ought in that procession of time to summon help, if she could, if the door was locked, if there was a door, she felt much too tired to find out. The air here, wherever she was, seemed close and oppressive, but that was no reason for her to be pumping

it in and out as if she had been running. It was breathing so hard
that made the pounding in her head anyway. . . .

Time passed. Herself, compact of body and heart, she could
sense in a dim way, vibrated ever more and more lightly now. But
a something, she knew this, it might be an outer self, gradually
rose to contemplate her body, lying wherever it was . . . Within
the blue cloud condensing around her, floating lower now, a brilliant circle of nearer scenes and persons swirled, resolved itself
into figures of amazing clarity, and stood still.

Pough at the zenith, a dark red Pough, his voice loud in the
ears of her weary body below. Never trust a martyr, he said. It
was all very plain who had done what had been done to her body,
but her mind floating clear did not care. No one cared. A gray
Goff laughed as an apricot Lee said in the morning, here's one
Burke forgot, and a brown Burke said, *what* may I ask?

But they did. In the cloud descending and descending dizzily
now, it was all very clear, it did not matter to her, but they did
care. Some one watching with a warning smile, he would know
what to do, he would know what they did . . . Fat rats pursuing,
that was it, the words came hard from the cloud, a lean gray cat
through the Popub Building. No, a courthouse, that was it. Words
came from the cloud with a choking sound. Pough, Lee, Burke,
Montefiore, Harris, Stock, chasing a lean gray cat around a courthouse. Words and one scene exploding into colors, all the colors,
as the cloud drew down. Never trust a lean, never trust a martyr,
he was right, never trust . . .

The cloud was so close now it could hardly be seen, all its colors
blending into gray and then like a closing iris into black. The circle
whirled into the cloud around her and she fell into a very quiet
sleep. . . .

XIX

"SAME answer, Captain." The young man at the window was silent for a moment then. "West Twenties don't look promising today. Empire State's out of key too. Nice snow."

"What's that got to do with it?" McLone's blue eyes were serious. His craggy nose made a sharp line above the hard set of his jaw. His chair squealed as he swung around. "Come back here and take another look at this thing."

"You know I never give sidewalk judgments." Van Kill did not move from his post. "Go on and twist the fellow's leg."

"We're not on a sidewalk." McLone skipped the third-degree disclaimer Van Kill had often heard from him in this third-floor office of the precinct station housing the Manhattan Homicide Squad. "Why do you suppose I got you out of bed at eight o'clock and on a Saturday morning at that?" The captain's upward inflection held the least degree of a brogue.

"Murder gets monotonous," said Van Kill. He stepped to the captain's desk.

McLone was still regarding two penciled scrawls, both on cheap blue-ruled tablet paper. *This* anonymous threat, he explained again as if repetition would make Van Kill come across, was found alongside the man in the gutter, *that* one, signed, in his room.

"*Are* they by the same person?" McLone wanted to know. A regularly appointed document examiner was one of the elaborate accessories which the captain's budget did not afford. Van Kill asked no payment for his advice except permission to ride with the squad when he cared to.

Van Kill adjusted the lens on his ring and with annoying deliberation scanned the documents. McLone shook his head then and, reaching behind him, opened a green-painted locker. From its floor under his overcoat he took a plain cardboard box. Among other things this held certain photographs which McLone considered too

revolting for the official file and a textbook on public speaking
presented by Van Kill at a time when the captain's sense of civic
duty plus a little surge of personal ambition had temporarily got
him down . . . He put the notes in the box and replaced it in the
locker.

"Murder *does* get monotonous," he said. "And scientific detection's all very fine if you can get the right material *with* constructive
co-operation." But there were very few clues you'd find on the
scene as interesting even as that note, that little memento of a
drunken altercation he'd just been showing Van Kill. An empty
shell, a slug or a gun, a knife or hammer, somebody's greasy old
hat or coat, that was usually what you got. "And it's usually ever-
lasting legwork *with* common sense that solves your murder," he
said.

Van Kill gave his usual nod of assent, forbearing to mention
good stoolies. The reason he got along so well with the squad was
probably because he did so little talking himself.

McLone brushed an imaginary particle of lint from his well-
pressed gray suit. He looked morosely past Van Kill toward the
back of the office, which held nothing but another locker by a dark
window giving onto a dim small alleyway. "We haven't had a thing
with decent color now for months."

Outside McLone's office Detective Harry Singer, wiry and slender,
was entertaining much the same line of thought as he policed up
the main squad-room floor. What was it Van Kill had told him
the squad lived by? Much skepticism, very little sleep, much curiosity, and a lot of friendly irritation. Singer surveyed the five
dormant detectives in view around the squad room. How right the
doc was. With a small dash Singer rounded a filing cabinet for
cleaning and laundry marks to the softly whistled tune of the
Zionist National Hymn.

At a desk near the captain's closed door Detective Alfred Birch,
dormant perhaps but far from mute, sat in the throes of dictating
a preliminary report, Detective Division No. 5, to a colleague, hunting and pecking on an ancient machine. Singer's tune came brightly

doleful over the clatter of his brush against a filing case that supported a dog-eared dictionary in front of Birch's desk.

Birch reared back and his freckled red face was redder than usual. "Cut out that cockeyed crying." Over years on the Force his accent had grown more Americanized as his temper grew worse.

"I'm not." Singer advanced cheerfully around the dictator's desk. "You limeys," Singer remarked with just the right insinuation, "have given us back our guns at Tel-Aviv."

"They'll have *you* in the *German* army, boy." Bevan the official squad stenographer tossed a cigar stub down from his perch on a long table in the middle of the room. "It's a scandal the way you go after those butts." Bevan put his nose back in an Eagle Edition of the New York Criminal Code.

Singer made a rude noise and rattled his floor brush against Birch's desk, sending the cigar stub under it.

"Go away," bellowed Birch and told Singer what he could do with his dusting tool. "I can't concentrate."

"Tsk, tsk." Stanley Poniatowski, half-asleep by a desk with two telephones opposite Birch's lair, lifted his bullet head from his barrel chest and raised his feet to let Singer pass the brush under them. "The mahn cahn't concentrate," he remarked. "What *is* this, a school?"

"For crime from some of the people I see around," roared Birch. "Where was I, Rover?" he asked the typist in a milder voice.

Jimmy Rovero grinned and joined the customary game of Birch-baiting. "Dis boid takes a gander across duh stem and makes dis guy wid a whisky bottle in his mitt," Rovero extemporized fluently.

"Nah, nah, nah," Birch roared again. "He observes this container of wine, I said." Birch hesitated. "Comes, uh, comes——"

"A pause in the day's occupations, that is known as the Children's Hour," Peter Swann filled in smoothly from under the hat that nearly hid his curly light hair. "Employ English," he said, moving part of his six feet to a new position on the desk by Poniatowski and the telephones. *"Boid gander makes guy mitt. What species of discourse is that?"*

"Why don't you cut out all that Brooklyn doubletalk, Birch, and just put down, during the course of an altercation?" Singer leaned on his brush and wanted to know.

"There'll be some new faces around here soon if some people don't learn how to do a simple DD5," George Bevan put in. . . .

New faces, it was a common enough threat in a business where, as McLone often told Van Kill, the sidewalk might come up any minute and smack you on the jaw. The gambit was an ancient one in those rooms, but of late the boys had developed a variation on the usual reply.

"New faces? That's okay by me," Birch growled, and in the midst of it began to yawn. "They're getting *good* business in the Bomb Squad nowadays," he wound the expected snapper up and while he did the telephone nearest Swann rang sharply, cutting short the Homicide squad room's expected laugh.

At its first ring Peter Swann hit the floor with both feet, scooped up the receiver, pushed back his hat, drew pad and pencil to him in what looked like a single move.

"Manhattan Homicide Squad, Detective Swann speaking," he said automatically and noted the time as 10:15 A.M. "Unidentified blonde, basement stairs, West Ninety—give me that street and number again."

He put the information down on his pad and his voice rose with interest. "She had *what* in her purse?" An official voice told him what once more. Interesting coincidence, Swann thought. He put the information down.

"We got one. Let's *go*," Singer called out to the squad room, now astir. He leaned his brush against the wall by Swann's elbow and Swann spoke briefly with him.

"Sounds good," Singer agreed. "I'll wake 'em." He already had his hand on the dormitory door through which he could see a radio, a card table, and nearer him Sergeant Mars and Lieutenant Roughead sleeping off another case.

Swann went to knock at McLone's office and deliver the usual semi-military report. Not until the last did he mention what he still thought was a mere coincidence.

"Dr. Van Kill's name and address," he said, "were found in the girl's purse."

Only then did the detective let his gaze wander from the captain to Van Kill, who had merely caught his breath inaudibly.

But Captain Frank McLone had been well acquainted with a certain leggy youth in the days when Van Kill's father had solved the Danforth kidnaping. It couldn't, thought McLone, looking at Van Kill's face sharply now, have been *that* many years ago. Captain McLone looked at Swann. The detective turned and walked quietly from the room.

So it happened that when Swann heard Poniatowski in the squad room bellowing, "Looks like we got a good one," to Mars in the dormitory, Swann said, "Shut up," and reached for his overcoat. . . .

After a silence which seemed longer than it could have been McLone who was standing said, "You don't want to go." He made it neither a question nor a statement of fact.

"Yes," Van Kill said, rising uncertainly. "Yes, I believe—yes, I do."

. . . Habit also reasserted itself with McLone. He gestured imperatively with his head and Van Kill followed him into the squad room. He saw the men standing around at informal attention, eyes on him, a friendly concern mingled with their sharp regard. Slowly, it seemed, though the whole circle of thought was one of seconds, Van Kill focused individuals in this circle of waiting men: hotheaded cockney Birch sitting at a desk with keen little Jimmy Rovero, Broadway Italian from the lower East Side. Mechanically he labeled the six who were going: Lieut. John Roughead, brokennosed ex-boxer, there in the dormitory door by Poniatowski, handy at Slavic dialects as at a brawl, and over there by the outer door, Bevan whom he had coached on his Freshman Greek at Fordham standing near Sergeant Mars.

Sergeant Mars had helped in the sequel of the Danforth kidnaping, but the record wasn't in that filing cabinet for open and closed cases. He had used the same labels describing all these men to *her* just yesterday afternoon. He had known every man in that squad room longer by far. Incredible . . . But he was glad for the heavy impact of curiosity and strength which the squad's presence always made upon him. . . .

Singer with the big black homicide lights and Swann with the green kit by the familiar long table in the middle of the room. Familiar as the barracks atmosphere, the battered furniture, the jokes and working habits of the men. For once it would not have been good to be alone by himself with anything so strange. . . .

The whole wait was one of seconds, but during it Singer noticed Van Kill's almost exaggerated military bearing for the first time. He mentioned the circumstance later to his partner Swann. At the time no one spoke except McLone, directing Birch and Rovero to hold the fort.

Then the eight of them were clattering down the iron stairs to the second floor, where McLone made a move to stop at the office of Deputy Chief Inspector Larkin, in charge of Manhattan Detective Squads. But Singer, leading them, called back in a stage whisper, "There he goes." They looked over the railing to see the Inspector's black raincoat and black slouch hat bob around the turning at the first floor toward the sergeant's desk. It was very familiar, all this, and McLone saying at Van Kill's elbow, "He'll get there first."

But the Inspector, as it had often happened before, did not. Van Kill thought, as conscious thought returned to him, that he had never seen the driver take wilder chances. Imagination probably. They had often gone recklessly with screaming siren through Times Square. Van Kill turned then to McLone, who was sitting next to him in the back seat. Briefly he told the captain about the connection between Popub and the Christian Cavaliers. . . .

~~~~~~

XX

"BACK here a little." Peter Swann sat just below the landing where the body of Betty Hargrave lay diagonally on its left side. "They missed something, I think."

Harry Singer, who leaned against the wall holding a squad lamp, understood Swann's *they* perfectly. It included precinct detectives, uniformed policemen and their commanders, who had got under foot as usual, Captain McLone, who had dictated a description of the scene to Bevan, photographers and fingerprint men from the Bureau of Identification, Inspector Larkin and the Medical Examiner, sundry tin and brass hats who had all come, surged about mingling with, controlling the customary gapers, and gone elsewhere upon their divers businesses.

"They often do," Singer said. Working together here, the voices of both men had the sort of clipped ventriloqual direction which is unintelligible to a listener not on the line of speech.

The lamp Singer held was a portable unit operating on its own battery. It shone across the marred heels of the girl's brown suede oxfords, pointing toward the steps, whose bare wood showed drag marks from bottom to top. At the edge of the girl's tweed topcoat which someone had spread over her, the tips of white petals glowed in the powerful beam.

"There?" Singer asked.

Beside the flowers, Swann indicated. Knuckles and a coral-enameled right thumb. He could have been a photographer posing a difficult subject. He had served his apprenticeship in the Bureau of Identification before coming to the Homicide Squad. He blew on the thumb. "See that?"

Singer slanted himself and the light. "Uh-hunh," he said pessimistically. "Not as good as the Gatti wax fingerprint we got on the Wilson gun."

"Beautiful latent," said Swann. "It's a right little finger. See how that delta goes left on the ulnar loop."

"Her own?"

Swann snorted. "Just try putting your own right little finger flat down on your right thumb so the top of your print runs toward your thumbnail tip."

Singer grinned, squatting companionably. "Man or woman?" he said.

"Am I a prophet? Whoever dragged the girl from the closet up here."

"I am," Singer said. "If you ask me, this is the color Cappy's been beefing for. No sex angle, the M.E. says. The girl's good-looking, has prominent friends, and now a latent like that. Every bit of it fit for the *Times* to print."

Harry Singer broke off in what might have been embarrassment. Cracking this case would be good for the team's already good record, but . . . he raised the topcoat slightly, lowered it almost at once, and jerked his head in the general direction of the basement.

"How's *he*—feeling?"

"How would you?" Swann said shortly. "Captain told him about those," he indicated the crisp flowers. "Said there wasn't any cyanosis except where she lay on her back. Eased his mind maybe."

"Did you hear the Inspector?" Swann shook his head. "You know how he stamps around and says 'Jaycee, Jaycee' when he's sore. He likes Van Kill."

"They'll be coming for the body." Swann was suddenly in a hurry. "Bushong's sticking around in the mailing room to get some pictures of that closet when the Lab's come up and smelled of it. Hop down and see if he's got his print camera and copper powder."

Singer stepped over Betty Hargrave and went downstairs to call the man from the Bureau of Identification.

Van Kill had given McLone a kind of answer about the piece of rough gray-brown paper which the captain was fingering dubiously. Van Kill put his feet a little further under Richard Lee's desk. He had been glad of anything at all to do.

"No prints. Bushong tried," the captain said. "But it *could* be from that party cake." He put the paper back in its envelope and tossed it on Lee's desk beside Betty's brown doeskin handbag. "I told you there was a contusion at the base of the victim's skull. I've seen prize fighters killed from a knockout no worse."

Van Kill's tone also was considered, professional. "Concentration of carbon dioxide doesn't seem to have been terribly high."

"We'll know when Doc Prufer sees what the aspirators suck up." For the City Toxicologist McLone had a certain patient tolerance, more than for the Police Laboratory, way out in the wilds of Brooklyn where a man couldn't get at 'em. "But," McLone tapped gently on Lee's green desk blotter, "why should anybody with brains enough to use CO_2 leave that wrapping paper on the closet floor? Was it a plant?"

"Could be," said Van Kill and had a passing fear that it was.

"Well," resumed McLone in the brisk objective voice which Van Kill found comforting, "I told you Doc Baumann says it probably happened eight to ten hours before we got here this morning at 10:35." He picked up Lee's phone, listened briefly. "Keep looking," he said, and put it down.

"Roughead?" hazarded Van Kill.

"The same. He says the boys can't find anybody yet around here saw or heard a thing out of the way between twelve and two."

"What about the landlady?"

"Mrs. Maude Rollins?" McLone smiled. "Couple of tenants heard her let out a screech about ten o'clock this morning."

"Did she," Van Kill wanted to know, "touch the body?"

"Nearly fell over it coming upstairs, yes," McLone said quickly. "But nothing more, she says, and I believe her. She just drinks to keep warm." The brogue piped in McLone's voice. "Nights when she doesn't the heat stays on until twelve, the tenants say, and last night was one of those nights. This morning it came on, such as it was, at eight." The captain paused. "Twelve, eight," he repeated half to himself.

"Yes?" inquired Van Kill, raising his head.

"By jiggerty!" It was McLone's strongest oath. He opened the doeskin purse and showed Van Kill where a cake of powder base had melted on opposite sides of the lining. He said rapidly, "This bag fell on top of that steam pipe in the closet, where else? This powder cake in the purse melted once around twelve—hardened again when the pipe got cold, and had melted some more at eight. When the purse was moved along with the body, it ran in the opposite direction, see? Body and purse clearly not moved till this morning. Maybe two men concerned, one who—look at it, am I right?"

Van Kill looked, but did not offer to touch the purse. "About the purse, yes," he said. "A man would have *carried* her upstairs."

"Murderers get excited," McLone, who always took a chivalrous point of view when possible, began, whirled in his chair, and made for the mailing room. A voice at the alley door was bellowing, "What the hell is this anyway?" and another, calm and official from the vestibule, saying, "*This* is a home-i-cide, friend."

Officer Ignatius Loyola Gallagher, Shield #23444, straight-backed and tall, was diligently detaining a muscular citizen who carried an attaché case. Van Kill cut in first with a wink to McLone.

"I know this man, Captain. Let me talk to him alone inside." And to Burke, "I'm Assistant District Attorney Weinstein from the Homicide Bureau. Come with me."

Gallagher, who recognized Van Kill, started . . . Van Kill closed the door of the Cavaliers' inner office.

"That was a big bluff, Burke," he said brusquely. "I'm from True American. Hand over that dictaphone record or we'll all be in the can."

The bloodshot eyes which the head Cavalier turned upon Van Kill were utterly convinced. Without a word Burke plopped into Lee's chair and fumbled with his case.

Van Kill snatched the paper-wrapped box from Burke's shaking hand. "You'll be hearing from the boss soon," he said, and left Burke gaping after him.

In the mailing room Van Kill put the package down on a perfectly bare table and gave its contents a glance. At the alley door he handed it to McLone.

"Play this over when you get a chance. Very important," he said and strode off up the alley. He left McLone gaping after him too. . . .

The closet was closed again. The Lab had departed with full aspirators and Bushong with a dozen used plates. McLone stood in front of the closet with Singer and Swann.

"I got a complete ridge count and one scar," Swann said. "Same print as Bushong got all over the addressograph in there."

"Perfect," said McLone. "But Crockett won't be here till 12:30. You'll have to see Bushong later on downtown."

Crockett, like Van Kill's fictitious Weinstein, was one among a large crew of young lawyers serving under Asst. D.A. Herman Lilienzweig, in charge of the Homicide Bureau for Clarence Daffin, the District Attorney in Chief. Assigned to the city by districts, they concentrated on homicide cases alone, taking formal statements from witnesses, seeing cases through their initial stage in the lower Homicide Court, preparing them for final prosecution in General Sessions by Lilienzweig, co-operating as the official phrase has it at all times with the squad . . . Or, as Singer and Swann put it now, fletcherizing the bacon the squad brought home. . . .

Swann moved over with McLone to Burke's desk at the back of the inner office. Singer brought Burke to them there and sat down with an arm upon the dictaphone. The head of the Christian Cavaliers made no bones about showing he knew the formula for police questioning.

"My name is Thomas Carroll Burke and I live at—" He mentioned a number on Mosholu Parkway in the Bronx. Singer, chin on palm, grinned slightly.

"Fair enough," said McLone. "Miss Elizabeth Hargrave worked for you?"

"As part-time secretary to the manager, myself," responded Burke. "We'll find it hard to replace her," he said with honest regret.

"What were you doing last night, Mr. Burke?" Singer put in casually.

"Playing stud and drinking rye in my apartment with some friends."

Swann said, "For how long?"

"From about eight in the evening till two hours ago." Burke gave some names and addresses which Swann took down with his other notes.

"Hope you kick those so-called friends of mine out of bed," Burke offered lightly while McLone relayed a checking call to a precinct in the Bronx. "They took me for plenty. I've got a hangover too." Burke held up a tremulous hand and flashed a ghastly smile.

"What does your organization do?" McLone asked.

"Promotes American ideals in business." Burke stifled a yawn and McLone let it go at that. Van Kill had told him what kind of ideals in the squad car on the way up.

Singer, neutral in complexion, hair, and eyes, was no longer neutral in attitude. He had taken his chin off his palm and was sitting up straight. He leaned forward suddenly.

"Why did you murder her, Burke?"

"In my *previous* career," Burke said to Singer deliberately, "the men I had to take care of all got well. I never laid a hand in anger on a woman in my life, let alone one so attractive as Miss Hargrave. Whose murderer," he told McLone, "I trust you will immediately apprehend."

McLone let it pass, inquiring, "Who was here yesterday afternoon?"

"Just before we closed, Miss Hargrave and myself," Burke said. "About five. Oh, yes, and I believe Miss Goff was around. Left after I did. Miss Daisy Goff." He gave her address. "She ought to be out there in the mailing room this morning. The rich kike she works for downtown," Burke said, showing his teeth to Singer, "closes on Saturday."

McLone was looking through the open door into the mailing room. "Miss Daisy Goff," he said, underlining the name almost imperceptibly. "You can go, boys. There's Crockett now."

Singer and Swann shut the office door behind them on their

way out. In the mailing room they stopped to tell Crockett and his stenographer Fielding what had happened thus far.

Crockett, a thin young man with a Law Review Staff look had never heard of the tradition that D.A.'s assistants should bellow at the squad. He did not inform them that they were getting nowhere with the case.

"Thanks," he said warily, as if he still had much to learn about homicide, which was the fact. "I'll put you onto something too."

The Chief (meaning District Attorney Clarence Daffin), had had this Cavaliers outfit under observation for some months of course, Crockett said. When the murder notification reached him, he saw it was time to let the police share his information. They'd all agreed the Chief had better not release anything to the newspapers about this Popub investigation which he'd known of for some months.

"There might be a big national security angle to it which would spoil if we let it out. I've got my orders to handle this strictly as a private homicide," Crockett concluded.

"We got ours from the captain," said Swann, who liked Crockett.

"Thanks for telling us anyway," said Singer, who did too.

It was therefore not until the pair of detectives had gone up the alley several paces that Swann growled, "Observation, balls!"

"Little dig-up-the-business Clarence," said Singer, who had performed duets like this with Swann before. "He's had them under observation for some months, yeah, on the moon."

"Got him with his pants down that shot."

"And a mess of termites right in the seams . . . That goddam harp . . . But somehow——"

"Don't let Burke fret you, son. Cappy'll let us work the case. I took the call, you know. Somehow, what?"

"I don't think Daffin'll go to town on this one," Singer said bitterly, tilting his aquiline nose. "Some of his rich backers have probably been paying out dough to these Cavaliers."

"He's coughed off worse than that," Singer was reminded by Swann. "Give the man credit, boy. He's hot for national defense."

"Of himself," said Singer. "That Boy Scout from Manhattan,

Kan. He'd hook his grandmother on a soliciting rap if he thought it'd step him up a notch. Piping down on the Popub-Cavaliers connection was Cappy's idea."

The idea had in a sense been McLone's. The captain, who would if pressed admit that the D.A. was a quick adapter, had himself adapted the idea from Van Kill, who had said that these rats, if given enough rope, would probably choke themselves.

The case, Van Kill considered, hung upon motives almost entirely personal. For him, he thought now, hurrying along Central Park West, certain features would always remain entirely personal. A private homicide, it would remain. Private—and as for its unexpected conclusion never fully explained to the press, though Poynton Darcy and Louie Lenz maintained that they had told all the true facts.

Mr. Thomas Burke had just finished telling McLone that his partner, Lee, had probably spent the evening in Weehawken, N. J. He was going there to call on a prospect, Burke said.

"Which reminds me, captain," he continued, a bit above himself from his run-in with Singer, McLone thought, "did you see a keyring around here when you searched the place? I was getting drunk already yesterday afternoon. Holidays," he explained. "I must have left it here."

"Keyring?" said McLone absently, his blue eyes on the office door.

"Yes," Burke went on, briskly emboldened. "I'd like to get at my files when you're through. I've got a hell of a lot of work to do."

McLone turned back to regard the head Cavalier. "Yes," he said. Even in the brief time before Van Kill had found what was possibly a piece of dry-ice wrapping paper and they had slammed the closet shut, McLone had used Burke's keys on the filing-case drawers. And every one of them was completely bare. "Yes," McLone said, actually smiling now, "I'm sure you have."

Miss Daisy Goff backed into a bookcase set against the wall of her furnished room. The top shelf, containing among other things her interlined copies of Caesar and Cicero, struck Miss Goff well below the waist. She jumped at the sudden contact, then as suddenly pressed back again. She couldn't get far enough away to suit her from those two men. One was tall, one was short, and their faces seemed to loom upon her larger than life, wolfishly menacing. Backed against her top bookcase shelf, her hair stringing over her ears, Miss Daisy Goff stood at bay.

She hadn't done anything thus far but hide under the bed when she heard them knocking, and scream when they told her who they were. But now like her heroes, it came to her she knew not whence, she ought to be brave. Cicero against the swords of Antony's minions, Caesar against the dagger of Brutus, she thought. She zipped her pince-nez from the chatelaine guard on her puny bosom and shakily put them on. She leveled a bony finger and, disheveled though she was, drew herself up to her best schoolroom height.

"Go!" she said.

But the horrible creatures just stood there leering at her. The big one looked like her flunking football stars (only the gesture always worked with *them*) . . . All men were beasts. Miss Goff's mind began to dally with a desperate expedient. It had classical precedent, Dido, and in the movies it always worked. The smaller one looked halfway decent, he might not take advantage of her.

"You naughty boys," said Miss Goff with genteelly seductive defiance, "you threatened to pull me out by the—by the ——"

"*Sollt mir entschuldigen,* leg," Harry Singer finished it for her. He wasn't leering, he had been trying not to grin.

They wouldn't give her the cue she wanted, the stupid things. They must be up to something worse. Miss Goff, more frightened than ever, decided to give her own cue. She half closed her eyes and swayed toward Singer. "Let me go, you beasts," she said.

Peter Swann, who was already about two feet away from her, moved back as he spoke. "When you tell us why your print was on the murdered girl's thumb," he said so matter-of-factly that Miss Goff jerked up and glared at him.

Harry Singer, essentially a gallant soul, indicated her little rock-ing chair. "Sit down if you feel faint," he said.

"You can tell us just as well sitting down why you murdered the girl," Swann conceded as Miss Goff tottered again. Whether it was an act he could not tell, but the look she cast at him was deadly enough.

"I didn't—I don't believe—I, oh!" she said and suddenly Harry Singer found himself holding a head. Miss Goff's pince-nez were cold on his Adam's apple, a musty smell came up to him from her hair. But some obscure impulse of sympathy (Singer had been good at Latin in high school) plucked at the detective's hard chest. He didn't push the head away. He even supported it with a hand, the better to hear Miss Goff moan:

"She was dead—stiff, when I came—about nine o'clock. I *had* to get her out of there, and her things, her coat and purse. She had no right . . . Making trouble—" Daisy Goff's voice thinned to a whine.

Peter Swann leaned over Singer's shoulder. "What about the keys?"

Miss Goff reared her head up like an ugly fowl. "I won't talk to you," she said, "you—you creature."

"Take it easy," said Singer. "Where were the keys and where was the girl?"

"Outside in the lock, she was inside, the hussy," Miss Goff said into Singer's overcoat lapel, and he could feel her thin body shiver against him with jealous hate of Betty Hargrave. "I was afraid they'd think," the rest came out as Singer urged it in a sort of croak, "I murdered her."

That was all Singer wanted. There was every evidence about Miss Goff's person, not to speak of what they had observed in her room, that the old maid had been violently upset. "Now, now," he said briskly. He grasped her by the elbow, eased her expertly up and around. "You'll be all right."

"Yes, indeed." Swann reached for the weeping Goff's left arm. Sex appeal, thought Peter Swann, who had never seen it tried by a more unlikely specimen. "Yes, indeed," he said, grasping her arm firmly. "We'll take *good* care of you. Just come along with us."

Bertram, the night elevator man at the Otranto Apartments, was still hanging around talking to Allen the day boy when Van Kill came in. Bertram's black Jamaican face showed no surprise at the question Van Kill asked; he only broadened his English accent as he replied:

"Lady Diana Brown? No, sir, definitely not. I was on duty continuously from 8:00 P.M. to 8:00 A.M. She could not have gone out without my seeing her, Dr. Van Kill."

That was one thing certain in a morning which had been completely otherwise, thought Van Kill, crouched over the telephone in his study making a tenth consecutive attempt to get David Montefiore . . . Lady Di had appreciated his thinking of her at all just then and said so. She had understood when he counseled her not to tell anyone about her household innovations . . . Understood perfectly. . . .

The bright empty ring-pause-ring of the dial system brought Van Kill back to all the anger he had pent up for hours. "May Abaddon, Asmodaeus, and Belial smash that idiot's bones to a pulp!" he shouted and banged the receiver down.

First David's apartment, then De Porta's, then Echo at Popub, with a double warning, then David's apartment again and several other places he might conceivably be on a Saturday morning for seven more mortal tries. "Damn him," said Van Kill, more mildly because it was plain David might eventually be. . . .

Van Kill arrived at the office of the Christian Cavaliers again as McLone took a telephone call from the precinct station, where the boys were working on Miss Daisy Goff . . . "Got her dead to rights," McLone said, swinging himself around in Burke's chair.

When you had a real lead like that fingerprint, McLone said, checking often took you to them in a matter of hours and *if* it was a citizen with no prior record, they never held out long on the cops . . . The document examiner, sitting on Lee's desk, felt

numbly aware that opposite him the captain was off on a favorite
lesson from experience. . . .

Of course the old lady hadn't admitted the murder yet, though
when they gave you the "visiting a sick friend last night" whom
they "couldn't bring into this," you knew it was coming . . . Van
Kill knew the beginnings of the first unparalyzed sensation he
had felt that day. Satisfaction and relief and something more indefinable. Maybe they would stay with Goff for a time. Van Kill
nodded decisively and McLone resumed his purposeful backtracking.

"This Cavaliers outfit here, Miss Goff puts the last word on them
for me." Most prisoners, he reminded Van Kill, got their likes
and their dislikes for particular detectives. In this case Singer had
been collecting all the information and Swann, pure American-
German, the right kind and proud of it, "she's calling *him* a dirty
Jew." McLone looked as if he wanted to spit. "*All* such name-
calling," the captain ruminated, "it's only an excuse for needing
to hate *somebody*."

Van Kill couldn't think of a better way of putting it. Just two
days ago he had been prating to Betty Hargrave about ambivalence.

"Bronx precinct's checked Burke's alibi for last night," the captain
growled regretfully. "Bound to have it ready-made of course, a lad
like that with one leg over the edge of stir for years, unless my
nose's gone wrong. Two things in his favor right now, he surely
is upset about his files being gone and the place cleaned out and
he surely had the father and mither of a hangover."

The captain had his blue eyes directed toward his feet, apparently
contemplating the delightful possibility of working with them on
Mr. Thomas Burke. But when he spoke again, he had gone back
to Goff.

Much more likely *she* did the murder singlehanded, last night a
little past twelve as the powder base clue had suggested, went away
to let the dry ice work, if that was it, and didn't come back until
this morning at nine. She then proceeded to move the body, perhaps with some crazy idea of making it look like an accident and
resuming her work. She found out the job was scarier than she
had bargained for, so she ran away and—McLone shot a glance

at Van Kill—"this we know," he said. "She hid in her room until the boys carted her off."

"I'd better drive down to the precinct and see what they're getting from her." McLone stood up and continued speaking while he donned his hat and overcoat. "Motive—hatred because the girl stood in better than she did with Burke. Immediate incentive, same as Burke's *could* have been—suspected what the girl was really up to, found her going through the closet and—" McLone hesitated over the bottom button and looked from under raised eyebrows at Van Kill. "If your theory tests, you'll not be asking me how I assume she got access to that particular dry ice? It doesn't *have* to be that particular dry ice."

"Anything you care to assume about Miss Daisy Goff is perfectly all right with me," said Van Kill, not getting up.

"*Do* you want to come along?"

"Not that much." Van Kill knew what the indefinable sensation had been. He was hungry, ravenously so. "After lunch perhaps," he said.

"You amateurs." McLone was struggling between the remnants of an old conviction complex and his chivalry. "No," he said, "I'm afraid the lady's going to fry."

"I hope." Van Kill got up with that, accompanied the captain as far as the squad car, and went back then to exchange a few words with Officer Gallagher on duty guarding the premises.

XXI

THE captain had given Mr. Benjamin De Porta a bad quarter of an hour. With less excuse really than he would have with Mr. Frederick Pough, whose office he was headed for now at about two o'clock. Who could blame a kindly man for doing a kindness? McLone asked himself. It had not been sensible of De Porta to employ such a misfit, but how could he know she would turn out to be such a villainous old mud hen?

And who, the captain was thinking as he conferred not exactly in private with Frederick Pough, could blame a sensible employer like this if an employee took a risk against which she had been specifically warned?

Not that Pough blamed Miss Hargrave. He looked altogether stricken to McLone. His brown face was drawn and he spoke with an effort. "I told your man Swann," he said. "I told Swann how I felt." The head of Popub had just come back from identifying the body at Bellevue with Swann and the experience had obviously shaken him.

He understood the District Attorney's motive for suppressing the Popub end of the case. "But," he said, "I wonder if the material Miss Hargrave collected for us might not be of use . . ." Here, Pough indicated a number of large manuscript envelopes on his desk, were Betty's notes on the Cavaliers' organization, everything she had got together over a period of nearly six months. The larger envelope, he said, contained a list Betty had made of the Cavaliers' small contributors. She had starred the names of the larger small fry, the $10 to $50 class, Pough explained.

"These are the backbone of the organization," Betty's employer said, tapping the package with his pen. "Regrettably. But they do not make news. Thousands of tradesmen, small professional people, clerical workers, they make the strength of such underground movements, but their names would add nothing to an exposé. It

160

was for that reason Miss Hargrave wanted to get into the Cavaliers' private files."

"It was for that reason, it appears, she was murdered," McLone said because Pough seemed to find it difficult to say. The list might be more important than Mr. Pough thought, the captain continued. "I'll give you a receipt."

"We'll want it back eventually, no doubt," the other said wearily. "But until this tragic affair is settled, I don't care to have that material of Betty's—Miss Hargrave's around. If there is anything I can do——"

The captain was a little embarrassed as well as impressed at the man's deadly sincerity. Pough had already, he knew, posted a thousand-dollar reward for information leading to the perpetrator's arrest with Commissioner Cantwell. That girl, the captain reflected, must have been a darn sweet kid. "I'll let you know," he told Pough.

"I should have insisted." Pough laid his palms flat on the desk and stared straight ahead of him. He had offered to see Miss Hargrave home from the dinner, she had refused, and he himself had said good night to the few remaining guests and gone home to bed. "If I had insisted, I might have found out what she was planning to do. But I didn't." The editorial director of Popub drew a hand across his forehead and down the side of his face. "I'd been feeling more like bed than anything else all evening . . . I dropped a considerable amount on the market yesterday," Pough explained, "and now—" The mute gesture he made with one hand, let fall quickly to the desk said plainly what else that was irretrievable he had lost.

The captain turned away to talk with Paul Harris and George Stock. His quiet conference with Pough had been private only in the sense that Pough had ordered his two minions to wait at the other end of the long room. To the experienced eye of McLone, who had taken a lot of it in his time, both men bore the earmarks of a recent bawling out. Probably, the captain concluded, about magazine matters which had nothing to do with the case. . . .

Pough had as a matter of fact been giving Harris and Stock a final word about Poynton Darcy's flagellation piece and he had also been telling Harris and Stock just where *Carnage* stood with regard to the murder of Betty Hargrave, which was nowhere. . . .

Both men took the slack out of their faces when McLone came up. They then proceeded to afford the captain what both termed that hearty co-operation all decent citizens owe the representatives of law and order in their eternal War on Crime. For years Harris had been trying to get McLone's by-line. The captain had thrown many better crooks than Harris out of his office and Harris knew he thought so.

Not waiting to be asked, Paul Harris plunged into a typically manic account of the *Carnage* dinner, George Stock contributing an occasional monosyllable. It was more honest than the captain, standing up with them and listening silently, had a right to expect. On the score of material details it was amazingly full, Harris drawing on what he called again his photographic plate memory. In every major essential but one Paul Harris's sinister narrative (he made it that) corresponded with what Van Kill had got from Montefiore, and in that one, strangely enough, Paul Harris agreed with Hendrik Van Kill.

In brief, the editor and the art editor of *Carnage* said they had gone immediately to their respective apartments after the party broke up: Harris to work on some story changes in a manuscript, Stock on some art layout revisions in the same. Stock lived in the West Sixties, Harris in the West Nineties not far from the Christian Cavaliers, oddly enough.

"I kept thinking even after I got home," Harris said in a level voice, "that Montefiore's little speech was in pretty poor taste."

Pough, who had strolled up casually, looked over Harris's head at McLone. "Not if you know Mr. Montefiore," he put in so quietly that it didn't sound like a rebuke. "You see, he's some-what ——"

"Screwy," Harris finished it. His slaty black eyes were on his art editor's face.

"Right," said George Stock, rising to the occasion. "That's putting it mild."

The captain knew when to go. He left the three men standing there looking at each other, while he tucked Betty Hargrave's *Cavalier* reports under his arm and headed for the reception room. He was careful to close the door behind him when he went out. Harris's attempted steer toward Montefiore didn't impress him much at the time. . . .

She probably wouldn't have been caught, Echo Newman told herself angrily, if the interrogation had been at all formal. Van Kill, attempting to reach David more than two hours ago, had led her to expect it would be. But McLone had walked meditatively past her desk like a man with his mind on something miles away. Then at the corridor door he'd halted and looked uncertainly back in her direction.

Did he want to see someone else in Popub? Echo, her office manners led her into it, was at his side asking him. She wasn't even sure he'd asked a single question. She'd literally pushed herself and David into the trap, telling how six or more of them lingered down at the *Hearth* banquet room after all the other guests had gone.

Mr. Pough, David, Harris and Stock, Echo remembered, were still there, a little before eleven, when Mr. Pough had seen Miss Hargrave and herself to separate taxis (*that* was all right) and it seemed she had no more than got home and to sleep at her hotel, the London in the upper Eighties near West End Avenue, when she. . . .

Put her neck straight into it, Echo Newman was telling herself two minutes after she'd seen McLone out. There was where the captain's technique had worked. She, who rather prided herself on her own technique for handling office temperament, had fallen for it.

Sitting at her desk, the heels of her palms pressing on her temples, Echo looked up at herself in the mirror-faced clock which David had put there some days ago. It was an expensive gadget and when she had refused it as a gift, David had stood on his rights as a minority stockholder. Mr. Pough had thought it was funny. Mr.

Pough was looking now as if he would never laugh again, she thought. The death of Betty Hargrave had seemed very remote to Echo this morning. Now. . . .

You fool, she said to the face in the mirror. Her eyes seemed a little darker than usual, but her forehead and the two oblique strokes of her brows were untroubled by the guilty panic leaping in her throat. You fool, you silly sheep. . . .

She turned away from the desk, one slender hand gripping the edge so that the knuckles stood out white, the other beating lightly on her knee . . . Like a sheep, blatting it all out, how she had been wakened by a telephone call from David. She hadn't gone down, no, captain, she was too sleepy.

All that, and McLone's noncommittal voice saying only, "So, Miss Newman, you don't know exactly what time it was when you got this call, or where Mr. Montefiore was calling from?" ·

"I could kill you for waking me up," she had told David . . . Now (terrifying, the murderous clichés of conversation, at a time like this), she deserved to have her own neck wrung for not going down to see him in the lobby. He was in the lobby of course, he *had* called her from there. She hadn't mentioned David's foolish after-dinner speech, thank heaven. Somebody else would though, somebody would be happy to. . . .

Going racial, Echo told herself sharply. The thing to do was to rig up some sort of agreement with that beloved idiot before it got too late. He couldn't look out for himself.

But who would look out for her? The thought intruded itself as she restored the lipstick she had bitten off. She dismissed it as completely as she dismissed her make-up kit when she was through with it . . . Now that her brains were working, Echo Newman had a very fair idea of what Captain McLone had on his mind.

Twenty minutes after he had talked to Echo Newman Captain Frank McLone had his mind on a series of matters. The first was the possible significance of the sharp flight of stairs he was climbing from *Hearth's* Domestic Science Laboratory on the nineteenth floor to the elevator by *Carnage* on the twentieth just above *Hearth.*

The second was his immediate need in an uptown-downtown combination like this for more help to sift the metropolitan straw-stack that he had merely shaken down. He'd have to put in to Larkin for special detail detectives today. Not as many as in the Opera House Murder or the Tourian Case (they took several hundred), but several dozen. This was, the captain directed a fleeting thought to the still unlocated Montefiore, going to be one of those cases with too many clues.

Singlehanded now the captain had fought through a terrific lot of chatter from the ladies at *Hearth* and learned from them the following:

The carton the cake came in from Raft's with the dry ice and the gray-brown paper that made it possible to handle the stuff, had been put out by the service elevator about eight o'clock. Two of *Hearth's* six helpers had put the cake on the table before the guests sat down and one of them had carried the carton into the corridor then. The service elevator ran up by the steps on which the captain had paused to think, around a corner but within a long arm's reach of the passenger lift.

At that point Captain McLone's mind gradually spread wings and took off a foot from the ground. He considered stairs almost as good as a bathtub for thought . . . Carton plus dry ice outside at 8:00 P.M. last night . . . Carton gone this morning when the staff came to work . . . Interview janitor and regular cleaning women of course. . . .

But anybody in the downtown Popub menagerie, two dozen guests, not to mention six help, could have taken the dry ice . . . Anybody uptown, including principally Goff, but also Mr. Thomas Burke (*and* maybe Mr. Richard Lee, who at last report hadn't turned up yet) would probably have got their dry ice some-where else. Dry ice, much of it protected by the same sort of gray-brown insulation that was around the stuff Raft's sent with their ice cream molds, was too easily come by. McLone didn't intend to worry too much about CO_2 until they got complete co-operation from Goff. But if the M.E. said that CO_2 had killed the girl, and they had to check every quarter-pound of dry ice used in the city yesterday, why, they'd do it.

Also noted was the fact that some of the men had come away from the *Carnage* banquet carrying brief cases which pertained to their work. Some of the women too. Miss Harriet Treach (the captain had been delighted with this city-gentled *Hausfrau*) carried a suit box around with her everywhere.

Guests at the *Carnage* banquet had been taken up and down by the night watchman, who was said to be in a state of coma when he wasn't buried in a sex or detective magazine. It would have been easy for anyone to sneak by that lad. . . .

But, and the captain considered it a large but, Goff had been put on the actual scene at the Cavaliers, *she* had moved the body, she had motive, could have got dry ice, had every opportunity, had— the captain, nearing the top of the stairs, got no further in his pondering.

He heard a scrabble of feet above him and a shadow fell across his face. He looked up to see a large bulk surge toward him and heave back as if pulled. The horse-faced individual who had surged was standing up against the service elevator with a shorter man who was panting slightly when McLone stepped around them. The larger man regarded the captain with owlish concern.

"You," he said, "are Cap'n Francis ExZavier McLone, Commanding Oss—Officer of the Manhattan Home-i-cide Squad. I," he continued carefully, "am greatest crimescribe in America and this is —where are you, Louie?"

"Shut up, Poynton," said Louie Lenz, weaving out like a sucker fish around a shark. "The captain knows us both."

"I do that," said McLone in much the same way he would have said it to Paul Harris, the by-line fancier. The captain didn't care greatly for sots either, as the cold eye he cast on Darcy might have indicated.

Poynton apparently thought so, for he instantly denied he was tight. He and the greatest fotog were trying to find Paul Harris, the greatest editor. Darcy seemed not to feel Lenz's warning kicks.

"He isn't around now, the lousy deadbeat bum," Poynton went on plaintively. "I gotta collec' what he owes me after last night."

The pair would afford Singer and Swann a little relaxation, McLone noted briefly. He was in a hurry to get back to Goff. "What about last night?" he asked without caring whether he heard now or not.

But Poynton Darcy, who had slipped down on the door a notch, hauled himself up and plunged into a confused story which was comprehensible enough to make Louie Lenz uneasy enough to forget his usual manners to cops. Like a bratling badger he bristled up at McLone.

"We took a passout home, from a models' party," he said in a rapid popgun voice, "in the Nineties near Broadway, about midnight, what's it to you?"

"Nothing personal," said McLone. He personally had never had any luck with drunks. The elevator came. He stepped into it. "We're investigating a sewer leak in that neighborhood," he said as the car door closed. . . .

XXII

~~~~~~

YANNI MAVROMICHÁLI sat in a booth at the Matapan, watching Van Kill polish off the rare steak and French fried potatoes which he had shocked Antoine by ordering with four jolts of rye.

Yanni, observing the good Greek custom of questions after meat, had withheld a piece of information which he was thirsting to impart. Between these two no comment on Van Kill's news had been needed; they had been close to this kind of thing before. . . .

It was a good sign that the kyrios was hungry. Tears of course were the proper accompaniment of funeral meat—and wine, but northern men found it hard to weep, and—this was important, they had not been formally betrothed. It was a waste, and Yanni could say no stronger word . . . But the kyrios was finishing his whisky. Yanni spoke in his native tongue.

"The person we know of," he began experimentally. He would never refer to Miss Daisy Goff in any other way. "The person we know of," he repeated, "has—" Yanni stopped, watching the ember-gray eyes of the kyrios change as if his words had fanned a flame of remembered anger.

"She moved the body." Van Kill lit a cigarette and drew on it deeply. Ever since McLone had told him about it, he had been trying to make himself adopt a sane attitude toward the fact that Daisy Goff had handled the body of Betty Hargrave.

Van Kill had no useless sentiment about those remains. What made them Betty was gone. He knew only too well how the Medical Examiner would with butcherly science lay open the body of Betty Hargrave to inquire of her lungs and heart whether they had stopped from lack of oxygen. He knew that the Medical Examiner would peel the scalp of Yanni's golden *despoinis* forward over what had been Betty Hargrave's pointed little chin and take out her brain to see if, rather, the blow on the back of her head had killed her. . . .

The Medical Examiner would do a particularly thorough job because the victim was a friend of Hendrik Van Kill. All this was regulation procedure and necessary. To Van Kill it was the skinny hands of Goff hauling and dragging Betty Hargrave's body out of the closet that had wrought desecration.

"She moved the body," he repeated in the same flat voice, "at about nine this morning. And since she can't account for her movements last night, McLone likes her, as the boys on the squad say, likes her very much for the murderer."

"Swell." Yanni said in English and repeated it in Greek, "*kalá*. She also did something else, may she burst . . . *She* goes to sleep." It was a bad beginning and Yanni became explicit in his own way. "This woman who would cross the ocean to view the Athene of Phidias and never look up from dusting its feet, goes to sleep. . . ."

"And what—" Van Kill, who had nearly forgotten Yanni's early morning job to help catch De Porta's prowler, flicked ash from his cigarette. "What is Hecuba to me?"

The returning arrogance of the kyrios was another good sign. Yanni got down to business. "This Mrs. Horowitz was told to go away, *amésos, immediately* last night after she had served the Kyrios De Porta his cold supper."

Van Kill was glad he didn't feel for everybody the friendly indifference he did for the efficient Mrs. Horowitz. *Odi et amo.* Thank god just now for hate. Ambivalence, that was what he had told *her.* . . .

"Instead this Horowitz falls to sleep in a chair and does not leave Kyrios De Porta's apartment until it would have been maybe eleven o'clock last night."

"Ben got in by one o'clock himself," Van Kill replied absently. *. . . This assumption of solidarity in the face of so much ambivalence,* he had told Betty in the car that day, *was wrong.* It might, just might be the keyword to join the fragments of what he was beginning to see as a manuscript obscurely torn. Cut rather, purposely cut, between the Christian Cavaliers and *Carnage.* Betty Hargrave's death was written on these two segments, the document examiner reasoned, while Yanni waited for his attention. The cleavage was emotional . . . *Hate-Love* . . . *Ambivalence* . . . Mc-Lone would need something less tenuous. . . .

"Kyrios De Porta," Yanni said, "was also up before this Mrs. Horowitz came this morning. Otherwise she would have started dusting and I might not——"

"What?" queried Van Kill . . . *Ambivalence*, yes, but whom did it fit? Someone both loyal to Popub and sympathetic to the Cavaliers. The extreme hate-love state was common among neurotics and children in the Oedipus stage. The emotions of such a person were two-edged, a sword that might turn in any direction. . . .

"——have got a full left-hand set of prints," Yanni finished proudly. Van Kill sat up. "Four fingers and thumb." The Greek wagged his head with modest self-approbation and did not see Van Kill's sudden frown. "From this person who leans her hand upon Kyrios De Porta's desk when she searched it, upon the glass of his bookcase, upon the door of his wardrobe, his medicine chest, his refrigerator——"

"Damn!" Van Kill exploded. *David,* the thought flashed to him painfully. "Nothing to do with you," he explained to Yanni, who was visibly hurt. "Splendid for you. I'll have to tell McLone."

. . . Tell him and give up my scapegoat, Van Kill thought realistically, and settled to talking at Yanni for his own illumination in the same way that McLone had talked at him. . . .

Betty Hargrave had been locked in the closet to die some time around midnight. This was fairly established from the way the powder base in her bandbag, which fell on the steam pipe, had melted. Precinct men were still experimenting with the Christian Cavaliers' furnace to see how quickly the pipes cooled off.

As for alibis, people whose lives had touched Betty's could account for their movements no better than usual in such a case. Cab drivers, apartment functionaries, barkeeps and suburban train schedules could be expected to eliminate many.

Meantime McLone had Goff, which was particularly convenient because Popub's interest in the Cavaliers was being hush-hushed. McLone's mind was still fluid, Van Kill said.

"But thanks to me he's further along than he usually is at this stage." Yanni inclined his dark head. It was a fine thing to hear the kyrios bragging again.

"I told McLone things Betty told me," the document examiner said . . . How Betty believed Burke had deduced that one *True American*, a pseudonymous contributor of literary hogwash to the Cavaliers' magazine *The Lance*, was identical with an anonymous contributor of financial inspiration. How Burke had either identified this angel, or was hoping to do so by making dictaphone records of their telephone conversations. . . .

"McLone likes Burke," Van Kill said. "Either as an accomplice of Goff or alone. He has the best alibi and the fact that the files are gone points to somebody interested in protecting the Cavaliers. But I ask you—" He put his elbow on the table and directed such a thinking stare at Yanni that the Greek felt uncomfortable. "Why would Burke steal his own files? McLone says Burke looked as if his own teeth had sneaked up and bitten him in the back when he found the files were gone."

The Maniote seldom speculated about human behavior, but his imagination leaped at material objects. They could be photographed. "This Burke had secrets in his closet to ruin his crew of traitors?"

"Names and addresses of important contributors," Van Kill told him. "Some undoubtedly who would be ruined if their sympathies were made public. But they're all gone now."

"Not gone," Yanni made a sardonic correction. "Hidden."

"I'm not so sure," Van Kill said. "I'm inclined to think they went in the furnace. Because that's where the little name plates from the Cavaliers' addressograph went. The furnace crew found slugs of lead in the clinkers."

"This Burke is a fool or he has copies of his lists elsewhere," Yanni argued.

Van Kill shrugged. "Overnight such a one as Burke may find himself liable to prosecution. Because of his organization. He must be prepared as a foreign agent is prepared to cut himself off from his incriminating evidence. Perhaps Burke's files are not destroyed. But if he knew about the murder before the police did and concealed his files to protect his clients, why was the big goon carrying that dictaphone record around?"

It was shock at hearing of Betty's murder as much as hangover that had made Burke hand over the dictaphone record, Van Kill said. "I haven't heard it myself. McLone says it's pep talk and market tips in a disguised voice."

Yanni waggled a finger outside the booth. "Brandy," he said when Teekee sailed up. "Do such people kill when they are on the right hand of the law?" he asked then. "And, saving your sorrow, kyrie, do they leave a body in their own closet?"

McLone was not forgetting the Popub angle, the document examiner said. He knew that everybody from Harris down to the little photographer Lenz had had his butcher cart upset by Betty Hargrave time and again, and hated her for it. "Not considering it was the job Pough gave her to do."

"I always dislike to mention motives," Van Kill went on after Dukas had brought the brandy. "People nudge each other when I suggest one. But there are some peculiar ducks in the *Carnage* pond. That little roach Lenz, you go round to the Flash and Shutter Club, Yanni, what's the word on Lenz?"

"He is not for women." Yanni lifted his Mycenean eyebrows. "Nor is his interest the other. What I have heard is very silly." Yanni, who took a classical attitude toward vice, spoke several condemnatory words in *kathomiloumêne*, the Greek of the people.

"Very peculiar ducks around *Carnage*," Van Kill repeated, "including our friend Paul Harris. Oh, yes—" Van Kill turned his hand on the table so that his thumb pointed at the arm which Yanni still carried a little stiffly. "—I gave McLone enough about Paul so that there was a tail on him before noon."

McLone now knew that Harris had been interested enough in Betty Hargrave to have her followed, knew that Van Kill had spoken to him disparagingly about this and about his refugee racket. But McLone knew nothing about a man who had mistakenly followed Yanni into Central Park.

"One of the *astynomía* is put to following Harris? So." Yanni lifted a hand and examined the nails. "We will persevere to look out for this Harris ourselves, I think."

Van Kill nodded absently. He and Yanni did look out for Paul Harris, but it was not, in the end, their doing that Paul Harris was looked out for.

"I wish I knew where Dizzy Montefiore went after he left me last night," he said. Yanni, who had been keeping half an eye out for his teatime trade, had already noticed the debonair youth wandering cheerfully in their general direction behind Dukas.

"You will ask him perhaps," Yanni said.

"So it's you, is it?" Van Kill spoke coldly. "You go phone Echo Newman. Listen to her. Then I invite you to come back here and admire the fine noose you've made for yourself."

Yanni knew the omens and excused himself. If one of *those* was coming on, the kyrios would be okay. But it was later coming than Yanni thought. When Van Kill did blow up, he had heard Montefiore's account of himself in full. Excluding attempts at ingratiation which Van Kill, unlike Echo Newman, frigidly ignored, the net of David's story was approximately what she had heard. . . .

Last night, could be around eleven-thirty, whenever he left Van Kill, David went, he said, to Echo's hotel . . . Walked . . . He called her from a lobby cubicle and tried to make his peace. ("For God's sake, Hal, I'm terribly sorry about Miss Hargrave, how can I tell you when you act like this?")

Echo was still annoyed. She would scarcely speak to him. So he left. Maybe the man at the desk or the stuffed uniform outside had seen him. He didn't know. Very institutional, these girls' clubs. Deserted by midnight. ("*No.* I said I didn't know what time it was.")

After that, he walked over to Ninety-sixth and Broadway, feeling very depressed. The cab driver was the first sympathetic personality he'd found all evening. Of course he didn't notice the man's registration. Who ever looks at hackers? David gave the man five dollars to drive him down, oh, but fast, to the Café Royal where Uncle Ben had said he'd come for a drink after the theater. De Porta had just been coming out as David started into the Royal, so he took the old boy home in the same cab. When they got to Random Street it was one o'clock, David added defensively. Uncle Ben said so.

This morning, why he had just sat in his apartment. Was there any harm in that? Of course he'd heard the telephone, doorbell too. "I finally stuffed the bloody things up with cardboard. When I got hungry I came down here."

It was then that the eruption occurred. Van Kill spoke in the quietest of tones, but Yanni began shepherding customers to distant booths.

Eavesdropping discreetly, the Maniote caught references to fools in Aristophanes whom he recognized, in Shakespeare with whom he was getting acquainted, and in W. S. Gilbert whom he did not know at all, but who sounded the worst fools of any. The entire exposition took half an hour and five languages, and when it was finished David Montefiore knew where he stood in the case.

Stepping into the booth to take an order then, Yanni knew that David Montefiore saw himself standing on the crumbling brink of a deep pit. His face was simultaneously flushed and haggard. His order was only a quick demand for a drink, any drink.

The kyrios, Yanni saw it for certain now, would be perfectly okay. "*Amésos, kyrie,*" he told the other kyrios and went to fill the order himself.

"I wasn't worried about Montefiore, but I'm glad you called." The captain's voice was completely impersonal. "Thought you'd like to know the Lab reports over 15 per cent concentration CO_2 in the air from the bottom drawer of that filing cabinet. The M.E. hasn't finished yet of course," McLone went on while Van Kill clamped his jaws together and took a deep breath. He had a split second's vision of Antoine the cook.

This telephone in Yanni's pantry was the one Antoine used. It had a faint aroma of retsina. For the rest of Van Kill's life the warm turpentine smell of that native Greek wine would call up an irrational image of solidified CO_2, whose odorless frosty vapor could make a death trap of an inclosed space. . . .

"Doc Baumann says in that case Miss Hargrave wouldn't recover consciousness after the blow on the head," McLone was saying.

Van Kill's reply sounded almost disinterested. "The drawer Burke said was empty? That rather points to its being the murderer who stripped the files, doesn't it?"

Captain McLone grunted. "Miss Goff admits she pushed the drawer shut right after she opened the closet door, when she stooped over the body. That kept the concentration in the drawer. The closet itself was fairly well aired out . . . She still says she was calling at the home of friends until around midnight last night." McLone's voice was wearily ironical. "Her relations with them are much too formal for her to ask them to oblige with anything so low class as a murder alibi . . . What's that you say?"

"I said," Van Kill repeated savagely, "it's too bad her relations weren't formal enough for her to keep her damn gloves on."

"He compared himself unfavorably to Balaam," David told Echo ruefully. "Balaam had a sensible ass . . . He made me wonder if it wouldn't go better with me if I gave myself up before the cops figure it his way." David sat on the edge of Echo's desk and studied the toe of his pendant foot. "Echo, do you know what happens to your brain when you're electrocuted?"

"David, for heaven's sake! Mr. Van Kill doesn't think you're a murderer. Just because you made a silly speech last night——"

"He thinks I'll make an awfully good stand-in." David shook his yellow head. "Hal can do a better job than any of Harris's ghouls describing the way the current slams one's evil form against the cruel straps. I went and phoned this captain of gendarmes friend of his as soon as I could totter. Wanted to talk to him right away, but the fellow wasn't in any hurry. Said he'd call me later. I guess they do that."

"They do." Echo frowned, remembering. "Oh, David, if I'd only gone down and talked to you last night. I had no business to be so nasty about your speech, it was mean of me to refuse your flowers." Echo turned her head away for a moment. "The carbon dioxide was an unlucky coincidence . . . They'll see when they talk to you that you're not the sort of person who'd——"

"Commit a murder? They're not psychic."

"The sort of person who'd be stupid enough to make a speech about it beforehand," Echo finished. "Anyway, you hardly knew Betty Hargrave."

"On the contrary, darling." David's voice was grave, but he was hearing the concern in Echo's with secret delight. The girl had never been so nice to him. "I am just the sort of person who'd be smart enough to figure *they* wouldn't expect *me* to be so stupid. And knowing Miss Hargrave is all against me."

"They've arrested a woman named Goff from the Christian Cavaliers," Echo faltered. "They can't connect you——"

"Oh, but easily. She works for my Uncle Ben. Pough will have to say, and so will you," David tried to look into Echo's eyes and failed, "that I didn't know Miss Hargrave was working at the Cavaliers or why. But I might have found out that she was, and how would I feel—that is, how would the prosecuting attorney say I felt? Believing Miss Hargrave was one of those American Nazis and knowing she had more to do than anyone with keeping *Carnage* a jump ahead of the post office?"

"David!" Echo looked up and gasped. "Don't say anything about *Carnage*."

"Darling, I'm just telling you. Hal explained it all to me very clearly." The blond youth sitting on the desk seemed to shudder. "Very clearly," he said again. "I'm the obvious link between the Cavaliers and the Popub banquet, the only person who'd want to hit both *Carnage* and the Cavaliers. I can't prove I never heard of the Cavaliers until after the murder . . . Hal said to tell you all this because you'd think of it yourself and you weren't the type to worry easily."

"Thinks I've got a soft core, does he." Echo pushed back her chair and got to her feet. "Did you ever notice," she went on, stabbing at the desk blotter with a pencil, "that I was not exactly crazy about Betty Hargrave? And you know how I feel about the kind of exposé Mr. Pough had her working on. Sooner or later Mr. Pough will find himself associated with the people who start petitions to abolish Passion Plays . . . Hasn't it occurred to you," Echo threw down the pencil, "that nobody knows I stayed in my room after I got home last night? I can't swear you didn't phone me from somewhere near the Christian Cavaliers to make a sort of alibi for yourself—because you might have known I wouldn't come down and find out you weren't phoning from the lobby. And if I failed you completely by not noticing the time, why," Echo paused for breath, "so did you fail me. You don't know but what I was just on my way in or out of my room when you phoned. And the people at the London ——"

"Dear Echo." Montefiore swung his feet to the floor and put his arm around her. "We will face this per-ile together," he said. "The octopus tentacles of a sinister, cruel, and appalling destiny will not separate we two . . . Together we will be arrested, together we will stand trial, together we will go to ——"

Echo slid away from him at the sound of footsteps in the corridor.

"Jael?" Frederick Pough called as he opened the door.

"Jail," Montefiore answered. "Puns he makes. Miss Newman's real name does have an ominous sound. Particularly to a person in my position, likely to be arrested any minute."

"You're as well off as I am." Pough smiled in almost paternal fashion at the fair young man and the dark young woman. "I'm staying alone in our town apartment now, and my man doesn't sleep in. And while your speech last night was rather ill-timed," he told David, "so they tell me was my dropping a packet in the market yesterday."

A nice man, Echo was thinking. David had made a lot of trouble for Mr. Pough already. Mr. Pough had every right to be annoyed at seeing them together, but he wasn't. . . .

"It made me look suspiciously glum, you see." Pough crossed to the door of his private office and turned the knob as he spoke. "You at least were cheerful last night, Montefiore."

"Thanks," David said. "Send me a penny whistle when I'm pinched, will you? To charm the mice." He gathered up his coat, tipped his hat to Echo, and grinned at the head of Popub, Inc. "Better you should make quick with the lordly dish now, Jael," he said. . . .

"What on earth?" Pough asked when David was gone.

Echo never blushed, but she looked uncomfortable. "It's in the Bible," she said. "Mr. Montefiore teases me about it. The song of Deborah says Jael brought Sisera butter in a lordly dish."

Pough laughed heartily for the first time in two days. "You don't butter *me*, Jael. What else did your biblical ancestress do?"

Echo looked at him from under her tilted eyebrows and made a little mirthless noise in her throat. "When Sisera was asleep," she said, "Jael took a tent nail and a hammer and nailed him to the ground through the temples."

XXIII

"I SHOULD have included freedom of speech," the document examiner took the cup of coffee De Porta handed him, "when I protested my inability to guarantee David's safety without curtailing his freedom of movement. Imagine me chiding Paul Harris about his ancient peccadilloes," Van Kill gnashed his teeth lightly, "while David was swatting up his speech on the perfect crime."

"The coincidence is too perfect of course." De Porta was like a troubled bodhisat with his coffee cup held at an umbilical level on the palms of both hands. They were sitting in his dining room again. Van Kill had just come from the Matapan. From behind the double doors, where Edward had played the phonograph three days ago, came the swish of soapy water. It was five o'clock. The Sabbath was over and Mrs. Horowitz was removing the last traces of Yanni's fingerprint powder. Mrs. Horowitz did her best to set an orthodox example for the bookseller.

"McLone says, sure it's coincidence," Van Kill told him. "David's recommendation of carbon dioxide being followed by the murderer, the fact that Betty Hargrave was important to *Carnage* which David had it in for, and the fact that Miss Daisy Goff works for David's uncle. All curious coincidences which may join hands around David as soon as we deprive McLone of Goff."

"You offer me a distasteful choice between two injustices," De Porta said. "By concealing poor Miss Goff's alibi for the time of the murder I can temporarily postpone suspicion from my nephew."

"Poor Miss Goff!" The porcelain cup rattled on the coffee table and Van Kill turned to stare at the bookseller. "David's as innocent as a puppy on the beach. He didn't know company was coming when he chose to roll in the dead fish. What for a tin martyr are you, Ben? If that pestilential old besom had pawed over *my* private possessions——"

"David was among the last to leave the Popub Building after the

179

Carnage banquet." Van Kill changed his theme. "There's always confusion at those big wakes. Not everybody had manners and said good night to Pough properly. Therefore—until McLone checks and rechecks, we won't know just when everybody left."

Van Kill got up and walked to the fireplace, stared blankly at his reflection over the mantel, and began walking back and forth in front of De Porta.

"David hung around trying to get a kind word out of Miss Newman, who was huffy about his speech. She left when Betty did. Went down in the elevator with her and Pough, who found taxis for both girls. When Pough came back, David was making his departure on a note of gay insouciance. So David says."

Van Kill was speaking in a reflective yet jerky tone as if his desire to tell De Porta as much as he could were interrupted by random thoughts.

"That left Pough, Harris, Harris's switchboard doxy and a couple of others," Van Kill went on. "It doesn't matter. The point is that anyone, whether he left early or late, could have snatched the dry ice out of the cake box by the service elevator. And whoever wants to make a case against David will have to prove he knew Betty was going to the Cavaliers."

"Do the police think Miss Hargrave had an appointment with someone?" De Porta asked unhappily.

Van Kill shrugged, turning away in his walk. "She got Burke's keys only by chance," he said and thought immediately of how Ben's key had been planted for Goff to get as if by chance. "The point in David's favor is that he was with me at the time Betty left her apartment to go to the Cavaliers. She took a cab from the rank there, the driver knew her and reported as soon as he saw the afternoon papers. He swears there were no cars behind them when they crossed the park. She left the cab at the corner on Central Park West and walked from there. If she was followed at all, it must have been by someone who knew she was going to the Cavaliers' office and picked her up along the side street, don't you think?"

"Unfortunately," De Porta said, pulling himself to his feet and moving around Van Kill to the coffee machine, "David does not know what time he left you nor what time he reached Miss Newman's hotel."

"The crucial period, Ben," Van Kill shot him an appreciative glance. "It was around eleven-forty, I judge, when David left me. *But he walked*. On a cold wet night in evening clothes the dope says he walked! I am afraid that even if every night flunky at Echo Newman's hotel saw him against the clock, we will never prove that David didn't have time to drop in at the Cavaliers' office on the way. Not," the document examiner added softly, "unless my own impression of the time he left me is wrong. And it could be."

"Don't be a fool, Hendrik," De Porta said sharply. "David can consult a lawyer. It is a pity he refused to answer the phone this morning. I wish you had told me more when you called me— there is a way of pounding on his door. I assumed of course that *you* had *been* to his apartment."

David lived in the Village, a good half hour by subway from either the Otranto or the Cavaliers' office. Remembering that frantic period between ten and three, Van Kill laughed.

"I'm sorry if you felt neglected, Ben, but David's not the only innocent person who might be drawn into this affair."

"Poor Miss Goff," the bookseller demurred. "I could have told you she had an alibi if you'd told me she needed it."

"An alibi for the murder. Goff left her prints in your apartment between eleven-thirty when Horowitz left and 1:00 A.M. when you came home . . . She'd have been pinched anyway. Her evidence confirmed McLone's deductions about the time Betty was knocked out, but she didn't give it willingly. Remember, Ben," Van Kill flung out an exasperated hand, "it's not up to you. Whenever Goff wants to *she* can tell how she lurked, down in the warm shop, probably, though I wish it had been outside, waiting for Mrs. Horowitz to finish her nap and go home, so that she could let herself in up here and burrow through your cigars."

De Porta took the stogie he was smoking out of his mouth and looked at it with fugitive alarm.

"I'd have the place fumigated if I were you," Van Kill laughed and the tension between them vanished.

"What was she after, do you know, Hendrik?" De Porta was not resentful, he seemed almost to be blaming himself for having possessions about which a fanatic old woman could be curious. "Theater programs, opera scores, catalogues from art exhibits I'd forgotten going to, my boyhood diaries from Vienna, are a matter of taste perhaps, but *why* waste paper like old market predictions? My private accounts, when I know she cannot add?"

"None of those things, Ben. Something more like a confidential advertisement from your kosher butcher is my idea. With a Sir Hugh of Lincoln flavor, you understand, saying, 'Be discriminating. Darmenweh your local shohet will supply fresh Christian babies for Passover.'"

"Passover is in April, Hendrik. Don't be silly."

"You'll find she was after something more like that than getting you for evasion of income tax," Van Kill prophesied. "I have no time for Goff, Ben. When I wasn't worrying about David, there were as I said other people quite as vulnerable."

"I suppose you know best, Hendrik," De Porta said courteously.

Van Kill halted in front of the bookseller and arched his neck. "Damn you, Ben, I will not be misunderstood. When you were being weaned in Vienna, Lady Di was being tried for murder by a jury of her peers in Edinburgh. She's been using dry ice to keep mice out of her apartment and I didn't want her mentioning it to anyone who came around checking on Betty's movements yesterday and David's last night."

"When I was—" De Porta's black eyebrows climbed his forehead. "Hendrik, are you telling me Lady Diana Brown is the notorious 'Ladydee' who poisoned her lover with lucifer matches and ——"

"Steady, Ben. The verdict was that admirably specific privilege of the Scottish court, Not Proven. Meaning, as connoisseurs of murder know, not Not Guilty, but Well, You Got By With It. Lady Di came to my father in '17," Van Kill went on. "The code and cipher division was looking for someone who knew both Swahili and

German. He had photographs of the disputed Ladydee letters and recognized her handwriting. Having to think of Lady Di at this time is just an illustration of all the witch lights and wayside morasses to be side-stepped in any civilized murder case."

De Porta seemed to ponder this characterization of the death of Betty Hargrave. Then he said, "Writing thrillers is a kind of sublimation, I suppose."

"Excellent, since she sells them," the document examiner agreed. "She's had a full life since then."

"You speak as if she continued to remove people who stood in her way," De Porta protested, then asked, "Does she ever talk about ——"

Van Kill said he thought Lady Di's had been a full life in other respects than homicide. "I happen to know she was ranee of a two-elephant principality near Benares at one time. Knowing her early history, I sometimes compare myself to the individual who went to visit a family in which there had been a hanging. He had been cautioned to avoid mentioning anything like a rope and he found them all out in the back yard learning to twirl lassos."

"Diverting their minds." De Porta nodded under a wreath of cigar smoke. "Are you trying to divert me from David's troubles with the mysterious Lady Diana Brown? You did, you know. It is a secret to be treasured." Van Kill gave him an affectionate if not a particularly happy grin.

"You can sit beside her tonight at Edward's school show. He said you weren't very enthusiastic when he called you yesterday." Lady Di, the young man went on to remark, was honoring the occasion by wearing her hair. "Edward's at the hairdresser with her now, watching its application," Van Kill said, rising and preparing to leave.

"It was not lack of enthusiasm but bewilderment, yesterday," De Porta explained. "The lad said he was collecting 'a sterling family claque' and requested I wear 'any respectable neutral or allied decorations' I might happen to own. I take it we are all to be very grand."

XXIV

‸‸

AND grand they were. Edward felt that Lady Di's tiara offset the
fact that his surrogate family went home in an ordinary taxi after
the Webster show, and not in the prodigal grandeur of a town
car. And his Mithra tableaux had been for those on the faculty
whose culture permitted exactly the one in the eye that Edward
had intended . . . A very satisfactory evening, the Cameron heir
reflected, hopping up and down on the curb in his Phrygian cos-
tume.

While Yanni and the cab driver were getting the bull fastened
onto the back of the machine, Edward observed a gentleman who
taught history, his name was Throop and he was a deacon at Riverside, descend the front steps and march past them muttering
angrily to his good wife. A most satisfactory evening, Edward
thought. He attended Webster some afternoons because he considered school part of a normal boy's life, but he made no secret
of the fact that he had chosen Webster, less because of its teaching
staff, than because of its forge.

Inside the cab they were talking about him. Gratefully, because
the boy's doings covered less pleasant thoughts.

"My fault entirely," Van Kill had just admitted to De Porta.
"My, as you say, spasmodic biography of Julian the Apostate, and
my theory that if Julian had not been murdered, it would be
Mithraism instead of Christianity today."

The Honorable Diana was thinking that Hal's words had a
hurried anxiety behind them. With the exception of De Porta
the whole group was nervy and her unaccustomed coiffure was
wearing on her.

"And would there be Mithraic Minions instead of Christian
Cavaliers?" David inquired.

"So marvelous that with everything else your ward retains a

184

child's absorption in his own world," Echo put in. "None of our troubles concern him."

One could never be perfectly sure of that, Van Kill told her. "He's given me some bad moments in the past."

The document examiner had been more interested in winning Echo Newman's confidence during the course of the evening than in discussing the psychology of the phenomenally gifted child.

"We thought you showed a real professional attitude," David said when the boy climbed into the cab. "Yanni told us between the scenes of your stunt how you *borrowed* shepherds and an infant from other acts so that you didn't have to rehearse and give away what you were up to."

Edward settled himself on Van Kill's knee with a jingle of his sword belt and smiled kindly upon his elders.

"The show was supposed to be 'Christmas Through the Ages,'" he said as the car started. "And all the little dreeps began working up Manger Scenes of course. So I thought Christmas was Mithra's birthday first."

The boy inclined his head toward the rear of the cab as it swung around a corner. "The bull's tied on behind," he said. "It was the bull that gave it éclat, don't you think? I built him up with newspapers and flour paste and he——"

"He is too savage." Yanni, who thought the little kyrios was getting above himself, turned in his seat behind the driver and spoke a critical word. "In ancient art the bull Mithra kills to save the world is placid bull."

"A placid bull is Ferdinand nowadays," Edward replied reasonably. "He cost only $2.58, not counting the flour Yanni sold me wholesale. Why are we stopping here?"

"David and I have some business in this neighborhood," Van Kill informed the startled Montefiore. "Echo is perfectly agreeable and it's for your own good."

"Highhanded as hell, aren't you," David commented as the cab drove away from them down Central Park West. "Where are we going?"

"Place you've never been and I'd like to prove it," his friend replied.

This section beyond the elegant frontages of Central Park West was, as Frederick Pough had said, not quite a slum. In Greenwich Village these ancient brownstones with their sour little boxed-in back yards would be garnished with bright shutters and potted ferns and rent for outrageous sums. Here they deteriorate slowly and between the high wooden fences their back yards are full of washing and rusty lengths of pipe.

David knew these things in a general way, just as he knew that New Yorkers are almost never murdered in back alleys, because there are almost no back alleys in New York. The inaccessibility of the back yards around the Christian Cavaliers was a matter he was willing to take on faith. He said as much, following Van Kill into and behind the counter of Feinstein's Fine Delicatessen on Columbus Avenue, where the document examiner nodded to the proprietor's wife and bore west through its kitchen and storage rooms into the gloom of its back yard. There it appeared Van Kill thought they should climb over the fence.

"Stop your noise, Dizzy," his friend said. "You didn't think about your evening clothes last night when you went mushing out in the wet snow. If you had, we wouldn't be doing this."

At the other side of the fence Van Kill stood on an ash can, reached over to give David a hand up. "We're going to meet a lady," he explained as David landed beside him. "Now the one across here," he went on, skirting the sooty remains of a snowman and a broken-down baby carriage, "has a width of chicken wire on top."

It was like a dream of being an insect, crawling from one open crate to another, David thought while negotiating the chicken wire. "What kind of a lady?" he demanded.

"Hush," Van Kill said. "We're in the Cavaliers' back yard. Listen."

A cat yowled from somewhere near by. Now that he could see a little, David observed that they were standing in a fairly sizable backyard, surrounded on three sides by a fence perhaps six fee high, but seeming to measure more because it stood on ground sloping down to a wooden barrier of about the same height just ahead of David and Van Kill.

This small barrier evidently stopped the back end of the Cavaliers' alley entrance, David reflected. Above and beyond the little fence, between the two buildings which it joined, Montefiore could see a muffled shine of night light from the side street in the Nineties on which they had originally started out. And that building whose fire escape he could now dimly descry, must be the one in which the Cavaliers had their basement apartment. But it might have been a black abode in another world, so far as David was concerned. Van Kill *would* be seized by this mad notion to come around the back way.

They might as well stay there, Van Kill said, after the cat had again announced its yearning for companionship.

"You didn't use to have such *outré* tastes, Hal," David complained. "What kind of a lady do you have to go crawling on fences to meet?"

"Merrower," answered Van Kill, bringing it up full-throated and letting it die away with a verisimilitudinous quaver.

"You needn't be coarse," David reproved him, but his interest was piqued, and when Van Kill miaued again, David miaued along with him.

"You be still." Van Kill's face was only a white blob above the darker shadow of his body, but Montefiore felt the look. "You'll drive her away. She's coming down that alley, I think." There was a plaintive call from beyond the little fence and Van Kill replied in kind.

This episode lacked the tone of japes David had been a party to with Van Kill in the past. A little group of nerves began to creep up the middle of David's spine. He drew back somewhat, wondering if Hal had gone mad, and saw the moving shadow at his friend's feet.

"Hal, look there."

"My God," Van Kill said as the animal began to strop itself on his legs. "I'm better than I thought . . . Will you come down, Maureen?"

David did not consciously hear any sound from the top of the little fence, but he looked up and saw the largest alley cat in the world, sitting there against the sky. It was a black cat with a white face; David could see the straight line of forelegs and the silhouette of its lean shoulders. It evidently fought tigers because its ears were chewed to semicircles. It sat quietly on a fence in the middle of Manhattan and looked at them.

"I got your message, Hal," the cat said in a kind of throaty purr.

David could feel his wits settle back just in time. He knew about the cat woman.

Van Kill was telling her so. "He's perfectly all right, really, Maureen. Loves cats and is very quiet." The last two words were spoken with a certain emphasis. "You've heard of Miss Carty, haven't you, David?"

There had been a write-up of Maureen Carty in *Lo!* David remembered now, but he took Van Kill's hint and contented himself with a friendly, "Mmmmm."

"Well, I don't know—" The queer head turned nervously and the sinuous shadow on the fence seemed about to flee.

"I'll send you a grocery order for salmon," Van Kill promised.

She looked at him through the darkness for a moment and then folded herself down off the fence in a movement as effortless as water.

"I've been working this neighborhood for about a week now, but how did you know?" The gentle voice was articulated in a minor key as if she did most of her talking to cats. She seemed a very small person standing beside them, although she had seemed such a big cat on the fence.

At the age of twenty-one, after a succession of unpleasantnesses with managers about stray cats in dressing rooms, Maureen had abandoned a career as an acrobatic dancer to devote herself to homeless and abandoned cats. Since then by night she had worked the boroughs of Greater New York, gathering up the surplus feline populations and carrying them to the SPCA.

Once on the ground most of her shyness vanished, but she gave them only a part of her attention now. She interrupted Van Kill's reply to her question to miau enticingly across the yard.

"I . . . saw some of your salmon tins," he repeated. "Listen to me, Maureen, were you anywhere around here last night?"

"You must always bend the edges together after you've emptied it or some poor pusser might get his head stuck," Maureen told David, who was so emboldened by this show of confidence as to say, "Oh, yes." Whereupon Maureen dove between the two men and vanished. She came back in a moment, talking to the cat which had previously stropped himself upon Van Kill.

"Was a bad cat," she said. "Wuzza baddy. Making me chase him when I didn't want him. Was a bad interfering cat, wuzza baddy."

"Why don't you want him?" David asked, though Van Kill's annoyance was a palpable thing in the darkness.

"Fat cats, pet cats, mamma cats and bachelors," Maureen recited her credo. "I send them on their way. Sick cats, tom cats, bitch cats, starving cats, they go SPCA."

"But," David objected rashly, "the SPCA puts them in a——"

"They're frightened," the cat woman flared at him. "Hurt, diseased, and afraid, and they have nobody to love them. You're one of the fat cats."

David flinched, quite expecting to feel her claws.

"What would you know about being afraid? The Society puts them to sleep, the poor babies . . . It's a better death than most humans get."

"David, I told you," Van Kill murmured. "That fellow you have there," he addressed Miss Carty soothingly, "is a bachelor?"

"He'll never be a daddy," Maureen answered with refinement and instant good humor. "Belongs to a delicatessen," she addressed the cat. "Was a baddy though. Made me chase him out of this yard and step on the man's stomach last night."

"What man?" Van Kill caught her by the arm.

The cat woman wound herself up and out of his grasp with a breathy cry. "Don't you touch me," she said. "Hal, you know I don't let anybody touch me." There was an odor of catnip about.

"I'm sorry, Maureen. This is important. To me, anyway. *Where* was the man when you stepped on his stomach?"

"In that entryway of course." Miss Carty gestured casually behind her at the Cavaliers' alley. "I nearly sprained my ankle. I was chasing this rascal and I didn't look. How was I to know he'd come along after the girl and ——"

"Who came along?" Van Kill drew a deep breath. "Look here, Maureen," he said slowly. "This gentleman here, this nice, quiet gentleman, who loves cats, is ——"

"—going to send me a case of salmon?"

Van Kill continued on the same breath, "—in danger of being accused of murder if we can't find out who was around here last night."

"You mean people," Maureen said. "You know I don't notice people, Hal." She clucked to the raucously purring cat in her arms. "The man had a big plaid coat over him."

David emitted a startled gasp. "Paul Harris!"

"Don't suggest things," Van Kill hissed.

But Maureen twisted her body to look up at David and said, "Why, yes, I guess it was. I remember he came to see me. There was an article in a magazine and a lot of people came to see me, but it's not true I scare magistrates. *He* wanted me to notice about some *people* while I was hunting cats. I thought he looked familiar, but so many people have the same face."

Van Kill put a restraining hand on David. "Maureen," he said, "there's no light in that passage. You can't see that well in the dark."

"I turned my flash on him."

The sudden light which the cat woman produced from somewhere about her person lifted David Montefiore's attention completely away from her next few words. Even in the dark there were, of course, indications that her appearance would be eccentric.

The boots and denim trousers showing below full-skirted coat were probably practical. It was her hat, an outsize bowler fuzzy with age, crushed in the center, and adorned with a padding of white hair under its brim that took David Montefiore's horrified gaze. The round yellow eyes peering through the hair and the triangular features were what he had expected too. Maureen Carty would naturally look like a cat.

"No," she was saying, "I didn't see him following the girl. The girl scared the cat back after he jumped into the passage, so that I caught him in the back yard here. Not *this* cat, you understand, but one I wanted."

"Maureen," Van Kill groaned.

But the cat woman had become conscious of David's fascinated stare. She turned her own steady but peculiarly off-focus gaze on him.

"You mustn't look at my hat. It looks terrible." She removed the hat, dropping the cat to lift it off her ears as if it were a beehive, which it rather resembled. "Somebody threw a milk bottle at me last night," she said, indicating the deep dent on top of the hat. "I'll have to get a new one. The switch looks lousy too, doesn't it?"

"Well," David hedged because the hair on the hat did seem to have coffee grounds as well as cobwebs caught in it. "What's it for, besides making the hat stay on?"

Maureen Carty's own hair lay in carroty whorls above her ears, and above her ears she was clean. Seventeen years of cat chasing had touched her very lightly. None of the obvious reasons for which spinsters devote themselves to animal uplift applied. David was more interested in her than in his own possible plight.

"A disguise," she was telling him while she poked at the inside of the hat with her flash to take out the dent. "I go all sorts of places. Up trees, elevator shafts, chimneys, in sewers, empty stores, freight yards. Nobody bothers old ladies."

"*David.*" Van Kill's was the patience of one coaxing the village idiot to tell where he's hidden the key to the firehouse. "David, this may keep you out of jail . . . *Maureen*," he went on, "if you'll put your mind on these people you saw in the alley passage *back* of you last night, this gentleman will get you a derby of chilled steel with asbestos hair."

"I'd rather have a horse and wagon," Maureen replied, but she did after her catlike fashion put her mind to it then. A recognizable portrait of every cat caught the night before was not entirely avoidable. But with Van Kill blocking these tangents, the story amounted to this. . . .

Maureen was in pursuit of a cat which had leaped the fence into the Cavaliers' alley entrance at the moment when a girl turned into it from the street. Maureen had just climbed the fence, that's how she saw the girl. Maureen thought the girl had stepped into the space between the buildings to get out of the snow and wait for a date. Maureen didn't notice anything about the girl except she had white flowers in her hair and she was humming a tune and she scared the poor kitty back into Maureen's arms.

This cat having been sacked up for delivery to the SPCA, Miss Carty set out to capture another which had been hanging around in a back yard responding to her blandishments . . . Yes, *here,* in the Cavaliers' back yard. But not getting close enough for Maureen to lay her hands on. So Maureen remembered the girl and hoping her presence would again turn the quarry, chased cat number two in the same direction.

But *this* cat (who later proved to be Wuzza Baddy whom Maureen didn't want after all) kept right on going after he had sailed over the fence, and that was how Maureen happened to step on Paul Harris *in* the alley behind her, *by* the side entrance to the Cavaliers' office.

Van Kill put a question, one of several dozen, "*Why* did you stop if you were actually chasing a cat?"

The answer to this was, Maureen couldn't tell without looking if it was a human she'd stepped on. Maureen sometimes did a good turn to horses and dogs and if it was one of these, she would have had to call the SPCA ambulance. "So I saw that the girl had hit him on the head and I went back to the back yard."

No, it developed, she had not seen the girl hit Harris on the head. She had not seen anybody hit Harris. "*Somebody* hit him,"

Maureen concluded restlessly. "I lifted his hat and there was a lump on top of his head."

The cat woman had begun stepping from one foot to the other and uttering sidelong miaus before Van Kill had got her to say that Harris, when she saw him, was resting flat on his back by the side entrance to the Cavaliers' office with his overcoat spread on top of him.

"Would you swear it was Harris?" Van Kill asked her. "Would you go into court and say you saw him there?"

Maureen narrowed her yellow eyes at him and backed away. Her cats were calling her. "Why not?" she inquired on a lifted querulous note. "I hate him, don't I?" She flicked off her flashlight. She was gone, but her voice drifted to them through the blind dark, "I hate all men."

"You see," Van Kill said as soon as their badly needed drinks had begun to warm them, "how much we want a little bit of luck. Nowadays, thanks to our enterprising D.A., it's possible to put a lady of easy virtue on the stand for what her evidence is worth. But *we* get Maureen. Imagine her telling the prosecutor that she's willing to testify because she hates all men. Besides we bribed her with promises of salmon."

"We know Harris was there." David removed a sooty scarf from his neck and dropped it on the bar of the little Columbus Avenue tavern beside his filthy gloves. "You believed her, didn't you?"

"You can believe anything Maureen tells you," Van Kill assented, "if you keep your head. We know Harris was there last night, but so far it's just for your own information."

XXV

VAN KILL found Lady Di waiting up for him when he got home to the Otranto. She had dressed Yanni's arm and sent him to bed and she was primed to lecture the document examiner about the physical repercussions of losing sleep.

He ignored her bullying until after he had phoned the offices of the Homicide Squad. It was Mars who answered, speaking around his cigar, which disappeared from his enunciation after Van Kill had reported on the evening's work.

"You drag in the goddamnedest supporting witnesses," Mars howled. "Don't you know you can put at least three Manhattan judges off their bridge game for the evening by simply mentioning the cat woman?"

Swann was asleep in the dormitory, Mars said, after he had apostrophized Maureen Carty. When Detective Swann (who had been holding the hand of Thomas Burke practically all day) was a uniform cop, he had gone on a riot call she put in when a couple dozen of her cats got loose in a subway. And he, Mars, would be personally damned if he would wake the boy up to tell him that the cat woman had entered the case.

Sure. Sure, they'd send somebody right out to get Mr. Harris out of bed and look at Mr. Harris's tummy. Of course they could identify Miss Carty's footprint if she'd left one. They were wonderful.

"Now that was a hell of a good angle you gave Cappy on Goff this after'," Mars reproached Van Kill.

The document examiner, lying back in his study chair, caught the overtone of reservation in the sergeant's voice and grinned tiredly into the mouthpiece of the phone. "She didn't admit anything, though, did she? . . . After I thought it over, I sort of fancied she wouldn't admit the evidence of her prints in De Porta's apartment."

"Cappy says it *proves* she's holding out something about the murder," Mars declared aggrievedly.

Van Kill said he didn't know.

"Well, maybe Singer does. He's been going around here laffing to himself like a psycho, but he won't talk."

Yes, Van Kill told the Honorable Diana, the boys did hold out on each other. "Because they don't want to be kidded if a lead they follow up on their own fizzles, because they want the credit if it pans out, and to prevent leaks."

Lady Di said she thought her way of having investigating officers be just like a big happy family was better. "A reader knows when a policeman holds out information, either he's protecting somebody, or he committed the murder himself . . . Doesn't that apply to Harris, though?" she asked then, and went on before Van Kill could answer, "I hope that wasn't a good stud you lost out of your shirt, Hal. When you came in, I thought for a moment you'd been in a fight. It's too bad. A fight's so relaxing."

Van Kill helped himself to the sandwiches Yanni had left out. "Drug store studs," he said. "You don't realize, old dear, I'm the lower third in this layout. Since Yanni and Edward have been leeching on the war through the stock market especially . . . Yes, it does apply to Harris," he added. He was very tired. Lady Di had forgotten her determination to see to it that he got some sleep, and the idea did not occur to Van Kill himself.

"We can suppose Harris committed the murder and was struck down by someone who saw him, or that he was the relatively innocent bystander and it was the murderer who struck him," Van Kill said bluntly. "I incline to the latter premise. Like your fictional cops, Diana, he's protecting someone. But not for love."

Lady Di picked up her knitting and shook her gray curls. She had removed her formal coiffure and her head felt comfortably light. "I have never cared for the idea that a character can't be a murderer because he's a blackmailer," she said. "I don't think you can make it convincing . . . When you rushed in here the other day, so annoyed because Mr. Harris was having Miss Hargrave followed, I thought it was going to be very interesting. But I'm sorry now that David Montefiore started all this and got you into it."

Van Kill was used to the fictional fourth dimension from which Lady Di sat and looked at life. "It would have happened the same way if David had never thought of bothering about *Carnage*," he said. "On the face of it of course Betty was murdered because Pough put her onto the Christian Cavaliers job. But the Popub magazines have been running exposés and articles about subversive groups here ever since Munich. None of those investigators came to grief. Why did Betty?" Van Kill had one foot on the seat of the chair he sat in so that his shoulder was resting against his knee; an ungainly boneless posture of the sort he affected when he was thinking hard and too weary to walk.

Lady Di looked over her knitting at him out of bland eyes which long ago a King's Counsellor in Edinburgh had called fair as Eve's and perfidious as Lilith's and said, "Miss Hargrave was careless."

The grate fire, upon which Yanni had exercised his mountain ability to arrange the smallest amount of wood for the most flame, was down to a charred ember. It was past one o'clock. Betty Hargrave had been dead twenty-four hours, the young man thought. Out of the corner of his eye he watched the cat Eo walk with elaborate indirection to the coffee table, rear on his haunches like the Shetland he more or less resembled, and hook a sandwich. Eo would eat bread if he could steal it. Bread was bad for him. Van Kill did not reflect on the human application of this incident. He had had enough of cats for the evening. . . .

"No, but Betty was self-centered. In fact . . ." Van Kill put his foot down smartly and stared at Diana with repressed excitement.

". . . A more pigheaded, teeter-tottering, uncompromising-even-on-issues-they're-not-clear-in-their-own-minds-about lot I never saw clustered around a case before," he said. "And I think that's important . . . Betty was told not to take chances, she knew I'd have the Cavaliers burgled for her whenever she wanted it, but she had to do things her own way . . . And Burke, with his anonymous sympathizer phoning him market tips, why did he want to risk killing the goose by tracing its eggs? Did he have a plan? I think it was pure perversity."

Van Kill sprang up and walked over to the liquor cabinet. "Look at Echo," he said and came back without touching it. "If Echo had given David some encouragement when he started to drag a wing in front of her, he'd have forgotten about *Carnage* . . . But no." He rocked on his toes and harangued Lady Di, who nodded encouragingly and plied her needles with animation. "Echo has to do things her own way, which is to side with Pough in defense of *Carnage*, and still not do anything definite to discourage David. She's in love with him, isn't she?"

"Well, she's worrying," Lady Di said. "And it doesn't become her . . . Is Mr. De Porta one of your teeter-totterers? He seemed a very well-balanced character to me. He knows all about South American poisons. I was telling him about my next book."

Van Kill agreed that the bookseller was well balanced. "Not that Ben's directly concerned in the murder. He went to the opening of *Love Is a Bore* Friday night and was drinking slivovitz at the Café Royal during the critical period. But . . ." Van Kill went back to the liquor cabinet and this time remembered what he was about. "Ben persisted in nourishing a bitch that was biting his hand at the same time that he thought David ought to give over on *Carnage* because of Pough's anti-Nazi activities."

"It's an old-fashioned idea of course," Diana said as she tasted her drink. "Heaping coals of fire. Never thought much of it myself."

"Pough," the document examiner said, "obviously expects David to lay off *Carnage* out of pure racial gratitude when his Geyer item is published. He doesn't know David."

"I should think the Nazis would simply say it's a forgery the way they do everything," Diana Brown spoke through the knitting needle she was holding in her mouth while she measured the balaklava. "But if Mr. Pough thinks it would appease the mad Montefiore, why doesn't he publish it? Is he afraid he'll find out it *is* a forgery?"

"No," Van Kill said. "Nothing like that. I included Pough in my line-up of strong uncompromising characters. His letter has a clear pedigree from Wagner's stepfather's family and the Wagner specialist in London said it was genuine. I haven't seen it myself."

Diana Brown chuckled softly and freshened her drink. "Too strong and uncompromising a character to suit you, Hal?"

"There are quantities of rich collectors, Lady Di, manger-dogging onto documents they can't appreciate or even read," Van Kill said. "While their betters write footnotes full of scholarly bile and hope their legatees will be more generous. Pough's not like that, you understand. He merely intends to handle his Geyer item in his own way, as he does everything."

"Don't be petty, Hal. You must admit having his own way has paid him well."

"Allow me a moment's unreasonableness then," the young man said quietly. "It isn't very damn often I meet a head I'd be willing to see on the pillow next to mine for the rest of my life. And Pough put her on a job that killed her . . . Pough is such a virtuoso of efficiency he can control a quasi-criminal like Harris and look out for delinquency among Yanni's busboys."

Lady Diana Brown sniffed. "Without Miss Hargrave do you think he can control Harris's magazine?"

"No," Van Kill told her. "Do you see how sooner or later the edge of the argument veers toward David? If *Carnage*, minus Betty, gets quashed by the decency act, David will have won his battle with Pough. But his victory will be a sword turning against him . . . Ah, well." The document examiner stretched his legs toward the now completely dead fire and observed the affectionate paw marks which Maureen Carty's bachelor cat had left on his trousers. "I had intended to put off worrying about that until tomorrow. What I started to say was that you can't blame Pough for guessing wrong about David's reactions. I do it myself. David has made it plain that he loathes and abominates *Carnage*, yet his account of the *Carnage* dinner showed that he was not averse to cauld grue when he himself had the dishing of it. A matter of ambivalence, as I keep saying."

"It's a matter of Harris," Lady Di insisted. "I do think a person with blackmailing tendencies would pay blackmail rather than murder if he had the choice. Blackmail, he would understand. But if the person who had something on him wouldn't *take* blackmail, I'm sure he'd rather commit murder than be exposed."

"Good lord, Diana!" The sleepy young man with cat tracks on his trousers and a stud missing from his shirt bosom got to his feet and shook himself. "I didn't say Harris was the type who would never kill anybody. That's a horrid idea, *I* think. And usually when people apply it to each other they mean to be complimentary."

"I think you'd better go to bed, Hal," the Honorable Diana replied.

XXVI

LATE the next morning, which was Sunday, Van Kill met McLone at the offices of the Christian Cavaliers. Their major purpose was to try Burke's dictaphone record over on the Cavaliers' own machine. They agreed that the voice was completely disguised and Van Kill took off the wording on the Cavaliers' old typewriter.

"The financial advice is okay," McLone told him impatiently. "I've checked on that. 'Manipulation of Amalgamated Air will result in a two to three point rise on Thursday or Friday,' says this tin woodman, and he was right."

The document examiner yes-yessed the captain and kept on at the typewriter.

Before noon Van Kill was sitting on Burke's desk with his feet in Burke's chair, a copy of *The Lance* and a sheet of his own typing in either hand, reading aloud.

"'American business efficiency in control will insure that Christian objectives are soundly supported'—from the dictaphone," he said in a level voice. "'He who objects to the Buy Christian movement to restore a fair share of business to Christians drops his mask and stands revealed as an enemy of all Christianity teaches'—from *The Lance*."

McLone sank his chin deeper into his overcoat collar and said, "Urr."

"Listen to it unemotionally," Van Kill encouraged him, "and you'll hear an obvious stylistic relation. Burke evidently did."

"If we had the original typewriting of whoever sent those editorials to Burke, or if we could do something with the record direct," McLone fretted. "But the typewritten stuff is gone and whoever's talking on the dictaphone did it with a strip of cellophane in his teeth . . . Of course I can see how a person who could give off one sample of that short con could write the other, but you'll never prove it in court."

"You're letting your prejudices hamper you, Captain."

"Prejudices are hampering *you*." McLone got up, took a quick walk through the rooms with the air of one making a last survey. They would let Burke back in here tomorrow, the captain had said. . . .

There was a little satisfaction in knowing the Cavaliers would be starting about from scratch, anyway. For a certain mutual confidence between Burke and McLone had resulted in Burke's discovery that the police were not responsible for the fact that every scrap of printed matter in the mailing room had been swept away. Even the five hundred envelopes which Miss Goff had prepared for Saturday night delivery were gone . . . Burke had also remembered a new box of dictaphone cylinders was missing from the closet. He was definitely not happy about it. Poniatowski who had been temporarily assigned to keep an eye on Burke's Mosholu Parkway apartment reported that Burke hadn't stirred out of it except for questioning.

"Maybe waiting for his angel to flap his wings," McLone said, asking himself if Betty Hargrave's murderer had intended to protect the Cavaliers' major contributors or actually to put a crimp in their business. "You're leaning over backward because you're prejudiced in favor of so many of these people, Van Kill. You hand me reasons for Goff and Burke and Lee and that *Carnage* fellow Stock falling for anti-Semitic propaganda, but ——"

"All essentially rigid personalities," Van Kill murmured, quoting Edward.

"They're hard-working and deserving," McLone philosophized cop-fashion. "Or think they are. Anti-Semitism's an easier answer than admitting they're not so smart as the next fellow. This Lee for instance . . ."

The captain had had varying reports of Lee, he said, but he would lay to it that Lee, when found, would consider himself deserving.

"What have you got on Stock?" the document examiner wanted to know.

"I'm considering general background," McLone said testily. "The

way you're not. Stock's one of these little wiry birds who didn't
grow tall enough to suit him. Belongs to a gym and believes in the
Alger books. Investigated the *Bund* for Pough. And like Burke and
Lee he's burned up every time he looks at a person with inherited
wealth like Montfiore. And Monte —— "

"How do they account for a self-made type like Pough?" Van
Kill interrupted, though he had known that sooner or later the
captain would grind out this damning generalization about David.
"That he married the boss's daughter?"

"Sure, they overlook the hard knocks a successful man takes on
his way up," McLone snorted. "Pough for instance put himself
through law school out West and had a pretty tough time of it,
minding babies and furnaces and keeping up with his studies until
the last year. Then, just when he got a municipal court job, the
draft took him. You," McLone looked at Van Kill from under his
eyebrows, "were just a short-pants smarty when the postwar depression hit. Pough stayed here after he was demobilized and made
good. Could Montefiore build himself a fortune if he started from
scratch?"

Van Kill stood down from his perch and adjusted the crease in his
trousers reflectively. He knew how the background and personal
habits of every minor associate of Betty Hargrave were being
checked. David himself was to complain that McLone's moles
had dug up when he'd slapped his first governess and where.

"The point is," David's friend answered the captain's question,
"*would* he?"

"The *point* is," McLone picked up *The Lance* and threw it back
on the desk, "plenty of men like this Montefiore helped the Nazis
get started in Germany. They wanted to hang on to what they had.
The anti-Semitic program applied to the unassimilated Jews, they
thought. Not the old established families. So I'm not overlooking
anybody just because he's supposed to be anti-Nazi."

"It's a very nice little point you have there, Captain," Van Kill
said sadly. "Did Mr. Harris put you onto it?"

"We don't need nibbles from sewer rats like him," McLone
said. "Though Swann says Harris would be an answer to prayer—if

he didn't lie. Got an eye for detail's's good as any man on the squad . . . Everybody drags in the kitchen sink when he's defending himself on anonymous information. You didn't expect Harris to deny he was anywhere around here Friday night and let it go at that, did you?"

The telephone rang. "Even you," the captain told Van Kill as he crossed the room, "have only your own say-so for being home around twelve Friday night."

McLone said, "Yes, Bevan," into the mouthpiece, grunted twice on different tones, and hung up. "Funny," he said. "Harris's tail reporting that Harris has gone to call on Pough. It's not very likely a bid for Sunday dinner, do you think?"

Van Kill replied that Harris had had nearly twelve hours since Detective Swann's visit about the cat woman's story to think up something.

"Wonder if he thinks we've told Pough on him, about his alibi for Friday," McLone said with sudden anger. "There's no associate of known criminals so immune as those lousy crime writers. Horning in, swiping evidence, inventing evidence, warning suspects, framing dumb cops—that Harris is one of the ripest. By-lines! By jiggerty, I'd like to tell on him."

"Pough would tell *you* what he's been telling David." Van Kill took a set of loaded dice, bought for Edward's Christmas stocking and rolled them across the desk. "Crime Does Not Pay, but *Carnage* makes money." He seemed pleased in a simple-minded way.

McLone glared at him. The captain was not naturally an irascible man, but he never got enough sleep and the Borough of Manhattan had produced four homicides over the week end and two attempts now held for investigation with the imminent prospect of the victims dying in hospital. . . .

"If we had a reason to tell Pough that Harris had a Comet Detective Operative trying to get something on him and Miss Hargrave," the captain demanded, "don't you think Pough would fire him?"

"I should think Harris could tell Pough's not the philandering type," Van Kill said, wandering across the room to get his overcoat. "From what I've been able to discover, Pough made a very solid marriage into a family which wouldn't admit that kind of scandal existed. His wife's gone South for her health now, but ——"

"Exactly," McLone said. "His wife's ill. And just the idea of such evidence would be embarrassing to a man who'd married above himself. That's what Harris was hoping for, *I* think."

The phone rang again.

"You were right." McLone replaced it with dour satisfaction. "Bevan says Harris has left Pough's apartment and Pough has phoned, asking to see me at my earliest convenience. Want to come?"

"No," Van Kill said. "You won't listen to me declaim from *The Lance* and orate from Anon."

"Having subjects like Harris throwing up dust in odd corners isn't so bad when you deal with citizens who really co-operate," the captain retorted. "You'd better come along. Any ideas Harris has spilled to Pough aren't likely to be in favor of any of *your* friends."

"I'm a document examiner," the young man said with the tone of one who releases a long-contained grievance. "How will it look when this case comes to court and I have to testify that you didn't find me a document to examine?"

McLone was inwardly thankful that the document examiner had declined to come along. An interview with him sitting by would have been fraught with unease.

XXVII

"You understand I'll lose my job," Detective Singer said with a catch in his voice. He sat on the edge of Daisy Goff's bunk in the precinct lockup, his forearms on his knees and his hat hanging from flaccid fingers.

"Oh, dear." Daisy Goff clasped her bony hands together and unclasped them as she walked up and down in front of Singer.

She had refused to talk to anyone but Singer. Although she was eating the meals which De Porta had arranged to have sent in, Miss Goff would see neither him nor the lawyer he had offered to provide. She had refused to attend Sunday services this morning. . . .

"If you don't tell them what you did Friday night, these Jews will take away my job," Singer said and released two large crystalline tears, raising his head so they would course down his cheeks and not fall on the floor and be wasted.

"Oh, dear." Daisy wept too. "It's just like a net." She turned in her pacing and faced the cell door as if minded to throw herself against the bars. However, the cell door was as usual during the daytime standing wide open. Daisy had not chosen to take advantage of this opportunity to mingle with her sisters in misfortune. She had taken a dislike to the matron who had made her wash her hair. "We're both caught in a net," Daisy said.

"Is there anybody you'd talk to?" Singer asked with a sob. They had been over the list of Daisy's friends and acquaintances repeatedly and either Daisy couldn't trust them with her secret or she didn't want them to *see* her in *jail*. Dr. Van Kill fell definitely into the first class, a cuckoo who had fouled his own nest, she said, and Prof. Devries of International into the second. . . .

Daisy came over to Singer now and laid a hand on his crisp dark hair. "A saving remnant, that's what we are," she whispered. "We must be brave."

Singer sat quiet under the weight of Daisy Goff's emotions,

mingled his tears with hers, and wondered where Swann was. He looked up at Daisy and gave a hiccuping sob, putting his voice into it. She stooped above him, closed her eyes, and gave him a musty salute on the forehead.

"We must bear the torch," she said.

"Ah, hah, I *thought* so." Swann loomed in the cell door, snarling at them. "Smootching, huh?" He came into the cell and stood with his feet apart, leering at them. "I thought if I left you two alone long enough you'd try to cook up something . . . What's she been telling you, huh?" Swann extended a brawny arm as if to grab Singer by the coat collar and Daisy stepped in front of him courageously.

"Don't you touch him, you beast. He knows nothing that would interest *you*." Her breast heaved.

Huddled on the bunk, Singer peered out from behind Daisy with streaming eyes and thumbed his nose.

"Oh, no?" Swann sneered now. "You'd be surprised at what interests me. That little rat hiding in back of your skirts for instance . . . Come out of there, you! Wait until the International Bankers hear about this. You know what they do to rats! Come on out, I say!"

Crabwise, arms raised as if momentarily expecting Swann's fist to fall, Singer edged into the corridor.

"Be brave!" Daisy called after him. "Remember, the torch!"

She sat down on the bunk then, sat in the place where Singer had left the warmth of his body. She was trembling violently and conscious of a hard knot in the base of her stomach which she identified as apprehension for Singer. What would Swann be doing to him, Swann and a shadowy complement of vile beasts like him? Torture him? Beat him? . . . She could see Singer tied down somewhere, and the others, their whips rising and falling on poor helpless Singer . . . Rising and falling. Daisy Goff clasped her hands convulsively in her lap and whimpered at the idea and the sensation it gave her. . . .

Swann waited until Singer had washed his face before he said anything in particular. Swann himself could cry a little if necessary and he knew Singer's easy tears could not be turned off like a faucet.

"I'm going to keep that old girl in mind if she doesn't fry," he remarked. "Now you take that pair of models Darcy and Lenz were partying with Friday night, *they* thought I was swell. Girls that good-looking don't have to be so sweet-tempered either. But they even had a good word for Darcy though he loused up their brawl . . . She's a good quick cure for a swelled head, that Goff, I'll keep her in mind."

Singer leaned against the wash bowl, lit a cigarette, and looked at his partner through swollen lids. The first puff of smoke came out of his lungs on the tail end of a sob, but the second inhalation steadied him.

"'s a shame," he said. "That was a good act we put on for her."

Both men were silent, thinking of the waste. Thinking how less than a month ago they had sat up and cried all night with a rape murderer because he had never had a bicycle and somebody had stolen his dog when he was little, and washed him into the death house on an incidental confession.

"I don't make it." Swann shrugged. "Guess she's a psycho after all. She sure thought I was taking you off to do you harm—I thought she was nuts about you."

"She is." Singer grinned. "The way I been living in her pocket, the rabbi should revoke my *bar mitzvah* . . . It doesn't matter. She doesn't know anything, nothing we want to know." He set his hat at an angle and was almost his chipper self again. "What about Darcy and that little fotog?" he wanted to know as they left the precinct and headed for the subway.

"Darcy passed out before 1:00 A.M. before the party'd got well started," Swann said impatiently. "They had to get the janitor out of bed to help carry him to a cab," he added, brushing Lenz and Darcy aside for good. "Now that old girl of yours," he went back to the subject that interested him, "is psychopathic, *I* say. What we need's a doc to ask her when she stopped sucking her thumb."

Miss Goff was no crazier than Swann, Singer asserted. And where would they find a Gentile psychiatrist for her anyway? "She's just average. This big secret of hers proves it . . . It wouldn't appeal to you," Singer continued with his low-voiced semi-ventriloquial articulation as they walked along and, dodging a pedestrian at Broadway, Swann lost part of it. ". . . But me I know plenty of Protestants, Lutherans prob'ly," Singer glanced at his partner, "who believe the same about Catholics."

Swann, knowing that Singer, if interrupted, might still dry up, controlled himself. And he had been a little jealous of his partner's private joke.

"She read it in a little pamphlet, see? And if it's in print, it's bound to be true, isn't it? From Seattle this was, not one of the Cavaliers', all about the Jewish Menace in New York. Here I suppose they know about the Menace in Seattle. The oldest synagogue in America is the Portuguese on Seventieth, no? And Benjamin De Porta belongs to it. She adds two and two. He's rich, influential —somewhere in his apartment must be records, notes, bills of sale, evidence about them anyway, if she can find it, and——"

"What? Find what?" Swann barked in exasperation finally, although Singer was always this way. "Evidence about what?"

"Guns," Singer replied mildly. "Under the synagogue. Guns to kill all the Christians when the time comes. They been collecting them there since the American Revolution."

XXVIII

"WHAT you have called my willingness to co-operate," Mr. Pough smiled at his caller, "might be laid to business expedience. However, I lost a valued young friend in Miss Hargrave as well as an almost irreplacable employee. I know that sooner or later your force will come upon this matter and clear it up, but meantime Mr. Harris's conviction of Mr. Montefiore's guilt may circulate among my employees. . . ."

Tacit between Pough and McLone was a mutual appreciation of the character of Paul Harris. The captain had also absorbed Pough's wordless warning that nothing about the character of Paul Harris which did not interfere with his editorial proficiency was of interest to the chief executive of Po Publications, Inc.

"Naturally, sir." McLone looked up from his notebook. "Now, just to be sure I've got it straight for the record: Mr. Harris told you this morning that, after the banquet Friday night, and at the time when you were down below seeing Miss Hargrave to a taxi, Mr. Harris says he saw Mr. Montfiore come around the corner from the service elevator where, along with other kitchen refuse, the container for the ice cream cake served at the dinner and the dry ice in which it was packed, had been placed . . . Mr. Montefiore was carrying a box measuring perhaps nine by twelve inches and wearing what Mr. Harris described as an angry determined expression, but you, Mr. Pough, as previously stated, while you saw Mr. Montefiore down below in front of your building, did not notice that Mr. Montefiore had any box . . . Is that right?"

"Correct," Pough said. "Do you always use such long sentences in your reports, Captain?"

"A matter of early training, sir." McLone savored the Havana Pough had given him and permitted himself an unofficial chuckle. "When I was a straight-backed lad, my old sergeant used to say a report you couldn't make in two sentences wasn't ready to give.

We do things differently nowadays . . . Mr. Harris didn't mention the color of the box or what kind it was, did he?"

"He wasn't sure," Pough said reflectively. "Gray or tan or perhaps brown, he told me. Mr. Harris is very observant of extraneous details. It's peculiar he shouldn't remember."

When McLone told him about it, Swann said it was not only peculiar, but downright bad judgment of Harris not to remember the color of Montefiore's box. "Harris is the kind of guy who notices necktie patterns without knowing it," the detective remarked as he set to work trying to locate Montefiore by phone.

He was found through locating Van Kill, who was lunching with him at the Matapan. "I'll bring him right along," the document examiner promised.

"God, what a pair of dudes." Mars, sitting on the window ledge in the squad room when the Van Kill-Montefiore taxi drew up on Twentieth Street, hoisted the sash and shouted down something about the duchess having moved.

The squad room was nearly deserted. Most of the men on duty were, like the evening's potential murderers, taking Sunday afternoon naps in the dormitory. Mars and Swann had got tired of talking to each other.

"Maybe they look fancy to *you*," Swann said as Van Kill waved his cane at them and drew David, who was disposed to stand and goggle up at the third floor, across the sidewalk. "You wouldn't want to tangle with either of that pair without putting down your bundles. The doc is heavier and in better condition, but the yellow-headed boy would remember to use his teeth."

Mars rather obscurely desired to be told whether Swann was telling him? Mars was a contemporary of McLone, though, having avoided responsibility, he looked younger. A remarkably thin man, he wore the thick shoes, derby hat and cigar of the traditional plain-clothes man and, partly because of his eyeglasses, contrived to look like a parson on the loose. A sardonic individual with keen intuition and mordant whimsy, he was a particular friend of Van Kill.

"I shall now mind read," the document examiner announced when he and David had climbed up to the squad room. "You want to see Mr. Montefiore because you have discovered that he has been dabbling in Amalgamated Aircraft. He didn't know it himself until I told him, because he leaves sordid commercial matters to his uncle."

"It's not that at all," David, still a little breathless from the stairs, protested absently. He was more interested in seeing the squad room where Van Kill had told him the men on duty sat around fretfully waiting for somebody to kill somebody so that they could exercise their profession. "I have good ideas about the market, but Uncle Ben doesn't trust me."

As a mind reader Van Kill was a variously qualified failure, Mars said. And after Swann had escorted David into McLone's office and closed the door, the sergeant made a kind of explanatory challenge.

"Name one citizen in this case who hasn't been fluttering his damn wings in Amalgamated Air," he said. The two men sat down at the long center table together and while Van Kill thoughtfully looked for cigarettes in all his pockets, Mars wedged his hard hat over one eyebrow and waited for the kickback. . . .

The document examiner was successively surprised, pleased, and annoyed with himself for untimely worry. If a lot of people in the case had bought the stock which Burke's anonymous tipster had recommended, then Amalgamated Air as a clue was all cold.

"Me," Van Kill said, answering Mars' question.

"I wouldn't be too damn sure," the sergeant told him. "Look at your friend. His uncle operates for him, he only collects. It's getting to be like '28-'29, the boys tell me. All sorts of little investors coming to life with defense industries."

"Interesting," Van Kill said, "and significant probably. Paul Harris and I are alike, I venture to say, in that we prefer to throw away our money on something that runs or rolls." He took Edward's Christmas dice out again and laid them on the table.

Mars repeated his caution against arrogant certainty. "Harris throws his money away on the dogs, but what he gives to that little squirt Stock to invest for him usually has pups."

"So Stock dabbles in—never mind." Van Kill rolled his seventh eleven under the sergeant's increasingly dubious eye. "Who else in the Popub layout is impatient with the fruit of his toil?"

Practically every unsanctified one of the lot they were interested in, Mars said. "Even that blonde pushover in Harris's reception room . . . Burke, for some reason, doesn't want to talk about it, but the Popub lot are talkative as hell. So it looks as if they had all done well with their air except Pough. He got caught and had to buy on the rise."

"Hard luck," Van Kill commented without sympathy. "He didn't take the same path as his lambs."

"Oh, it's Stock, the dear lad, that most of 'em take advice from," Mars said. "Except that Newman girl, I guess, and of course some people would say she came by her talent natural . . . I'm only telling you this," Mars moved his cadaverous body out of his chair, "to save you the trouble of finding it out yourself. We haven't had time to check on it yet anyway."

Mars crossed the room to his locker and returned with a fresh cigar. There was a tradition that Mars's cigars would lay any one but Mars low, and that even Mars showed the effects. The sergeant did not offer one to Van Kill.

"I never quarrel with the leg work you boys do," the young man said genially. "Cavalier Burke may tell you more if you tell him how freely this Air has been circulating. At present I imagine he feels that, if you connect his True American dictaphone voice with the murder, as I hope you will, it will be equally embarrassing to admit taking or not taking its advice about buying Amalgamated Air."

"A kind of accessory if he bought, an indication of foreknowledge of the murder if he didn't?" Mars balanced the cigar in his teeth as he pronounced the words. "Too damn entirely subtle. Why are you so hot to prove the Cavaliers' True American and the dictaphone voice are the same?"

"Because if you identify the voice, you'll have your murderer," Van Kill said. "What have you got against George Stock?"

"Didn't you know?" Mars took his cigar out of his mouth and turned the speculative gaze of a dissipated raven on it. "I like him. Too sweet to be wholesome as they say. What's all this fuss about Harris? A bad boy and we all know it, when Stock's got no better an alibi for Friday around midnight at all. Working by himself in a walk-up apartment, he says. Why, it fits him like a glove! He hated Hargrave, I don't like the tone of his voice when he mentions Miss Newman, and he's got a plaster bust of Napoleon above the door of his dark room."

"Subtle, am I?" Van Kill asked.

Because Swann had inferred that Harris's failure to provide an exact description of the box which Montefiore was supposed to have carried away from the *Carnage* banquet proved there was no box at all, McLone was a little taken aback by Montefiore's remembering it perfectly.

"The box was green," David said, "a kind of fetid color you know, tied with that tough fiber ribbon that has holly berries printed on it, on account of Christmas."

To be sure he had gotten it from the pile of refuse by the service elevator. "That was where I had put it," David explained, looking from McLone, who was sitting erect at his desk, to Swann, who had his heels hooked over the rung of his chair and appeared half asleep. The blond youth resembled a collegian with a clear but wary conscience who has been called in by the dean, Swann thought.

"You told me yesterday that you did not remove anything from the collection of trash by the service elevator," McLone said, his eyes on a typewritten page before him.

"No," David said politely. "No. You asked if I took anything pertaining to the dinner off the garbage pile. And I said—why didn't you just say, did I take the dry ice? Then I told you I didn't take any dry ice, or if you insisted, anything pertaining to the dinner.

You didn't ask if I took anything of *mine*. And the box was mine, that is it was Echo's, only she got angry afterwards and I——"

"Mr. Montefiore," McLone exchanged glances with Swann, "would you mind telling us what was in this box of yours?"

"Some lotus."

"Some what?" McLone's voice had the same tone of dogged patience, but his eyes were points of concentrated suspicion directed at the elegant young man.

"Lotus, you know—" David laughed nervously. When Van Kill turned that sort of gaze at him, David was accustomed to shriek, "Don't look at me like that!" But he hesitated to do this now. "Not to *eat* of course," he said and the captain tilted his head toward Swann whose shift of position was a sign he wanted to speak.

"Flowers," Detective Swann said. "He means he had a box of flowers."

McLone dropped his eyes to the pad on the desk. "Would you mind telling us about these flowers, Mr. Montefiore?"

"Do you mean about the man in Florida who has the swamp where they grow?"

Police officers know that most people become voluble when the sort of pressure David had endured for a moment is lifted. But McLone and Swann learned more than they would ordinarily have expected to about the cultivation of Egyptian lotus in the United States, about the florist on Sixth Avenue, who handled them sometimes, and about how the big thick-stalked golden blossoms had, it was regrettable to remember, looked frightfully phony in the girdle of the silver gown which Echo Newman had worn to the banquet.

After the banquet Echo had been annoyed and had refused to take the box home with her. Whereupon David had tossed it on the trash pile by the service elevator. But he had experienced a change of heart when he was leaving and had taken it with him. Mr. Montefiore had gone to call on Dr. Van Kill then.

Did he think Dr. Van Kill would remember his having the box?

No, David said, because Mr. Montefiore had not intended to say anything about his disagreement with Miss Newman, and Dr. Van Kill would have known about it immediately if he had seen the box. So Mr. Montefiore had *left* the box on the private stairs which led to Dr. Van Kill's penthouse from where you got off the elevator. Wasn't that natural?

Natural, perhaps, the detectives agreed, but unfortunate. Mr. Montefiore would likely have kept the box out of sight if it had contained something less innocent than flowers.

Carrying the box then, David had walked the cold wet streets to Echo's hotel near West End Avenue.

"In case it becomes advisable to find someone who saw you walking during this period, had it occurred to you that a man of your appearance in evening dress, carrying a bright-colored box would be more noticeable than one who wasn't?" McLone asked with gentle reproach.

"I don't see how anybody'd notice the box if they didn't notice *me*."

The box, McLone explained still more gently, might if they could trace it, be called circumstantial evidence in David's favor. He did not consider it necessary to say that only a defense attorney would think so. McLone at this time was quite convinced of David's innocence. It was not until later, when David had managed to do as many as possible of the things a man with enemies can do to make himself look bad to the police, that McLone felt otherwise.

"I'm sorry I didn't keep the flowers then," the elegant young man said regretfully. "After I talked to her on the phone at the London Miss Newman still didn't want them, you see. So I threw the box in a DSC can on Broadway just before I flagged the taxi I took downtown to meet my uncle. . . ."

The Commanding Officer of the Manhattan Homicide Squad and his detective sat back in their respective chairs and looked at each other. The desk clerk at the London had admitted such a very cautious remembrance of seeing Montefiore in the lobby

some time after Friday midnight that McLone had no hope of
his recalling a green florist's box.

"Just the same," David went on more brightly, "it goes to
show how amazingly thorough you people are. I can't imagine
how you found out I took it off the trash pile at Popub in the first
place. I'm sure there wasn't anyone around who noticed me going.
Everybody was in the gents' cloak room as I remember (ordinarily
it's just a little reception room, you know, corresponds to the one
Carnage has on the floor above) listening to a joke Mr. Harris
was telling. I couldn't see him of course, but they were all laughing
so his voice was loud enough for me to hear him while I waited
for the elevator . . . About why the bus conductor wanted the
lady with the marmoset to pay two fares. . . ."

Peter Swann checked the box of flowers with Echo Newman
while McLone engaged Montefiore and Van Kill in polite conversation in the squad room. The thing was accomplished without
trouble, but when Swann emerged from telephoning, Van Kill
asked him to call Miss Newman back and tell her Mr. Montefiore
was on his way to take her to the Philharmonic.

"Hell, no," Mars said after the pair had gone. "That Bond Street
cowboy couldn't make up a lie like that. Ordinary working clay
like us don't realize what carrying a package means to a citizen
like Montefiore. A goddam crisis, that's all."

"Maybe I should have got Singer in there too," McLone said
doubtfully, but Swann shook his head at this.

"Singer's folks came from Pinsk," he explained and left it to
Mars to elaborate:

"They're both Jewish, but how confidential do you get with an
Orangeman, Cappy?"

"All right, all *right*," McLone snapped. No one but Mars pre-
sumed to call him Cappy to his face, but he suspected some of the
squad did so behind his back. "If you're going to make anybody
carrying dry ice out of the Popub Building Friday night, either
in a box, on horseback or in his bare hands, you're going to have
to scratch harder. If we believe Montefiore and his girl about the

green box of flowers which Harris *couldn't* have seen Montefiore carrying away, what do we say about Harris's box, which was gray or tan or maybe brown that he says he saw Montefiore take?"

"I say we keep *that* box under our hats," Swann answered. "Harris saw *somebody* with a box come away from the trash pile. Somebody who feels perfectly safe now . . . So Harris arranged for us to get just enough secondhand so we'll soften up this prospect for him. So by the time Harris goes around to the guy he really saw and puts in for a contribution to disremember, the poor bastard will fall on his neck with gratitude . . . I say we sit on this box, watch Harris, and see what happens."

"Nothing is what will happen," Mars opined. "All his tails say he knows he's being watched. You got anything more on that fat doll of his in the Seventies, Cappy?"

"Name's Morna Maye," McLone answered, shuffling papers. "Harris hired the apartment last week and went to see her there yesterday morning. Since then he's been living like a monk. Point is we had the tail on him for anyway two hours before he heard of the murder. Whether he knows he's being watched or not, it's plain he thinks he ought to be."

Sergeant Mars and Detective Swann understood the glow of placid satisfaction which the captain's features assumed as he contemplated Harris's narrow existence. "He can't stand it long," McLone said. "I believe you're right, Swann. If we just watch Harris, he'll *make* something happen."

At the moment Mr. Harris was verbalizing in front of the mirror in his bedroom. "Was it Montefiore I saw, or wasn't it? Why'ncha *ask* me?"

Mr. Harris was rather drunk. He had eaten a lonely dinner in a tavern and come back to his lonely apartment with two bottles obtained on the way. "Whyncha ask me?" He left the mirror and went into his living room to look into the street.

Ordinarily Mr. Harris was content with his apartment and his own company in it. Its location on the top floor of a converted private dwelling gave him a feeling of security that he sometimes felt the need of and it reminded him of Paris. He had floor cushions, a mirror over his bed, and a few well-chosen lithographs to enhance this latter impression. Mr. Harris's living-room window was a cosy bay whose carved gingerbread canopy usually gave him a *quartier Latin* feeling too.

But not now. Standing at his window now, Mr. Harris could not see McLone's plain-clothes man, but he knew the man was there. The angle of the French gable which held the window was in fact such that Mr. Harris could not see the street without standing close to the pane. "Can't see *me*," Mr. Harris growled at the invisible watcher below.

When he sat down to read here, he could see nothing but sky. Opposite him was an empty lot where an apartment house had recently been torn down and the nearest window facing him was that of an empty rear flat in the next block.

But today Mr. Harris's physical privacy seemed to accentuate the fact that nosy cops were interfering with his private affairs. He was even doubtful about using his own telephone, a fact which would have warmed McLone.

"How would I know what was in the box?" he went back to ask the mirror. "Did I *see*?" Bracing himself with one arm, Harris leaned on the dresser top and looked himself in the eye. "Think you got something on me, doncha? Holding it over my head."

Through the mists Mr. Harris's little black eyes considered their craftily triumphant expression and approved. His elbow bent suddenly and the editor of *Carnage* rested his lower ribs on the dresser edge. In this position, as if leaning forward across someone's desk, he whispered, "Everybody knows, even the cops know, how I notice things. I remember afterward, if I care to. . . ."

Mr. Harris brought up his free hand abruptly and rubbed the thumb and forefinger together under the nose of his reflection. "What if I don't care to?" he asked the mirror. "What's it worth to you?"

XXIX

~~~~~~

ONE of the fascinating things about New York City, Edward Cameron liked to remark, was how people minded their own business. "You have to go out of your way to attract atention," was the way he put it after listening to his guardian summarize the alibi situation for Ben De Porta, calling at the Otranto Apartments expressly to hear Van Kill.

On Sunday night, forty-odd hours after Betty Hargrave's murder, there was still only a handful among her Cavalier associates and those who stayed late at the *Carnage* dinner who could satisfactorily account for themselves for Friday around midnight. These were: Poynton Darcy the crimescribe, Louie Lenz the photographer, Paul Harris's receptionist Miss O'Bryan usually called Baby, Thomas Burke and Daisy Goff. Those who wished to include De Porta in the list of suspects because of his relationship to David Montefiore might include the bookseller in the company of those with alibis. "A fine lot of people," Van Kill told him warmly.

For the non-alibied, one had only to consider the ease with which city apartments could inconspicuously be gotten into and left by their tenants. Where walk-ups like those of Stock and Harris were concerned, it was obvious. Of loftier edifices with bat-eyed attendants (like those inhabited by Echo Newman, Frederick Pough, and for that matter Hendrik Van Kill) the document examiner said:

"Doormen and elevator operators are supposed to keep out undesirables and notice strangers. Notes and comment on what time tenants come in or out do not swell the Christmas largesse."

Meantime, Van Kill added, the police were waiting to see if the dawn of the working week would produce Mr. Richard Lee. "I would not wish the son any more bad luck than he deserves, but if, having been bumped by a hit-run, he should rest unidentified in some suburban hospital for a week or ten days, it would be very convenient for me . . . But I look for no such luck. . . .

The luck of apprehending a citizen wanted for questioning was not anticipated by Officer Ignatius Loyola Gallagher, who was on duty again in and about the offices of the Christian Cavaliers on Monday morning. "New light on the murder of Miss Elizabeth Hargrave is anticipated when all members of the Christian Cavaliers business promotion agency return," the morning papers had said. A man who has already left town for the week end when a murder occurs at his place of business may have a dozen excuses for not returning. He may not have read the papers. Mr. Lee was therefore not a suspect. Not yet.

However, if he should develop into a suspect, it would look nice on the record of whatever cop happened on him first. On such fortuitous items promotions are built. Gripping pessimism firmly in his conscious mind, because he was by nature a hopeful man, Officer Gallagher strolled out of the Cavaliers' side entrance a little before ten. He stood just beside the spot where Maureen Carty declared she had seen Paul Harris lying with a bump on his head and looked toward the street. The fact that Mr. Thomas Burke had not yet come striding down the little walk confirmed Officer Gallagher's belief that Burke was sitting in his apartment on Mosholu Parkway hoping that Lee would phone him before he talked to the police. . . .

A fine place for any kind of monkey business, Officer Gallagher reflected again. There were no windows in the side wall of the adjoining apartment and the little fence which blocked access to the yard behind the Cavaliers' building was anyway six feet high. Gallagher left the alley doorway, walked back to the fence, and measured himself against it. When he turned and faced the street, he saw a handsome sick-looking young man step cautiously along the narrow passage toward him.

Officer Gallagher recognized that Mr. Lee was not trying to sneak into the Cavaliers' offices. He was walking easy to spare his head. Hangover, Gallagher observed to himself. A worse hang-

over than Burke had had on Saturday . . . Mr. Lee saw the uniformed cop standing against the fence, but he closed his eyes against
the vision and kept going. Officer Gallagher followed him through
the vestibule and into the Cavaliers' mailing room.

"Hello?" Lee stood in the door of the inner office and called in
non-vibrant tones. The bare desks and tables evidently told him
something. He faced around and seemed to believe in Gallagher
this time, for he spoke to him.

"Has there been any trouble?"

"You will be Mr. Richard Lee?" Gallagher went to the telephone
and dialed his precinct.

"Somebody pinched?" Lee asked. His features were pale and as
expressionless as if the facial muscles were paralyzed.

"Gallagher talking," the young officer told the desk sergeant and
announced the arrival of Mr. Lee.

There were two detectives from Twentieth Street at the precinct
now, the desk sergeant said. "Hold him."

"Our business is perfectly legal," Lee was protesting, *Burke said*.
Perfeckly legit'mate. Did Burke—did youall pinch Burke?" Lee sat
suddenly in Burke's desk chair and his gaze traveled up Gallagher's buttons to his face. You could almost hear his eyes grate
in their sockets, the young cop thought. "You gonna pinch me?"
Lee asked.

"They just want to ask you a few questions at the precinct,"
Gallagher said carefully.

"Well, where is everybody? Why's nobody here?" Talking jarred
Lee's head. He took out his handkerchief and wiped his face.

Officer Gallagher had recently attended a lecture on interrogation
at the Brooklyn Police Academy by a Detective Inspector from the
West Coast. (Blushing, squirming and perspiration were indications
of nervousness, the expert had said, but need not be interpreted
as signs of guilt.)

"Miss Goff's in jail," the officer saw no harm in telling Lee.

Lee took off his hat now and wiped his forehead. "In jail too?"
he croaked. "Miss Goff?" He put his hat back on, gripped his knees
as if to steady both hands and knees, and seemed to huddle into

his overcoat. (Pallor, tension, and cold sweat meant shock or fear and were *much more* likely signs of guilty knowledge.)

Lee licked his lips. "Where's Bet—where's Miss Hargrave?" he asked . . . *Dry mouth,* Officer Gallagher thought. He could almost hear the keen-faced man from San Francisco saying, "A subject displaying such symptoms is 'hot.'"

"Miss Hargrave?" Officer Gallagher prayed he was doing the right thing. "Oh, they was supposed to put her in the baggage coach on the Commodore this morning. I guess she's pretty near to Albany by now."

Lee stared at the policeman. "Baggage coach . . . Betty? No! No, officer. Say it ain't so—say it's not." Richard Lee's handsome features became unrelated entities and his face went to pieces. "She's not, she can't be," he cried. He attempted to stand, his knees buckled, and it was only because Gallagher caught him that he did not fall full length. He was crouched on the floor, holding on to Gallagher's hand while he implored the officer to say it wasn't so when Swann and Singer walked in.

"I always heard Nazis were inclined that way," Swann commented.

"He's hot," Officer Gallagher whispered proudly. "I bet he'll tell you anything."

Singer watched Richard Lee pull himself up into his chair and sit there drawing long hiccoughing breaths and looking at the two detectives numbly. "That guy's not hot," Singer said. "He's just scared."

Everybody who talked to Lee that Monday agreed he was scared, but opinion varied as to whether the Junior Cavalier's fright was connected with his refusal to talk. Mr. Lee himself said he couldn't tell where he had been from Friday to Monday because of a highly respectable lady whose name he couldn't bring into this. Nobody believed him.

It was unfortunate that no one really *liked* Lee for the murder. If this had happened, he would have had a champion on the Homicide Squad, and being detained for questioning might have been as easy for him as it had been made for Miss Goff. Yet in contrast to her Lee was co-operative and polite to everyone.

He had a bad time at the Tuesday morning line-up because Captain Levy in the announcer's pulpit was half Irish and wanted to know if Mr. Lee wouldn't at least tell the detectives assembled the nationality of the lady whose name he was protecting. Captain Levy mentioned a number of nationalities . . . At Center Street, when he was mugged and printed, several cops agreed that Lee was certainly what Lombroso meant by a criminal type.

The young man either didn't know, or was afraid to tell any more than Burke already had about the Christian Cavaliers. His whole attitude toward Burke was peculiar and he was only sullen when the Number One Cavalier came to see him and shouted at him not to be a fool.

"I can't help you," Burke told Captain McLone with apparent honesty. "He scares up a lot of his own prospects. Meets 'em at parties and like that. It's his job of course."

It was Swann's belief that Lee's refusal to tell where he had been, to let Burke send him a lawyer, or to co-operate in any way with Burke was a sign that Lee wished to wash his hands of the Cavaliers. "He's a nice social-minded, two-tasseled boy from the South," Detective Swann said. "He wouldn't have gone into this racket if he'd expected any violence to happen."

There were two other new developments early on Tuesday. Bertram the night elevator boy at the Otranto seemed to remember that Mr. Montefiore had had a package when he called on Dr. Van Kill the Friday night previous . . . and Mr. Luke Laros, the Sixth Avenue florist, recalled Mr. Montefiore's purchase of lotus vividly. Sure, absolutely the blond young man had often talked about lotus to him, Mr. Laros declared . . .

The newspapers tossed Lee up Tuesday morning and dropped him to the back pages by night . . . "They're leery," McLone said unhappily. "Since the Christian Fronters practically got acquitted of treasonable activities as if it was candy stealing, they don't dare land on a little thing like the Cavaliers operating in restraint of trade. What's needed," the captain shook his finger at Singer who happened to be within range, "what's needed is a little co-operation between all you orthodox and reformed and Zionist. You ought to organize and fight this sort of thing. Really organize, I mean, throw a scare into 'em."

"That's certainly an idea, Captain," Singer answered. "We should borrow those guns under the Portuguese synagogue maybe, huh?"

McLone glared at him for a moment and reverted to Lee, who would, he said, spend a sober Christmas anyway . . . And late Tuesday afternoon, the day before Christmas, Burke, who had on three separate occasions told McLone that his entire mailing list had disappeared at the time of the murder, came down to the Cavaliers' offices and addressed about two hundred envelopes . . . Just a few he'd been able to remember, Burke told Swann with a dazzling smile.

Singer and Swann were still weighing the probabilities of this feat of mnemonics with McLone when Richard Lee's alibi came out of the Christmas Eve dusk into the Homicide Squad room and bowled them over, for they were essentially simple men. The widow from Weehawken wore a hooded fur cape, like a lady menace in a spy story, and she carried her head high. She was flanked by a Filipino chauffeur, a colored cook and a French maid. Between them they accounted for every breath drawn by Mr. Lee from Friday at dinner time to early Monday morning in Weehawken, New Jersey.

Very definitely, Mr. Lee's entertainment over the holidays was not to be charged to the taxpayers of New York City . . . Singer phoned the news to Van Kill and was invited to drop in on the tree-trimming party and tell about it.

XXX

"CAPPY says this rich widow of Lee's shows what kind of names were on Burke's confidential list," Singer remarked as Van Kill took his coat. "Cappy says he wouldn't be surprised if the D.A. decided the Cavaliers angle was too hot to handle."

"Not as hot as a Popub exposé would be," the document examiner said. "What's Lee's lady like?"

Singer hesitated. "Sort of like what I can see of your party, from here. Looks normal, but I can see at least one person who's ready to drop everything and run up the wall."

Van Kill stood beside Singer and considered the group in the big living room through the detective's eyes. Montefiore on the stepladder wrestling with the upper branches of a huge evergreen at this end was obviously having a wonderful time. So was the small boy standing below and being bossy. The white-haired lady with the walloping drink who was watching Yanni set up a crèche on the fireplace mantel was not nervous, neither was the plump gentleman with the little beard who was waiting to hand him a donkey.

"If you mean Miss Newman," Van Kill indicated Echo whom David was reproving for tossing him thick instead of thin tinsel for the top of the tree, "she's overworked, doing both her own job and Betty Hargrave's at Popub now, and she's worried about Montefiore . . . I'm just worried. Every twenty minutes she and I go out in the kitchen and howl like wolves. Come on in. You can at least stay that long."

"Yes, do come in." Edward had not been able to restrain his curiosity about who was in the foyer any longer. "There's more champagne," he said after Van Kill had introduced him.

"Not for you, I think," his guardian replied.

"It's supposed to make you feel ebullient, *you said,*" Edward countered as Singer stepped back to the hall table where he had placed two packages on arrival. He handed the larger and lumpier one to Edward, saying he had purchased it for a good boy. Edward tucked it under his arm and thanked Singer nicely.

Lady Di said Singer was the type of detective she personally always used and demanded to know if he regularly went armed. Singer grinned and lifted his coattail for her to see. Yanni greeted him as a guest of the kyrios rather than as a policeman and De Porta asked if he had seen the new seventy-ton tank which the synagogue had just acquired. But for David and Echo the atmosphere would have been entirely what Edward called "a family party for us orphans."

But Echo made Singer feel like a cop for making what sounded even to Van Kill like a harmless enough remark, "Bet you never did that as a kid." Echo dropped the red bauble she was reaching up to David and backed against the stepladder. Echo Newman had the close-grained complexion that does not change color, but tears could have been no more patent than the fear that welled into her eyes.

"Why shouldn't she?" David on the stepladder looked blue icicles down at Singer. "Good old Druid custom, decorating trees for the winter solstice." The cat Eo, who had been lurking in the nether branches, lashed his tail and batted the red glass ball between Singer's feet.

"Tougher than they look," the detective commented as he handed the ornament back to the girl.

Edward plucked at his sleeve. "Come in my room with me and I'll give *you* a present," the boy said.

"That blond kike," Singer muttered to Van Kill. "Just because his folks haven't had pogrom trouble since the Inquisition he gives me the Polish brush-off. I'm Russian."

Van Kill leaned in the door to Edward's room. "The United Front of Israel," he moaned faintly. "I don't know how you did it, but why did you have to go scare his girl?"

"She's got guilt reactions." Singer couldn't help absorbing some of the stuff Swann read. "You know how she was brought up, don't you?"

"Well enough so she didn't expect to be anybody's private secretary," Van Kill answered as indifferently as he could. It was true he had contented himself with the most general information about Echo: daughter of one of the Newman Importers on Fifth Avenue, educated in the city schools, left Barnard to go to work in the fall of '32. . . .

"Sure, sure," Singer shrugged. "Ten years now they're living off their fat in the rug business. What I mean, that girl was raised *kosher* and disowned, regular *echt* don't-darken-the-door, when she was eighteen, for going to a dance with a goy. Just how strong do you expect her to be against anti-Semitism?"

Van Kill would have followed Singer into Edward's room to argue this out, but there were Christmas presents of his, Edward protested, still unwrapped . . . He crossed the room and spoke to the tree-trimmers, who were bickering amicably again.

"I wouldn't ask you to stop fighting when just anybody drops in," he said. "But when it's a detective, you might give him ideas."

David as usual denied that people in their right minds could quarrel with him. "One has to be patient with Echo. Letting Mr. Pough walk on her all day gives her a terrible disposition after hours."

"David's annoyed because I'm going to work tomorrow," Echo explained. "It's unreasonable because Mr. Pough is, too." She hesitated, looking apologetically at Van Kill. "It's the Letter to Aunt Louella for *Hearth*, you see. We've sent nine drafts down to Miss Treach and she's still dissatisfied. Miss Hargrave used to write them on the subway on her way to work, Mr. Pough says."

"Wait'll he has to put out the next *Carnage* without her," Montefiore rested his elbows on top of the ladder and spoke with quiet satisfaction.

"David!" Echo gasped. "It's that sort of thing gives the police ideas, isn't it?" she asked Van Kill.

The document examiner shrugged. "I'm beginning to think I've wasted worry on David. After all, it's actions they like best in court . . . Why did you go to church with brass knucks in your

pocket? How came you beside the victim with a smoking revolver? . . . With words, unless they're on paper, or a dictaphone
sometimes, it's a matter of, 'Your Honor, I was misunderstood.'"
Van Kill made a face. "Right now for instance the boys are a
little miffed about the cavalier way Burke has gone back to work.
Even if he has an unshakable alibi, they feel he might curb his
exuberance. As Mr. Harris seems to be doing, for instance."

Echo said nothing. She seemed absorbed in her own thoughts
and puzzled by them. *I wonder if I could make you tell me,* Van
Kill thought, looking at her.

"We'll be kind to your little shamus when he comes out of
Edward's room anyway," David promised. "I could see he hadn't
been warned about your *Wunderkind*."

Edward's room, originally the master suite of the apartment,
was full of contemporary data on the private life and cultural
growth of Edward Cameron. Now when he stopped to think of it,
Van Kill realized that its contents, from the trapeze hanging
functionally over the bed to the geoponic tomato vine, might
stagger an unprepared visitor. Chemical experimentation in general was limited on account of the tropical fish, although Edward
had an apparatus for making perfume. Van Kill had imposed
no rules except one relating to the removal of bulky projects which
went untouched for over a week. This, owing to the season, did
not apply to the patent hive of bees attached to the terrace window. . . .

"Mr. Singer's got one of Edward's ash trays," Echo laughed.
"Look at him."

As David had prophesied, Singer had the appearance of a man
in need of reassurance. Edward's bedside kiln was an economic
triumph, besides insuring him against the embarrassment of unexpected gifts. The initials which could be riveted to the ash tray's
handle while the recipient waited were his own idea and De
Porta had complimented him on the glaze.

Edward stopped when he came back into the living room and
told himself that his party was a success. They had come to the
point of putting silver rain on the tree, with Echo being over-

ruled by Van Kill and David, who both declared that it should be thrown rather than hung on neatly. Edward put Singer's gift on the floor, tucked in his shirt, and said, what about the rest of the champagne?

As if Detective Singer had been waiting for the opportunity, he pounced on his gift with a cry of well-simulated amazement and declared he had given Edward the wrong package. Having made the substitution, he sat down and accepted a drink with the air of one who needed it. Meantime Yanni had answered the house telephone and reported a strain on his Christmas spirit.

"It is the little Smart on his way up. Saying he is expected."

Edward began to defend himself before Van Kill and Yanni turned to look at him. "He fascinates me. He's horrible, but he has the most *amazing* ideas. And he's a great comfort to me because I know I shall grow up and get over this condition I'm in. . . ."

"Don't encourage him to stay," Van Kill said earnestly. Edward promised to retire to his room after a minimum of courtesy. "I have some presents to wrap for you," he told his guardian, implying by his tone that he had peddled papers and collected old bones to buy them.

Rudi looked like Major Mite in his silk-lined cape and top hat. He was full of Christmas cheer and his manners were out of Graustark. He kissed Lady Di's hand, referred to Yanni as the patron who had furthered his career by getting him an engagement in Yonkers ("My first real break since the Fair," he said honestly) and he was so attentive to Echo that she left her glass of champagne on the stepladder by the tree and went to sit beside Lady Di. Eohippus the cat retired to the kitchen.

Edward Cameron seated himself cross-legged under the Christmas tree, where he could philosophize about human nature, while observing the group of adults around the fireplace. He thought that his guardian, leaning against the mantle with his face in shadow, was doing the same. Edward held his measured potation of champagne against the firelight and watched the bubbles. His nose tingled sympathetically. By turning his head he could see the glass which Echo had left on the ladder—the bubbles started at the bottom of the hollow stem there, slid through the reflected colors of the Christmas tree lights, and shimmered on the surface like molecular Roman candles. . . .

Edward listened critically to Rudi, who was talking about vaudeville coming to life with the death of the double feature and receiving Lady Di's assurance that they would come and see him when he reopened in Yonkers tomorrow night.

"Yanni's Uncle Yoryi's Cousin Spiros is having a Santa Claus Bingo tonight," Edward spoke from under the tree. He noticed that Rudi, who was well under his own four feet in height, was starting his second whisky-soda.

The Honorable Diana, with an eye to possible novel material, asked if Rudi had liked living in the Midget Village at the Fair . . . The best thing about the Midget Village, Rudi said, was the plumbing. As for the inhabitants, "I have ever thought Nature erred in putting ladies among the Little People. A man midget," Rudi said, getting out of his chair and clicking his heels to Echo, "is a man. He is eminently capable of *appreciating* a full flower of womanhood."

Edward could see from the set of Van Kill's shoulders that he was frightfully amused. Edward could understand almost everything about adult life except occasionally the things that made people laugh. He understood what Yanni, keeping the midget supplied with a steady flow of their second-best whisky, was up to. Edward thought Rudi was being merely tiresome instead of horrible enough to be fascinating. This story Rudi was telling now to illustrate why show folks thought those on the outside were hostile . . .

A Try-Your-Skill pitch near the Aquacade, this friend of Rudi's had had, with chained rifles that the customers shot at moving targets, and a very nice layout of prizes. Rudi's friend could afford this last because the endless chain carrying the targets passed a mirror arrangement, so that what looked like the bull's eye was really the far edge. And on this rainy night of the story, when Rudi had come out between acts to talk to his friend about how bad business was, this customer came along. He shot down all the targets and swept the booth virtually clean of lampshades and smoking sets and Detty Wetty Baby Dolls.

"First he lets Milton show him how to hold the gun, and then he shoots it all down." Rudi spoke so bitterly that Edward suspected him of having an interest in the pitch. "Then when he's piled all the prizes in his arms, he turns around and grins at us, walks across the road, and throws it all in a big oily puddle . . . If he didn't want the stuff, why'd he have to do *that*? There wasn't hardly anything we could save except a couple of candy dishes. I can still see that mean grin of his," the midget declared. "I'd know him if I saw him again anywhere."

Edward moved quietly around the tree and went to his room to wrap presents. When it suited him, Edward took full advantage of the fact that he was only a child. Aside from Lady Di (toying with an idea for a good quick spy story about a midget who traveled in a suitcase), they were all rather bored with Rudi. David rose when Detective Singer cut short a low-voiced conversation with De Porta and began to ask specific questions about Rudi's mind-reading act. Montefiore looked at Yanni as he passed behind the midget and made a neck-wringing gesture. Yanni acknowledged the sentiment without change of expression and David wandered after Edward.

Montefiore found the Cameron heir kneeling on his bed wrestling with a package as big as himself.

"Could I help?" David inquired. "I had a job once when my great-aunt Ruth thought I might be a department store executive. I learned to tie a pretty good bundle before I got fired."

Edward disengaged himself from a coil of metal ribbon and sat back on his heels. "Thank you," he said with unnatural calm. "I seem to be all thumbs." Then, as David's long fingers began to smooth and fold, "Was it discrimination made you lose your job?"

David looked up and saw the boy's round cheeks flushed and his eyes brimming. "My word, no," he said hastily. "The head wrapper, a horrible woman who could break rope with her bare hands, claimed I was a disrupting influence."

"Well, I'm glad of that." Edward spoke with sudden vehemence. "I've got so tired of hearing about the Christian Cavaliers and this magazine *Carnage*, and the harm they do, and nobody appreciates the trouble *I* have. Nobody should believe anything he reads without checking his authorities, but the lies people tell to children are *criminal*!"

Edward's tears spilled over now. He rose to his feet, walked across the room to a small display tank where two male bettas ruffled their fins at each other through a glass panel. Edward looked at the fish for a moment and faced David.

"Amalgamate!" he shouted at Montefiore and waved his arms. "That's all *you* have to do, amalgamate! But look at *me*! Me with the mind of a man, a good man's mind confined in the body of a child. And nothing can help me. Nothing!"

"Oh," Montefiore stood up and sighed with relief. "You're drunk."

"It's that damn liquor," Edward acknowledged.

"Everybody gets fooled by champagne." Montefiore squatted beside the boy and spoke reassuringly. "I remember when I was twelve—you don't feel sick, do you?"

Edward shook his head blindly. "Just very, very sad." The faintly-scented square of linen David handed him seemed to increase his grief. "I'm sorry for the Jews and the English and Greek orphans and I'm sorry for myself. I'm even sorry for midgets who invest money in devices for cheating the public. And I'm sorry for Echo because you think she's in love with Mr. Pough, but most of all I——"

"Shut up, Edward." David took the boy by the shoulder and shook him gently. "You mustn't say such things."

Edward dashed the moisture from his lashes and looked the blond youth in the eye. "You've been thinking it," he accused. "And last Friday when Miss Hargrave was here, I saw Hal doing it. Why shouldn't a girl be wrapped up in her job? I

said . . . But now he's lost her and I'm sorry for him because
he's a lonesome sort of person too and ——"

"Stop thinking about it," David said desperately. He knew how
an encircling arm, a little gift of money perhaps, would dry the
tears of an ordinary child and many women, but this tragic manikin . . . "Stop thinking about it. You'll be crying again."

"I—I intend to." Edward sat on the floor and wept with quiet
vigor. "I've never seen it so clearly. All my life I've been trying
to understand everything. B-but I see now the people in this world
don't try to—understand each other. That's the trouble."

"Stop thinking about it," David repeated. "People with ordinary
minds learn they have to. You can't take the woes of the world on
your shoulders."

"No," Edward said. "One of your folks did that."

Montefiore compressed his lips and raked his fingers through
his hair.

"I don't understand it," he said at last. "You had only two small
glasses at least an hour apart. Let's go into the bathroom and
run cold water on your head."

"Echo put hers by the Christmas tree and left it to go to
waste," Edward replied. "Tap water dries up the natural oils of
the scalp."

Almost at the same moment that Edward had said he was sorry
for Echo, Van Kill was reflecting that the evening's entertainment
had been curiously hard on her nerves. He was sure too that the
second and worse fright Singer gave her was quite unintentional.
The detective from the Homicide Squad was leaning forward,
chin on hand, in the way he had, listening to Rudi discourse
about the function of memory in the art of mind reading.

"Stage presence comes from experience and native gift. Outside
of that there's nothing to my act but memory," the midget was
pontificating. "Even your little boy understands," he assured Van
Kill. "The first question I pretend to guess from a sealed envelope
is a phony, see? There's a note and an envelope corresponding to it
slipped into the basket we have on stage for discards, just in case,

see? Then I pretend to confirm my reading of this phony from the first *genuine* audience note which the usher holds out to me to open. I memorize that genuine note at a glance, and I breeze right on through the rest that way. A fool with a good memory could do it if he had a natural stage presence, see?"

Detective Singer framed his question just as Yanni signaled the number of Rudi's potations. Rudi had consumed an apparently impossible quantity of liquor for his size.

"Suppose you had a list of names and addresses," Singer began. "Like a city directory in a small town. Say ten thousand. You send out advertising, from here. How many names and addresses would you happen to remember if you lost your book?"

Rudi stared hard at Singer. His eyes opened wide, narrowed to slits, and opened wide like two camera shutters. "Say that again," he demanded.

There was a covert exchange of glances at this first sign of a limit to Rudi's capacity, and Van Kill looked at Echo. She had made only one movement, a slow lifting of her hands to her throat, and her expression had not so much changed as set, but her hands were clenched so tightly against her neck they left a mark when she took them down and her face with its wide utterly blank eyes was like an Egyptian funerary mask.

"How many of those names and addresses would you happen to remember?" Singer finished, repeating his question.

"Without I ever looked at them with the idea I intended to remember them?" Rudi asked slowly and distinctly. "None."

He got down from his chair then, walked over to where Echo was sitting, and fell like a log at her feet.

"Hah!" Yanni Mavromicháli shot out a powerful arm and plucked Rudi off the floor by his coat collar. *"Syngnómee, desposúna,"* he said to Echo. "Excuse me, miss. We remove this worthless burro to taxi ere he burst on premises."

"I don't take any credit to myself," David said. "But it's what one means by the shock treatment for sobering up."

"Well, I certainly think it's too bad." Edward wiped his nose on

David's handkerchief while his words dripped scorn on David's last proposal. "Here is a poor little boy nine years old trying to get along in the world and learn what he needs to know . . . And not only are people so careless of his welfare as to let him drink too much champagne, but it is then suggested that he drink *coffee.* Coffee!" Edward abandoned the third person in an access of indignation. "At my age! Do you want me to stunt my growth?"

With the removal of Rudi, Singer announced that it was time he got along too. He was going to take over on a shooting for Ponia-towski and Rovero while they went to midnight mass. He wished the party a merry Christmas and departed, carrying the lumpy package which he had first given Edward.

Van Kill took advantage of the general movement to have a private word with Echo.

"Of course I'm jittery," she said. "Isn't wondering what out-rageous thing David will say or do next enough?" She was standing in the curve of the piano looking up at him, her face in the shadow which Van Kill himself cast on it.

He said, "I won't urge you. If you must think it out by yourself, you must. Only remember to think *by yourself.* If you don't it may be dangerous."

Echo Newman met his gaze steadily. "You're supposed to be a frightening sort of person, aren't you?" She smiled. "David said he found six white hairs over each ear the morning after you took him to meet the cat woman . . . I'm only worried about David."

Van Kill took hold of her chin with his thumb and first finger and tilted her head into the light that came over his shoulder. He had helped Echo with her coat and into cars during their short acquaintance, but this was the first time he had really touched her.

For an instant his touch and his look made her think of De Porta as she had seen the bookseller recently holding a porcelain up to the light. Then the contact of this man's strong impersonal fingers told her things about inner hurt and leashed fury and a drive for revenge that shook her as if someone had struck a mighty chord on the piano at her back.

"I think you're lying," he told her kindly. He turned away and left her trembling. It was not a reaction to his words. It was because Echo had heard the voice of Betty Hargrave speaking behind them.

When Edward returned to the room, he showed no signs of his recent spiritual crisis except a newly washed face. He was sorry he had not been present to say good-by to Mr. Singer, he said. "However, I can open *his* present now."

The box contained three pounds of an imported licorice candy, a variety much favored by Captain McLone for solitary consumption at his desk, Van Kill said. It was difficult to get now.

"Licorice settles the stomach," Edward said, helping himself. "It's all right with me. But what do you suppose made Mr. Singer think I wouldn't like a little red fire engine?"

XXXI

A JANUS model locomotive whistled loudly, pulling a long string
of freight cars up a rocky gorge and into a tunnel of real cement.
Edward Cameron, who lay flat on the temporarily rugless living-
room floor, gave a happy sigh.

"It's the very largest line I've ever had," he said.

"It must be the largest in the world," said Van Kill, resting his
shoulder blades on a divan with his feet up on an armchair, the only
two pieces of furniture in ten yards of living room which hadn't
been pushed back against the wall.

Yanni, sitting beside Van Kill, did not show the strain. But the
Van Kill-Mavromicháli construction gang had been driven so hard
they hadn't had time to open many presents except David's to
Edward, and it was now after noon of Christmas day.

Edward, still lying on his stomach, had digested Van Kill's
remark. "You're tired and you're not a specialist in this line," he
said soberly. "A big Morgan man here in town has one that covers
his entire basement. Why doesn't Mr. Montefiore come up and
look at this?"

"He's probably played with it already," Van Kill said, and let the
wrapping of a small parcel which he held rattle to the floor.

"An old book," Yanni said doubtfully.

"What kind?" Edward sat up.

Van Kill grinned. "A first edition, measuring nearly six by
eight inches, and," he added, "worth about three hundred dollars."

Yanni gazed respectfully at the black morocco binding and gilt
edges of the pamphlet.

De Porta had given him the 1680 London copy of the vain prodigal life and tragical penitent death of Thomas Hellier, the document examiner informed them.

"What did *he* do?" Edward wanted to know.

"Born at Whitchurch near Lyme in Dorset-shire," Van Kill

skimmed the contents title, "he murdered his master, mistress, and a maid, and was executed according to law at Westover in Charles City, in the country of Virginia, near the plantation called Hard Labour, where he perpetrated the said murders."

"Very interesting." Edward turned back to his train.

"There's a moral in it." Van Kill twitched his nose. "A moral to be derived from such a wicked career, this three-hundred-year-old ancestor of *Carnage* tells us. It says the First Families of Virginia, although they may have deserved the gallows in England and come to this country in shackles, have in Virginia done very well. 'Leading,'" Van Kill read, "'a creditable, comfortable, and for aught I can understand, a plausible, honest life . . .' That was before their descendants took to stockbroking," he added meaningfully.

Edward was unperturbed. "You mean they were doing that sort of writing a long time before Mr. Harris," he said and lay down again with his train.

Yanni attempted a mild diversion. "Did the captain have muts new to say?" Van Kill had been called out to an early morning conference with McLone.

"About stockbroking, yes," Van Kill replied maliciously. "They know about everything all of us have been up to in the last five months along that line."

Van Kill thought he saw the slightest of signals travel between Yanni and the boy, the same kind of fractional nod he had seen them exchange when he came back from the police conference earlier that morning. . . .

He had found Teekee out in front of the Otranto with an anxious dustcloth and a face as bright as the new Hermes cabriolet he was presiding over to the amusement of a swipe from the garage. Van Kill had made a suitable Christmas disposition of car and attendants and gone on upstairs, where he thanked Edward and Yanni, laboring even then at the train. . . .

They must have made a real killing in the market, he thought now as they turned their bland gamblers' faces on him. They had both been a little too sweetly thankful, Edward for the pair of

Police Positive Target revolvers, Yanni for an order on Van Kill's tailor to replace the outfit he had burned . . . Hoping he wouldn't make any inquiries . . . But now they got the works. . . .

"While we were reveling last night," Van Kill said sternly as the train whistled around a sagebrush bend, "the Homicide Squad was laboring with Mr. Burke. He had to throw the cops some kind of a bone, after inconsistently *remembering* several hundred names and addresses from his general mailing list. So now, McLone tells me this morning, Burke's remembered, by inches, that good old Anonymous contributed several thousand dollars to the Cavaliers in the past few months—with his market tips."

Yanni took a deep breath. "No money?"

"Anonymous sent no money to the Cavaliers." Van Kill was emphatic. "He telephoned market tips, and none of them went sour until the very last, the one we have on the dictaphone, which was why Burke got drunk. I think that *was* why he got drunk, damn it."

Yanni rolled his eyes and Van Kill took a new tack.

"The Homicide Squad knows a lot of other things about market angles in this case. Almost everybody connected with Betty Hargrave's murder seems to have been playing the market in the past five months: De Porta, David, Miss Newman, Frederick Pough, Paul Harris, George Stock, and Louie Lenz have all been taking mild flyers on utilities and industrials, outright buys and small-rise marginal hauls, as you and Edward call them in your joyless jargon . . . Aircraft too, Yanni, especially Amalgamated Aircraft. *All* of them except Daisy Goff, more's the pity."

Yanni frowned, but said nothing. The train was slowing up.

"De Porta of course advises David, Stock seems to do the same for Harris and Lenz. Pough is his own tipster too and he occasionally advises a friend." Van Kill shot a glance at Yanni, who was about to speak. "He merely uses broker Snell as a convenience and Miss Newman——"

Van Kill hesitated and Yanni tried to change the subject. "Miss Newman," he said, "will be coming here tonight? You can——"

"Miss Newman," Van Kill ignored him, "is a better prophet

than most professionals. She wouldn't say why she's coming over
the phone," he added. "But I suspect Pough wants us to work
on the Cavaliers. He's begun to see what a spot he's in, losing
Miss Hargrave. I shouldn't wonder if Pough gave us permission
to photograph the Geyer letter now to soften me up."

The document examiner slid down a little farther on his shoulder
blades and stretched his legs. He was enjoying at least the human
element in this dim mathematical game which he always compared unfavorably with roulette. "*Any* one of the seven could have
contributed those market tips to the Cavaliers, police assume, re-
gardless of personal sympathies. Any *one* of them could have wanted
to thwart the Cavaliers in some devious way, to test their strength,
to horn in on them. Harris for blackmail, of course. He's a blackmailer born and bred. There are so many possibilities."

"Yes, kyrie," Yanni said. "But I don't see how—" The wily
Mavromicháli knew perfectly well this would lead to three persons
in about one minute, and to nobody else.

"And now, Yanni, it gets really interesting, all this sordid grade-
school arithmetic." The train stopped as Van Kill sat up to stab
with a long forefinger at the Greek. "Just before the murder all
of our seven were into Amalgamated more or less heavily. Burke
too. Only this *last* time, as I told you, Burke got left because he
followed the advice of his anonymous telephone tipster as usual
and went along only for a short ride of a point or so. He pulled
out Thursday morning, the day before the murder. He saw Amalgamated Aircraft continue to rise. Friday afternoon he started
getting drunk. Interesting *and* significant, Yanni."

Edward was propped up on his elbows facing Van Kill and the
briefest exchange of glances flickered from Yanni on the divan
to the boy on the floor.

"This is what is significant," Van Kill continued evenly. "Some
mysterious person or pool of persons was buying up all the Amalgamated in sight, before it began its unusual rise. Thursday afternoon, that was, just about the time Miss Hargrave and I saw Mr.
Pough and his broker Mr. Snell lunching at a certain restaurant

on Pye Street . . . Do I have to tell you, Yanni," Van Kill asked, "or will you ——"

"It was perfectly legal," Yanni spluttered. "It looked like a sure thing. Besides," he added sulkily, "I had a hunts Amalgamated was due for more than its usual ups-down flutter."

"Of course." Van Kill was soothing. "But just to make sure you had a *dead* sure thing you ran out and bought the block of stock your temporary busboy told you Pough had promised a friend at the prevailing price. Then you turned around, through your broker, oh, I admit it was perfectly legal, and sold Mr. Pough back the block. You *did* speculate when you plunged further into Amalgamated," Van Kill added wryly. "But that was just to make dead sure Mr. Pough couldn't pick his block up cheaply anywhere else."

"Mr. Pough is soch a stubborn man, so honorable," Yanni justifying himself, lost control of his consonants. "The little kyrios tell me he overhear Mr. Pough is promise that stock to pay mpack mpig business favor, I know he will mpuy it no matter what it cost. I myself have heard Mr. Pough give Mr. Snell pig pawling out for not obey orders once before."

"And that," Van Kill said thoughtfully, "was why Mr. Pough looked sick at the *Carnage* banquet. Because we hadn't seen the end of the busboy. I don't mind your holding out on the police, Yanni, but *why* do I have to learn this kind of thing from comparative strangers?"

"Entouard is not to blame," Yanni asserted vigorously. "I took responsibility."

A small snort was heard from the vicinity of the Janus model train. "I'm entirely to blame," said Master Cameron. "And a lot of the money was mine. I wanted to get even with him for interfering with me learning the restaurant business."

It was plain that Mr. Pough's particular brand of interference weighed harder on Edward than on the Greek. Irrationally the episode of Edward picking up tips at the Matapan and Rudi Smart the midget substituting for him when Pough sent the Society's investigator round had worried the document examiner more than he cared to admit. He drove the needle in harder this time.

"Disgracing the firm by getting your name brought up before the Squad as a suspect in a murder case, Yanni," Van Kill said. He only half-smiled at Mavromicháli's startled face. "Want us to lose our license? Remember how much it cost, that piece of paper you *will* keep framed on your bedroom wall? Three hundred dollars cash money we put up to the State Department in Albany and a surety bond of ten thousand besides."

But this time quoting costs and measurements in their own sad way didn't take the financiers down. Van Kill had given them an opening.

"You cannot detective in New York without license," Mavromicháli asserted, and then as if some people's minds were beyond him, "*Ee astynomía* will suspect every person who ever took a tsance on Amalgamated."

"It was your idea," Edward stated severely. "You said your document examiner's credentials were not enough. You said there were times when every examiner ought to go into the human background of his case."

"You can't, it was, I did," said the badgered document examiner. "But you're wrong, Yanni, about the police. They may check all sales of Amalgamated for some time past, just as a matter of form. But they have enough people now to suspect: the seven I named in addition to Burke."

Yanni was perverse to the last. "Asking your parton, kyrie," he said, "I cannot see how this concerns me."

"Don't you see," Van Kill went on in a not very confident tone, "that what you've been doing amounts to discrimination against a customer? Remember, Miss Hargrave included a mention of those telephone tips in her report to Mr. Pough. Police might think Mr. Pough was framing an alibi for himself, so to speak, by deliberately losing money. Giving himself an excuse to look glum the night of her murder, I mean."

In the pause that waited upon Yanni's reply Edward could be heard, talking to himself. "Calls himself a good American. *I* was showing initiative." Master Cameron petulantly yanked his two-faced Janus engine from the front and attached it to the rear of his train. . . .

In Yanni's opinion Mr. Pough and the police could take care of themselves. "With customer my rule, keep mouth shut. In this case I figure it will emparrass Mr. Pough muts more if I speak, and Mr. Pough is very fine customer inteed."

"He is indeed," said Hendrik Van Kill, and paused as if he knew that Edward had been revolving a last word. Apparently soothed by his activities, Master Cameron hopped to his feet and came up to his guardian.

"You know, Hal," he said, leaning on Van Kill's arm. "You know, the important part about the whole financial transaction was the fact that we saw a chance to give you a little backlog and," he finished with boyish candor, "and we simply took advantage of it."

Van Kill laughed, but he was moved. "You win," he said.

Lady Di wandered in to admire the presents and have her gift to Van Kill, an ivory Hellenistic plaque representing Dionysus with goat, admired . . . Wednesday was liver day in Edward's bright lexicon of health. They would have a Christmas dinner at the Matapan that evening, but now it was liver . . . No, she couldn't stay, she told the boy. "I'm not dressed, I'm revising."

She had come and gone in the midst of her obvious abstraction and Van Kill, somewhat similarly afflicted, was taking time off and following a smell of frying onions out to the kitchen now. Yanni was tending the skillet. Edward, buzzing around underfoot, pointed out how Eo, weeping strong tears from the onions, was nevertheless waiting for his slice of liver like a well-mannered cat.

Van Kill absent-mindedly reached into the refrigerator and flung the cat a piece of liver.

"You'll spoil him," Edward objected.

Van Kill smiled vaguely and meandered back to his study and a piece of prose uproar entitled, WHAT MAKES DEPRESSION? He had shoved the other issues of the Cavaliers' *Lance* bequeathed him by Betty Hargrave to the floor beside his desk. All of the anonymous front-page essays in them said the same thing.

He turned to a paragraph on the first page. Betty had thought that the anonymous telephone tipster was identical with True American, the pseudonymous Lancer. Burke had shown he believed it too by letting Van Kill as an emissary from True American have the dictaphone recording. Unlike McLone, Van Kill did not think Burke knew the identity of either voice or writer.

There was a striking similarity between the style of tipster and essayist, both of them low-grade political campaign, typical fat-cat merrowling . . . He tried a sentence from *The Lance* once more. . . .

" 'We must re-establish our free American Society, based upon Christian solidarity, co-operation, and justice,' " Van Kill read aloud. " 'If we are to become happy, prosperous and unified again, it will be necessary for us forever to put an end to socialistic experiments and to re-establish our original Christian form of nation.' "

Details, rhythmic details. Like those of campaign speeches—and how were *they* usually composed? . . . Almost eagerly Van Kill took another specimen:

" 'Christian schools, Christian culture and the church can only be supported when Christian business is contented. He who objects to the BUY CHRISTIAN movement to restore a fair share of business to Christians drops his mask and stands revealed as an enemy of all Christianity teaches.' "

Dictated, of course, Van Kill answered his own question . . . And who had access to a dictaphone? De Porta, David, Lenz, and Stock . . . Every one of the seven. Plus Goff and Harris. Mustn't forget Harris. Harris dictated *all* of his stuff. Boasted about it. . . .

Details, the rhythmic details, how deaf he had been not to hear them before, but the rhythms of so many voices and personalities had been shouting at him in the past few days, trying to distract him. Van Kill's face wore a look of almost revengeful satisfaction.

" 'Christians! Mobilize your buying power to save your jobs, your homes, your church and your nation from those who would bring them to destruction!' "

There it was again, anybody but a man temporarily deaf would have noticed it before. All the end rhythms were trochaic, a long and a short, half of a trochiambic drumbeat roll. . . .

Justice . . . nation . . . contented . . . teaches . . . destruction . . . Van Kill repeated the words to himself and heaved a sigh of relief. These keys, he thought, blending tropes joyously, would be important fulcra in the manuscript to settle the hash of *Carnage and Cavaliers.* Thus he was thinking when Edward shouted from the kitchen:

"Come and get it."

"I think I *have* got it," the document examiner shouted back. He marched out happily to eat liver and onions in the kitchen with Edward and the Greek.

XXXII

~~~~~~

IT WAS about eight-thirty Christmas night when Echo Newman came out of the Otranto Apartments on Central Park West and passed David Montefiore without seeing him . . . David stood in the entrance, more noticeable than the average elegant young man with his dark fedora arrested in his hand and the light on his hair.

"Indeed," he said to Echo's back. David did not like not being noticed and he did not like the look on Echo's face. He watched her walking rapidly northward. Her slim back in the high-collared black broadtail coat that she wore to business had an indefinably unfamiliar aspect. David changed his mind about visiting Van Kill.

Echo had told him on the phone that she was too tired to see him that evening, and David was perfectly capable of understanding that this might not mean she was too weary to see other people. When he started to follow Echo, David told himself it would be fun to catch up with her and deplore her high-hat manner. He also admitted to himself that he was incorrigibly nosy, and wanted to know why she had been calling on Van Kill. For several blocks, until Echo turned west in fact, David managed to repress the alarm he had felt at the look on Echo's face.

Van Kill had noticed the girl's abstracted manner, but the fact that she brought him, not merely what he had been anticipating, permission from Pough to examine the Geyer item, but an insulated folder containing the document itself, distracted his attention from Echo and her almost rude self-absorption. Van Kill's *amour-propre* had been more wounded than he would probably have confessed by Frederick Pough's refusal to let him examine the manuscript in the first place. Now, though the editorial director of Popub's gracious note, which he also sent with Echo, had suggested no time limit to the loan, Van Kill was in a tearing hurry to get at it. Before Echo had reached the street and snubbed David, Van Kill was triumphantly helping Yanni arrange lights and set up the document camera. . . .

Echo may have failed to see David partly because her mind's eye was full of him. But David, following her, could only tell that she was not walking with her usual free stride, that there was a stiffness in her carriage as if she were consciously keeping her head up. By the time she reached Riverside Drive, where she crossed to the west side but did not enter the park, David was heartily disgusted with himself for dogging her. Yet he found it impossible to turn back.

He continued after the girl, keeping on the east side of the Drive. David knew that Echo liked to walk on Riverside, that she liked walking infinitely better than he did, and that there was nothing unusual in her walking home from Van Kill's apartment to the London. Also he was perfectly sure, even before she passed the corner where she should have crossed and headed back for West End, that she was not on her way home.

From being ashamed of himself for trailing her, David, who did not care for walking, became annoyed with Echo. She quickened her stride as they passed Eighty-fifth and David should have been grateful for the change of pace. His dark overcoat was none too heavy, a cold wind rode down the Drive. At Eightieth, looking across at her slim-legged figure silhouetted in the clear moonless night beyond relays of swishing cars, he was furious. He felt now that the tension born of reluctance in her gait meant she was going somewhere she didn't want to go. Why should Echo do that?

He thought he knew where she was headed when she turned into Riverside Park at Seventy-ninth Street. Both as motorists and as pedestrians David and Echo had argued about the Rotunda, Echo maintaining that it possessed a certain individual beauty, David positive that its Mayan-Renaissance architecture below outweighed its functional use to traffic above. . . .

David ran across Riverside Drive at Seventy-ninth Street without waiting for the light. He had stopped giving himself reasons for his actions. . . .

From Seventy-ninth Street and Riverside Drive pedestrians who

want a close look at the Hudson may get it best by going down
through a kind of public patio that is known as the Rotunda. To
reach this belvedere from Riverside Drive they have a choice of two
angling walks. These descend to become tunnels, north and south,
under two angling motor roads which, like the walks, branch off
from the westward continuation of Seventy-ninth Street and which
then strike up a rather sharp ascent into the Hendrik Hudson
Parkway above.

Like the stem of a bulb with its adherent roots the westward
prolongation of Seventy-ninth Street is rejoined, a few yards beyond
the tunnels, by the angling walks and, flanked by them, under-
passes the Hendrik Hudson Parkway bridge. Just past the bridge
the walks become two broad stairways, curving north and south
into the Rotunda below, while the westward-running stem of
Seventy-ninth Street broadens out into the bulb which is the Rotunda's open top. About the Rotunda rim traffic coming from and
reversing to Riverside Drive goes full circle in a turnaround, traffic
dipping down from the Parkway goes a half circle and then ascends
to the Parkway at the bridge above by filter roads similar to those
on the Drive side.

Both Echo and David were on foot, but the fitful movement of
passenger cars around and away from the Rotunda was to figure
prominently in the next few minutes of both of their lives. This
was because Echo Newman had promised to meet Paul Harris in
the Rotunda.

Standing at the edge of the Seventy-ninth Street stem, David
watched Echo pacing away from him, quite slowly now, down the
cement walk toward the north tunnel. There were no other pedestrians to interfere with his view of her. The river air was cold.

David was aware of the traffic flowing in beautiful intricate pulsa-
tions around and past him only as an urban pedestrian is aware of
traffic moving normally. Even as he hesitated on the sidewalk, looking after Echo, two sedans, moving abreast, separated and took the
ascents, one north, one south to the bright elevation of the Parkway
beyond him against the dark western sky.

At the same time a coupé immediately behind drove rapidly

straight west under the Parkway bridge, circled the Rotunda coun-
terclockwise, underpassed the bridge again, whizzed back by the
sidewalk where David was standing, and, whimsically, continued
along on Riverside Drive.

David was not in a mood to appreciate manifestations of other
people's whimsy. When he was asked about it later, he could only
reply that everyone knew a driver could play hide-and-seek with
himself endlessly on and off the Parkway, in and about the Rotunda. And who noticed cars?

At present, seeing Echo nearly at the north tunnel, David began
to run again, down the walk to the south tunnel. He shot under
the lights of this fifty-foot barrel and up the back-angling path to
the base of the bridge. Here by one of the tall helmeted lamp posts
which illuminate the entrance to the Parkway bridge underpass,
he slackened pace enough to glance over his shoulder. Echo had
not yet emerged from the other tunnel's mouth. . . .

David dashed under the bridge and checked his speed to take
the first of a flight of fifteen broad steps leading around and down
into the Rotunda proper. He took the second step and the third
more rapidly. From here the rim of the Rotunda (from which a
motorist or reckless pedestrian may look down into its fountain
and the space below) becomes invisible to an observant man of
little more than medium height, but David was not being observant
that night. It took Paul Harris to notice such things.

There was unfortunately no one taking official cognizance of
Echo's and David's movements this Christmas night. Captain Mc-
Lone had requisitioned special detail men from Inspector Larkin
for the Hargrave case, but these he had put onto past rather than
present movements of Betty Hargrave's associates. The only exception to the general axiom that non-criminal citizens always behave
with the most uninformative circumspection after a murder was
Paul Harris. And ten minutes after David Montefiore and Echo
Newman crossed Ninety-sixth Street at Broadway Paul Harris in
the subway beneath there shook, the phrase was his own, his tail.

The tail in question, a short nondescript detective by the name
of Oscar Miller, was one of Larkin's best. The Inspector really

shouldn't have called the misfortune, and it was that, Miller's fault . . . Three times in the distance between Forty-second and Ninety-sixth Street Harris had traversed the length of the train, sitting down momentarily, moving on.

Thus it happened that when the uptown local pulled in at Ninety-sixth Street Harris was standing near a door, Miller just pushing up toward it from the middle of a crowded car. It happened also, by a most unlucky chance, that when the local pulled in, an uptown express was standing across the platform and next to it a downtown express. Their doors, irregularly open, made an inviting and unorthodox thoroughfare to the downtown platform beyond.

Harris jammed through the opening door of his local, streaked across the uptown platform, and into the uptown express. Miller line-bucked into second position with the ease of an old New Yorker, leaped through the uptown train and gained the downtown express as Harris passed through it. Harris pulled up on the downtown platform as the automatic door closed in Miller's face and the express began to carry Miller away.

For the first time then Harris, raising his thumb to the middle of his face, indicated he knew he had a shadow. Then leisurely Harris caught a downtown local, got off at Seventy-ninth Street, and also made for Riverside Park. . . .

Having followed the north flight of steps a few moments after David Montefiore had disappeared down the south, Echo Newman stood at the paved bottom of the Rotunda and gazed up toward its rim. Rather like a goblet, broader at the base than at the top, it contained her, looking smaller than she truly was in that deep deserted bowl. No cars could be seen passing above the rim, though they were visible along the Parkway, and still above that, Echo could make out three or four tall apartment tops with their water towers black against the stars.

Her appointment was for nine o'clock. She had plenty of time. Too much. The reluctance David had noted in her stride had become nervous waiting anxiety as her gaze dropped below the Rotunda's eastern rim to dwell on the pilaster pseudo-arches, the black lanterns, the evergreens in tubs which Montefiore had deplored . . . Familiar, yet not reassuring. She had chosen to meet Paul Harris here because this private-public place was familiar to her.

Echo Newman's dark eyes swept the circular fountain beside her, drained now, its blue tiles unlovely and cold. It was different in summer with the lighted water spraying up to the motor road above. The small comical turtles around the edge were gone now too. . . .

This circular stone room open to the sky was not really cold, though a random wind came leaping through the entrance archways from north and south at intervals and dashed itself around her . . . The girl shivered and pulled up the collar of her coat. Her knee, pressed against the circular stone bench of the fountain's rim, was trembling. Behind her, if she had turned to face it, was a cloister effect giving onto the Hudson and the boat basin just below. The girl stood up straight and made a half movement which brought her left shoulder around . . . She might have meant to sit down and wait looking through the cloisters to the dark river. . . .

Like Echo Newman, Paul Harris chose the north tunnel, but according to his habit he noticed more and he took his time. His manner too was far different, and upon the muscles of his face rested a suspiciously complacent expression. Harris ambled up the angling walk when he had emerged from the tunnel. He reached the tall helmeted lamp post at the base of the Parkway bridge opposite the one where Montefiore had stopped to glance over his shoulder a few minutes previous.

The editor of *Carnage* magazine paused under the bridge to look down through the grillwork on his right at a complaining engine on the tracks far below. Pistons. Psychoanalysis, with which Mr. Harris possessed a running acquaintance, had an explanation for that. Seeing engines always gave him a sense of power. Mr. Harris grinned.

He took his time moving on to the Rotunda stairs. Automatically (he always noted his surroundings) Harris marked the four wooden signs atop the Rotunda's rim. ONE WAY, said the sign nearest him. Not for *me*, Paul Harris said to himself, and took the top step slowly, the second, and then the third. At this point the Rotunda rim on his left and any cars that might be circling it became invisible to a man of about medium height. But ahead he could see a stone retaining wall and above it a bit of helmeted lamp post to the left of a barren tree. This light evidently marked still another line of access to the Rotunda from a filter road. . . .

Some moments after Paul Harris paused on the third step to survey the scenery (the time was never exactly ascertained) Echo Newman made a half movement with her left shoulder and that was all she could remember doing for a long interval. It was not even certain that she clearly heard a shot.

But she felt a sudden sharp heat and a jarring impact in her left side as she fell on the stone bench. She did not see David Montefiore's face appear between the pillars of the cloister archway behind her, nor Paul Harris, running from the north archway entrance of the Rotunda. She did not see the revolver lying on the bench at her side. She never knew when the two men met beside her.

"Echo," David said, bending over to touch her. He did not seem to notice the revolver. "Echo," he said and became aware of Harris's presence then. He stood up and drew back his fist.

"Don't be a damn fool," Harris said sharply. "Want her to die? Go call an ambulance."

David turned and ran. Dodging through the pillars of the cloister, he reached its southwest corner, threw open a heavy door, and hit the big landing platform at the head of the stairs before the door had well closed, although the light was not especially good. At two jumps he took the eight steps down to the middle landing, the ten from there to the vestibule just outside a basement garage in two more.

Montefiore remembered a telephone booth and directories against a white kalsomined wall at the west end of the vestibule . . . Close up in the light of the wire-caged electric bulb over the bracket that held the directories his clear-cut features and blue eyes showed, if anything at all, an expression of numb haste. His hat was askew upon his blond hair . . . He pushed it further back and dived for the telephone booth. . . .

"Trafalgar 4-7533," he told the operator and gave the address . . . He called three private hospitals and the police. . . .

XXXIII

THE questioning of those who might have witnessed the affair at the Rotunda took place in the office of the lieutenant commanding detectives on the second floor of a precinct station not many blocks away from Riverside Park. This office was like several dozen others of its kind in Manhattan, clean, but seeming to carry an aura of age-old municipal tobacco and dust.

William Crockett sat in it about ten o'clock that night at a long table with his stenographer. Sergeant Mars alone represented the Homicide Squad. Singer, Swann and the rest, with some precinct detectives, were still talking to Paul Harris and trying to talk to David Montefiore in an outer room. . . .

The squad and the precinct had already disposed of the first among three witnesses who might have seen the shooting of Echo Newman. This was a jumpy individual named Wilfred Carr, who sat on Crockett's left near the head of the table. Stenographer Fielding and his notebook occupied a place at their right. Mars was slouched on a near-by bench, chin in overcoat collar, and apparently asleep. His derby hat rested on his knee.

Crockett had found it hard to get the witness going. The green leaf on the cap Carr held in his hand and on his khaki coat marked him as a Park Department man. It was his responsibility, Wilfred explained, to keep the Rotunda clear of debris as well as to maintain order in it if necessary and keep an eye on cars driving around the rim.

"In a manner of speaking," Wilfred said with the bright air of an aging professor which had marked his account throughout. "In a manner of speaking, you might say my close attendance upon these duties estopped me from witnessing the unfortunate affair."

Wilfred put the hand which wasn't holding his cap up to touch his heavy clipped mustache and with another nervous movement adjusted his eyeglasses. It looked as if he couldn't go on from there.

254

Crockett gave him a boost. "Where were you when the shooting occurred?"

Wilfred floundered. "I had the water running." He gave a fussy academic giggle. "In the gentleman's, uh, that is, I was detained." Wilfred caressed his mustache. "You might say upon a combination of official and personal business."

"I see. Then you did not observe, you did not hear what occurred?"

"Uh, no. I just got out there when those three ambulances arrived. I had not terminated until then, uh, you'd better make it my official duties in there."

Crockett took him over it again with the same result. He said, "That's all, Mr. Carr. You may go."

Wilfred made a jerky salute and went. . . .

Crockett leaned back and lit a cigarette. Many things in the business still surprised Crockett, including a Park Attendant whose native language seemed to be English. Nothing surprised Sergeant Mars. He did not stir. . . .

Crockett took a few quick drags, crushed out his cigarette, got up and opened the glass-paneled office door. "I'll talk to Mr. Harris now," he said.

Harris walked in calmly and sat down in the place Carr had vacated.

"My name is William Crockett and I am an Assistant District Attorney," Crockett began the customary formula. "Do you want to tell us what happened now? You don't have to of course and it is my duty to warn you that anything you——"

Harris seemed to be enjoying the situation. "I always co-operate with officers of the law," he interrupted. He explained why, officially and in full.

"Oh, yes," said Crockett with perfunctory enthusiasm. "When did you arrive at the Rotunda tonight, Mr. Harris?"

"Exactly nine o'clock by the Mazola sign across the river."

"Why did you go there?"

"I had an appointment there with Miss Newman at that time."

"Who made this appointment?"

"She did."

"When was that?"

"Yesterday afternoon in the corridor just outside her office, about five o'clock as she was leaving work."

"Why didn't you discuss what you had to right there?"

"I never waste time on anything that isn't *strictly* business during office hours. But this thing," he hesitated, "had been worrying me and I ——"

"What did you tell her?"

"I just said there was something *personal* regarding the business I'd like to talk to her about. She named the place and the time then. Said she was going to be busy last night and today."

"What was this personal business matter, if you don't mind telling us?"

"Not at all," Harris said briskly, his face still expressionless. "I wanted to warn her to steer clear of David Montefiore."

"What has he been doing?" Crockett tried to keep his voice natural.

"Making threats against me," Harris said. "Not that I'm worried about myself. But I was afraid he'd make the attempt on her that he actually has . . . That fellow's capable of anything," Paul Harris added with the first emotion he had shown.

"What has all that to do with *business*?" Crockett wanted to know.

"Everything," Harris declared. "I thought I'd made it clear that Montefiore's trying to sabotage my firm. And next to Mr. Pough Miss Newman is the brains of that firm," he said with handsome sincerity. "Montefiore knew she'd never fall in with these crazy schemes of his any more than Mr. Pough would. As a minority stockholder he couldn't really do anything within the law. But he was desperate enough to strike back at us through her. I saw it coming. I wanted to warn her," Harris said with what sounded remarkably like a sigh.

Crockett was severely practical. "Why couldn't you have talked to her on the premises of your firm?"

"I couldn't be sure how she would take it," Harris explained with nice restraint. He would have turned down any yarn for *Carnage* that didn't pep up the woman angle in a questioning more. He had dictated hundreds of better scenes than this himself. "I didn't want to embarrass her, there are people coming and going all the time. You never can tell how women will act. Unfortunately she's personally interested in Mr. Montefiore, I understand. It wouldn't have been the decent thing to do."

Crockett, his thin face reflective, asked, "Are you quite sure you didn't have a personal interest in Miss Newman?"

Harris shook his big head slowly from side to side. He said, "My relations with women in a firm where I work are always on a strictly business footing."

The Assistant District Attorney changed his angle of attack. "What path did you take to the Rotunda?"

Harris described how he had got rid of the detective following him. His tone indicated that there was a vast difference between the co-operation he was now affording the Law and the co-operation the Law had been affording him. With considerable detail he described the course he had taken from Seventy-ninth and Broadway to Seventy-ninth and Riverside Drive. From that point on he practically gave a Bertillon of every crack in the path. "When I arrived at the Rotunda," he concluded, "I descended into it by the north flight of steps."

"Tell us exactly what happened then," said Crockett, a gleam of unwilling admiration in his eye.

Harris told of descending the first three steps and of noticing ahead of him the light pole and the tree which marked the north access to the Rotunda from the Hendrik Hudson Parkway.

"Did you see anything else ahead of you at that time?"

Harris paused to think. "Nothing except the sky," he said finally.

"Proceed from there."

"I walked down seven more, I notice such things, and got to step ten. At that point, on my left, I observed a plate marked—" Harris paused "—7930 below a black iron lantern set in the Rotunda wall. After that on the left side I noticed five tile ventilators in the wall extending from step ten to step fourteen. I was proceeding

slowly because I was on time. I usually am. Just about as I got to
step fifteen, the one below the ventilators, I heard a noise."

"Was it a loud noise, Mr. Harris?" Crockett interrupted to ask.

"Not very, more like a muffled berroom. I thought at first it was
a backfire from a car. But I had seen no cars anywhere from
Riverside Drive as far as the Rotunda, and I thought it might be
a shot. I started to run."

Harris was in his element, but with admirable self-control he
managed to approximate a detective report. "I turned into an archway, which is the entrance to the Rotunda on the north. It leads
by a ladies' lavatory on the left."

"What did you do then?"

"I continued running toward the fountain, which is in the center
of the Rotunda."

"What did you see there?"

"I saw Miss Newman lying on her left side on the stone bench
which surrounds the fountain. It really constitutes the wall or
outer rim of the basin," Harris said.

"Did you see anyone else?"

"I saw David Montefiore."

"What was he doing?"

"When I first saw him he was crouching by a pillar in the
cloisters as if he had just jumped from the motor turnaround above.
He got up and started running toward Miss Newman."

"What did he do when he reached her?"

"He started to assault me, but I persuaded him to summon the
proper authorities."

"What else did you do?"

"I removed Miss Newman's coat, took my knife, and cut away
her blouse where she had been shot in the left shoulder behind. I
tore up her scarf to make a bandage and laid the coat back over
her. I also found the slug on the bench where it had come through
under her arm." Harris was calm and factual. He did not show the
strain of avoiding adjectives.

"Did you see the gun from which the shot was fired?"

"I saw a gun."

"Where was it?"

"On the right side of the girl, the side behind which Mr. Montefiore was crouching."

"Ever see the gun before?"

"Yes."

"Know who owns it?"

"I own it. It is a forty-four Frontier Model Colt and matches an 1873 Winchester rifle, I mean it will take the same caliber shell, that I have in a private museum in my office."

"When did you last see this Frontier Model Colt revolver?" Crockett asked.

"Not since—this is Christmas, let me think now . . . I haven't specially noticed it since six days before Christmas."

"Why did you happen to notice it at that time?"

"I showed it to a middleman Montefiore sent up."

"Who was this man?"

"Dr. Hendrik Van Kill." Harris's face and voice were wooden.

"I see." Crockett flicked a glance at Sergeant Mars, but Mars still appeared to be asleep. Crockett said, "Has Mr. Montefiore ever seen this gun?"

"I suppose so." There was a shade of what might have been disappointment in Harris's tone. "I remember him looking at the shelf it's kept on."

"When was this?"

"The day before I saw Van Kill. Week ago today, last Wednesday, the afternoon I was telling you about Montefiore made those threats."

"How did Mr. Montefiore happen to be looking at the gun?"

"I didn't say he was," Harris corrected. "He was looking at my whole crime collection and made some belittling remarks about it."

"Did he *seem* to notice the Colt revolver?"

"He didn't say that he did."

"Do you keep the cabinet which contains this collection locked?"

"No."

"Then Mr. Montefiore might have abstracted this Frontier Model Colt?"

"He might, or anybody who came into my office when I wasn't there," Harris said judicially.

"Has Mr. Montefiore been in your office since that time?"

"Not that I know of. He's often around on that floor bothering Miss Newman."

"Would you say Mr. Montefiore probably took the Frontier Model Colt?"

"I've got no right to say that," Harris rejoined in a virtuous tone. "I'm only telling you what I personally know to be true. I always——"

"Of course," Crockett cut it off. "That will be all for just now."

Mars raised his head from his coat collar and spoke in an amiable growl. "Mr. Harris, you claim to have noted all this stuff like lantern plate number 7930 and five ventilators between step ten and step fourteen."

"I do." Harris was calmly elated.

"What's to hinder your studying all that up as a part of planning the crime yourself?"

"Nothing," Harris said and grinned. "Except *my* good sense. I never was in the place before in my life. That's just the way my mind works. I can prove it."

"How?"

"Give me a detective night duty list from the precinct here."

The demand was so brash and unexpected that Mars got up to comply . . . Harris seemed to do no more than glance at the list. He recited off the whole of it.

"Let me have some numbers, any numbers," he said then.

Mars gave out a long list of shields; Harris threw them back at him with hardly a pause . . . Harris proceeded to describe the first floor of the precinct station which they had come through rather hurriedly an hour ago. He detailed it down to the last cuspidor and a cartoon on the bulletin board.

"This showed a man asleep at a party," he specified. "A balloon coming out of his mouth said, 'We had a very very very nasty night.' Like the one we been having," Harris observed.

"You want to *make* it that for Montefiore," Mars said. He did not mention Harris's story to Pough about the box which he said he saw David carrying away from the Popub service elevator on the night of the *Carnage* banquet, the box which squadmen had agreed to keep under their hats. But Harris felt unjustifiably elated at what Mars did say:

"You keep putting Montefiore out in front every chance you get. He tried to frame you for a murder, but he couldn't shoot straight, and he didn't duck away fast enough. Isn't that what you want us to think?"

"I'm telling you what I observed and I just finished proving I'm a good observer," Harris retorted with respectful firmness.

"Well, then, you observed he looked as if he had just jumped," Mars reminded Harris. "From the Rotunda rim about twenty feet down? What would be the sense of that?"

"Don't ask me to make sense out of that saperoo," Harris countered with some heat. "Maybe he got overbalanced when he was throwing the gun down on the bench and had to jump."

"Or else thought he'd just hop down and let the girl see who shot her before she died?" Mars asked sardonically.

"Who knows what he thinks?" said Harris with even greater warmth. "I won't say anything more about him. I got my loyalty to the firm. Can I help it what kind of screwball holds stock? I wouldn't have told you what I have if I didn't make it a practice always to co——"

"Yeah, yeah," said Mars wearily. "You saw the wound. In your opinion could the shot have been fired from a car at the rim?"

Harris was pleased to be consulted. "From the angle, yes," he said. "It came in fairly high just under the shoulder blade and went out low under the arm. But," he added stubbornly, "I told you I saw no cars from Riverside Drive to the Rotunda. If there had been any, I would have seen 'em."

"Okay, Bill," said Mars and Crockett took Harris through it again, but Harris brought them out at exactly the same hypothetical hole. . . .

After the last question, which was about the wound again,

Harris's face continued to wear a look of concern. "Have you got any report?" he asked. "They told me out there——"

"You might say she's semiconscious," a grizzled precinct sergeant had told Harris when he asked about Echo Newman in the outer room. And Harris knew this veteran would tell any witness the same unless the witness had seen the victim in a state of advanced decomposition.

"We have no official report," Crockett had learned enough about homicide investigation to parry. He told Harris to wait outside.

"Gladly," said the editor of *Carnage* magazine. "I always," he continued, surveying Crockett and Mars with an injured expression, "I always co-operate with officers of the Law." He moved out upon these words. . . .

Paul Harris would have termed David Montefiore distinctly unco-operative. He let William Crockett get no further than the "want to tell your side now?" part of the formula when he said:

"It's rather a long story. I don't believe you're capable of understanding it." Crockett, who had got the highest Gentile grades in his class at International Law School, felt hurt.

In the heavily populated outer room David had refused to talk at all. Here in the office with only Mars, Crockett, and Stenographer Fielding at the table he was almost as taciturn. . . .

No, he wouldn't say how he learned Miss Newman was going to the Rotunda. "It's a personal matter," Mars extracted after a round of patient prodding.

He refused to discuss his relations with Harris and *Carnage* magazine. "I won't dignify that drip or his drippings by further speech."

It wasn't, Crockett decided, the silence of a sullen or of a defiant man. Condescension rather, or cheerful despair . . . David was willing to tell the little which he said he could recall. . . .

He came down those big steps, yes. Of *course* he didn't know what side of the Rotunda they were on. He walked through by the fountain and Miss Newman wasn't there. Sorry, but he didn't think they'd understand why he didn't wait and speak to her then.

He'd passed on back through the imitation cloisters toward the river and strolled down the esplanade. What difference did it make if the damned thing was west of the cloisters or not? He believed them if they said it was. North or south? He supposed he went off the north end of the esplanade, this in response to a series of questions from Crockett, and then, "What I should have done was save you trouble by going straight off into the river from there."

Dramatizing himself, Crockett thought. He ought to be watched.

But David said, "I didn't mean to be melodramatic. I wanted to see if there were any battleships, I suppose."

Mars' bony fingers drummed on his bowler. David, shaking his head, bright gold in the harsh gleam of light from the green-painted cone above the table, couldn't say how long he stood there looking at the river. He just knew that after a time he heard a noise, an alarming noise, from the Rotunda. He didn't know if it was a shot or not. He wasn't a gun-fancier like Harris. He heard a noise, so he ran back into the cloisters again, and there——

"And there," Mars came in suddenly, "Harris states that when he first saw you, you looked as if you had jumped from above."

"An acrobat! I stumbled running. I wanted to get to her as fast as I could."

He didn't spot Harris until they met at Echo Newman's side. He didn't see the Frontier Model Colt. "I couldn't really see anything but her lying there," David said stonily.

The rest of Montefiore's account tallied too well with Harris's. He supposed he did make to hit that filthy blister. He did run to telephone. He knew the place, of course. He had often parked his car in the basement garage when he came to use his boat in the basin last summer. Why not? . . .

Over and over it they went with David quietly. The time for sustained noise and psychological duress, if it ever came to that, would be later days in Crockett's office on the upper floor of the District Attorney's Building which houses the D.A.'s Homicide Bureau. There Crockett and a colleague, with relieving pairs, would pound away, one pacing the floor, the other sitting down, one threatening to stay there all night until they got it, the other protectively paternal, professionally menacing by turns. Detectives in remote precinct stations, trying to elude newspapermen, might do the same with such variations as long experience and the inspiration of the moment might suggest, from wisecracks and ridicule to rosaries and tears. Then before they let the suspect go, the District Attorney's physician might examine him to make sure he didn't claim physical damage afterwards. . . .

Over it they went now, with only an occasional tentative bellow, Mars and Crockett at the table, precinct detectives and Homicide Squad men wandering it and out to ask apparently casual questions from time to time . . .

But David neither added nor subtracted much from what he had already said. "Oh, for God's sake, what's the use!" he burst out when they tried to get him talking freely about Echo Newman. "Why don't you lock me up and be done with it?"

"We might at that," Mars said with a strained smile.

Bullying would never get anywhere with this kind. The moment for "hot" interrogation, trapping a perpetrator into contradictory accounts by sympathetic silent listening soon after the deed had long since gone past. So it was more from a sense of duty than anything else that Mars resumed his usual technique, shifting suddenly from questions about David's boyhood hobbies, his travels and schooling to the matter in hand.

David seemed to sense this and it was he who ended it at last. He ran an impatient finger through a little runnel of varnish his own cigarette had made on the table, dying out unsmoked. He yawned unaffectedly and stood up. "Now I'm tired," he said. "I won't talk to any of you any more."

"All right, son." Mars knew when he was beaten. "Is there anybody you *would* talk to?"

David drew a hand over his face as if wiping it clean. "I don't know."

"Van Kill?" queried Mars.

"Van Kill," said David Montefiore, seeming to assent.

XXXIV

The document examiner was at his desk when Sergeant Mars' call came during the hour before full dawn. With its attached bookshelves this desk formed the long east wall of the study where Van Kill sat, elbows propped on the Wagner and Geyer biographies he had cited while talking to the president of Po Publications less than a week before. The beams of a daylight lamp, reflected from the pages of the mammoth Burrell volume and the Bournot book on top of it, limned parenthetical furrows around the document examiner's mouth which had not been there when he visited Frederick Pough.

Van Kill raised his head from his encircling fingers when the telephone bell cracked the silence in the room. He peered vaguely across a sandwiched heap of papers and instruments toward a toppled pile of books as the telephone rang behind them a second time.

Careless the jumble looked as Van Kill reached a long arm over it to seize the telephone and plant it upon the volumes in front of him. But between the curve meter, the angle measure, the protractor and other glass plates ruled with black lines, lay the most careful data for a conclusion upon a night's work of driving speed.

A thousandth-of-an-inch worm's job Van Kill would say when asked about his business . . . The bottom sheets of the pile of papers before him dissected every curve of bulb and loop, every angle and tilt of letter, word, and line in the questioned Geyer script. The second sheaf up paid attention to spaces between lines, letters, and words, to margins left, right, bottom, and top. A third devoted itself to beginning and end strokes, letter-crossings, and punctuation marks. A fourth observed shading and repairs, while a fifth noted the width, the quality and speed of the lines . . . In sum the whole anatomy and rhythmic impression of the entire hand. . . .

To the left of the main stack the young man had placed a separate report, comparing the measurements of the questioned Pough item with those which years ago Van Kill's father Pieter had taken from the unquestioned Geyer manuscripts available to Burrell and Bournot. On a sheet atop this Hendrik Van Kill in his own hand had reproduced every style of letter which the Pough item used. To duplicate any hand was a genius the late Pieter Van Kill had supremely possessed. His friends always insisted that he could have made a better living as a forger than as a pedagogue. His son had something of the same ability. He used it now for his own enlightenment, as not long after the murder of Betty Hargrave was solved he used it in the King's business.

Now as he took up the telephone, Van Kill could not yet explain his instinctive haste, had not yet probed the source of his jabbing conviction that this night's task might prove uncommonly significant. Nothing in the contents of the questioned letter could have alarmed and excited him so. They were precisely what Frederick Pough had said: A sentimental German avowal that Richard Wagner was the pledge Johanna and Geyer had given to Fate; a sidelong reminder to Johanna Paetz that her own true sire (the language got more flowery and chivalric than ever here) had been "an Hebraic Maecenas and creator of all that is most beautiful." . . . Nothing in the letter had put that fine-drawn tensity which showed on the young man's face as he lifted the receiver and said, "Speaking."

The outward appearance of the letter was ordinary enough too. It lay (while he listened to Mars' voice over the telephone) on a transmitted-light table between the slotted desk and the great north windows at Van Kill's left: a fold of pseudo-parchment, yellowish brown in tone, spread out so that a solid page of handwriting showed on its front and about a half of one on its back. The strong electric bulb under the glass table top illuminated the paper's leathery mottling and every detail of its spidery almost womanish script.

"Dresden, d.31, Dez. 1813," it read in the upper right hand corner of its first page. "Liebste Freundin," the salutation in the upper center ran on.

Thus Ludwig Heinrich Christian Geyer (presumably) had begun to his *dearest friend*, and where he had finished one might observe a micrometer caliper for measuring paper, a special Brown and Sharpe design. (Van Kill had measured the thickness of the paper and found it matched the standard of other originals.)

The instrument's parallel non-rotating knife-edge jaws could be seen pressing upon the last line of the missive, the simple "Geyer" signature. Its grip lay flat across part of a three-line postscript, written along the left-hand margin of the back page in Geyer's usual way. . . .

Too much in Geyer's usual way? . . . The individual letters were mechanically correct and the rhythm of the lines well made in the Geyer mode . . . *Made too well?*

Van Kill had been testing the feel of the style, reading the Burrell and Bournot letters aloud in the early morning quiet and comparing them with the questioned document just before the telephone rang. . . .

Mainly the Pough document harked back to the language of the Bournot item, dated just two days before it: December 29, 1813. There was much play in both upon Geyer's need for himself and Johanna to banish jealousy, bring up the purer metal in themselves, and cast out the slag. Now that they *both* faced the truth about their birth, they had a great and noble summons to cast out the dross, to bind their covenant of friendship closer over the dying year—thus the Pough document adapted a sentence from Bournot which ran in part:

"Ueber den Sarkophag des 1813th Jahres lassen Sie uns unser Freundschaftbuendnis noch fester schliessen." The very sentence upon which Van Kill had been concentrating when Mars' call disturbed him. . . .

Most ambiguous of all the Geyer letters, Bournot had called his own exhibit, and Geyer, if he had written the Pough document, must have intended it as an explanation of his earlier one which Johanna would easily recognize . . . Remarkably alike the two letters were in everything, even to the same formal close: *"Leben Sie recht gluecklich!"* Written with a flourish of emotion in the Pough item, where the downstroke of the *g* in the *gluecklich* crossed with the *Geyer's* G.

A lucky life to you from Geyer—how formal in the century's mode, how full of egoistic male sentiment at any time, how German, thought Van Kill. The sort of sentiment, distorted in others of the breed, which let them blubber into their beer over their neighbor's scenery and children, then go out when the edge turned lightly to self-pity and cut their lucky neighbor's throat. Pathetic, though, in Geyer's case. Much of Geyer's bad luck, Van Kill mused, down to his death from overwork, had been brought on him by his own folk. . . .

Hetéra lúpe, the words of the Aesop fable lined out so long ago by Edward, opened a vagrant bypath for Van Kill's one interval of brooding thought in the night that was almost gone . . . *A crowning grief—from her own* . . . Could that have been the way of Betty Hargrave's death? . . .

Fighting off the odious conviction, Van Kill turned away from his work. He sat staring at the apartment towers beyond his north windows, funereal in the slightly graying dawn, and shivered as if danger's very finger had traced the Geyer script. . . .

But his heart, more than his mind, rebelled at the thought. Two words, four syllables in a trochiambic rhythm were forming on his lips as he turned back sharply to the Bournot book in front of him. Words in a drumroll rhythm, the summoning beat he had made with his fingers and impatiently thrust away from his mind when he and Betty sat at lunch together in the Matapan Restaurant one week ago. . . .

And then the call from Mars drowned the rhythm out. "Be there after I pick up De Porta," Van Kill said.

XXXV

Some hours after dawn Van Kill and De Porta were finishing breakfast in the Kitty Hawk Restaurant. Draining his third cup of coffee as De Porta called for their bill, the document examiner spoke from a silence he had scarcely interrupted since they left the precinct and set out for La Guardia Field.

"His memoirs! He tells us he won't write his memoirs till they take him to a better jail." . . .

De Porta watched one plane arrive and another taxi off in the space when he might have replied. . . .

It was true that, proof against threats and bullying and coaxing from Van Kill, against entreaties from De Porta, David had told them *exactly* that when they tried to find out how he knew Paul Harris had a date with Echo Newman at the Rotunda last night. . . .

"I knew. I went there," David had said stubbornly. "If you want any more, you can read the D.A.'s stenographic notes."

They had hoped David would explain himself when McLone joined them and he learned how Echo Newman was. It was either an accidental miracle or purposeful sharpshooting that the bullet missed her heart, the captain said, she was in a critical condition from loss of blood and wound shock and much too ill to be questioned.

But Montefiore's only reaction was a kind of dull hysteria. "A murder trial would be a new kind of excitement for me. I'll be guilty if she dies."

David didn't want a lawyer, he said. All he wanted now was to sleep. . . .

That was what they had left him doing in the precinct lockup, while Van Kill had a mysterious conference with the captain, telephoned Yanni, who brought baggage in a taxi and saw them on their way to the flying field. . . .

"I believe David's really in love," the bookseller said. "I believe that's what his behavior signifies." De Porta was a troubled Buddha counting change with quite unnecessary care at an airport restaurant table, not at all an ageless Buddha now. He was completely mystified by Van Kill's determination to leave town at this time when if ever David needed him.

"I hope so." The vowels grated in Van Kill's throat. "I can tell you something else that's significant."

Replacing his billfold, De Porta waited.

"Pough's Geyer item is spurious." Van Kill's voice was dogmatic.

"A forgery?" This was a reality, a familiar reality, and De Porta's bewildered mind clutched at it. "But I'd understood Ainsworth said it was genuine."

"Ainsworth is a *Wagner* specialist. What would he know about documents?" said Van Kill.

De Porta was curiously apologetic. "Pough's been imposed upon since Ainsworth saw it," he said quickly. "There must have been a substitution. Harris must——"

De Porta broke off. He had been insisting only a short time ago to Captain McLone that Harris *must* have shot Echo Newman from the rim of the Rotunda if for no other reason than the fact Harris tried to make out that *David* had done so and jumped.

"It is a very good forgery, Ben," Van Kill said, "above a genuine Geyer signature, on genuine Geyer correspondence paper, too."

The document examiner set forth his reasons and watching De Porta's face, was pleased at the distraction he had brought about.

The bookseller put a question then.

"Why do confirmed fist-makers and doodlers do it *now* on a blank fold of paper?" Van Kill was close to being exuberant. "A slip to mark a pile of goods laid out for moving. Poor Geyer was always moving. Identification to keep a servant from swiping his personal paper. Paper was not cheap in those days. One reason's as good as another. It is a sound signature in any case and over it a very good duplication of the Geyer hand. *Too* good."

Van Kill went into technical details and from time to time De Porta nodded with the quiet comprehension of one who had refereed many a battle of books. . . . De Porta could engage in such a discussion although his only nephew was detained by the police on suspicion of attempted murder. This was because of De Porta's personal philosophy of life and because in even the most troubled part of his mind he knew Van Kill's present interest in a century-old letter was in some way connected with Van Kill's conception of the case.

"By itself," he was saying, "by itself the crossed stroke, the *gluecklich* upon the *Geyer*, isn't decisive at that range of time. Taken with other features, though, the lack of a certain spark and pickup in the rhythm, it's completely conclusive."

"Where would you date the hand?" There was a lively curiosity in De Porta's voice.

"Last third of the nineteenth century, I'd say," Van Kill's was tentative. "When the Nietzsche crowd was bearing down on the charge that Wagner, the prince of anti-Semites, was a Semite himself. Some disgruntled stepnephew of Wagner's, let's say, some champion of Geyer at any rate, who found a sheaf of Geyer's correspondence paper in an old wardrobe, probably thought Wagner needed damping down for denying the Nietzsche charge with such heat. Hence our document. I've always thought," Van Kill wound up on a tangent, "there was too much rabbinical interrogation of characters in the Wagner *opera*. Who now is this so-handsome blond young man faring through the dangerous wood?"

De Porta nodded. "Kreowski and Fuchs," he said. "You've seen their book on the satirical novels and cartoons that were being turned out by the score in Vienna seventy years ago. Cartoons of the Rabbi of Bayreuth with a very racial nose directing kosher Valkyries in an orthodox Nibelungen Ring, I've seen some ribald ones myself Fuchs and Kreowski didn't reproduce." The bookseller smiled.

"Viennese in provenance, probably," Van Kill said with a kind of urgent abstraction. "I wouldn't wonder the find Nachmann wished off on Pough goes back to Vienna by way of Lisbon and Prague."

"Pough believes it's genuine, you think?"

"He has no reason not to. That's just our trouble," Van Kill said, as the waiter announced his plane. "Just one of our troubles," he added, getting up.

"I understand," said De Porta. There were so many things to understand. "David—" he ventured almost hesitantly and rose with Van Kill.

"Jail's the only place for David," the document examiner said flatly, and then as if the two were unconnected observations, "I can't have him ruining my investigation now."

De Porta went no further with Van Kill than the circular island of the Information Desk. He said good-by there and watched Van Kill striding away with a touch of weariness in his gait, as familiar a figure as his father had been before him coming into, going out of the Random Place shop. Familiar and yet strange. Hendrik Van Kill might yet take quite unpredictable steps to keep anyone from ruining his investigation of this murder, Benjamin De Porta was afraid.

XXXVI

FREDERICK POUGH telephoned the Otranto apartment as Yanni was packing the bag Van Kill had asked him to bring to the precinct station . . . Dr. Van Kill was preparing to go out of town, Yanni said cautiously and with his best enunciation. However, a message could be sent him, if it was important? . . . It was, rather, the publisher said. He would be glad to talk it over with Mr. Mavromicháli, if he cared to make an appointment. Meanwhile perhaps Mr. Mavromicháli would exert his influence with Dr. Van Kill to take the commission Mr. Pough had in mind . . . Yanni smiled as he would have done face to face with his good customer and made an appointment for eleven o'clock. . . .

The Greek saw a sardonic humor in Mr. Pough's calling Van Kill before business hours. When the kyrios had requested a look at the Geyer document a few days before, Mr. Pough had temporized. Needing his help then, after the murder of Betty Hargrave, the great editor had sent his Geyer letter to the kyrios to examine at his leisure. In due course, Yanni reasoned, he would anyway have requested the assistance that the kyrios could give. But the timing of this business diplomacy had been upset by the attack on Miss Newman. . . .

Yanni's unemotional analysis of Frederick Pough's state of mind was that the murder of the golden *desposúna* had (in an entirely respectable fashion) touched first his heart, but the attempt to murder Miss Newman was a blow at his head which the editorial director of Po Publications immediately recognized. Yanni's business instincts were as subtle as his intuition and he was right in feeling that the president of Popub would not quibble about terms . . . He told Van Kill as much when he relayed Pough's message to the precinct station with the bag and was partly satisfied at the answer Van Kill gave. . . .

An hour or so later the Greek spoke of this to Edward in the

273

foyer of the Otranto apartment. Yanni was on his way to keep the appointment with Frederick Pough.

"Under the circumstances I approve of the contact," Master Cameron said as he held the door open. "A little more money never does any harm. Hal's a brilliant man in his particular line, but a trifle irresponsible where business matters are concerned."

"He *said* he would take it," Yanni answered with sober content. Edward nodded back at him. It was remarkable how the man from the wilds of Mani and the boy whose ancestors had emerged from Highland fogs showed the same grim financial certainty in their liquid dark eyes. "You," the Greek's sternness carried over into this, "are not to do any of the things you will think of while I am departed."

Edward nodded again. "No," he said. And observing that Yanni was feeling in a vest pocket to make sure the firm's detective card and badge were there, he added a bit of familiar advice on his own part. "Just remember to think in English. Wait a little every time before you speak and avoid the consonants that give you trouble."

"I will," Yanni said, turning away briskly. *"Addìo."*

"Addìo," Edward said.

"He will undertake to execute your commission when he returns," Yanni quoted Van Kill.

"Splendid." Pough made a memorandum on a desk pad.

They could talk terms when Van Kill came back and took over in the Cavaliers' investigation where Miss Hargrave left off. "One doesn't," Pough said, "often find a combination of intelligent instinct and discretion like Dr. Van Kill's."

Yanni found he needn't do much more than assent. It came easy to him with a good customer like Frederick Pough.

The attempt to murder Miss Newman, who had known about the Cavaliers' assignment from the first, coming so close upon the murder of Miss Hargrave in the midst of her work with the Cavaliers, was *not* an accidental sequence, Pough told the Greek. "They knew more about Popub than we guessed they did."

"*Lee and his partner* have a large crew of traitors," Yanni came tactfully to the point.

"Miss Goff is still in jail, I'm not accusing Burke or Lee," Pough said judicially. "I'm not blaming Harris either, though time and again I've told him that Crime Cabinet's a standing invitation to violence for irresponsibles and not a few of them come around *Carnage*." The use to which Harris's museum had been put last night was enough to make a man lose his interest in firearms, and he had never cared much for them, Pough said. . . .

Yanni, who preferred a knife, had to agree. But he said, carefully, "I should make it clear, Mr. Pough, that Kyrios Van Kill does not guarantee to protect the members of your firm in this matter. He is interested in your commission only because you are concerned to investigate the relation of these Cavaliers to Miss Hargrave's death."

There was no need, Yanni thought, to tell Pough outright that Van Kill had already been commissioned to investigate the editor of *Carnage* magazine, but he was relieved to hear that Pough understood.

"This firm does not stand or fall with any one man," the publisher said guardedly. "I also am concerned only with having every angle of the Cavaliers' connections exposed."

"I mean to look into this Burke and this Lee myself," Yanni shifted the emphasis. "I have had a certain experience with such types."

Lee was a type who showed up in surprising places, Pough said, unless his identification was all wrong. "At the Weatherlys' last night. You must remember Weatherly, Mr. Mavromicháli——"

Yanni nodded. Leonard Weatherly was a Wall Street banker, an amateur of classical archaeology who came to the Matapan sometimes. Scholarly and artistic celebrities or demi-celebrities from in and out of town frequented the Weatherlys' annual Roman holidays, Yanni believed he had once heard Van Kill remark.

"I don't *know* he's the Richard Lee Miss Hargrave described to me," Pough continued. "But he's the same type and I heard some woman he was hanging about refer to him as a promising young promoter from the South. I didn't want to start him thinking, so I didn't ask."

"*I* shall ask him," Yanni said bluntly, "not mentioning you, sir, of course."

"Splendid. If it's action they want, it's action we'll give them," Pough said in a decisive voice and then, referring back to the Weatherlys, "Not my favorite kind of party, one of those four-to-four serials, with no formal food between cocktails and scrambled eggs. But they're such delightful hosts they deserve some of Antoine's *kottópoulo bámies.*"

Yanni waited with modest anticipation for what he felt sure he was about to receive.

"Can you arrange one of your large booths for me New Year's Eve so late as this?" Pough said.

Yanni smiled. He said, "There is always a place reserved for you, Mr. Pough."

Yanni Mavromicháli had hardly settled in the deep green chair across from Frederick Pough to discuss the job the publisher had in mind for Van Kill when Edward Cameron in the Otranto apartment heard the telephone ring. He shut off his train and went into Van Kill's study to answer it.

"Miss Beggs? Yes, this is Edward." Master Cameron paused, listening intently. Miss Beggs was one of his instructors in manual arts at Webster School.

"You probably won't recognize my voice. I have a very bad cold," came over the telephone to Edward.

"Sorry," he said, "I didn't catch all of that." He looked very young and solemn, ingulfed in Van Kill's big swivel chair.

"This is Miss Beggs. You probably won't recognize my voice. I have a very ba—" The woman's voice suddenly stopped with the throttled choke which is sometimes heard from people who have a very bad cold. Then it continued, pedagogical, precise:

"One of our school patrons was much pleased by your Mithra figure. He wants to exhibit your drawings for it in a display of school art which he is making at his private museum. Will you bring your drawings for the Mithra figure up to the school corner? Come right away, please. Our patron will meet us there in his car and take us for a field trip to his museum. Won't that be nice?"

"That would be nice," said Edward, pausing reflectively again.

It was a little space before he answered, "Is it all right if I come in riding clothes? I'm going to the Park later on."

"Surely," said the precise voice on the other end of the line.

"That will be very nice," said Edward. "I'll meet you there in forty-five minutes then."

Yanni caught George Stock rushing through the reception room of *Carnage* magazine.

"Hello there, Mavromicháli. What are you doing up here?" The art editor had a chatting acquaintance with Yanni at the Flash and Shutter Club, but the Greek had never seen him so friendly.

Yanni, doing what he called "tsecking," was not the affable proprietor of the Matapan. When Mavromicháli of Van Kill and Mavromicháli Detectives was checking, he was polite but unpredictable, his quite considerable muscle assumed an implicit menace, or where women were concerned an implicit promise, and his presence filled any room he happened to be in. Yanni had derived a wry satisfaction of late from people realizing at last that the men of his native land were fighting men.

The Greek said, "Hello," with cautious reserve, and waited while the art editor parked on Baby's desk to talk. Baby herself was out.

"Don't tell me," Stock said, his bleached face twitching in a grin. "I'll tell you. Only got a minute. Gotta go grab some layout changes offa that lazy bum Lenz. I know more about you than you think," he said, the grin fading. "You want me to tell you if I tried to bump Newman off. I didn't and I'll tell you why."

This man was not friendly, the Greek calculated. He was nervous.

"Because, next to the big boss, she's the brains of this firm, and if I'd taken a shot at her, she'd be dead right now." Stock threw open his coat with a sudden jerk.

It was like a peepshow, Yanni thought, the way Stock flashed the marksman's medal on his vest. And Stock was a Punch prating on of his achievements with a gun. He'd been runner-up for the Leech and Wimbledon teams several times, the art editor said. Yanni clucked his appreciation and Stock went on.

"Whoever missed that short try was a lousy shot," the art editor asserted, "or he wanted to miss. From a car driving around that Rotunda of course, when you consider the angle and all, a deliberate miss that close would be damn good. But it wasn't me. At 9 P.M. I was driving past the corner of 125th Street and Amsterdam, fifty blocks away."

He drove a dark-blue sedan, Stock said. He mentioned the name of his garage, showed his driver's license. Yanni took the information down.

"At that corner at just that time there was a water main break." The art editor put his feet to the floor and started to get up. "Which is how come I snagged my right front tire on a piece of cast iron." Stock rose. "How could I be wise to that break unless I was there? How could I be in two places at once, huh?" he wanted to know. "Gotta run now, good-by, see you later." He rushed out, trailing an aroma of dark room in his wake.

Yanni's interview with Frederick Pough took little more than fifteen minutes and his chat with George Stock less than five. Accordingly it was not much past eleven o'clock on the morning after Christmas when nine-year-old Edward Cameron set before the Honorable Diana Brown the idea that had come to him as he was promising over the telephone to bring his drawings to the corner by Webster School.

Lady Di's opposition was mostly a matter of form. She had seen for some time what ailed Edward, perhaps more clearly than Van Kill because she had come to know the boy in a more tranquil way. This unease of a rapidly maturing mind sought outlet in Edward's forays through the city with the Greek.

Mavromichàli, she thought, would probably have lifted the boy out of his post-Christmas boredom (mixed a little now with loneliness for Van Kill) by running him down to the Matapan, having Antoine teach him how to fry fish. She hardly saw how she could blame herself, she told the document examiner later on. Nevertheless it was with a poignant recollection of his panic over the affair that, when he came at last to write up his recollections of this case, Van Kill set down, as nearly as he could arrive at it, the very minute of Edward's telephone call. . . .

As has been said, the argument between Lady Di and Edward was perfunctory on both sides. (Yanni, consulted later, thought the move would take the young kyrios further out of the danger zone. Being very busy, he put off thinking what Van Kill would say.) When Edward Cameron made a telephone call of his own, it was therefore about 11:10 A.M., quite near the moment when Frederick Pough was congratulating Yanni on getting the aid of Hendrik Van Kill against the Christian Cavaliers.

Edward had little notion of what he was starting when he took out his book of private addresses, ran through it with a grubby finger, and called the number he had in mind. . . The damage, such as it might be to various parties, had been set in motion and the ground for the panic of Van Kill (flying west to Kansas City now) had been laid by the time Yanni finished talking with George Stock. . . .

The Greek didn't try very hard to find Paul Harris. He was out, Baby told Yanni when she returned to her desk. How long had Mr.—Uh?—been waiting, she inquired . . . She needn't bother to leave a message, Yanni told Baby, and left her with a smile which somewhat jumbled her next two calls.

Yanni didn't try because he believed, with one of those superstitious convictions of which he was capable, that Harris had not only murdered Betty Hargrave, but attempted the life of Miss Newman as well. The solution of the case, the proof against Harris, must surely rest with Burke and Lee at the Christian Cavaliers. He felt more certain of this than ever as he came out to the new Hermes cabriolet, parked near the Popub's glass-canopied marquee, and slid under its wheel.

Just *how* Harris was concerned with that abode of buzzards the Greek, driving downtown now at a sober pace toward the Matapan, didn't feel so sure. As a tipster, may be. A stingy man like Harris, Yanni told himself, would not lay down any cash. As a (what was that word the kyrios had used, Yanni wound it experimentally around his tongue) as an *ambivalent* person, Harris was the logical candidate. Like a child Harris did not really know where his affections lay, thought Yanni, who knew well whom he hated and whom he loved. . . .

Thus considering still, Yanni showed Leonard Weatherly to a booth and bowed himself away toward the kitchen, where he called George Stock's garage. But as he sat by the pantry phone, the Greek's mind was not on the art editor of *Carnage* magazine. He was congratulating himself on Mr. Weatherly's having chosen to lunch at the Matapan this noon. He could follow the lead Mr. Pough had given him about Lee without going out of his way.

Mavromicháli grinned his private satisfaction so fiercely that Panayoteekee, switching his fustanella into the pantry after butter pats, retired immediately to the waiters' washroom to examine his conscience . . . George Stock's alibi checked in every detail as the Greek had expected to find that it would. He got up and went back to Weatherly's booth without having noticed Panayoteekee at all. . . .

Yanni had noticed Leonard Weatherly's superficial characteristics before. He was a prim bilious-looking little man who reminded Mavromicháli of the poor wizened figs one paid fifteen cents each for in New York. He remembered Weatherly's likes and dislikes about food, one did that automatically, he had chatted with the Wall Street man about Greek vases, Weatherly favoring red and black, Yanni black and white though tactfully, and that was about all.

Today the Greek listened with his ears after he had nudged Weatherly into talking about the party last night. "Unfortunate how many people don't consider themselves entertained unless they have more to drink than they should," the little man said grimly. He'd personally spent most of the evening arguing with Frederick

Pough, whose knowledge of Erechtheum reconstruction lore would have *astounded* Mavromicháli, no doubt . . . Yanni, who had been engaged in restoring art objects when Van Kill first met him as foreman of a dig in Corinth, was frequently astounded by rich American collectors of antiquities. . . .

"Yes, sir . . . No doubt," he responded.

"I'm afraid I was selfish about Pough," Weatherly said. "Never got such a chance to talk to him before."

Yanni was interested only in the whereabouts of Dick Lee last night and Mr. Weatherly had never even heard of the big promoter from the South. The Greek saw that Mr. Weatherly was the sort of host who considers his duty done if he takes a guest out of circulation at his wife's parties. Mavromicháli thought it lucky Mr. Weatherly could identify another of his Christmas guests lunching at the Matapan.

This gentleman, a pudgy customer's man, Yanni didn't often pronounce his name, Bernard Flather, had a vivid recollection of Dick Lee. A demon with the ladies, he said. The customer's man, a party-crashing guzzling lion-seeker (the Greek had words for him) *would* remember an unfortunate incident, Yanni reflected, an incident at an affair which was probably no more a "brawl" than any party where some people drink a lot and some don't.

Flather recalled Dick Lee quite well on account of a certain guest who should be nameless since he had been taken flat drunk shamefully early. "He shouldn't have inhaled sherry on top of all the corn he had driving up from the South. He certainly was corny, get it?" the customer's man inquired boisterously.

Yanni had a large tolerance for festival behavior, but this afternoon, he observed to himself, Mr. Flather had been dog-hairing all morning.

"Dick Lee was the bright genius who suggested we pour some more corn down him, and he was perfectly all right, I give you my word," Flather assured Yanni, "about an hour after we found him passed out on the floor . . . Lee? Why Lee went back to the ladies then."

Harris, the ladies, Dick Lee and a car from the South which

might have hugged the Rotunda rim last night, Yanni juggled these images with orders, suggestions, and complaints. Yanni, who had started his life in America as a hacker, know how screwy ladies could be . . . A lady from Weehawken swore Lee had been with her last Friday night, the night of Betty Hargrave's murder. Yanni was willing to bet his last drachma that any lady of Dick Lee's persuasion would swear to anything Dick Lee told her to.

Nothing like bearding the buzzard in its lair, the Greek assured his own doubts. He swung through the kitchen as the luncheon rush subsided, headed back for the pantry and called the office of the Christian Cavaliers. The telephone rang in the midst of a vast cold silence on the other end. No birds in the nest . . . Yanni had a long telephone conversation with Kyría Diana Brown a little later which took his mind back to Harris, but for the most part he was thinking of Burke and Lee. . . .

Between one and five o'clock Yanni tried the Cavaliers a dozen times with the same result . . . Plenty chance to lime and pluck their bough before the kyrios came home. The advertisement he had been revolving amid the click of silverware and the muffled plunk of dishes might give him a needful ingredient to make the lure stick, the Greek reflected, pointing the Hermes cabriolet for Barclay Street and then uptown. . . .

"Oímoi hos phanerón!" said Yanni to himself. "Alas how obvious!" Continuing to think about the case, he deftly dodged the Hermes around a jaywalking garmentmaker's push truck at Thirty-fifth Street and Eighth Avenue . . . Obvious, but not in the way he had thought. Mustn't let your prejudices run away with you, the kyrios was always saying. . . .

Lee and Paul Harris it had been who followed the kyrios's despoinís to her death last Friday night. That was sure. But Harris was the type of spy, not of murderer. The Greek saw this clearly now. Lee set forth to murder, Harris to spy. Lee on his murderous errand struck Harris down for prowling after him. Lee, drunk with a murderer's arrogance, covered Harris up with Harris's own shepherd's plaid overcoat and the cat woman had stepped on his stomach . . . There was a time when he himself would have admired a glaring garment like that topcoat, the Greek mused inconsequentially, and drew to a halt near Times Square. . . .

"Anybody seeing automobile on or near rim of Rotunda above 79th Street boat basin, 9 o'clock, Christmas night, will learn something to advantage." When he stepped into the Times Building, the economical Mavromicháli had his notice boiled down to the point where it was practically sinister.

Thinking the tired young man at the desk looked a trifle suspicious, Yanni produced his detective card. The young man waved it away, took the notice wearily. He looked as if he considered himself above divorce evidence. . . .

The Greek's mind played back and forth upon Paul Harris and Dick Lee as he drove to successive newspaper offices, leaving the same notice for a single insertion under a box number that carried no name. Going in and out of doors, his smart steps rang in tune to the rhythmic sequence of suppositions his mind was forming about the two men.

Harris as a tipster recommending Amalgamated Air over the telephone to Burke, fattening up the Cavaliers for blackmail of them and their crew. (How could he *ever* have supposed Harris was the murderer when he knew the cat woman saw Harris flat on his back in the alley? Why should a *spy* knock a *murderer* down? To keep the murderer from knowing he was spied on? *Léros*, Yanni chided himself in mild anguish, *nonsense* sometimes you think, Mavromicháli. It was what Van Kill would call emotional fixation no doubt, trying to oblige Van Kill, whose original job had been to investigate Harris.)

Lee waiting then for a chance to frame Harris, Yanni's mind took up the interrupted rhythm of connection between murder and attempt. Lee, informed by some detective or confederate that the coming together of Echo Newman and Paul Harris would take place (let the kyrios speculate how). Dick Lee using the Weatherlys' party as an alibi, taking the drunken Southerner's car, driving around the Rotunda, firing the shot at *Desposúna* Newman . . .

Find someone who saw that car (Yanni left his last stop, the

Daily News office, with the sure sense that he could—modernistic buildings uplifted his practical brain). Find someone who could describe its driver, and the roast would be ready to serve when the kyrios returned. . . .

Shortly after five-thirty, as Yanni headed for the Otranto, Paul Harris glanced down at a stack of typescript by his easy chair and yawned. Having been out of the office a good deal that day, he had made some ado about carrying a loaded brief case home. The editor of *Carnage* sat in his favorite spot for reading, in front of the broad bay window in his living room.

The editorial eye flickered upon the ruck of typescript and caught at a title that spoke to it, THE VANISHING VIRGIN AND THE TRIPLE TOMBS. Harris was about to reach for this when the telephone rang on a cellarette at the other side of his chair.

"Hello," he said, then sharply, "I told you not to telephone here."

"I thought you'd want to know how I came out."

Morna Maye's fruity voice sounded a little doleful, matching the basement room in the Seventies where she sat by a pseudo-colonial desk before a pseudo-fireplace on top of which was a pseudo-marble figure advertising a popular brand of port.

"Get it over with quick."

Harris had visited Morna Maye in this apartment once, before he heard of Betty Hargrave's murder, as a detective from Inspector Larkin's office, assigned by McLone to shadow the editor, had duly reported to the Homicide Squad. Harris didn't like to think about the place. Its shabby rugs, dirty closets and cockroach-infested kitchen reminded him of his past. But the layout of the place, which had been a speakeasy once, was ideal for what Harris had been contemplating even when he visited Morna there. Its back room, which the Albany discard faced as she sat at the telephone, had good thick walls, one small high barred window, and a stout back door looking onto a tiny fenced yard which was never used. To disturb the other ephemeral inhabitants of the building would have required a mass murder at the least.

"He came like a lamb. I didn't have to tape him or anything."

Morna lifted her eyes to the connecting door of the back room.

"Hurry it up, I said," Harris rasped.

There was a certain relish in the way Morna took her time. "I did just like you said. I met him with the car and told him we would wait for the school patron, who had been temporarily detained, in my apartment. I just put a blindfold on him. I told him it was a game."

"Forget I ever told you anything." The editor's tone was casually brutal . . . "If anything happens, it's all on you."

"I know that," Morna Maye replied dismally. "I just wanted to ask, what do I do now?"

"Wait'll the doc gets back. I'll pass the word to you some way then."

"I mean after he wakes up." Through the door of the back room the woman at the telephone could see a little figure in riding clothes on the bed. "While he was awake he was *terrible*, I mean after we got in here. He kept asking for whisky, and that wasn't *all* he kept asking for."

There was a short silence while the editor of *Carnage* figured this out. "He's supposed to be precocious," Paul Harris said then with a mirthless chuckle. "Just you keep on giving him what he wants."

Yanni went home to feed the cat, who remarked upon the lonely apartment disapprovingly. This done, with a few well-considered pats and a few apostrophes in the vernacular Greek (to the general purport of, "Oh, cat, thou must believe the kyrios will soon return, oh, cat, and everything will be okay"), Yanni fared forth to his Uncle Yoryi's Cousin Spiros's Olympia Palace Motion Picture Theatre in Yonkers.

Arriving well before the first show began, he sailed through the empty lobby with all the assurance of a distant relative. He paused briefly to look askance at the decor, which was Roxy on a *retsinata* jag. He went on back stage. As the person who had persuaded Uncle Yoryi's Cousin Spiros to hire Rudi Smart's mind-reading act, Yanni felt a certain responsibility.

He returned in a few minutes. If Cousin Spiros wasn't worrying, why should he? Yanni settled down to enjoy the newsreel. Part of it showed the Italian army knowing no obstacles in Albania. A fine people, only their bosses are bums, Yanni observed to himself. And they run well, he thought, ignoring most of the featured picture, which was some Hollywood director's notion of Viennese sophistication before the First German War. Mavromicháli preferred knee-pants and quill-pen pictures about the American Revolution.

The Greek had stretched his satisfaction over the newsreel thin by the time the chief usher, in a uniform of more than admiralty splendor, stepped up to a microphone at the center of the stage before heavy velvet drapes and began bellowing, in what he evidently regarded as an Oriental wail: "Calling Swami Kalikal! Swami Kalikal, appeaaar. Minoot man, mighty mind, appear!"

Very ham, Yanni thought. But he sat forward as the drapes parted and a small figure in Oriental robes stalked out to a rumbustious burst of melancholy swing music from the organ. It will be okay, it must be okay, Yanni told himself nervously, concentrating on the small figure's solemn face. . . .

XXXVII

YANNI spent Friday morning calling up some of Weatherly's female guests . . . Expensive at wholesale, was his estimate, after wading through an assortment of trilling sopranos and gushing contraltos . . . *Koúkleh zalisméneh,* giddy dolls, was the Greek's unspoken comment. To listen to them you will think Mr. Lee does nothing at the party but make donkey's eyes on the person you are talking to over the telephone. . . .

Mavromicháli got exactly nowhere until he called personally at the Weatherly house in the lower Seventies off Riverside Drive and talked to Roberts, the Weatherly chauffeur. Roberts had been directing cars on Christmas night.

"Saw a man looked like you say this Lee did," the chauffeur asserted. "Going out to some car with a southern license at the end of the line. I went in the house for a bite to eat then. Hope you win your bet."

It was a dark-colored sedan, Roberts answered Yanni's question. And he was doing damn well to remember that, there were so many of them. . . .

A dark-colored sedan, Lee in a dark-colored sedan . . . Yanni telephoned his luncheon instructions to Dukas and called up the office of the Christian Cavaliers.

"Richard Lee speaking," said a saccharine male voice. "Who is this, please?"

"A friend with money who'll be seeing you," said Yanni and hung up.

"Mr. Lee, a dark-colored sedan with a southern license—" Standing in the open doorway of the Christian Cavaliers' office, Yanni did not finish the sentence, for Lee whirled at the sound of his name. Red, pale, and guilty, Yanni noted Lee's face as he turned.

Yes, it did look a little like roast beef rare properly streaked with fat.

The Junior Cavalier started to take a step forward, thought better of it, and leaned on his desk, by which he had been talking to Thomas Burke, who stood up, completely poised, grinning sardonically.

"Did you call up a lil' piece back? Who are you?" Lee said in one breath. "What about my car?"

Yanni did not answer the questions. "Wednesday night, Christmas night," he said slowly and distinctly, "you were at a party at the home of Mr. Leonard Weatherly."

Lee stared at the waiting Greek. "Great day in the morning, man," he said, "what have I done now?"

"At about eight-thirty on Christmas night," Yanni said deliberately, guessing at it, "you went out on the sidewalk by the corner of Riverside Drive. You got under the steering wheel of a dark-colored sedan having a southern license plate." Burke, Yanni saw without apparently noticing him, was listening with unsympathetic interest.

"Oh, that car!" Lee's whinnying tone of relief seemed as forced as the spluttering confusion with which he went on. "That wasn't my car. I came in a taxi, that car belonged to a lil' ole boy got drunk."

He took the boy's keys out of his pocket when they found him under the piano passed out. Lee knew there'd be more corn in the car, that was the only thing to bring him around. "I just eased out to his car for that," Lee said. His speech was gumbo thick with apprehension and Yanni thought how inconsistent native Americans were who urged the foreign-born to lose their accents, as the Junior Cavalier went on, "I brought his own jar of corn liquor in to him and that's every blessed thing I did."

Yanni sliced into it. "You must have found your expert marksmanship useful in the car."

"I told you all I did in that car, except I left the keys there," Lee said, flushing angrily. "That was 'cause I stopped to take a lil' taste. What's this you handin' me out about marksmanship?" He gave a thin laugh. "Why, I couldn't hit a barn at six feet."

"That," said Yanni Mavromicháli ominously, "is left to be seen." He turned on his heel and walked out. He had at no time identified himself.

Glancing over his shoulder as he neared the little alley entrance, Yanni saw Burke stride up behind.

"He drives down South to see his folks every spring," Thomas Burke said without preface. "He makes the cheap license he gets there do all the rest of the year in New York. That's why you got him going," the Senior Cavalier explained as if he thought Yanni must be a member of the traffic squad. But Burke went on, "Did you ever see a southern boy who couldn't handle his gun?"

Either one of those buzzards would throw the other to the wolves, Yanni thought, when he left them Friday afternoon . . . Lee a good deal further than Burke, Yanni was convinced Saturday morning as he sat parked on the north side of West Twentieth Street and fingered a typewritten sheet.

A document easily come by in Burke's apartment last night, through a contemptible outer door lock, under some old dirty shirts, this page grasped in the Greek's fingers above the steering wheel. Yanni was not particularly happy. It was harder than starving a goat for him to give up anything to the police, particularly this sample sheet from the Cavaliers' list of small customers. His document-fishing trip besides had taken Mavromicháli to a section of the Bronx where in Prohibition days he was known simply as Black Mike.

Mavromicháli slid out of the Hermes and walked slowly across Twentieth Street, reflecting that with the *whole* document to keep he could have made the *Carnage*-Cavaliers link up which the kyrios so much desired. But Van Kill had expressly told him to hook only a sample and leave the rest to the squad. . . .

Lee, alas how plain it was that Lee had fed this carbon list of customers anonymously through the mail to Thomas Burke. It might have been Harris with his memory for detail duplicating the list for Burke, but much more obviously it was Lee. . . .

Yanni strolled past a warehouse which exuded a smell of pepper and spice toward the Tenth Precinct Station entrance, while considering the obviosity of the Number Two Cavalier . . . Lee, Richard, klepping the lists and the Cavaliers' propaganda the night he murdered Betty Hargrave. Lee the Number Two Man, saving all that material to feed back a bite at a time to Thomas Burke as from an omniscient contributor, promoting himself to be Number One Man while he waited to frame Harris. . . .

Harris where, think English, Mavromicháli . . . The devious Greek took himself hastily past the desk sergeant and an idea sprang full-armed upon him . . . Harris *who* was also trying to be Number One Man through blackmail of the Cavaliers. Number Two Men, that was the psychological connection for making which the kyrios must certainly congratulate him, Yanni carried this consolation along as he went up the steep stairs toward the Homicide Squad. That was the natural affinity between Lee and Harris, they were both Number Two Men, trying to be Number One. . . .

Yanni found Mars alone in the squad room with his feet up on the long center table and his derby hat tilted morosely over his eyeglasses. All policemen look like crooks, thought Yanni.

"Dr. Van Kill," he held out the typewritten sheet and spoke with laborious care, "Dr. Van Kill told me, give you this, from Thomas Mpurke's apartment in the Bronx. There is more."

"Thanks." Mars sized the Greek up from under the rim of his derby and extended a hand. "How did he get it?"

"He does not know."

"I see." One short appraisal had told the sergeant more about the Greek than the Greek would have cared to know the sergeant knew. "I'll attend to the rest of it personally," said Mars. "You give him this from us, soon as he comes back. Roughead's detail've turned up a witness saw Miss Hargrave and somebody, the murderer maybe, following her last Friday night."

This witness, Mars explained gloomily, lived in the same block as the Cavaliers' office. About midnight the night of Miss Hargrave's death this citizen was walking his dog. From across the street he saw a girl go into the Cavaliers' alley. He noticed little about her except she had something white in her hair. But he did get a good look a minute after that at a man in a dark overcoat who ducked into a sort of street extension of a basement apartment entrance near the Cavaliers' alley mouth. This witness didn't see the man come out, though, and he didn't spot Harris at all. Presumably Harris and the murderer didn't come up for air until the dog-walker had reached Columbus Avenue.

"But hell," Mars, working his eyebrows under his derby, came to a dismal conclusion, "that was across the street and a week ago. Roughead thinks he can build this citizen up to identify. But I guess we wait till the doc comes back and see what he's got on Harris. Anyway this dog-walker ought to stack up with the doc's cat woman, tell him that for us too when he comes back. He'll understand."

"He will." Yanni wondered what the cops would like in the way of a witness, a retired policeman with a candid camera? "Thank you very muts," he said. . . .

Mavromicháli returned to the cabriolet and began reading replies to his advertisement which he had picked up at various newspaper offices on his way to the Homicide Squad . . . The Lucrative Loan Co. desired to know if the advertiser needed money on easy terms; the Coverall Car Insurance invited him to consider his folly in having an uncovered crackup; the Comet Detective Agency would investigate anything for him discreetly and thoroughly. One by one, from the small pile on his lap, Yanni tossed these and other more personal blurbs into the glove compartment with neat systematic scorn. . . .

"I saw a car near the Rotunda about nine o'clock Christmas night. I'll be back in town Monday morning. Call me up then and I'll try to pin it down for you," wrote a certain Lawrence O'Dell, who gave a number in the Academy exchange.

Yanni put this letter in an inside coat pocket and drew a sharp breath through his teeth. It *had* to be a dark-colored sedan with a southern license that O'Dell saw, he thought prayerfully . . . And should it be, they would strip this Friday night Ixion pantless from his dark overcoat. They would roll him out bare-faced in the dark-colored sedan around the Rotunda like Ixion from the cloud. Oh, *he* would come out of it. They would—they would jointly pin a double carnage on Cavaliers for Frederick Pough.

This assurance gripped the Greek through Saturday and Sunday, most of which he spent at the Matapan, alternately hounding the help like a Cerberus to preparations for New Year's Eve, alternately smiling in a curiously remote way. He always took fear for his job when the boss grinned like that, the Spartan headwaiter was reduced to telling Antoine the Athenian chef by Sunday night.

By that time Mars had called up. "We got the rest of Burke's list. It's legal now," the sergeant said bluntly.

"What does he say?" Yanni's question was diffident because Mars didn't have to tell him *anything*. "Burke first says there are some names of clients he remembers. How does he say he has these many more names in writing now?"

"Santa Claus," Mars growled amusedly and told Yanni how Singer and Swann had called on Burke with a search warrant and left him with stern admonitions in place of an inch-thick sheaf of typewriter flimsy bearing the names of several thousand Cavaliers' sympathizers.

"Says he got it through the mail last Monday," Mars explained. "Thinks it was his patron saint, True American, again . . . Hell, no, Burke didn't save the wrapper," the sergeant answered Yanni's instinctive query. "We're thankful we got the list. We think it matches what we had, *before* you gave us the sheet, I mean, but we'll have to wait for the doc, cappy says, to tell us definitely if it's a match and why he thinks it's so damn important. We all hope he hurries home."

So did Yanni and as he took Mars' call Saturday afternoon he reassured himself by glancing at the telegram he had got that morning from Van Kill. "Finished K. C. Flying Santa Fe. Home Monday late. Go see Echo and David. Don't meet me," it advised.

Yanni had inquired over the telephone about Miss Newman and Mr. Montefiore several times. He went Sunday morning to see them both personally. . . . He came away from his visit to Montefiore with feelings very mixed. The Greek couldn't conceive of anybody being contented in jail, but he was pleased to know David was pleased with the food. Making a lot of notes about jailhouse life, David said, and getting next to himself in a lot of ways. The Greek wasn't sure what all this meant, but he would report it to the kyrios with Homeric fidelity and hope the kyrios would be pleased . . . Calling on Miss Newman in the hospital was of course more complicated than going to see Mr. Montefiore in jail. Mr. Montefiore was not suspected of knowing something that endangered his life. As yet nobody had tried to kill *him*. . . .

Miss Newman was mending steadily, said the round-faced jolly little nurse who showed Yanni in to the private wing at St. Luke's. She was so jolly and so much a nurse that Yanni almost forgot she was also one of the new generation of policewomen. Particularly after viewing the aseptic elegance De Porta had arranged for Miss Newman to mend in.

But Echo was only distantly cordial to the Greek. She looked like a Cretan goddess whose religion had collapsed, Yanni fancied to himself, with the loose black volutes of her hair against the pillow.

"I'm feeling much better," she said in response to the Greek's double question. "But I don't want to say anything about the case. They tell me I have no fever, but I must be delirious, because the only thing I can think of can't possibly be true."

Yanni asked no further questions. Van Kill had said she would be like that. Yanni went home to the Otranto, fed and comforted the cat, and examined a piece of mail which had come special delivery. Still wearing his gloves, he handled the dime-store envelope, addressed in block pencil letters to "Van Kill and Mavromicháli, Detectives." He held it up to his mouth and breathed on it all around, then scrutinized it carefully in various angles of light at Van Kill's study window.

The Greek satisfied himself similarly about the fold of dime-store stationery inside the envelope after he had perused its contents. He was about to drop the note on Van Kill's desk when an idea struck him and a slow smile replaced the scornful anger on his dark features. He walked rapidly through the connecting door into Lady Di's apartment. On the wall of her study, where she habitually stuck personal reminders and professional memoranda, newspaper clippings which gave her story ideas or which she thought might do so if she left them there long enough, Yanni transfixed the note and envelope with a pin. . . .

Sunday night Yanni felt justified in catching the mind-reading act at Uncle Yoryi's Cousin Spiros's Olympia Palace in Yonkers again . . . Quite professional by now, he thought. . . .

That same night Paul Harris managed to slip Inspector Larkin's detective long enough to phone Morna Maye from a drugstore booth. She hadn't stirred out once, she said. She'd been having food sent in from a delicatessen and liquor from a near-by store. Her guest seemed to be having a fine time, she added with a giggle.

"Keep him that way," Paul Harris said. He slid out of the booth into a side street, from the side street into Broadway, and walked up the main stem slowly as far as the Nineties, letting Larkin's detective keep him in plain sight.

Late Sunday night Detective Stanley Poniatowski, assigned to help the Bronx precinct in keeping tabs on Thomas Burke, had nothing new to report to Captain McLone. Burke and Lee were keeping themselves cloistered, as you might say, in Burke's Mosholu Parkway Apartment, the barrel-chested Polish detective announced.

"What do you suppose they're up to?" Captain McLone behind the desk in his narrow office was sleepy and a little querulous.

Poniatowski turned to go. "They've taken a vow of silence, those birds, it looks like to me."

On Monday afternoon, some two hours before Van Kill's plane was scheduled to arrive, Lawrence O'Dell wore his overcoat into the Otranto living room and sat down with Mavromicháli. He was a senior law student at International University and he had no hat. He was in town only because he didn't have time to go home to Chicago for the holidays, he told Yanni.

His caller had the cross doll-like gravity of many fat young scholars, the Greek observed now as he set forth what he thought it was necessary for O'Dell to know. There had been a big accident at the Rotunda Christmas night.

"It is fortunate you saw the escaping car," Yanni remarked with somber joy.

"I usually walk around there every night," O'Dell said. "It's about the only time I take off. I'm cramming up for my bar exams."

He lived just a few blocks from the Rotunda, which he had the habit of walking through down to the Hudson, usually about the same time, eight-thirty, and by the same route, the north tunnel, up the sloping path, then under the Hendrik Hudson Parkway bridge, the law student carefully explained . . . The very same route, Yanni recalled, that Paul Harris admitted taking Christmas night. . . .

"I took my customary route Christmas night. It's just your hard luck I didn't go far enough to see the smash. Was anyone fatally injured?" O'Dell interrupted himself to ask a second time.

"Not likely to be," Yanni said guardedly. This young man might be *too* obliging if he thought it was too important. "Tsust a question of exacting damages," the Greek declared.

"I see." O'Dell asked leave to light his pipe, puffed at it thoughtfully. "Trouble is, I didn't specially notice the car, except it was a sedan, some dark color, and it carried a southern license tag, I think, but I don't remember what state, I merely glanced at it driving off. Did any witness catch the number on the scene?"

"No." Yanni masked his elation. A double carnage was as good as pinned on Cavalier Lee and Pough's money in the kyrios's pocket, he thought.

"Too bad we can't connect the two, I'd just finished tying my shoestring and I caught a straight line on the driver's face," O'Dell said cryptically. "I notice faces, you understand."

He intended to be a prosecutor, the law student stated. This rather cross young man, who didn't get enough exercise and thus was probably a bit sluggish in certain important physical respects, would no doubt make a very good district attorney, Yanni admitted to himself.

"Going back to my story," O'Dell continued with a fine forensic air, "I pursued my customary route through the north tunnel and up the path toward the bridge. I didn't get quite as far as the light pole by the bridge underpass. You can't see the Rotunda from where I stopped, I can't swear I heard a crash, just the ordinary tire noises and backfires from the Parkway. I stopped because I noticed my shoestring was dragging."

"Most annoying, but most fortunate," Yanni remarked.

"Quite," the law student said severely. "Well, then, I was just straightening up when this dark sedan came driving out from under the bridge. Not fast, maybe ten miles an hour. He was on the far side of the street of course, fifteen-twenty feet from me on a guess, but there's good illumination from those light poles and he had his left front window rolled down. That's how I happened to catch a direct line on the man's face, his profile, to be exact, his left cheek, his nose, his mouth, and his chin. I always look at faces carefully and that's why I looked at his . . . I didn't go any further that night. There was a tough tort I'd been working on I wanted to get back to." One could see Mr. Lawrence O'Dell stepping down from the witness stand. "Did you," he asked, "secure a description of the possible perpetrator from any person on the actual scene?"

"We did not," Yanni had to confess with a sigh.

"Too bad. An unsupported identification may mean little in court," the fat young man declared as he stood up. "However, if you run across somebody for me to look at, I'll be glad to cooperate."

O'Dell put his pipe in his pocket and shook down his overcoat. "Sorry I couldn't give you something more to build on," he said.

Somebody to build up, Yanni corrected the phrase when O'Dell had gone. But that was a job for the kyrios and the cops. They could build this young man up the same way they would the dog-walker, Yanni told himself, going to telephone a message to La Guardia Field for Van Kill.

The roast was all garnished for the kyrios now. It was just a question of what end he should begin to carve from, the Greek thought. He called a taxi and for the third and last time set out to catch the mind-reading act at Uncle Yoryi's Cousin Spiros's Olympia Palace in Yonkers.

XXXVIII

~~~~~~

HENDRIK PIETER MINUIT VAN KILL stepped off the plane at La Guardia Field into a busy night which with the calm morning that followed it would bring Betty Hargrave's murderer very much into the public view.

"Dr. Van Kill?" The messenger boy saw the tall young man in the politician's sombrero shake his head. "Message for Dr. Van Kill?" The long drink of water with a hat like the mayor's looked like he belonged to such a name, but the boy didn't argue. He turned hopefully to the next man in line.

The document examiner brushed past the messenger as if he sensed how the tide of events was setting in Manhattan and hastened ·to plunge into it. There was an urgent detachment in his movements as he strode ahead of the other passengers and ducked the airport bus. Yet anyone noticing him, and he was not sure someone wasn't, might have observed that he followed the advice of Sherlock Holmes about the choice of hacks (neither the first nor the second which may present itself) in the cab rank.

Van Kill was eager to execute Frederick Pough's business with the Christian Cavaliers, also he hurried for a cause closer to his skin. He hadn't the slightest intention of being fingered by—one of Harris's gunsils, for instance. Not until he'd delivered the sack of news that had cost him a trip to the West and nearly five days of unsavory if not so dangerous company to collect.

There was an impatience about his caution which the studied blank of his features did not reveal. He told the cab driver to hurry . . . Van Kill was a man perfectly adjusted to his own company. But a person who knew him well, De Porta for instance, might have seen that the past five days of living with himself had been hard on him. It was not entirely the black sombrero (purchased in a fit of brittle humor and worn home to electrify his conservative ward) which made the ridge of Van Kill's nose and the triangular planes of his cheekbones seem unusually prominent. The document examiner had been looking at the roots of crime. Finding them unrecognizable except by their foliage gave him a sick recklessness of spirit which was to stay with him for months.

He understood now why Betty Hargrave had died and was as sure as he would ever be, since she was dead, that her death had been an unnecessary precaution on the part of her murderer. He knew that on the contrary Echo Newman was safe only as long as she remained in the hospital. For never, Van Kill was later to say, had he met a murderer so quietly balanced while letting an alibi or the lack of one carry him along, so quick to swim with the moment's surf as the murderer in this case . . . David, glimpsing the Columbus statue at Fifty-ninth Street while the taxi swung into Central Park West, David, he said his friend's name aloud, was still in jail, he hoped. . . .

Solving this case, giving the threads he and Yanni had gathered to the police to pull, was bringing him no sense of a thing finished. The thing that had killed Betty Hargrave, the motive if one insisted on the term, was too general. The murderer of course, the faster the police could arrange to finish off so consideredly wasteful a murderer the better, he thought, grabbing the safety strap as the taxi jarred to a halt. . . .

Thus by the tenor of his thoughts Van Kill was badly prepared for the empty apartment into which he walked a little before eight o'clock. Only Eohippus came to meet him, uttering diatonic observations which may have referred to the new hat, but certainly hinted of food. With the little beast trotting at his heels Van Kill made a thorough compass of the two apartments. Both looked unlived in, their own, except for the tree which the cat had been climbing, alarmingly neat. No train, no projects, no child's purposeful confusion, no message anywhere. . . .

The document examiner had a vivid imagination, made livelier by a varied police experience. Pictures rose to his mind which he tried to black out as he opened doors. Pictures of what he had seen found in thickets, floating in the water, not every kidnaping case came out so well as the Danforth affair his father had solved.

Enough clothes gone from Edward's closet for a visit of some days, he saw. But where?. . . Harris, the name rang sibilant in the picture, once Harris got Lady Di and Yanni out of the way, nobody else in the right camp would know about Van Kill's private war against the editor of *Carnage* magazine. . . .

With trembling fingers, cursing himself for his meticulous unease, Van Kill wrenched open faucets, ran water. It came out discolored with disuse from all but the ones in Yanni's bathroom. A damp towel was in the Greek's linen hamper and a recently used shaving set in his medicine chest. Used by Yanni though? Would an FBI man use Yanni's old-fashioned cutthroat razor and shaving bowl? You never could tell about the FBI. . . .

Van Kill fetched up at the kitchen in a growing panic which neither ridicule nor reason could down. The fact that breakfast materials and a carton of raw beef for the cat were in the refrigerator should have reassured him too, but it did not. He threw down a portion of meat for the cat and stalked back into Diana's quarters.

"Where are you all?" he called. "A fine welcome home," he shouted with foolish anger and in the heat of it strode into Lady Di's working room. He brought up with his hands upon its wall against a sheet of dime-store stationery whose penciled block lettering assailed his eyes.

"We have your boy," it apprised Van Kill and Mavromicháli, Detectives . . . If they had, the document examiner's purely homicidal look melted as he read on, if they had, this note wouldn't be here, by God. It would be in the hands of the FBI. Yes and a G man lurking in the closet with tear gas and another good man with a gat waiting to put anybody out of commission who came around, he thought with happy impracticality. For all his distrust of the municipal *astynomía*, Yanni as a patriotic Greek-American reverenced the FBI.

"If you want him back," Van Kill read on and an angry mirth showed in the corners of his mouth, "lay off the Cavaliers. Put a personal in any morning paper. Just say, 'Laying off. Frank.' If

you don't, you know what to expect," said "The Christian Cavaliers."

Van Kill was reaching for Lady Di's telephone when he heard
his own ring, distantly. In two dozen strides he was at his desk
and gripping the receiver.

"Van Kill here," he said. He listened for a moment, the grin
flickering around his mouth again, to a Western Union girl prepare
to parrot a message from one "Y. Mackmacaulay" which "we were
unable to deliver to you at the airport."

He waited no longer than to hear where Yanni was. The guess
which had been forming when he smiled at the Cavaliers' message
took swift possession of him. "Harris, the homunculus, Yonkers,
what a fool I was," he babbled. "They worked Rudi off on Pough
one time," he was running on into the girl's headphone. "Now
they've done it on Harris. My God, what a jape," he exulted and
hung up. . . .

"Must be nuts, the poor guy," one telegraph girl muttered to
another.

"Well, sure, if he's got a friend in Yonkers," the other asserted
reasonably.

In a taxi again and headed north Van Kill began to laugh, a
little hysterically. Never in his life had he expected to hurry to
Yonkers for a mind-reading act . . . The tall young man came up
a side aisle of the Olympia Palace at eight-fifty-nine so quietly that
only a few people in the crowd, intent upon the stage, noticed
him. From the wings Van Kill watched a small solemn Swami
take the last two questions of his act.

The Swami closed his great dark eyes and concentrated. He
waved a small hand as if summoning thought. "I am told that
you want to know about Aircraft," he opened his eyes after a
space and announced. "Beware of Amalgamated. It will slump
three-quarters of a point."

The chief usher, who faced the Swami before a microphone in
front of heavy velvet drapes, ripped open the plain envelope he
had been holding up, presented the note inside it for a moment to

the Swami, threw note and envelope into a Byzantine wastebasket on the stage.

"I was correctly told," the Swami observed to the microphone. "Thank *you*," he said and made an upward gesture. . . .

"And now in farewell I am told that a gentleman wishes to know where his family is." The Swami did not close his eyes on this last question. He seemed to be looking around the usher straight into the wings. "Let me say to him," the little Swami wheeled and spoke earnestly into the microphone. "Let me say to him that all his worries will in a wonderful manner be resolved this night."

"I was correctly told," he concluded the formula, familiar to him now from five nights' use. The usher took it on from there. Note and opened envelope rattled into a Byzantine wastebasket on the stage. "Thank *you*." The Swami made an upward gesture, prolonged it outward. "Thank you all," he said to the crowd, "and *au revoir*."

In the taxi on his way to Yonkers Van Kill had felt like the parent who is tempted to beat his precocious child with an old hobnailed shoe. Now, seeing Edward Cameron walk smiling not at all, solemnly toward him into the wings, walk to loud applause in which the wings joined, Van Kill felt like that same parent who is always changing his mind, always wanting to take the precocious child in his arms. And this time he did. . . .

"I have found out why vaudeville died," Edward murmured sleepily from the rear seat of the taxi in which with Van Kill and Yanni he and Lady Di were leaving Yonkers for good. Plainly he thought he had got enough of acting to last him his life. The monotonous enthusiasm of his fans had begun to pall. Their questions were always the same . . . Where is my dog? What should I do about my husband? Where is my money, when will I get some, will I take a trip, will I meet a tall dark handsome young man?

Edward had got weary too of telling autograph hunters it was against his religion to sign his name. But the worst were his colleagues, old hams who wanted to put the bite on him for a loan. "Good eggs, but frightfully dumb," Master Cameron remarked with a touch of the monetary grimace which always amused Van Kill. "They learn one act and never change it. They know nothing else. Except human nature," young Cameron amended in a gracious voice and apparently fell asleep. . . .

"The boardinghouse was good material," said Lady Diana, who held Edward's head in her lap.

"I'm sure it was." Van Kill meant he was sure that the Yonkers boardinghouse where Lady Di and Edward had stayed while the lad was substituting for Rudi Smart would produce at least four novels, set in variations of the same milieu, full of jealous tension and murderous thoughts. He did not mention his own fright or the possible hazard, in two senses of the word, of Rudi Smart.

Rudi Smart (Minute Man, Mighty Mind) was not a particularly winsome character, and as Edward had implied, he had a number of psychological quirks which were doubtless adducible to his stature. His intelligence and his conversation however deserved more respect than these were ordinarily given. And if he had been a full-grown bore, the chances were that someone present besides Van Kill at the Christmas Eve tree-trimming party would have remembered the midget as a remotely possible help to the case which the police were trying to build against the Christian Cavaliers and the person who had shot Echo Newman.

Van Kill did not recall Rudi's story about the man who had shot out his friend's try-your-skill pitch until he was in the air on his way to Kansas City. The idea was too tenuous even to be called a hunch, the document examiner thought then. And if it were not, if it turned out that the murderer had wandered alone through the amusement area at the World's Fair one night last summer and revealed a phenomenal marksmanship under the eyes of Rudi Smart, what would McLone say to such a witness? What had he said of Maureen Carty? Van Kill had gone about his business in the West with the thought that if Rudi were the unwitting vessel of any embarrassing identifications, he was safe enough so long as no one suspected it. Realizing that Paul Harris had the midget in his custody had given the document examiner a kind of tertiary bad moment.

Yanni seemed to know what the kyrios, so happily returned, was thinking about. "Will you rescue the little man now?"

"Let a man have his fun, can't you?" Van Kill demanded rather obscurely. "Being Edward Cameron has been something *special* for him."

"My being Rudi Smart has been something special for him too," Edward murmured. Several Broadway columns, it seemed, had mentioned the ham act that had suddenly gone big-timey. Financial biggies, the columnists hinted, were trekking to Yonkers for the market comments they got from the act. "*My* notices will insure *his* future for some time to come," said Edward Cameron and was definitely asleep. . . .

They reached the Otranto about midnight. Van Kill had to subdue sentiment on his part and garrulity on Master Cameron's in order to get the boy to bed.

"I'm going to type up my notes while my impressions are fresh," Lady Di excused herself. "Don't stay up long."

"It won't be long till morning now." Van Kill waved her off affectionately and moved toward his study with the Greek.

At his desk the document examiner dialed Benjamin De Porta's number. Yanni waited, quivering with eagerness to tell what he knew, delighted that the kyrios was back.

"Ben?" said Van Kill . . . "Yes, intact so far as I know. How are Echo and David?"

"Both getting along nicely *in statu quo*," Van Kill heard the bookseller reply.

"Good old *status quo*," Van Kill said with a cheerful despair. "I'll have bad news for *Carnage* tomorrow, I'm afraid. Tomorrow we spill a certain editor's soup, if you know what I mean."

He did, De Porta said. Would the document examiner mind explaining how.

"He has a record," said Van Kill. "Sorry I can't tell you more over the telephone. Public decency . . . I'll be seeing you early tomorrow after I see McLone. Maybe to tell you how we'll settle the editor's colleagued conspirator's hash too."

Yanni, who sat beaming close to the desk, heard the bookseller make an unintelligible protest.

"Yes, yes," said the document examiner impatiently. "I'll come in one piece to our dinner date tomorrow night . . . Of course you didn't, I'm making it now." He turned to Yanni and said, so that the question was audible to De Porta, "Are you too full up with New Year's Eve business to give us a booth?"

"Not too full for you, kyrie," the Greek said reproachfully.

"All set then, Ben. We meet at the sign of the Cerberus at eight o'clock tomorrow night."

"Be careful, Hendrik," Yanni could make out the bookseller saying.

"*Shalom alekhem,*" Van Kill said rather gently. "I won't keep you up."

"You say this Harris and his traitorous colleague in the Cavaliers both have criminal records, kyrie?" Yanni spoke upon the click of Van Kill's telephone receiver.

"I said Harris did." Van Kill's gray eyes surveyed his assistant quizzically. "That's one bit of news McLone will consider plausible . . . I'll open my budget after yours. Something tells me yours is more important than mine."

Yanni shrugged expressively. But there was no false modesty in his attitude as he began with Pough's having spotted Lee at the Weatherly party and a tangential mention of Mr. Pough's reservation for New Year's Eve at the Matapan. "A fine company we shall have for your setting out of the case," he said, and Van Kill agreed.

The Greek related how Pough's lead had taken him, through Weatherly and Flather and Roberts the Weatherly chauffeur directly, *amésos,* Yanni said, to Richard Lee. "Now placed going out from the Weatherly party to a dark-colored sedan with a southern license half an hour before *Desposúna* Newman was shot on Christmas night."

Van Kill reached into the drawer of his desk for his pipe and filled it as Yanni talked. The Greek watched the kyrios's fingers perform this operation and noted that they were thinner and more tobacco-stained than usual. Yanni was used to the feeling that Van Kill was thinking ahead of him, but as the pipe was lit he had an uneasy impression that his listener was not so much anticipating as redistributing his, Yanni's, blameless deductions.

But Yanni had still to reveal the sedan seen near the Rotunda by Lawrence O'Dell. He went on confidently to tell of Lee's guilty manner and what Burke had said about a southern boy's ability to handle a gun. He was sliding quickly over how he had established Burke's possession of a carbon copy of the Cavaliers' small contributor list, and given proof of the same to Mars, when Van Kill interrupted with a "Splendid, Yanni. That *is* important."

The words came from Van Kill's lips on small clouds of pipe smoke and there was no mistaking the accolade. Gratified, but puzzled, because he had never considered his discovery of Burke's list as proof of anything but Burke's dishonesty, Yanni went on to Lawrence O'Dell's story of the man driving away from the Rotunda Christmas night.

"He will be a great co-operator, this student, I think. But that, kyrie, is police work." Of the dog-walker whom Roughead had found Yanni said, "Saving your grief, kyrie, I think *astynomía* will also make this dog-shepherd remember a loud overcoat following that Lee in a dark overcoat the night *Desposúna* Hargrave was murdered. Thus bulwarking the cats woman."

"No doubt," said Van Kill.

Yanni went on freely to voice his suspicion of Harris as the telephone-dictaphone record Amalgamated-Aircraft tipster and the True American of *The Lance*; of Harris attempting to blackmail Lee and throwing Montefiore to the cops (first by his lies to Pough and again after the affair at the Rotunda). The fact that Mr. Pough had put Yanni onto Lee showed Mr. Pough guessed this, as also perhaps he guessed Lee had tried to frame Harris by pistoling *Desposúna* Newman.

How Lee discovered Echo and Harris were meeting at the Rotunda was also police work, the Greek said. "We ourselves can persevere to skewer those Number Two Ruffians, Lee and Harris, upon their double job of carnage, I think," Yanni finished proudly with a pun of his own.

"*Kállista,* Yanni. Congratulations," Van Kill told the smiling Greek. "I'm afraid the cops will think my dish is very small garlic upon yours." The document examiner paused to consider his pipe. "All I know about Harris is that some twenty years ago he left an unserved sentence for pandering behind him in Kansas City."

Yanni was not surprised. He couldn't think of a more logical preparation for Harris's kind of true crime work or for anti-Semitic propaganda, he said.

"The connection was as you say logical," replied Van Kill. "I heard Harris say he'd known Morna Maye in Albany, it was obvious in what profession, and he dropped an acquainted-sounding reference to Kansas City. I therefore went to Kansas City and asked around among the cops."

Yanni's classic features became a tight mask which said plainer than words that Van Kill's time would have been better spent on Pough's commission in town.

"Somebody had to do the job, Yanni," Van Kill grinned. "In person. You can't ask a community via teletype to check over its old dirty linen for you. McLone told me he was glad the Department had somebody with funds enough to make a plane trip . . . I found the honest cop who arrested Harris," Van Kill went on. "We got a line to the crooked police and court employees who swiped the evidence and lifted Harris's fingerprints. That was before the days when they could have sent duplicates to the FBI. We can prove what magistrate under the old regime looked the other way . . . Kansas City officials are ready to call Harris's number as soon as we line things up on this end."

"On this end Mr. Pough will act," Yanni assured Van Kill, who had been leaning back in his swivel chair, discoursing easily.

"Of course he will." Van Kill swung up and put a hand on his desk. "Pough has never countenanced stupidity of any kind. *Trying to kidnap Edward to make us lay off the Cavaliers while he squeezed True American is Harris's brand.* His cunning, like his viewpoint, is two-dimensional. Pough knows Harris's limitations.

So long as Harris stuck fairly close to *Carnage*, he could make Harris's abilities profitable . . . Pough's record is quite clean. Pough was a municipal court stenographer at the time Harris was convicted in Kansas City."

Yanni looked startled, but he did not speak.

"Don't jump to conclusions now," Van Kill smiled. "Pough wasn't attached to the court where the evidence was swiped . . . So far as I know he never met Harris personally until *Carnage* was about to have its throat cut and Harris guaranteed to give it a transfusion. If Pough checked Harris's checkered editorial career across the country, he found that Harris had a record as a circulation-builder. Pough indicated as much when I talked to him about the Geyer letter. Pough is a business man. Harris with Pough to keep him on the job was a business asset. Frederick Pough, you see, has been a keen judge of values ever since he was in college.

"In New Mexico," Van Kill resumed, "I could catalogue Pough's career in the small town where he was born. A self-made lad from a good poor family. Just as McLone told us. A contrast to Harris whose origins are not the sort one digs up in five days' time. In college Pough made himself what is called a well-rounded student, Yanni. Fine scholastic record, popular socially, good enough at sports to make teams, but a bit of a lone wolf—like many students who work their way."

The Greek, a lone wolf himself, could understand all this. "But where, kyrie," he added in a somewhat desperate voice, "where does all this leave us with Harris and Lee?"

"It leaves us with a man like Frederick Pough stuck with a man like Paul Harris," Van Kill said. "It leaves us with such a close connection between the *Carnage* setup and your Cavalier, that I'm personally in doubt," he reverted to a metaphor the Greek had used in his narrative, "what end we ought to carve from."

Yanni was pleased that Van Kill thought of carving, but he was still uneasily aware of the kyrios's mental, not reservations, but redistributions. "You approve of my analysis, then, kyrie?"

"Oh, quite," Van Kill said offhand, "except perhaps you're bearing down too hard on alibis . . . Walk-up apartments, George

Stock's street accident he had all the time in the world to do research on before he saw you, doormen and assorted flunkies lying
like gangsters—both classes have to think of their jobs. As you say,"
Van Kill proceeded in a mollifying voice, "the connection between
Cavaliers and *Carnage* in this case is very close, so close that the
fat Cavalier who shot Echo Newman had only to reach out a hand
to get the Colt revolver from Harris's Crime Cabinet. The person
who shot Echo Newman also murdered Betty Hargrave, as you
assume correctly, and from approximately the motives you assume,
being as you have agreed from the start, Yanni, ambivalent about
Jews.

"An efficient person, Yanni," Van Kill said with bitterness, gazing
as he spoke at a point above the Greek's head where a light swirl
of snow had begun to powder the windowpanes. There was quiet
in the room. Yanni staring at Van Kill sat forward in his chair,
his feet well under him almost as if he were crouched to spring.
For an instant it was all the Greek could do to keep from turning
to look over his shoulder where the kyrios was looking. "A very
efficient person," Van Kill said.

Yanni took a deep breath. "Lee is not ambivalent about the
Chosen People," he said slowly. "He hates and fears them, being
stupid and lazy himself. George Stock is very efficient, he is the
closest person to Harris I can think. George Stock investigated
the *Bund* during much time for Mr. Pough, he is I think loyal to
his employer, but it might have been *too* much time if Stock ——"

The telephone cut across Yanni's painful admissions then.

"Maureen?" said Van Kill. "Yes, of course."

But for a certain stillness in the set of Van Kill's head, as if the
muscles in the back of it had tightened, the Greek who was watching him might have thought he had been expecting the cat woman
to call. Yanni's own scalp crawled. He half rose from his chair,
bending over Van Kill as if the danger could reach from the telephone.

("You saw our taxi drive along Central Park West?")

As Van Kill spoke the fingers of his free hand made a one-two-
three-four beat on the desk.

("Certainly I want to know anything more you have to tell me.")

For some reason the nervous thump-thump-thump-thump of Van Kill's fingers sent a cold wind through the roots of Yanni's hair.

"I'll meet you back of the Cavaliers in half an hour."

XXXIX

FIFTEEN minutes later Jake Feinstein of Feinstein's Fine Delicatessen sat gingerly in the side entrance doorway to the office of the Christian Cavaliers. The base of Jake's tail hurt, the wind hunting down the alley had a cold breath, and Jake was disillusioned with the human race. A moment ago he had been minding his own business in the Cavaliers' back yard when a man whose shape was dark against the whirling snow climbed the alley fence.

Now Jake regarded this inclosure with several others between there and Columbus Avenue as his own private domain. But he was a friendly cat as well as a dignified neighborhood character. He deserved the epithet of misanthropic as little as he did the spinsterish one of Wuzza Baddy which Maureen Carty had bestowed upon him. During the past week he had formed a strong attachment for Officer Ignatius Loyola Gallagher, who still walked a casual beat in that immediate neighborhood.

Stepping nicely through the snow, Jake had therefore advanced with a hospitable chirp toward the man coming down from the fence. The man halted his progress through the yard as he saw the cat and drew something from under his long dark coat. Jake, being curious, turned, but did not retreat. What the man had hauled out looked rather like a broom to him. The end of this instrument was much smaller than that of Mrs. Feinstein's broom and infinitely harder as Jake learned when it landed on his hinder parts. Jake gave a yell of surprise and of, it may have been, horror; he had never been hit so hard before in his life. Bristled up to twice his normal size, he had sailed over the fence, taking refuge in the doorway, where he now was proceeding to examine his injured members and lap them solicitously . . .

Officer Gallagher would have taken an active hand in these proceedings if he could have witnessed them and a very professional interest in the long weapon carried by the man in the long dark

311

overcoat. But at the time when the man came boldly down from Columbus Avenue, entered the Cavaliers' alley, and as boldly climbed the fence, Officer Gallagher was proceeding westerly toward Amsterdam Avenue. Consequently no human interrupted the man in the dark coat when he crossed the Cavaliers' back yard to the fence at its extreme rear, climbed this barrier also, and took up his station behind it, resting his rifle in a crack between two boards . . .

It was not much after one o'clock in the morning when Hendrik Van Kill walked from Columbus Avenue toward the Christian Cavaliers. Until he reached the mouth of the alley Van Kill set a determined stride which kept his legs, but not the upper part of his body warm. There he felt a puzzling combination of cold and heat. In his head too, which some malign humor had moved him to keep topped with the sombrero he had bought in Sante Fe.

What he felt wasn't fear, he was sure. Wrath? Danger—he went to face danger gladly in a sombrero, he thought, remembering something Betty had told him Pough had told her. It was the chill of cautious retrospect that tempered the prick of an exciting prospect, sent those waves of feeling over him . . . You *would* make gestures . . .

Maureen Carty had never called him up on the telephone before. She never used one so far as he knew except to summon SPCA ambulances and such. The voice in the receiver had been too cooperative . . . A frame, that call? . . .

"If you think it's a frame, edge up behind the picture and see," Mars had counseled him years ago. Exactly what he did *not* intend to do now, Van Kill decided. David had talked to Echo about Maureen. If Echo let fall a word to any member of Popub, the rest would know it sooner or later. Some one in Popub would assume that Van Kill, having come the back way behind the Cavaliers to meet Maureen Carty before, must come that way again . . .

The document examiner therefore sidled through the mouth of the little alley that led to the Cavaliers side entrance and went forward against its left wall. Unfortunately Betty Hargrave's murderer had figured that Van Kill might figure that way about his route to the Cavaliers . . .

How did he expect to catch Betty Hargrave's murderer? Keeping a cautious eye up the alley, Van Kill continued his catechism of himself. Redhanded? How idiotic. Nobody except Yanni and Harris's lug had used a knife in this case . . .

Yanni had known the call was a frame. All the Greek's nymph-harassed ancestors who lived on Cape Matapan at the fabled mouth of Hell protested it a frame . . . I ought to be kicked, Van Kill told himself, taking advantage of his mores, his native convictions. Van Kill knew that if the situation had been reversed, he would have clipped Yanni on the jaw and sat on him until he had phoned the police. He wondered how soon Yanni would think of calling McLone . . .

But because Yanni did believe that murder was a private matter, believed in a primitive unself-conscious fashion that a man robbed of his mate had a right to personal vengeance, he, Hendrik Van Kill, was being a stinking egoistic show-off. "Shut up, stay home and look out for Edward," he had told the Greek unfeelingly. "She threw hers away, can't I even risk mine?"

Risk it *how*? Provoke the murderer into shooting, Van Kill halted his progress along the wall to ask himself. Catch the bullet in his teeth? Van Kill was letting a grim humor play upon his mind and Van Kill's sense of humor was taking his mind off his work . . .

Jake Feinstein had chosen the moment of Van Kill's stealthy footing down the alley to reconsider his injuries. To each cat himself is deity and Jake was as much absorbed in himself as Moses upon the mount. Thus Van Kill saw the cat first and stepped out into the alley around it, a little step, but enough . . . Across the downsloping back yard a long rifle behind the Cavaliers' back fence came instantly to a carefully rested sight. Beyond the alley fence the sombreroed head of Van Kill was for an instant silhouetted against the street glow. Behind the gun Betty Hargrave's murderer was smiling a little smile of efficient satisfaction.

The cat looked up during this moment and seeing another man in a long overcoat, dived for the nearest hole, the high moving bridge of the man's legs. The cat gave a scream of deathly alarm as the bridge collapsed and they both went down together, six legs tangling just as a twanging crack split the dark alley air. No cat gut ever sang like that, Van Kill remembered thinking as the back of his head hit the cement walk. And then in the suddenly complete darkness he remembered no more . . .

Nearing the end of his beat, Officer Gallagher heard the shot and ran for the alley mouth with his revolver ready and his whistle in his teeth. Officer Gallagher was not a foolish specimen of young cop. He knew what a fine target he would make pounding down the middle of the Cavaliers' alley. He went cautiously sidewise and when he stumbled upon a body, he crouched over it and shielded his electric torch with his hat.

Gallagher made a little twitter of surprise when he recognized Van Kill. Having his whistle in his mouth, he had only to draw a good breath to summon help. And all this took place a number of minutes after Yanni Mavromicháli had decided to telephone Captain Francis Xavier McLone . . .

The light of Gallagher's torch and the shrill rain of sound beating from the narrow enclosure must have touched a fiber of anxiety in the stunned man. For Van Kill moved his lips and Gallagher stopped blowing long enough to hear him mumble, "Harris—will get" before he lapsed into complete unconsciousness . . .

It was nearly two o'clock before Mr. Paul Harris could fix his mind on THE VANISHING VIRGIN AND THE TRIPLE TOMBS. The same emotion was gnawing the editor of *Carnage* magazine this night that had ridden him now for some days, making it hard for him to concentrate on the pile of manuscript he'd begun last Thursday when Morna Maye phoned.

Worry about that quiff was no piece of what was biting him, Harris concluded, pulling his easy chair to a position in the window embrasure where he could get his feet up on the ledge. He needed no report from a Comet tail to know she hadn't stirred from her squat in the Seventies. Van Kill didn't worry him. *On* the job that long-legged son was bad news, but he was home,

Harris's operative had tipped him, and Harris would soon see to it that he got *off* the job. Who could stop Paul Harris? Not the lowdown perversity-disseminating dumb copper illegitimates . . .

Why look, Harris told himself, you knew they were trailing you from the start, didn't you? Didn't you duck away and meet Newman? Meet Morna in a telephone booth and make her talk like a lady to the brat! Thank God for public telephones . . . Didn't you sneak off and post that first note to Van Kill right under their nose? . . . Will there be any more notes? There will *not* . . . They got no plant on the mail you post, they won't have. Didn't you have those Comet ropers report to your office? Do they look any different from the most of the ex-cons that come in? Business, my boy, nothing but business. Smart of you, Paul, the editor told himself thickly. Where then, he asked himself, was the thread that would unravel, ravel, no, unravel his unease? . . .

No, no connection. Coppers could prove positively no connection. It was this lousy job that was biting him! The thought came in a blinding flash of inspiration as it had come many thousand times before to Mr. Harris when he was a little drunk. This lousy job he was going to say the hell to when he pulled Van Kill off the Cavaliers. The little snatch, the pressure he had to put on the right Cavalier was all a means to a legitimate end.

"Spiritually isolated in this burg, that's what you are, Paul, fed up, bored, restless for bigger things," the editor articulated into his rye. He took a last gulp, pulled the floor lamp closer, and bent to his work. Harris could read when he could scarcely talk.

He had gone through the synthetic discovery-of-virgin's-unclothed-body atmosphere, the murderer had appeared on page five, and a few synthetic suspects were being grilled by eagle-eyed cops, when there was a curious double noise above Harris's windowpane. A sharp cracking contact, then a sound as of split wood that tumbled with a rattle to the window sill.

Harris might not have done what he did then if he had been sober, but Harris was a very inquisitive man. As it was he got up without a second thought, threw open the window, and stuck out his head.

There was a twanging plop when the editor's face appeared and a distant report. The expression of curiosity on Paul Harris's countenance changed to surprise, to a swift sardonic grimace. He put his right fist in which the manuscript was now clenched on the window ledge to support himself. He went to his knees and his head fell on the manuscript and from the hole between his eyes there came out upon the title in due course what the Homicide Squad was later easily able to recognize as blood . . .

On this particular night Detective Miller had had the task of taking Harris out of his office and putting him in, as the jargon goes, at his top-floor walk-up. At around two o'clock the detective was still watching the editor's light from a doorway in a building next to the vacant lot across the street.

A little after two o'clock Miller heard the crack and rattle of wood falling from the gingerbread ornament at the front of Harris's apartment. He saw Harris look out, saw the editor's head fall on the window ledge.

By the time Miller roused the superintendent of Harris's apartment the murderer was on his way home. The man in the dark coat, who had murdered Betty Hargrave, threatened the life of Echo Newman, and now rid the community of Editor Harris, had long since gone from the empty rear apartment a block away where he had fired the two shots.

The man took pains to scuff away all recognizable footprints. With his gloved hands he put the Winchester 1873 down on the floor below the open window where he had rested it, as if he wanted to leave a clue for the police, whom he so much admired. To replace the gun in Harris's Crime Cabinet would be overextending his luck, and this man of quiet efficiency did not often stretch his luck too far . . . He left the apartment door which he had forced open a crack . . .

His face as he softly left the building showed no regret. There were some jobs a man had to do for himself, where loyalty to what he was supposed to believe and indeed his position were at stake. A man could fall from his position easily in these trying times . . . The man in the dark coat walked to Ninety-sixth Street and took the subway home. He went to bed and slept soundly until seven o'clock when he was awakened by a call from the Manhattan Homicide Squad . . .

Severally and in groups between about 3:00 and 8:00 A.M. the Manhattan Homicide Squad verified the fact of Harris's death, did the rest of the necessary on the scene, and located the Winchester 1873 . . . McLone wakened George Stock and Frederick Pough, who jointly identified the rifle and later identified Paul Harris at the Bellevue Morgue . . . Singer and Swann roused Morna Maye and her midget guest. It was this contingent that, at the behest of Van Kill, now conscious and in his most dictatorial and uncommunicative mood, was accompanied by Yanni Mavromicháli . . .

Rudi Smart, a little gentleman to the end, informed these three that when they talked to Morna they were talking to a lady whom he could give an alibi for the past five days and nights, and did they want to make anything of it? . . . Singer and Swann decided they didn't . . .

"Keep him sober now," the irrepressible Singer advised Miss Maye. "He's gotta work tonight."

Yanni carried a bundle of photographs which he stayed behind to show Rudi. Newspaper clips, candid shots, a cabinet photograph, and some police posters with the writing cut away were spread before the midget.

"Among these there is perhaps someone who has done you an injury?" Yanni inquired.

"It don't matter if there is, does it, honey?" Morna folded a quilt around Rudi and kissed the top of his head. "Let the dead past bury its dead, is what *I* say."

But Rudi did recognize the picture of someone who had done him an injury. This was why Yanni Mavromicháli came home, as Van Kill said, walking on his heels. The Greek had been thinking of the case as a roast to carve from either end and the kyrios had turned it upside down in the platter . . .

Roughead and Mars woke Thomas Carroll Burke and Richard Lee in Burke's Mosholu Parkway apartment. The two were being questioned at the precinct now in conjunction with Daisy Goff . . . "The squad and Yanni did all that. I did nothing but bump my fool head. Not even a souvenir bullet hole through my sombrero, thanks to a cat," said Hendrik Van Kill.

He lay on a divan in the Otranto living room around 8:30 A.M., smoking angrily and talking to David, a sober, much chastened Montefiore, it seemed. On the floor under the Christmas tree Edward was leafing a book Van Kill had brought him from Chicago. Near the boy Lady Di sat knitting a sock. From the study Yanni could be heard at the telephone, yes-noing Rovero, who had sent them occasional front-line flashes through the night . . .

Van Kill raised his bandaged head to listen. "Spying on me for fear I'll sneak out on 'em," he said, including the pair by the Christmas tree in his glance. "Yanni and Gallagher had the squad, Doc Baumann, and what looked like half the West Side uniformed force packed in that alley when I came to. McLone said I had to go home and stay there and Baumann said it was a slight concussion, the old liar, and backed him up. But I told you that."

"At least twice," David said mildly, and the blue eyes he fixed on his friend were compassionate. "I don't suppose McLone wants you throttling the murderer with your bare hands."

"McLone doesn't even know who the murderer is yet," Van Kill snapped. "I haven't the strength to try to convince him till he gets over this excitement about Harris."

"How will you convince him then?" David asked.

"It won't be easy." Van Kill flung up a hand and shoved back the compress Lady Di had just arranged. "McLone is a little disorganized after losing his chief suspect and his chief witness at the same blow. After all Harris did see the murderer carry dry ice in a box away from the Popub service elevator that Friday night and he did see the murderer follow Betty Hargrave to her death."

"But *I* was supposed to be the chief suspect," David objected. "I still can't understand why McLone let me out this morning."

"He went over my head." Van Kill was disgusted. "*I* don't want you wandering around loose to maybe get popped off too. But McLone can't have you suing him of course. Think what the defense would do to him if he tried to introduce the written evidence of a character with Harris's record."

"I wouldn't think of it. I'm grateful to McLone. I learned a lot in jail," David said with disingenuous sincerity. "What surprises me is that you didn't let McLone know what you had on Harris as soon as you located your family."

"I was just about to when the murderer phoned." Replying evasively, Van Kill tugged at the bandage. It fell off. "Who am I to snoot so accomplished a gentleman when he does me the honor of suggesting a private interview? . . . I suppose I thought I could bring McLone the murderer and Harris's sentence on the same tray."

"It's too bad you didn't set a police trap." Lady Di crossed over to replace the compress and went back to her chair. "You really ought not smoke, Hal, if you expect to be an agreeable host tonight."

"With the bobbies in your books, Lady Di." Van Kill grinned and put out his cigarette. "I can see myself persuading McLone to set a police trap when I myself was only half-persuaded I had been talking to the murderer. On such short notice our coppers, who are wonderful but only mortal, would have had themselves a stirring melee falling over unfamiliar back yard fences and some absent-minded siren would have been sure to scream in the rush."

Edward, who was liking *Mathematics for the Millions*, but finding it a trifle popular, had been able to follow the conversation too. He might have made a remark then, for he also had ideas about police procedure. However, he had just happened to turn to the title page of his gift, where Van Kill had written a fact for Edward's guidance.

"A nineteenth-century French academician once paid a great deal of money," the boy read, "for the autographs of Julius Caesar, Alexander the Great, Judas Iscariot, and Mary Magdalene, written in modern French script on modern French stationery. This scholar was an internationally famous mathematician."

The passage, Edward concluded, had implications a great deal more tart than Van Kill's overt remarks about specialists sticking to their last . . . Besides, Mr. Montefiore was speaking now.

"I should think the cops could still use Harris, even if he is dead, and Maureen Carty, even if she is fey, on the right man," David said. "That is, if they have any other witnesses to back up the cat woman."

"Police have two, Yanni and I one and a half to build up," corrected Van Kill, lighting another cigarette. "I don't think the dog-walker, Echo Newman, Lawrence O'Dell, and Rudi Smart will have any trouble among them toppling the right man from his perch."

"Smart, dog-walker, O'Dell?" David spread his hands. "Is this more stuff you've held out on McLone?"

"Lieutenant Roughead dug the dog-walker up." Van Kill let his cigarette smolder in the ash tray while he explained about the citizen who had seen Betty Hargrave and her murderer on the Cavaliers' street the night of her death. "They're rechecking the better alibis now and McLone now hopes the dog-walker will identify Burke or Lee. Burke, Rovero says, still denies knowing anything about that Cavaliers' list which came to him so mysteriously through the mail. It's a good enough story. Better than ever with Harris dead. Because with Harris's demonstrated behavior—having Betty shadowed for purposes of blackmail, trying to have Edward kidnaped for similar reasons—it's too convenient to put every irregularity except the murders on Harris."

"Too convenient." David's voice echoed the ironic amusement in Van Kill's. "The murderer is a close associate of Harris, I presume."

"One of his colleagues," said Van Kill. "As for our half a witness, you heard Rudi Smart yourself say he'd know the man who threw all his prizes in an oily puddle anywhere."

David's eyes roved to the fireplace where Rudi Smart had strutted before Echo. "I should forget it," he said.

"Our murderer is a marksman, he's never *denied* it." Wincing, Van Kill raised himself on his elbows and ground out his cigarette. "Our murderer is Rudi's man . . . Christmas night he tried out his marksmanship on Echo Newman at the Rotunda, and there's where our best witness, the one Yanni found, comes in."

Van Kill gestured at the Greek, who had just entered and im-

mediately been pressed to hold yarn for Lady Di. Yanni registered
a modest complacence as Van Kill told about Lawrence O'Dell
and the profile view this law student had got of the murderer driving away from the Rotunda Christmas night.

"You can see, David," the document examiner said, "why we
can't let McLone waste anything as good as that or the rest of
Yanni's evidence on the wrong man."

"I can," David said and smiled at Edward, staring up round-eyed
from his book. "What about the rest of the evidence you *hope* will
convince McLone?"

"I don't think Betty's murderer wanted to kill Echo," Van Kill
said tangentially. "I think the reason Echo still won't talk, the real
reason why she wouldn't talk to you in the hospital, Yanni, is that
she knows ambivalence deflected the murderer's aim. The fact that
you were there in the Rotunda, David, when Betty Hargrave's
murderer shot Echo Newman was so much velvet for him. He
never liked your attitude toward *Carnage*."

"Nobody liked my attitude." David's faun face was mournful and
he spoke to the room at large. "But Echo—that psychological stuff
will mix McLone all up. Tell me what you'll tell McLone to tell
the murderer."

"The psychological stuff, matters of style and so on, can be saved
for me," Van Kill said grimly. "If I have to use it and I can trust
myself. But what I tell McLone will be perfectly simple, mostly
what he already knows and I've been telling you . . . I can tell him
to tell the murderer, for instance, we've a dictaphone record of his
voice recommending Amalgamated Aircraft over the telephone to
Thomas Burke. We know Betty Hargrave's murderer also sent
Burke a carbon copy of the Cavaliers' small contributor list, the
one I mentioned just now which Yanni located in Burke's apartment and told Sergeant Mars about. McLone, you see, can effec-
tively tell him that."

"I can." David looked at Yanni, but the Greek had his eyes and
hands on Lady Di's yarn.

"He knew Echo suspected him of abstracting that list from the
Popub safe. That's why he wanted at least to frighten her off. Mc-

Lone can tell him that too. But principally I can tell McLone to tell him he shot Echo Newman because he wanted to frame Paul Harris, who was about to demand money for hushing up what *he* knew about the murder of Betty Hargrave."

Listening closely, Montefiore fancied he heard in Van Kill's savage repetitions a restated symphonic theme, a harsh demand for requited doom. Its coda, David thought, sounded in Van Kill's voice as he went on.

"McLone can tell the murderer he knew I could force the truth about Betty Hargrave's murder from Paul Harris and get Echo to talk," said the document examiner. "Let McLone tell him that's why he tried to kill me and did kill Paul Harris last night. McLone can tell him all that happened on the night of the *Carnage* banquet, on Christmas night, last night, and how and why," said Van Kill, "with my compliments."

David waited until Van Kill lay back on the divan and looked normal again. Then, "Perfectly simple," he said. "You just go from Harris and the dog-walker and Carty to Rudi Smart and Echo and Lawrence O'Dell. You just pound in the things you say your witnesses are sure they saw and knew."

"McLone will do more than that," Van Kill said evenly. "It's a practice the Department of Justice officially frowns upon, but neither McLone nor the D.A. would hesitate in a case like this to make *quite sure* their witnesses saw and can tell the right things."

"Quite sure," David said absently. "Yes, yes, of course, I can see they would have to do that."

"After all," Van Kill said, "the dog-walker and Lawrence O'Dell saw our murderer from some distance, and our murderer is very sure of himself. He is, in fact, David, a very efficient man. In his quiet way he was coolly reckless about taking the normal risks of identification and will, I *think*, fight them to the very end. On such matters I believe he seldom listens to any voice but his own."

"I think he'll listen to this. It seems very conclusive to me." David got up to go. "Well," he added a little awkwardly, "thanks a lot, Hal."

The rest of them went with David to the door. "Give our love to Echo," Edward told Montefiore, smiling up at him. "We're sorry we didn't get to see her in the hospital. We'll miss you both at the party tonight."

David smiled too, as warmly as if he remembered the understanding he had reached with the boy at another party not so long ago. "We'll miss *you*," he said. "Since I'm just out of jail I've some business to catch up with and I expect I'll be around St. Luke's pretty steadily the next few days."

They were all very cordial and a trifle constrained in the manner of good friends. Yet David's blue eyes avoided Edward's dark ones as he bowed himself out of the door, and Edward alone was not surprised at what happened soon after that.

"I'm surprised at *him*," the boy said of Van Kill to Lady Di and Yanni. "He'd never dream of telling me anything like that. He'd be afraid I'd go right out and tell somebody else."

XL

〜〜

DAVID MONTEFIORE took a taxi from the Otranto Apartments to the corner of Fiftieth Street and Sixth Avenue. Walking away from his cab, he noticed a television truck across the Avenue near Radio City with a small crowd around it. Seeing this sight made the Avenue look, David could not tell why he thought so, look like spring. The last morning of the year was sunny, the sky beyond the tall buildings appeared to vault away from them, and the small trees along the curbs looked as if they might surprise themselves and suddenly leaf out.

Montefiore glanced at the crowd more than at the televisor and smiled. It was pleasant to be out of jail. He went westward at a brisk pace toward the Popub Building. Under its glass-roofed marquee Poynton Darcy and Louie Lenz stood with their backs toward Montefiore, chatting lugubriously. Intent upon his mission, David did not notice them. He took the elevator and got off at the twentieth floor, facing the reception room of *Carnage* magazine . . .

Poynton Darcy had a certain amount of influence with certain members of the Force. One of these, a uniformed cop attached to the precinct in the Cavaliers' neighborhood, had phoned him about Paul Harris's death not long after it occurred. Darcy had picked up Lenz a little before nine o'clock. They had paid a short visit to George Stock in his office twenty stories almost directly above where they were standing now.

"I'd've bet you money George would step into Paul's shoes," Darcy was grumbling. "Way he talked you'd've thought Pough thinks George rubbed Paul out to grab his job. Shame about Paul," Poynton mumbled mournfully. "He was a fine type in his line."

"A fine type," Louis Lenz agreed, with pious abstraction. "Think Pough will stand for Paul's bills? What say we see *him*?" Lenz

324

fingered the strap of the miniature camera slung on his shoulder and half wheeled around.

"What's on the books," Poynton conceded.

"Now," urged Lenz, fidgeting. "What say we see him now?"

Pough had come in very early and talked to him before doing anything else, George Stock had already informed them with considerable eloquence.

Darcy woke up. "Nuh," he said. "Pough'd just hand you a line about letting it pass through the regular channels. I'd rather not see Pough personally at any time."

Lenz said something functional about the president of Popub's business economies which made Poynton smile childishly, and Louie, who felt some slight need of backing, followed it up.

"Ah, come on, Poynton. We can tell him what it means to the company's reputation," said Lenz, his face set in a wicked little grin. But the crimescribe hung back. "Okay then, be a chump all your life. None of mine were personal. I'd just as soon see him any time," the cameraman snapped. He took a tentative step toward the Popub door.

"Good-by then," Darcy said firmly. "I should be halfway done with my piece on Paul for *Legitimate* right now."

Lenz faced toward Sixth Avenue where Poynton was headed. "Gonta use Cassidy's by-line?" he said, referring to the precinct copper who had phoned Poynton about Paul's death.

Darcy nodded. "He's due to get kicked off the Force as it stands, he might as well have the cash, and I can make him claim he was first on the scene. Wish I could snag somebody higher up though," the crimescribe said moodily.

"Agh, we'll play up old Cantwell's pan anyway." Louie Lenz was turning back toward the Popub Building when he heard the same noise that Darcy did and eventually looked up.

The noise was a scream, several screams by the time Darcy and Lenz had lifted their eyes to the window ledge which the people crowded around the televisor on the east side of the Avenue were pointing at now. Louie Lenz unsheathed his camera. He backed up with Darcy against people who came racing across the Avenue to join them on the west side. A man was stepping out on the ledge.

Stepping out deliberately, they all saw, there was nobody visible behind him at that time. The man on the ledge at the twentieth floor was straightening up and standing there athwart the Popub Building with an almost arrogant demeanor. High up in Radio City a pair of startled television technicians watched his image on a screen.

Standing sidewise, the figure on the ledge glanced back for the space of Lenz's shutter click. Coolly resting a hand against its frame, like a yachtsman by the mast of his own boat, he looked back into the high open window at a face which had appeared there.

"Stop him," the face was mouthing, thought an engineer on the television truck, or perhaps he had only shouted that himself.

"There he goes," a supervisor by the engineer's side indubitably said, and, "Here he comes," a voice went up from the crowd as Poynton Darcy ducked for the marquee and Louie Lenz dashed to the street in front of it. A policeman's whistle went crazy. In the space of a very short time exposure the man on the ledge had stepped off and down into the winking eye of Louie Lenz's camera.

Down the man plunged close in to the building, past the fifteenth floor and the tenth, smoothly, but at the ninth he struck a ledge which ripped off his left shoe and sent him spinning away. Glimpsing the man's face full on, Lenz drew a harsh breath, but he stuck to his work, his cheek and eye muscles pulled back, his bent arms steady.

The man hung in mid-air for an instant, plunged on, and Lenz had stilled the whole of the three seconds' drop in well-spaced shots, his fingers manipulating the film shift automatically, the click of the shutter sounding softly in his ears.

When Lenz thought about it later, it seemed fully two or three minutes until the figure, spinning from that ninth-floor ledge, went nearly horizontal at the fifth, tilted head down, tilted, plunged on and cracked against the marquee head foremost with a sound like a pistol shot, and then a spill of tinkling glass. Lenz waited long enough to snap the body in that grotesque pose, head and shoulders bunched down like a boneless gymnast's, feet up and then toppling over as Lenz jumped forward.

Lenz jumped and halted and focused the end of the body's fall, its feet down and close together like those of a dancer ending a leap. In the ground glass those last fractional seconds, Lenz could see the bottoms of the trousers bellied out with the wind, the coat and shirt ripped exposing the body's waist, the necktie blowing up toward the left arm, extended as if to balance the dancer's descent, the face still recognizable, and then, in the top speed shot Lenz had time for, turning as if to conceal its mask.

The body dropped toward the sidewalk and there was a sound as of a collective breath long-held suddenly let out. The body appeared to pivot on its shoeless left foot and like a dancing scarecrow then fling its right foot wide into the gutter an impossible space. Body and face landed flat with an audible splash and a small sucking noise very close to Louie Lenz, kneeling to focus the scene.

"Get up from there," a policeman's rough voice was saying and Louie Lenz heard it the second time. He got up and became conscious in a moment of a wetness on his cheek. He took out a clean white handkerchief from his coat pocket, rubbed it across his cheek, and looked at the stain on the cloth. His first instinct was to drop the handkerchief in the gutter, but Louie Lenz's cold bird brain worked fast. *Souvenir,* he thought, the first conscious word that had crossed his mind, except *exclusive,* in all of that time.

Louie Lenz put the handkerchief in an inside coat pocket and his hand was steady enough. But something in the cameraman's stiff face made the policeman ask, "Did you know him, Mac?"

"Know him?" Lenz repeated and his reflexes asserted themselves. "Not me, officer," he said. "I'm a press cameraman. Just let me catch this other shot, will you?" he wheedled, gazing ahead at a knot of people under the marquee.

Grouped almost as well as he could have done it himself in the studio, Lenz was to admit when he had developed the photographs. In the immediate foreground a policeman, avoiding the sight on the street, had his back turned and was half stooping, while beyond the officer, left to right, ran a regular funnel of interest the way they did it on the stage.

Sorta modern with those backs turned, one hundred per cent copaseetic, Lenz thought, a small central group staring straight in front of them, blanking out what they had partly seen, one woman with a handkerchief to her face, next to her a mournful rear elevation which could belong to but one man, and on the right end two Popub elevator boys whom Lenz also knew. These held their hands and fingers stiffly straight, their elbows bent at a right angle, their mouths and eyes tense and bulging in the accepted pattern of best horror. A trifle too realistic, Lenz thought. But they were coming out of it a little now—*that* was better.

"Hold it," Lenz very nearly said as he snapped the group.

He walked over to the mournful backside, which did an about face as Lenz spoke. When the crimescribe had had a few seconds for recovery, he and Louie Lenz whispered briefly inside the Popub Building door.

"Don't ask me why he did it. Let's get it to *Legitimate* right off," Poynton Darcy suggested.

"*Legitimate* and *Authentic*, you chump," corrected Lenz. "And that's only just a start. This is big," he said.

It was big, Poynton Darcy agreed. It was worth taking a little trouble to get the true facts in this case, and of course he and Lenz would always maintain that he had all of them. Hadn't he actually been on the scene this time?

Bizarre business troubles, appalling worry over fantastic and ghastly series of murders, draining life blood from colossal firm with octopus tentacles—Poynton could see it take shape. This was one weird suicide that would rate front position in any book. As a long serial for sure, with a rehash of the whole case from beginning to end. As a yarn it was tops the way it would run, but Poynton had a loyal nostalgic wish that it might have appeared in artistic form where it really belonged.

Carnage, Lenz thought practically as he glanced around to make sure the guard wasn't looking, the book might go out of business now . . . *Carnage,* Poynton Darcy's mind lingered fondly over the name. *Carnage,* it would have been a natural there, but he knew that the story would never run there now . . . *Carnage* . . . Oh, monthly promise of horror most lush on shiny bright cover where near-naked girl beholds lustful approach of Fate worse than Death . . . The chances are *Carnage* is on the skids . . .

And that may perhaps have been the reason why the crimescribe and the cameraman seemed a bit distrait as they commandeered the service elevator and rode up in it to the twentieth floor . . .

~~~~~~

XLI

"FREDERICK POUGH jumped to his death because he was True American of the Cavaliers' *Lance*. Yanni and I had found it out, Echo knew it, and David told him so," Van Kill told De Porta.

They were sitting in the booth which Frederick Pough had reserved for New Year's Eve at the Matapan Restaurant. Yanni had called in person at the Weatherlys' and expressed his regrets that Mr. Pough was unable to dine with them tonight. The Weatherlys had made other arrangements then.

"I presume by this time Weatherly has drawn another blank," De Porta said.

"Certainly by this time," Van Kill agreed. "By eight o'clock Christmas night Weatherly was out on his feet. Pough had overheard Echo make her date with Harris and was planning a little business trip around the Rotunda for nine o'clock. Riding an alibi with the same bland *sang froid* as he did the lack of one, Pough took advantage of the southern passout's car—and of Weatherly's brand of drunkenness which he knew from of old."

It was the hour between eleven and twelve when at the end of each old year the minutes seem to hurry and halt on their way to the new. In Pye Street at the sign of the Cerberus business was good because people had war nerves. Yanni was eminently satisfied at the pounds of meat, the gallons of wine and spirits which had been consumed this night. The discreet native musicians he had not without dubiety established between the fishpool and the foyer railing had evoked no complaints from single-minded gourmets. The Matapan's orchestra played Near Eastern music and gypsy tunes with polyglot cheer, and outgoing patrons stood around it and tried to discover how its members kept up their hose.

"Like Bordeaux when the Germans were entering Paris," Van Kill said. He gave an ear to the hum of satisfied dining around him. "There's been something guiltily gay about this Christmas week. I noticed it everywhere from here to Santa Fe."

"It is the fear that very soon business might be stopped from going on as usual," De Porta remarked.

"Under new management," the document examiner said reflectively. "Pough, suppressing his Geyer letter because after May tenth he more than half saw German plane carriers anchored off the Rotunda come another spring. He set Betty Hargrave investigating the Christian Cavaliers just to see how strong the American wind blew that way. He started feeding the Cavaliers market tips to test their business judgment and see if they had any other head than Burke. He wanted at least two big good conduct marks to show he'd been on the right side of the ring in case the world challenger became the world champion."

"Not a surprising inconsistency for a business man of that type," De Porta said a little sadly. He struck a match and waited for the aura of sulphur to subside before he set it to one of his small cigars. Flame glinted upon the black and white crest of the bookseller's hair, drew an answering gleam from the black pearl in his shirt front. The black brows and eyes were those of a placid Pharaoh now, Van Kill noticed, as the bookseller raised and lowered the flame of the match in successive puffs.

"He advertised that inconsistency," Van Kill said, "on the newsstands every month, what David's been complaining of from the first. Pough didn't know what he liked except that he liked what brought in the cash. I recognized it myself, a *Hearth* for mother and the girls, a *Carnage* for every sublimated rape killer, but I didn't push it to its logical conclusion. That policy of get them coming and going was Pough's only principle, David told us at the Centre Street conference this afternoon."

"You mean Pough's secret support of the Christian Cavaliers had nothing to do with anti-Semitism?" De Porta asked.

"It had everything to do with anti-Semitism," Van Kill said. "It would never even have occurred to Pough to take the way he did to get his good conduct marks if he hadn't been ambivalent about Jews . . . A boy named Blumberg nosed him out of a law school scholarship and a boy named Montefiore inherited too damn much Popub stock. But David didn't touch on that. David simply took the line that Pough bit off much more than he could chew and David proved it."

"Pough jumped, then, not so much because he was a proven hypocrite—" De Porta blew a smoke ring which, settling, melted against the table top. "—as because his megalomanic ideas failed."

"Megalomaniac, no." Van Kill dissented. "Simply a nosy managing executive completely on his own for once and for once completely out of his depth, David told him. When Pough left the pond of popular ideas and tried the same stroke in the ocean of popular ideologies, he couldn't keep his head up. When I unwittingly coached David this morning, I was thinking mostly of how I'd tell McLone what a weight Harris must have been on Pough's shoulders after he left the Popub ring and went into the wider one of anti-Semitism. How when Pough failed to kill me he *had* to kill Harris because he knew as soon as McLone and I began to keelhaul Harris, he'd crawl to us and whine, 'What I saw Mr. Pough do in a dark overcoat Friday night if you'll whittle my pimping sentence down to a misdemeanor, what I saw Mr. Pough do in a car Christmas night if you'll wash my sentence out entirely.' . . . But David, smarting from old wounds, being yes-yessed and told to run away and play every time he came up with a beautiful big business idea in his teeth, David simply took the line that as a champion executive Pough had turned out to be a ham-and-egg stumblebum. It was David's proving to Pough that he was just a prelim-bout Machiavelli that made Pough jump, David told us."

"Continuing metaphorically, then, you would say Miss Newman was the chief nail David used to hammer home that fact," De Porta said. His calm was in marked contrast to Van Kill's restless dissatisfaction.

"Echo Newman," Van Kill said, "was the living link between Betty Hargrave's businesslike carbon copy of the Cavaliers' small contributor list which Pough *implied* to Echo he had given McLone along with Betty's original. Exactly as he implied to Yanni that he was no marksman, never cared much for firearms, he says . . .

Echo comes to our tree-trimming party and hears Singer hinting around to Rudi about what sounds to her very much like Betty's carbon copy in the hands of Thomas Carroll Burke. I saw the shock it gave her myself. But the thing which really crystallized her suspicion was not Pough's unbusinesslike move in supposedly giving the carbon copy to Captain McLone. It was the copy turning up with Burke in conjunction with Pough's sending me the Geyer letter after once refusing it to me. Locating that copy in Burke's apartment so that Mars could get it was Yanni's most important job, though he also charted the murderer's entire course from the night he left the *Carnage* banquet and followed Betty Hargrave down the Cavaliers' alley into the closet to the night he drove around the Rotunda and shot Echo Newman. Except that Yanni pinned it on Lee instead of Pough . . ."

"The truth was," De Porta ventured mildly, "Pough made the mistake of underestimating his office wife."

"To some extent," Van Kill said. "When Pough overheard Harris making a date with Echo, he probably thought no more of it than now Echo could tell him what Harris was planning next. Then she stumbles across Singer's information, starts doing the very thing I told her not to, which was think for herself in company, and Pough sees her at it when they work together all day Christmas . . . David told Pough this morning that underestimating Echo's prescience was the worst of the four mistakes he made as an executive and had to cover up by two murders and two attempts . . . Misjudging Betty's loyalty was the first, David said. I don't think myself that Betty would have done anything but laugh it off if she'd found Pough's name on Burke's list of big contributors . . . Overestimating Burke——"

"And he turned out to be the kind of man who accidentally leaves his keys lying around," De Porta interrupted ruefully, "who betrays an unbusinesslike curiosity about his anonymous benefactors."

"Precisely," the document examiner smiled. "And fourth, underestimating the trouble anybody like Harris could cause when he hired him in the first place, knowing the creature's record . . .

David telling us at the conference in Commissioner Cantwell's office this afternoon just what he told Pough this morning sounded so plausible that McLone was furious with him for settling a fool-proof case out of court. He's inclined to be a little furious with me still, though he admits he wouldn't take time to come listen to me this morning."

"McLone's conviction complex operating," De Porta observed. "Pough had one of a different sort, the totalitarian, scuttle-your-ship kind."

"Don't be thinking David anticipated that," Van Kill said. "He knew Pough was dictator-minded, but it was the unique chance of making Pough listen to him that drew David up to that office this morning. We gathered from what he said at the conference that David was in the midst of a beautiful periodic sentence and didn't notice when Pough got up and went to the window. When he did, Pough was already on the ledge. David told us Pough looked back and said, 'You must help Jael carry on.' And after that Pough wasn't there any more."

"Not a bad decision," De Porta said, glancing up.

"Too good a death for an appeaser," Van Kill shrugged. "But as Pough recognized, a far, far better thing for Popub than anything else he could have done. The D.A., I think, was gratified at the turn of events. He almost said so in formally exonerating David from any blame for Pough's suicide."

"Psalm-singing Clarence gratified?" De Porta was skeptical.

"Why not?" the document examiner said. "This way he's spared the embarrassment of maybe having Burke get up at the trial and remember some big Cavalier contributors who are maybe big Daffin backers too. He doesn't have to admit that he let a local situation like the Cavaliers develop while he ran around cobbling up a national reputation as the Kansas boy who already had the big bad city thoroughly deloused. He can let Pough be a martyr to the anti-Semitic cause, blame the murders mysteriously on the anti-Semitic hydra which Pough was trying to hack down, and co-operate with David's forthcoming *Lol* exposé as if he had initiated the investigation himself."

De Porta said, "I'm beginning to see why you're dissatisfied, Hendrik."

"Too many people in the country like Pough wanting business to go on as usual no matter what happens to the country," Van Kill agreed.

"Business will be better than usual," David Montefiore said. The sole owner of Po Publications, Incorporated, was sitting by Echo Newman's bed in St. Luke's Hospital, holding her free hand. The other one was still involved in a sling and bandage, but there was enough of it visible to show the emerald it wore.

"Not with scrapping the March *Carnage* and hiring all those experts you've mentioned for the new one," Echo disagreed. "You can't just snap your fingers and coax those star reporters and psychiatrists down from the learned journals and big slicks."

David disengaged his hand in order to talk. "*Carnage* is going to be a big slick," he said. "The war on crime must give any real psychiatrist a pain in the neck. The reporters will be glad to say what they really think for once."

"Not for love," Echo's dark head moved on the pillow. "You've got to offer them either professional prestige or important cash."

"We'll give them both," David said. "We can economize some place else. I was reading in jail that English publishers are using both sides of their stationery now."

Echo took a deep breath through her fine nose and looked away. At this moment she didn't want to start any arguments.

"Lotus," David said, following her gaze which had gone in the direction of the bedside table where the flowers were. "Lotus *is* a little too heavy for a sick room . . . Acushla, what do you suppose Harris wanted to tell you Christmas night?"

"About the box, I suppose." Echo made a little shrugging motion with her good shoulder. "Captain McLone and Mr. Van Kill agreed when they talked to me here this noon that Harris would probably have told me that same story he tried on Mr. Pough about the gray or tan or brown box which you never carried and Mr.

Pough did. Personally I can't see what Harris hoped to accomplish with that story about the box."

"Hal explained about that at the conference," David said, enjoying himself. "That was Harris's way of telling Pough he had seen him carrying the dry ice off from the *Carnage* banquet. It was a covert demand for blackmail, Hal says, which Pough countered boldly by reporting to McLone. Pough could do this, you see, because Hal says when Harris got conscious that Friday night, he obviously hopped up and scuttled away from the Cavaliers' alley without any idea that Betty had been murdered inside. But since the cops kept the box story under their hats and didn't ask him about it as they did about the cat woman's story, Harris thought he had Pough coming his way until he saw Pough at the Rotunda and recognized that Pough had tried to frame him by killing you. Pough let it drop at that, however, so Harris went right on protecting him. Harris didn't guess Pough put two and two together when Yanni told him Hal had gone West. For Pough that trip West meant just one thing: if Hal dug up Harris's unserved sentence, Harris would squeal about the murder to protect himself. Pough couldn't take any chances, so he planned to kill Hal. Meanwhile Harris was thinking he could still collect blackmail if he kidnaped Edward and thus pulled Hal off of Pough's neck. He probably went right on thinking it until Pough shot him between the eyes."

"Mr. Van Kill ought to have a house and grounds," Echo said abruptly. "He'd have more space to keep that little boy out of mischief if he did."

"He will have." Smiling, David took her hand again. "Uncle Ben's going to try to buy back the old Van Kill house on Staten Island for him. He won't take any money from Uncle Ben, which Uncle Ben thinks is quite unreasonable."

"I don't know," Echo said. "He didn't manage to keep you out of trouble, did he? He let you go to jail, didn't he?"

"Yes," David said, "he let me go to Jael."

"Too many people like Pough," Van Kill repeated, "hating the

People and calling the People anybody they happen to hate. Blaming Them for their own lack of thrift and brains and competence. Such a quick and easy way of summing up the persons you fear and envy, whose politics you can't stand. One small three-letter word. It's the best little persuader the international gangsters have. How many people in this country can even *name* their eight great grandparents?"

"You don't seem too hopeful that we can do anything about it, Hendrik," De Porta calmly observed.

"Short of a direct assault on its source, how can I be hopeful?" Van Kill leaned back and waited while redheaded Teekee, whose twenty-yard kilt was like a fluted snowdrift, gave them fresh ash trays.

"Twenty minutes, *kýrioi*," he said eagerly. "Twenty minutes to a happy New Year."

"You can't be too hopeful," the document examiner resumed. "There are too many Burkes and Lees and Goffs who don't get exposed by being dragged into a murder case. I wouldn't have caught Pough if, after refusing even to let me see the Geyer manuscript less than a week before, he hadn't sent it to me at the time when my ears were running over with dictaphone and *Lance* sentiments. I remembered the similar rhythms of a letter I myself had heard Pough dictating in his office and it all began to mesh. After I had examined the Geyer manuscript I began to see how it might not be the fear his document was a forgery that was making him suppress it, but a belief that it was genuine."

"I shall not soon forget, Hendrik, when and where you told me that it was a very *good* forgery," De Porta said. "Psychologically I must admit that Pough's possession of the Geyer letter was a very considerable block to my understanding how May tenth jitters made Pough the two-faced individual he turned out to be."

"A very good forgery," Van Kill said. "When David publishes it he can get more than one competent man in the field to disagree with me . . . Mars' call coming just as I saw that the Geyer must be a forgery lifted me out of the tenuous into the definite. I knew that Pough must be our pigeon then because I knew what Echo had on her mind was Betty's carbon copy of the Cavaliers' small contributor list. Both Betty and Echo had to be put out of Pough's employment because they'd started doing entirely too much thinking for themselves. Burke was just careless and inquisitive and merely needed discipline."

Van Kill lifted his head from his hand and gestured at the room outside their booth. His attention was caught, not so much by the rising hum and animation of Yanni's diners as by the flutes of the Matapan's orchestra finishing a defiant crescendo on the dominant word of the Greek National Hymn, *eleftheryá*.

"*Liberty*," Van Kill said. "There are too many Poughs at liberty in this country playing both ends against the middle. Too many plug-uglies like Burke willing to do the actual dirty work. Too many unwitting stooges who, if they don't help shovel the stuff out like Goff and Lee, think there must be something in it because they see it in print."

"What about your own Burke and Lee and—" De Porta added hesitantly, "Goff?"

"Don't call her my Goff, Ben." Van Kill gave one of the fleeting grins that had lately been rare with him. "Just because I told you I'd picket you if you took her back in the shop. Matter of fact Singer's gone and got her a job running an addressograph for the Anti-Nazi League. He told her the Germans were suppressing Latin . . . Lee seems about to marry his Weehawken widow and become a potential patron of the Cavaliers' successor . . . Burke," the document examiner sighed. "Burke may crawl into one of the old-established anti-Semitic ratholes in the South or on the West Coast. And there's a dandy little new opening I ran onto while I was away that would be ideal for a harp like Burke. The Ku Klux Klan is starting a newspaper in Indiana to help businessmen keep the Big International Bankers from giving the United States back to the British."

Van Kill had had to raise his voice above the mounting noise. Edward appeared on the crest of it, wearing a candy-striped paper hat. His cheeks were flushed, his coat was belted untidily about him, and he carried an armful of Roman candles. He was in a fit of chattering anxiety.

"We're going to have fireworks," he scolded. "Don't you know it's nearly New Year's and we're going to have fireworks? Diana and Yanni are out there now. If you don't come right away, you won't see them."

The boy pranced with impatience as De Porta and Van Kill rose. "There's going to be fireworks," Edward Cameron said.

"I shouldn't be surprised if there were," said Hendrik Van Kill.

THE END

www.ingramcontent.com/pod-product-compliance
Lightning Source LLC
Chambersburg PA
CBHW032235010726
47494CB00002B/503